Victor Pemberton was born in Holloway, in the London Borough of Islington, in the early 1930s. His first job was as a Fleet Street postboy but after two years' National Service he went to work in the travel industry and wrote his first radio play, 'The Gold Watch', which was broadcast by the BBC and has since been repeated five times. He went on to write radio and tv plays full time and in 1971 became script editor for the BBC's 'Dr Who' series, later writing for the series himself. In recent years he has worked as a producer for Jim Henson and has set up his own production company, Saffron.

His first novel, OUR FAMILY ('a wonderful story' – Nerys Hughes) was based on his highly successful trilogy of radio plays of the same name and is also available from Headline.

Also by Victor Pemberton

Our Family

Our Street

Victor Pemberton

First published in 1993
by HEADLINE BOOK PUBLISHING

5 7 9 8 6

ISBN 0 7472 4144 9

Phototypeset by Intype, London

Printed and bound in Great Britain by
Mackays of Chatham plc, Chatham, Kent

Reproduced from a previously printed copy.

HEADLINE BOOK PUBLISHING
A division of Hodder Headline PLC
338 Euston Road
London NW1 3BH

www.headline.co.uk
www.hodderheadline.com

To
Oliver J. the second.
Welcome.

Chapter One

That evening, the back streets of Islington seemed to be filled with the grey November fog. Thick, choking palls swirled endlessly, obliterating almost everything in sight; it was a real peasouper. Along the busy Seven Sisters Road, people made their way home from work in the dark, often bumping into each other despite the dim beams of light from their cherished handtorches. Some shops closed early – there was obviously not going to be much custom while people could hardly see a hand in front of their face. Even Digby's, the greengrocer's, had had enough, and by five o'clock in the evening they had pulled down their long green window shutters. By seven o'clock, only Dorner, the butcher's shop in Hornsey Road, remained open. It took more than fog or Hitler's bombers to deprive Dorner's customers of the best savaloys and hot pease-pudding in the district.

Ever since the start of the war five years before, this small corner of north London had

had its fair share of death and destruction. On too many mornings shopkeepers in the main Holloway Road had arrived to find their windows blown out and the pavements pitted with glass and, in the Seven Sisters Road, a high-explosive bomb had once torn through five shops, leaving a great smouldering gap in the long terrace. In nearby Hornsey Road, only quick action by the ARP had saved the Emmanuel Church when an incendiary fire bomb had landed on its roof. But although most of the inhabitants in the surrounding back streets were becoming worn out by the intensity of the nightly bombing raids, they were defiantly determined to put up with anything Hitler decided to throw at them. Some of those inhabitants, however, seemed to resent any of their neighbouring streets that had completely survived the nightly bomb damage.

Despite the fog, the Merton Street gang were out in force that night. Hadleigh Villas was always their favourite rendezvous, for it was a quiet cul-de-sac just off the Seven Sisters Road, with large, grand houses that were absolutely perfect for the ritual game of 'Knock Down Ginger'. Not that the Merton Street gang was really a 'gang'. They were just a bunch of youngsters, most of whom lived in the same back street, which was sandwiched between Hornsey and Tollington Roads. The oldest, Jeff Murray, was sixteen. He was a well-built boy, with a reputation for being a first-class goalkeeper in the street football team, and he was, naturally, a constant hit with every girl in the neighbourhood. In contrast, at fifteen years of age, Frankie Lewis seemed a little backward for his age, for he was only just starting to experiment with life.

That evening, there were only five of the gang huddled together in their usual hiding place in the doorway of Pascall's, the bicycle shop on the corner.

'Right then,' whispered Jeff. 'It's my turn tonight.' To the others he was nothing more than a ghostly shape in the fog, but they recognised his strong, firm voice. 'I'll take the old Kraut's place.'

'That's not fair!' snapped Alan Downs, who was just a couple of months younger than Jeff, and his rival in practically everything they did. 'The Kraut's place is dead easy on a night like this. She couldn't see yer even if she tried.'

'It'd give 'er a good fright, though.' Patty was the only girl in the gang, and she loved it because it made her feel special, as though she had power. She also acted older than her fifteen years – and her snogging with Alan in the old shed behind the Emmanuel Church sometimes went further than even he had ever thought possible. But Patty really preferred Jeff, who kissed her the way her screen idol, John Payne, kissed Betty Grable. 'I bet on a night like this the old Kraut's in 'er cellar, tappin' out morse code messages to 'er pals in Berlin,' she said, excitedly.

Frankie hadn't thought about that. Of course, like everyone else he knew that the old sauerkraut in number 19 *had* to be a spy because she was a German, but it had never occurred to him that she was probably sending back secret information to the Nazis every night . . .

'If she really is a spy, she won't send messages 'erself,' sniffed 'the Prof', who was also fifteen. He'd been given his nickname by his mates because he was a bit of a swot at school and knew practically everything there was to know about scientific things. His real name was Pete Moosey but he much preferred 'the Prof'. Even though he couldn't see a thing in the fog, Prof was busily cleaning his fragile, tortoiseshell spectacles on the now-tatty woollen scarf his Auntie Hilda had knitted him. 'Spies always have someone else to pass the information on to,' he said firmly, in his slightly la-de-da way which was frequently a source of jeering amusement to his gang mates.

The truth was that these die-hard members of the Merton Street gang knew absolutely nothing about the inhabitant of 19 Hadleigh Villas. All they knew was that the woman who lived there was a German and, so, logically, she just had to be a Nazi. Which was why, a few weeks before, Jeff and Alan had made a perilous expedition to the house late one evening and painted a huge white swastika on the front wall at one side of the street door. None of them had actually seen the 'spy' in question, but in Frankie's imagination she looked something like a female Adolf Hitler. Once or twice during the day they had seen someone moving about inside one of the upper-floor rooms of the house, but at night it was impossible to see anyone because the blackout curtains were always tightly drawn.

'You lot can do what yer like!' Jeff, the only one who wasn't wearing a warm coat, stood up and defiantly pulled his knitted bobble-cap over his ears. 'I'm gonna take the old Kraut's place!'

Whether it was the fog getting to his chest or an attack of the asthma that had plagued him since he was a small child, Frankie was suddenly convulsed with a coughing fit. The others tried hard to shut him up while Jeff stood up and emerged from their hiding place in the shop doorway. He disappeared into the swirling fog and after a moment, Frankie recovered, but his eyes were running and he was very breathless. From nearby came Jeff's voice, calling back in a loud projected whisper. 'As soon as yer 'ear me shout, get ready ter run!'

The next few minutes were very tense. After Jeff had called back, there was absolute silence in the road, for apart from the Merton Street gang, nobody was out on such an evening. It seemed ages before anything happened. Frankie kept wondering why he'd ever got involved in a silly game that was meant for young kids, not blokes of their age. After all, what did it achieve? What fun did they really get out of bringing someone to their front door just so that they could shriek with laughter and rush off into the night like a bunch of lunatics. Now, the fog was getting thicker than ever, and what air there was smelt of burning coal-fires. But just as Frankie was pulling his scarf over his mouth and tucking his short brown hair up under his school cap, there was the distant sound of banging on the door-knocker of number 19, followed by Jeff's hysterical yell: 'Knock Down Ginger! Yahoo!'

A second later, Alan, Patty, and the Prof were screeching out at the top of their voices: 'Knock Down Ginger!' Although he felt stupid, Frankie did likewise, but his voice was too hoarse to he heard above the others, and when they all rushed off into the fog he felt totally disoriented. From the distance, he could hear the whooping and yelling of the others, but he couldn't see them. He had no idea which direction he was attempting to run in, stumbling along as though blindfolded. Suddenly, he tripped over the kerb and found himself sprawled out on the pavement. Soon he was coughing and spluttering in the stifling fog, his short trousers no protection against the cold paving-stones. Gradually, he pulled himself up and, for a moment, just stood there, rubbing his eyes, trying to get some sense of direction. But in the eerie silence that followed, he started to panic. He could sense something in the fog directly above him. It didn't move, it didn't talk, and it didn't seem to breathe. 'Jeff? Is that you?'

Frankie's voice was almost a whisper, and very unsure. 'Stop muckin' about now, Jeff!'

A small puff of wind suddenly arrived from nowhere, but it was just enough to scatter the swirling fog and give Frankie a chilling view of the ghostly image staring down at him from the top of some stone steps. Gripped with fear, he realised that he was standing by the front gate of number 19. 'Was wunschen Sie?' The deep-throated voice was that of a woman.

Frankie was paralysed. It was the old Kraut herself, the Nazi spy! Through the grey evening fog she looked like a towering monster, just waiting to pounce and eat him. All he knew at that moment was that he had to get away from number 19 Hadleigh Villas.

Most of the houses in Merton Street had been built in the last decade of the nineteenth century. Each of the three floors contained two small rooms, with a minute lavatory on the landing between the first and second floors. There was also an attic, usually only big enough to take either a small bed or to use for storage. None of the houses had bathrooms, so most families used a tin tub in their sculleries. But everyone had a small back yard, although since the start of the war most of these had been dug up to accommodate the arch-roofed galvanised-steel Anderson bomb shelters. During the worst part of the blitz, in the early years of the war, Merton Street had

had its share of bomb damage. Chimney-stacks had tumbled down into the gardens below, slate tiles were ripped off roofs, windows were shattered, and plaster was brought down from the walls.

The Lewis family lived in the corner house at number 1 and still spent most of their nights in the Anderson shelter, despite the fact that the air-raids these days were by the pilotless 'doodlebugs' and more recently by the dreaded V-2 rockets, which gave no warning when and where they would strike. Frankie hated going down the shelter, for it was claustrophobic and the air was damp and stifling. But by the time he got home from his horrific encounter with the ghostly apparition in the fog, even the Anderson was a welcome sight.

''Ow many times do I 'ave to tell yer? I don't want yer 'angin' round the streets after dark!' Frankie's mother, Gracie Lewis, was half-way through a fish-paste sandwich when Frankie appeared through the blackout blanket that was draped across the shelter entrance. 'What 'appens if there's an air raid?'

'There's no air raid ternight, Mum. The siren 'asn't even sounded.'

'I doubt we'll get a raid ternight, Grace. Not in this fog.' Frankie's father, Reg Lewis, was half-dozing in his easy chair, his face covered by the morning's edition of the *Daily Mirror*, which he had read from cover to cover several times over.

Gracie finished her sandwich and wiped her fingers on her apron. 'Planes can fly above fog. Them devils don't care where they drop their bombs.'

Ever since the bomb had fallen in the nearby Seven Sisters Road, Gracie had been obsessed with the family going down into the shelter night after night, regardless of what was going on in the skies above. In fact, over the past year or so, she had turned the Anderson into a second living-room, despite its ridiculously small size – no more than six feet from wall to wall. But at least there was an electric light and it was, at most times, quite warm, thanks to the small paraffin stove. Nonetheless, Frankie hated the place, and always referred to it as 'the Cell'. It was a killer for his asthma, and he spent many a night coughing into his pillow.

'I 'ope you and your pals 'aven't been playin' that stupid game agin,' Gracie said now. 'You keep knockin' on people's front doors like that and yer'll 'ave the law down on yer!'

Frankie's sister, Helen, who was squatting on the top bunk, flicked her eyes up briefly at her brother. She was nearly three years older than Frankie, and was very protective of him. Frankie caught her eye, and they exchanged a grin. Then she returned to the jigsaw puzzle which she had completed at least a dozen times before.

Although it was only half-way through the evening, Gracie yawned. In fact she always yawned, for though she was only in her early forties, she had settled for doing work only when she had to. Her family were fed as well as the war-time rations would allow, and their clothes were washed and ironed. But that was the extent of Gracie's energies.

'Is there anythin' to eat, Mum?' Frankie knew the response he would get and, sure enough, it came.

'If yer'd come 'ome for tea at the proper time, yer'd get a proper meal. D'yer think I wanna keep cookin' all times of the day an' night?'

Frankie, who was still just peering through the blackout blanket lowered his eyes.

'There's some spam on the scullery table. And don't cut the bread too 'fick. Yer farver wants some for 'is breakfast in the mornin'!'

'Fanks, Mum!' In a flash, Frankie was gone, leaving his father to chuckle to himself behind his newspaper.

The fog was beginning to clear by the time Frankie had finished his spam sandwich. He shared it with Winston, the family's black and white mongrel dog, who Gracie Lewis never allowed to join them in the shelter. The white-washed walls and stone floor of the scullery made the room very cold, so Frankie lit one ring of the gas stove. As he warmed his hands over the flame, his mind kept going back to that horrifying encounter with the old Kraut. What would have happened if she had caught him? She could have shot him down in cold blood, and nobody would have found him until the fog had cleared. His thoughts were interrupted by Winston, who was licking one of his knees. 'Cut it out, Winnie. It's not my barf night!' When he looked however, he discovered that Winston was licking some dried blood from a small cut, a result of his fall on the pavement in the fog.

'Better not let mum see those trousers. You've got a great big tear in yer seat.'

Frankie looked up, to find Helen standing over him, looking exactly like her mother must have looked at her age. She had the same flashing brown eyes and auburn hair, small ears and a nose that seemed to undulate to its tip, and a long, thin neck. Only her mouth resembled her father and brother's and she was very sensitive about her skin, which was covered in freckles.

'It's OK. Take 'em off. I'll sew 'em up for yer. She won't know nuffin'.'

Frankie looked relieved. Once again Helen was getting him out of a potential row with their mother. 'Fanks, sis.' While Helen went off into the adjoining back parlour, Frankie slipped off his shorts and put on his father's old raincoat which was hanging on a hook on the scullery door. ''Ave they got the wireless on, then?'

'Yeah,' groaned Helen from the parlour. '*Music 'All*.'

Frankie knew what that meant. It was Saturday night, and that meant *In Town Tonight* on the wireless, followed by Norman Woolland introducing *Music Hall*. It was the highlight of the week for both Gracie and Reg Lewis, especially when their favourite comedian, Robb Wilton, was on the bill. Frankie and Winston joined Helen. She was threading a needle with some black cotton. 'I wish they'd let me sleep in the 'ouse,' said Frankie, kneeling in front of the remains of the fire in the coal stove. 'I'd sooner take my chances wiv the doodle-bugs than go down the Cell.'

'You wouldn't, if one landed on the roof, Frankie.'

Frankie's ears were almost numb from the cold and, as he rubbed them, they really hurt. Although there were only a few embers left in the fire grate, Winston was leaning his chin on the brass fender.

Helen took Frankie's shorts and started to sew up the seam that had ripped apart. 'You shouldn't keep goin' on at that old girl in 'Adleigh Villas,' she said, scoldingly. 'It's not fair.'

Frankie looked up with a surprised start. 'Wot yer talkin' about?'

'Yer know what I'm talkin' about!' Helen stopped sewing for a moment, and glared at him. 'That poor woman at number 19. You and Jeff and Alan should learn ter grown up, and leave 'er alone.'

'We 'aven't touched 'er!'

'You're always playin' that stupid game –

knockin' on 'er door and rushin' off. You're like a buncha kids!'

Frankie looked indignant, and glared back at her. 'I've never knocked on 'er door!'

'Well, if you 'aven't, that stupid Jeff Murray 'as. *And* all the rest of 'em.'

'The old Kraut deserves all she gets. She's a *Nazi*.'

Helen looked up from her sewing again. 'You're bonkers! They wouldn't allow a Nazi to live in the middle of Islington. Why d'yer 'ave ter keep 'angin' round the streets upsettin' people? Knock Down Ginger's a kid's game! Why don't yer try an' find somefin' useful to do fer a change?' She finished her sewing, tied a knot in the thread, then bit off the end with her teeth. 'There!' She threw Frankie's shorts back to him. 'Be more careful next time!'

'Fanks, sis!' Frankie grabbed the shorts, got up, and gave her a quick kiss on the cheek. 'Let me know anytime I can 'elp *you* out.'

To her brother's surprise, Helen came straight back at him. 'Fanks, Frankie. I'm glad you said that, 'cos there *is* somefin'.'

Frankie looked at her suspiciously. Helen was the one person in the world he could trust. Ever since they were small kids together, she was always the one he could turn to when he was in trouble. But he had never considered the possibility that there might come a time when he could help her.

Helen went to the parlour door and closed it. Then she knelt close by him on the floor and whispered, 'Listen, Frankie. I've met someone. We've bin seein' each uvver for the last few weeks.'

Frankie looked puzzled. 'Seein' each uvver? Yer mean – a boyfriend?

Helen lowered her eyes shyly. 'He's more than that. I love 'im.'

'Love 'im!' Frankie roared with laughter. 'You ain't old enuff!'

Helen shushed him. 'I'm nearly eighteen, and I'm old enuff ter know when I'm in love wiv someone! I tell yer, Eric's really nice.'

'Eric?'

'He's in the Army – Royal Fusiliers. I met 'im at that Servicemen's Dance at the church 'all.'

Frankie scratched his head. His sister had had boyfriends for years, but it hadn't occurred to him that she would get serious about someone. 'Well, what d'yer want me ter do about it?'

Helen bit her lip anxiously, and looked guilty. 'E's asked me ter go away wiv 'im – for a weekend.'

'Go away wiv 'im? What for?'

Frankie's rampant naïvety caused Helen to blush. 'Eric's goin' away on active duty any day now,' she said, awkwardly. 'I might not see 'im for ages.'

Frankie got up and struggled to put his shorts

back on under his father's old raincoat. 'Where's 'e wanna take yer, then?'

Helen stuttered with embarrassment. 'We're – we're goin' ter stay – wiv – wiv his aunt and uncle. They live near Bognor Regis somewhere.'

'Bognor Regis!' Nobody Frankie knew travelled that far these days. Ever since the war started, the family hadn't even been away on a day out.

'Well, are yer goin' ter 'elp me or ain't yer?' Helen was getting guiltily irritated with Frankie's questions.

'What am *I* supposed ter do?' snapped Frankie. 'Why don't yer just go?'

'Yer know very well I can't just go. Not wivout tellin' mum and dad.'

'Then tell 'em!'

Helen clutched her forehead in despair. Why *was* Frankie so naïve? Why couldn't he understand about these things? 'Mum'd kill me!'

'Just because you wanna go away wiv a friend for the weekend?'

Helen got up from her kneeling position. In a low voice she whispered, 'Listen, Frankie. Mum and Dad 'ave always said they'd never mind if I spent a weekend in Essex wiv Ivy and Joyce and their family. All I want yer to do is ter back me up when I tell 'em I'm goin' wiv 'em.'

'Back yer up? 'Ow?'

'By tellin' 'em that you've bin invited too, but that yer don't wanna go.'

'But Ivy and Joyce are *your* pals, not mine.'

All of a sudden, Helen felt as though she could strangle her young brother. Why couldn't he have a girlfriend of his own so that he'd know what she was trying to say? After all, most boys of his age knew about girls, and asked them out for dates and things. 'It doesn't matter whether they're my pals or yours,' she sighed, desperately. 'Just tell me – will yer do it, or won't yer?'

As she spoke, the air-raid siren wailed intrusively from the roof of Hornsey Road Police Station just around the corner. Not even the fog was going to keep Hitler's doodle-bugs away that night.

Early on Sunday morning, the Merton Street gang were out as usual, searching for bits of shrapnel that had fallen from anti-aircraft shells during the night. It was quite a risky task, for it involved climbing up on to flat roofs and poking around people's front gardens. The shrapnel pieces came in all shapes and sizes, and were usually jagged and very dangerous to handle. Every piece that was collected was taken to the ARP post, which was situated in the playground of Pakeman Street School, and sent back to the munitions factories for re-use in Allied bombshells.

Frankie and Prof usually teamed up and, together with dozens of other kids in the neighbourhood, scoured the streets, filling their old enamel buckets with the remains of the night's deadly aerial bombardment.

By about nine o'clock, most of the surrounding streets had been covered, and the gang met up in the playground to pool their catch. It was only when they had deposited the contents of their buckets at the ARP post that Frankie was able to tell the others about his horrifying encounter with the old Kraut.

Jeff Murray laughed the loudest. 'It's yer own fault, Frankie. I told yer ter run as soon as yer heard me shout!'

'I did run!' insisted Frankie, who was sucking a small gash on one of his fingers, caused by careless handling of a piece of jagged metal. 'But there was so much fog, I ran straight into 'er.'

Jeff, watched admiringly by Patty, ran his fingers through his long blond hair. He was the tallest of the gang, making him look a year or so older than his real age. 'I say we 'ave anuvver go at 'er ternight.'

The others all agreed. All except Frankie, who suddenly panicked. 'No! We can't!'

'What d'yer mean, we can't?' asked Alan. He had rather a flat way of speaking. 'She's a Kraut. We should make life as difficult for 'er as we can.'

Frankie picked up his enamel bucket and draped it across his shoulder. 'There's no point, Alan. We should try someone new. What's the point of goin' to the same 'ouse every time? It's borin'.'

Patty grinned at Frankie. She was a thin, but attractive girl, with long brown hair tied with a ribbon behind her head and she loved to tease Frankie, who always got shy and awkward whenever she talked to him. 'Of course, *you* don't 'ave ter come if you're too scared, Frankie Lewis,' she said. mockingly.

Frankie squared his shoulders defiantly. 'I'm not scared!'

'Good!' announced Jeff, immediately. 'It's your turn to knock anyway. So *you* can take the old Kraut.'

Frankie's face crumpled with horror.

That evening, a thin layer of mist still hung over Hadleigh Villas. It was very cold, and the pavements were already glistening with frost. Of course, there wasn't a light to be seen from any of the houses, for the blackout blinds were drawn for the night. Two Air Raid wardens, with torch beams preceding them, made their way around the cul-de-sac and quickly disappeared into the Seven Sisters Road. As they passed Pascall's Bicycle Shop, they didn't notice the Merton Street gang crouched in the doorway.

Patty had her arms around Jeff's waist and, every so often, kissed the back of his neck. She loved the excitement of the moment, and watched eagerly as Frankie left the group and hesitantly made his way across the road towards number 19.

Frankie felt as though his knees would give

way before he even reached the other side of the road. Why, he asked, had he allowed himself to be talked into this? Suppose the old Kraut telephoned the police and then sent them round to see his mum and dad? By the time he had reached the stone steps leading up to the front door of number 19, a cold chill was running up and down his spine.

The house itself was in total darkness, and Frankie could just see the outline of it against the night sky. To him it looked like the giant's castle he'd seen in a Walt Disney film, alive and just waiting for him. To his terrified mind, it looked ugly and distorted.

'Get on wiv it, then!' Jeff was calling from across the street while the others whistled and jeered.

Frankie cursed them then took a deep breath and made his way up the stone steps to the front door. The first thing he noticed were the Victorian stained-glass panels in the door itself. It was too dark for him to see them in detail, but as the moon kept ducking in and out of the clouds, he could just catch a glimpse of what looked like a man on a horse slaying a dragon. Hardly daring to move, he gently put his ear to the door, and listened. There was absolutely no sound at all coming from inside, and this made him even more nervous. Before he made his move, he decided to wait until the moon had disappeared behind the clouds again.

It seemed to take ages. Gradually, however, the thin beam of moonlight on the stained glass door vanished in the darkness and in one swift movement, Frankie reached up to the large door knocker and banged hard three times. But just as he was shouting at the top of his voice: '*Knock Down Ginger!*', the door suddenly opened and he was grabbed by his coat collar and yanked inside.

Across the other side of the road, the remainder of the Merton Street gang looked on in horror as the sound of Frankie's panicked yells disappeared, and the door of number 19 slammed with a thud behind him . . .

Chapter Two

'Was wunschen Sie?'

Frankie could hear the low, sinister voice, but couldn't see the face that it was coming from. Apart from the penetrating torch beam that was shining straight into his eyes, he could see nothing, for it was pitch dark. All he knew was that he was sprawled out on the hall floor of 19 Hadleigh Villas, his back pressed against the front street door.

'Was wunschen Sie!'

This time the voice was louder and to Frankie, it sounded like someone from every war-time spy film he had ever seen. He wanted to say something, but his voice was so dry the words just wouldn't come out. Suddenly, the hall light was switched on, but the bulb was of such a low wattage that he still couldn't make out the features of his captor. All he could see was that it was a woman who was standing over him, a small woman who did not look to be even as tall as Frankie himself, but for the moment she was merely a silhouette, with the light bulb and its multi-coloured shade dangling from the hall ceiling behind her.

'Was wunschen Sie!' His captor was growing impatient. 'What do you want – boy?'

At last, Frankie was able to understand what his captor was saying. Summoning up all his courage, he croaked, 'Nuffin'. I don't want nuffin', miss – 'onest.'

'If you want nothing, why do you knock on my door?'

Frankie found his captor's accent to be quite different to what he had imagined, it was not hard and ugly, but really rather soft and gentle. 'It's only a game, miss. Just a game,' he said desperately squinting from the penetrating beam of his captor's torch, which was still directed straight into his eyes. 'I didn't mean no 'arm, miss – 'onest I din't. We do it to all the 'ouses 'round 'ere. *All* the kids do it.'

'But you are not a kid. You are a young man.' She finally switched off her touch. 'Get up, pleass.'

Frankie struggled to his feet. But when he eventually managed to stand up, his legs felt as though they were about to give way.

'Wie heissen Sie?'

Once again, Frankie didn't know what his captor was saying.

'What is your name, pleass, young man?'

For a moment, Frankie hesitated. He was

fearful that if he told the old Kraut his name she would pass it on to the police. 'It's Francis, miss.' Almost as he said it, he wished he hadn't. 'But my mates call me Frankie.'

'Frankie?' The old Kraut considered this briefly, then nodded her head, which Frankie could still only see as a silhouette. 'Yes. And what is your family name?'

Now Frankie was really starting to panic. This time he did not answer, but lowered his head guiltily.

'Don't worry,' she said. 'You don't have to tell me if you don't want.' As the woman spoke, she noticed that the boy was shivering with the cold. She was not surprised. The hallway was almost as cold as the street outside. 'If you want, you can come and warm your hands by the fire.' Without another word, she disappeared into a room off the hallway, leaving the door open behind her.

As soon as she had gone, Frankie tried to open the front door but he found the Yale latch was down, and he was so agitated he didn't know how to release it.

'It's much warmer in here.' The old lady's voice was calling from the room she had just entered. 'Why don't you come in?'

With his back to the door, Frankie waited a moment. His hands were frozen, and he blew into them to try to warm them up. Eventually, he plucked up enough courage to walk a few steps into the hallway. To Frankie the Nazi's house seemed like a huge mansion. On either side of the hallway were doors to other rooms, and the staircase was wide and curved perfectly up to the first floor. Beneath the stairs were two more doors, only just visible because there was no electric light turned on back there. Frankie found this very sinister and, remembering all the thriller films he had seen, imagined that they led to the kitchen and the cellar, where no doubt the old Kraut sent back all her morse-coded messages to the Nazis in Berlin. The wallpaper was old and faded, so much so that it was almost impossible to make out what must have once been a rich yellow-and-blue floral pattern.

'Why don't you come in?' The woman's voice again called from the room off the hallway.

Frankie slowly made his way to the open doorway of the room and his eyes widened in astonishment. The room he was looking at was completely different to the shabby hallway outside, with elegant antique furniture and a vast, rich-coloured Persian carpet that covered almost the entire room. The ceiling was very high, fringed with delicate blue-and-white plaster mouldings, and was sharply reflected in a huge gold-leaf mirror which was fixed to the wall over the wide, open fireplace. But the real shock was the books. There were hundreds of them, crammed on to heavy oak shelves which covered every available wall-space in the room. Frankie was overwhelmed by the sheer numbers of them, the different shapes, colours, size. The only time he had ever seen anything like it was when he once reluctantly visited the Islington Public Library in the Holloway Road. But this was different. This wasn't a *library*. It was a *house*, a place where someone lived . . .

'If you want, you can come and warm your hands by the fire.'

Frankie was still hesitating in the open doorway. But at least he could now see his captor quite clearly – and she wasn't at all what he had expected. The first thing he noticed was that she wasn't old at all – well, not *really* old. She was probably about forty-five, and her hair puzzled Frankie. It was an odd gingery colour, although her eyebrows were dark brown, like her eyes. At this point Frankie realised that he had seen his captor somewhere before, but for the moment, he couldn't quite remember where . . . Taking a deep breath, he entered the room and made his way to the fireplace, where the not-so-old Kraut was warming her hands by a crackling coal fire.

As Frankie approached, his captor moved away from the fireplace and eased herself down in a favourite armchair with a high back, but she didn't say anything until she had given Frankie the chance to use the warmth from the fire to rub some life back into his frozen hands. 'And so, young man', she said finally. 'What do you have to say for yourself – Frankie Lewis?'

Frankie swung round with a horrified start.

Yer know my name! 'Ow do yer know my – ?'

The Kraut smiled. 'Yes, I know your name, Misster Frankie Lewis.' She sat back in her chair, and folded her arms. 'I know the names of *all* your friends in Merton Street. It isn't too difficult to find out such things, you know.'

Frankie felt his stomach turn a somersault. All his mates in the gang were right! The Kraut *had* clearly been gathering information about them and sending it back to her bosses in Berlin. She *was* a Nazi spy. ''Ow?' The word almost stuck in Frankie's throat. ''Ow do you know?'

Frankie's captor leaned forward in her chair, with a mischievous smile. 'You would be surprised. Oh yes – you would be very surprised how the "old Kraut" knows.'

Frankie stared at her. For the first time he could see her face clearly. It was quite pale, almost totally white, in fact, as though it was covered in too much face powder, and her cheeks were highlighted with rouge, which matched the colour of her thick lipstick. The lips themselves were shaped in a kind of cupid's bow, making them look smaller than they really were, especially when she pursed them.

'And what about *me*, Frankie Lewis?' She leaned back in her chair again. 'Do you know what *my* name is?'

Frankie shook his head.

'Do you want to know?'

Frankie shrugged his shoulders.

She sat up straight in her chair, hands folded in her lap. 'Barclay,' she said firmly, casting a proud glance at a framed photograph of an Army officer on the mantelpiece behind Frankie. 'Mrs Robert Andrew Barclay.' Then she turned her look to Frankie again.

'In the old days it was Lieberman. Elsa Lieberman. But that was a long time ago . . .'

Frankie felt the back of his legs being scorched by the fire, so he quickly moved away.

'Do you like apple cake, Misster Frankie?'

Frankie was rubbing his legs, which had turned a deep red colour. 'No.'

'Have you ever eaten it?'

Frankie shook his head.

'Then how do you know?'

Frankie shrugged his shoulders.

Elsa rose from her chair and went to a small cupboard in the arched recess beside the fireplace. She took out an airtight biscuit tin, opened it, and offered a piece of sliced applecake to Frankie. 'Here. It's homemade.'

Frankie flinched and shook his head.

Elsa pursed her lips. 'Where I come from, applecake is a great delicacy.' She put the tin down on the small table by her chair, but did not replace the lid. 'A boy of your age should be more adventurous.'

'Please, missus. Can I go home? I 'ave ter 'ave my supper.'

'Of course you can go home,' said Elsa, returning

to her chair. 'No one is a prisoner in *my* house.'

Frankie hesitated for a moment, then shuffled awkwardly towards the door.

'Tell me something, Misster Frankie.' Elsa called without turning. 'Do you like to read books?'

Frankie reached the open doorway, and turned. 'Pardon miss?'

Elsa swung round to look at him. 'Do you read books?'

'Not really, miss.'

'Why not?'

Frankie shrugged his shoulders. 'Don't know. Ain't got the time.'

'Time!' Elsa spluttered with indignation. 'A young man like you has no time? Ridiculous!' She quickly rose from her chair and crossed the room to the endless rows of bookshelves. 'Do you see these books, Frankie? I have been collecting them ever since I was a little girl at school – much younger than you. Without them I couldn't breathe, I couldn't exist.' She ran her fingers along a row of old books, the bindings of some of them ripped and worn. 'They are my food!'

Frankie stared at her as though she was mad. He wanted to turn and run, but he found something mesmerising about this strange woman.

'Do you know something, Frankie?' Elsa's eyes were scanning her beloved books. 'I have spent my life reading these books – every one of them.'

For a brief moment, she turned to look back at Frankie. 'Some I have read more than once – two times, three – sometimes even more. They are like old friends to me. I like to visit them as many times as I can.' One of her fingertips caressed a row of books. 'For example – this one.' She pulled it out slightly. 'It's by my favourite author, Thomas Mann – such a storyteller. It's about a young Prince, who could not face up to reality.' She turned to look at Frankie, who was watching her with awed fascination. 'The story is so important, Frankie. Without it, there is nothing.' She pushed the book into place again. 'No good for you, this one. It's in German.'

Frankie watched Elsa as she continued to run her fingertips along the rows of books. He couldn't work out why she hadn't been angry with him when he banged on her street door. He could not understand why she wasn't beating him instead of treating him like an old friend.

'Ah! Now this you would like! *Treasure Island* by Robert Louis Stevenson.' She pulled out the book, and turned back triumphantly to Frankie. 'What boy could resist such a story!'

'I saw the picture!' said Frankie, quick as a flash. If there was one pastime that really excited him, it was going to the pictures. 'Wallace Beery played Long John Silver. I saw it at the Marlborough a coupla weeks ago!'

'The picture?' Elsa snorted indignantly and pursed her lips. 'The cinema is no substitute for a good book! A story should be *read*. It is the imagination that should paint the pictures!' She took the book down from the shelf, and thumped the cover with the palm of her hand. 'Did you ever *read* this book?'

Frankie shook his head. 'I don't like readin',' he confessed. 'I only read what I 'ave to fer school.'

Elsa seemed close to a heart attack. 'You don't like to read? Mein Gott! What's wrong with the young people of today? You don't like to read a book!'

She sighed deeply, then held out the book to Frankie. 'Here. Take it.'

Frankie didn't move.

'Take it! It won't bite you!'

Frankie approached her and tentatively took the book with both hands.

'Take it home with you. And don't give it back to me until you have read it from cover to cover.' Elsa pursed her lips, and stared Frankie straight in the eyes. For some unknown reason she liked this boy and wanted to help him. 'Don't go to the cinema until you have read it. Now pleass go, young man.'

Frankie, still in a daze, turned, and made his way out into the hall, clutching the book in both hands.

Elsa followed him, but before they reached the street door she stopped him. 'I trust you with my book, Misster Frankie Lewis. It is a friend to me. Do you understand that?'

'Yes, miss, ' he said.

'Good!' Elsa opened the door. Outside, the mist was just beginning to clear. 'Do you know the jumble shop on the corner of Hornsey Road.'

'Yes, miss.'

'When you have finished my book, bring it to me there. Now go home, Frankie Lewis. And from now on, stop playing silly games on my street door.'

Before he could answer, Elsa had eased him out on to the doorstep and closed the door behind him. Within a few minutes, he was hurrying along Hadleigh Villas and out into the Seven Sisters Road, still clutching the old woman's book in both his hands. On his way home, he made a slight detour so that he could pass the jumble shop on the corner of Hornsey Road and Tollington Way. The windows were shuttered so he couldn't see inside but as he stood there in the dark, staring up at the legend above the doorway, '*BARCLAY. ANYTHING BOUGHT OR SOLD*', he remembered where he had seen Elsa Barclay before.

The following Friday, Helen Lewis went off to Essex to spend a couple of days with her friends, Ivy and Joyce – or that was the story she told her mother and father. Frankie, keeping his promise, backed his sister's story. The fact that Helen was going off for a dirty weekend with her soldier boyfriend in Bognor Regis hadn't really occurred to Frankie. But he realised that if his mother found out she was out with a fella there'd be more damage to the home than anything Hitler could throw at them!

Friday evening was bath night, so after collecting a clean towel from the wardrobe in his parents' bedroom, Frankie made his way to Hornsey Road Public Baths. It was a brown-brick building, snugly situated on the other side of the main Seven Sisters Road. Further on up the hill lay Hornsey Rise, which eventually led to the posher areas of Crouch End and Muswell Hill, where a lot of people had bathrooms of their own and didn't have to turn out in the cold every Friday night. Frankie always thought the Public Baths were a depressing place – even more so since the police station next door had been bombed early on in the war. Since that terrible night, when so many policemen had been tragically killed, the clock in the tower high above the Baths had stopped so many times it was now totally unreliable. But despite the fact that there was a piece of broken glass missing from its face, the old girl was still there, a kind of symbol of defiance against everything that Hitler had thrown at poor old Holloway over the past five years.

As Frankie rushed through the main gates he asked himself yet again why it was that they had to have their bath on a Friday night. Why not a Tuesday say, or Thursday? Even Monday would be better. At least it would relieve him of the boredom of his school homework. But no, it always had to be Fridays, because – because, well because it was Friday, and that's all there was to it. Frankie hurried as fast as he could across the yard so that he could avoid the smell of chlorine coming from the swimming pool in the other part of the building. He hated the smell of chlorine because it triggered his asthma.

'You're late!' Frankie's father, wearing his grubby white bath attendant's apron, was waiting for Frankie by the cash counter in the main hall. Reg had been a bath attendant since before the war, ever since he'd had to leave the building trade after an accident in which he fell off some scaffolding. It left him with vertigo, which was also the reason he got turned down for conscription. ''Ow many times do I 'ave ter tell yer? If yer come late, yer miss's yer place in the queue. I've 'ad to put the Gorman bruvvers in front of yer.'

'Sorry, Dad,' Frankie said apologetically, I 'ad to take Winston out. 'E piddled in the kitchen.'

'Bleedin' dog! 'E's too fat an' lazy ter do anyfin' on 'is own.' Reg collected his enamel bucket and mop, nodded to Elsie on the cash counter, who smiled back at Frankie indicating that, as usual, he could go in without paying. Frankie then followed his father through the swing doors marked *MEN'S BATHS*, nearly bumping into a hefty middle-aged female wearing a hair-net, who was trying to edge herself through the doors marked *LADIES' BATHS*. Frankie reckoned she looked more like a woman than a lady, especially when she glared back at him as though it was his fault she was having difficulty. As Reg made his way along the steamy corridor, he called back over his shoulder to Frankie, 'So yer sister's gone orf for 'er dirty weekend, 'as she?'

Frankie was puzzled. 'What d'yer mean?'

'Don't worry, I weren't born yesterday. She's got 'erself a feller. Everyone seems ter know 'cept yer muvver.' When they reached the wooden benches outside the bath cubicles, Reg put down his bucket and mop. He wasn't much taller than his son, but he looked older than his fifty years, and his dark hair was greying at his side-burns. 'Whatever yer do,' he said, lowering his voice to make sure no one could hear him, 'don't breeve a word to yer muvver. If she knew what 'elen's up to, she'd cut 'er up wiv a bleedin' chopper!'

All of a sudden Frankie realised what his sister Helen was getting up to and the thought horrified him. His sis' goin' off for hankey-pankey with some soldier boy? How could he have been so *stupid*!

'Frankie boy!'

Two voices greeted Frankie simultaneously. It was the old Gorman twin brothers, Mike and Bert, perched side by side on the wooden bench, towels clutched under their arms, waiting for their turn to take a bath. Most people found it difficult to tell them apart, which gave them a lot of opportunity to get up to all kinds of mischief. They always dressed identically, an art they had perfected during their long careers as a comedy double act on the Music Hall stage. This evening they were wearing pre-war navy blue overcoats, and flat tartan caps worn at cocky angles.

'Evenin' Mr Gorman.' Frankie's reply was directed at both of them.

'Been to any good pictures lately?' asked Bert, the younger twin by one and a half minutes.

'Your dad tells us you went to see *Gone with the Wind* for the seventh time,' said Mike from behind his bifocal glasses.

'Actually, it's the ninth time,' replied Frankie proudly. 'I saw it twice in one week when it came back to the Savoy last year.'

'Nine times!' spluttered the twins.

'That's means 'e's spent more than a whole day in the picture 'ouse watchin' one film!' said Mike, turning to his younger brother.

'Blimey!' replied Bert. 'That's longer than we ever played the 'ackney Empire!'

They roared with laughter at their own joke, but Frankie couldn't even raise a smile.

'Right, gents,' called Reg, as he came out of one of the cubicles having cleaned the bath after the previous occupant. 'Could you take five and six, please.'

In a flash, Mike and Bert were on their feet and, doffing their caps briefly to Frankie, disappeared into their adjoining cubicles. Because each cubicle was partitioned to less than ceiling height, Frankie and everyone else in the men's bath house had to listen to the old-timers' banter. Frankie didn't mind, he knew that the twins missed the Halls, and this was their way of keeping their memories alive.

A few moments later, the bather in cubicle number seven came out and, after his father had cleaned out the bath and turned on the hot and cold water taps, Frankie was shown in. He was soon soaking in the relaxing warm water though because there was a war on, everyone was only allowed half a bathful of water. But Frankie always loved these five minutes he was allowed in the bath tub each week. It gave him the chance to lie back, close his eyes, and imagine he was Spencer Tracy or Clark Gable in a scene from one of their films, living it up in some luxurious hotel bathroom, with a huge cigar in his mouth and a glass of champagne in his hand. If he opened his eyes, of course, reality soon took over, and he found himself back in the old white chipped bath tub, with rusting taps, shabby white tiled walls, and the half tablet of Lifebuoy soap he was allocated by his father which had to last for at least four Friday bath nights.

Mike and Bert's comedy routine was a background echo which finished with a closing song.

Tonight it was *By the Light of the Silvery Moon*, and Frankie found himself joining in. But when it came to an end Mike called out, 'Oy, Bert! When are you gonna fix Elsa's sink in the jumble shop?'

Frankie's eyes sprang open.

'I'll go in over the weekend,' Bert called back. He was the handyman of the duo, and made the odd bob or two on the side. 'She really needs a new sink. The one she's got 'as just about 'ad it.'

'Poor lady.' Mike was splashing around so much in his bath he sounded as though he was swimming the English Channel. 'She's 'ad a tough time since 'er old man went down at Dunkirk. We oughta keep an eye on 'er, if only for 'is sake.'

'I know.' Bert's voice across the the tops of the cubicles. 'She's a good type, is Elsa. Even though she is a Kraut.'

Frankie leapt out of the bath, quickly towelled himself down and, after saying cheerio to his dad, made his way home. On the way, he could think of nothing but Elsa Barclay. Ever since he had left the house in Hadleigh Villas a week before, he had tried to put the whole experience out of his mind. But what he had now heard about Elsa had brought it all back. And if the Gorman twins thought she was a 'good type' then there had to be something more to her than he had imagined . . .

By the time Frankie reached the traffic lights at the junction of Hornsey and Seven Sisters

Road, he found himself impatient to get home. After his warm bath, the cold November evening air made the blood in his veins tingle and, without warning, he suddenly dashed across the road before the last car had cleared the traffic lights. Almost involuntarily, he found himself trotting, then running. As he turned into Merton Street, he was met with a wall of darkness, for everyone had drawn their blackout curtains for the evening. Without a torch he had to run carefully, and even though he thought he knew every inch of the road, he knocked against a pig swill bin by one of the lamp-posts, sending a stream of household left-overs on to the pavement. The sound of the bin lid clanging to the ground made every dog in the street howl with rage, including Winston. Frankie continued to rush on. He didn't know why . . .

As soon as Frankie got the front door of Number 1 open, Winston leapt up at him. 'No, Winnie! Not now! Down boy!' he yelled.

'Is that you, Frankie?' Gracie Lewis's voice called out from the kitchen. But she wasn't really interested – the wireless was turned up full and the sound of *Forces' Favourites* was filling the house.

'Yes, Mum, it's me!' Frankie called back, then rushed straight up the stairs, leaping them two at a time, hotly pursued by Winston.

Frankie's room, which he shared with his sister Helen, was tucked away at the back of the house on the first floor. Helen's part of the room was sealed off from his by a floral patterned curtain which was draped across a piece of metal wire. As Helen was away for the weekend, Frankie drew back the curtain, threw his wet towel on to the bed, and pulled off his school blazer and pullover. Winston leapt on to Frankie's bed, clearly believing that his young master had come home to have a good game with him. But Frankie had another matter on his mind. Kneeling on the floor, he reached under the bed and pulled out the thick, leather-covered book Elsa Barclay had given him. He had hidden it there after he had got back from his encounter with her the week before, and hadn't looked at it since.

He stretched out on the bed and looked at the cover: *TREASURE ISLAND* by Robert Louis Stevenson. He casually turned the first page, and looked at the picture there. Then he turned another page, and another. Finally, he reached the page with the heading *Chapter One: 'The Old Sea Dog At the Admiral Benbow . . .'* With his chin propped up on one hand, Frankie started to read . . .

Chapter Three

Highbury Boys Grammar School was spread out on the corner of Highbury Grove, just a stone's throw from Islington's Upper Street. Its grey stone façade was depressing and unwelcoming and even during the height of summer, the majestic sight of the huge oak and elm trees bordering the main road could not hide the sheer awfulness of the building.

The interior was no better. Classrooms were not only too small to take more than thirty boys in each, but they were freezing cold in the winter months because the only form of heating in the school was coal fires and, during lessons, these were usually blocked from view by the teaching staff warming their own rumps. In the early part of 1944, a doodle-bug had landed on the block of flats nearby but, much to the disappointment of the pupils, the building itself withstood the worst of the explosion.

Frankie hated school. He couldn't see the point of sitting in a crowded classroom for six hours a day and to him Highbury Grammar was just a place where he could meet up with pals and have as entertaining a time as possible. However, this Monday morning was somehow different. He was much more subdued than usual, and even in 'Boggy' Marsh's maths lesson he found himself making a half-hearted attempt to understand what boring old algebra was all about.

It was not until Mr Wood's English lesson however that the Prof first noticed the peculiar mood Frankie was in. The two boys shared one of the twenty double desks in the ice-cold classroom.

'The English novel,' Woodsie proclaimed pompously, 'is admired in every country throughout the world. Without doubt, this country had produced some of the finest writers in the world. Shakespeare, the Brontës, Henry Fielding, Jane Austen . . .' At this point his mind went blank, but, as usual, he was able to disguise the fact by quickly folding his arms, revealing the leather patches on the elbows of his rather tatty sportscoat. 'Right, let's have you then!' he called, scanning the classroom. 'Some more English writers. Names! Names!'

Prof's rather squeaky voice called out first. 'Charles Dickens, sir,' he said. The Prof, after all, had won a scholarship to gain his place at the school.

'Right – Dickens!' Woodsie's beady eyes darted from one side of the room to the other. 'More!' he yelled.

A sea of hands was now raised and names were called back at him from all directions.

'Sir! Charles Kingsley!'

'Sir! Agatha Christie!'

Sir! Oscar Wilde!'

Woodsie leapt up from his perched position on the guard-rail in front of the fireplace. 'Don't be an ass, boy! Oscar Wilde was Irish. Come on! What's the matter with the lot of you?' Woodsie was now at his intolerable worst. 'What about the rest of them? What about Thackeray? What about Robert Louis Stevenson?'

'Sir!'

Prof swung with a start to look at Frankie. He couldn't remember the last time he had seen his friend hold up his hand in class.

Woodsie too was taken aback. He had never liked Frankie Lewis. Not since the first day the boy arrived at the school after winning one of the Government's so-called 'Special Places', a scheme set up during the war as a kind of compensation for not quite passing the scholarship exam. To the English master, Highbury Grammar School was no place for a boy whose idea of the world was fashioned out of the make-believe tinsel and technicolour dreams of the Gaumont, Astoria, Savoy, and Marlborough cinema screens around Islington. 'Yes, Lewis?' Woodsie clearly resented having to respond to the boy who had fulfilled almost all his expectations of non-achievement.

'Please, sir. Robert Louis Stevenson wasn't English. 'E was a Scottish writer.'

A sea of disbelieving faces immediately turned to look at Frankie. No one had ever dared to argue with Woodsie, let alone correct him. And Frankie Lewis of all people!

For a brief moment, Woodsie did not reply. His beady eyes were lowered, his expression like marble. Then quite suddenly, without moving from his perched position on the guard-rail, his eyes flicked up and darted across to Frankie. 'How perceptive of you, Lewis,' he said, with a suggestion of the smile that could fell any victim stone dead from twenty paces. 'I presume you can also tell us precisely *where* Robert Louis Stevenson was born?'

Frankie was already beginning to wish he had never spoken. But as he opened his mouth a shaft of wintry sunshine beamed through the window beside him. It was as though a spotlight had been turned directly on to him for his reply. ''E was born in Edinburgh, sir. November 13th, 1850.'

There was an astonished gasp from the entire class. Prof, always protective of Frankie, quickly lowered his eyes, covered his mouth with one of his hands and whispered, 'Don't, Frankie!'

But it was too late. Woodsie was on the attack. He raised himself up from the guard-rail, and moved slowly between the rows of desks. 'Congratulations, Lewis. I had no idea you were such an authority on Scottish writers.' He reached Frankie's desk, crossed his arms, and stared straight at the boy. 'Perhaps you can tell us the *titles* of some of the books written by Robert Louis Stevenson?'

Prof bit his lip hard. There was nothing he could do to help Frankie now.

Frankie felt a tight band across his chest. He was only a short breath away from having an asthma attack. ''E wrote *Kidnapped*, sir. And *Dr Jekyll and Mr 'Yde.*' He was starting to wheeze. ''E also wrote *Treasure Island.*'

Woodsie remained stone-faced and his large ears seemed to wiggle as he tensed his jaw. 'Did he now?' He unfolded his arms and leaned with one hand on Frankie's desk. As he did so, Prof moved out of his way, almost stifled by the raged heat from the English master's body. 'And would you care to tell us what *Treasure Island* is all about, Lewis?' leered Woodsie, moving in for the kill.

Frankie took a deep breath and wheezing badly, replied, 'It's about this pirate, sir. 'Is name's Long John Silver. 'E tries to stop Jim 'Awkins from findin' the 'idden treasure.'

'Fascinating! Well done, Lewis!' Woodsie turned away and made his way back to the fireplace, still calling out his remarks to Frankie. 'And who played the part of Long John Silver ?'

Frankie looked puzzled. 'Sir?'

Woodsie reached the fireplace, and resumed his

sitting position on the guard-rail. 'The film, Lewis. The film of *Treasure Island*. Wasn't it on at some picture-house around here lately?'

For some reason, Frankie deeply resented this particular jibe, despite the fact that Woodsie was well-known for his sarcasm. Sitting upright in his seat and peering over the heads of the boys in front of him, he started to protest. 'Yes, sir, but—'

Woodsie was far too vain to allow any further discussion. 'Since you are an authority on the works of Robert Louis Stevenson, I think it would be a good idea for us *all* to take the subject for tonight's homework.' Smiling broadly at the entire class, he called, 'Four foolscap pages, please.'

If looks could kill, Frankie would have been struck stone dead by every boy in the room. But the moment was saved by the distant wail of the air-raid siren coming from Highbury Corner Police station, a sound they rarely heard these days. Almost immediately the siren wail was picked up by the ringing of handbells throughout the school, and every boy in the room hurriedly left his desk and made for the door.

'No rushing!' yelled Woodsie above the clatter of boys' feet on the wooden floorboards. 'Did you hear what I said? Take – your – time!' Nonetheless, Woodsie wasn't far behind them.

Despite Headmaster 'Boggie' Marsh's instructions that air-raid drills were to be carried out 'in a quiet and orderly manner', the excited yells and the clattering hundreds of feet clip-clopping down the stairs into the bowels of the old Victorian building, echoed stunningly from the walls. Most of the pupils were leaping down the stairs two at a time, but Frankie and the Prof took their time.

'You must've been out of your mind!' yelled Prof, his voice battling to be heard over the sound of cat-calls, whistles, and excited laughter. 'You *know* what happens when you try to pick a fight with Woodsie.'

'I wasn't tryin' ter pick a fight wiv no one,' protested Frankie, avoiding being pushed down the stairs by two rowdy kids from one of the lower forms who were trying to pass in a hurry. 'But Woodsie was wrong, Prof an' that's all there is to it.'

But how come you know so much about Robert Louis Stevenson – where he was born, and all that stuff?'

'It was in the front cover of the book.'

'Book? What book? What are you talking about?'

'*Treasure Island*!' Frankie came to a halt on the stairs, allowing the stream of boys to push past at a relentless pace. '*She* gave it ter me. The woman in 19 'Adleigh. 'An you know what? The book's much better than the film.'

The Prof stared through his tortoiseshell specs in disbelief. '*She* gave you a book?' There was shrill incredulity in his voice. 'The old Kraut in 19 Hadleigh Villas gave *you* a book?'

At the bottom of the stairs they had to join a long queue of boys who were slowly shuffling into the air-raid shelter.

'I told yer the uvver day,' said Frankie, making quite sure he could not be overheard. 'She *collects* books – lots of 'em. You should just see 'er 'ouse. It's like walkin' inter a library or somefin'.

Prof was thoroughly curious. 'Frankie, you didn't tell me the old girl gave you a book. All you said was that she dragged you into the house and gave you a good telling off.'

'She did!' Frankie was beginning to get irritated. 'But she give me a book 'cos she said reading was far better than goin' ter the pictures. Now give over, Prof – I don't wanna keep talkin' about it!'

The air-raid shelter was no comfort to anyone, for it was nothing more than a large stone hall surrounded by what looked like Victorian prison cells. Most of the boys imagined that it had been used as some kind of children's borstal in the old days and nobody seriously thought for one moment that if there should be a direct hit by a doodle-bug, or a V2-rocket, there was even the remotest possible chance of survival. However, it at least gave the *impression* of being somewhere safe to go, even though it was bitterly cold in winter, with no form of heating. Most of the boys crouched on the floor in any available space they could find, and that included the empty cells, each of which was lit with nothing more than a bare electric light bulb. And there was even less space today, for a class of twenty or so girls from the nearby Highbury Hill Girls' School was among the shelterers. Because of the emergency exchange system between the two schools they had come over for one of old Charlie Garrett's history lessons. Both schools adored Charlie, for he was a real character, always sucking one loose front tooth.

'It's funny how I've never seen the old Kraut 'round our way before.' Prof, scarf covering his head and ears, was shivering with the cold. He was a delicate boy with a wonky heart, the result of a bout of rheumatic fever when he was small. But at least it got him excused from School sports, a subject he loathed. 'I mean, I've been past that jumble shop in Hornsey Road dozens of times, but I had no idea it was *her* running the place.'

Frankie wasn't paying much attention to his pal. His eye was fixed on a group of girls from 'the Hill' sitting just opposite him. In particular there was one girl who fascinated him. She was about fifteen years old, with bright, violet-coloured eyes and long blonde hair and she kept her eyes lowered all the time, only looking up when she thought that Frankie wasn't watching her.

'I heard that the woman who runs that shop lost her husband at Dunkirk . . .' The Prof's nose was running and he wiped it with his sleeve. 'My Auntie said he was an officer or something. Buried up at Finchley.'

Frankie didn't answer.

'How come they allow a Kraut to run a shop right in the middle of London?' Prof persisted.

Suddenly, Frankie turned on him, eyes blazing. 'She's *not* a Kraut, Prof! Why can't you stop callin' 'er that? She's *English*! She told me she was 'an I believe her.'

Frankie's raised voice caused the blonde girl to look up with a start. But when Frankie turned to look back at her, she lowered her eyes shyly.

Prof felt quite hurt at being talked to in such a way by Frankie who was supposed to be his pal. So he rested his head against the stone wall behind him, closed his eyes, and for a full minute didn't say another word. But eventually, he couldn't resist speaking. 'Have you told Jeff and the others yet?'

Frankie was still watching the girl opposite. 'What about?'

'About the old – about the woman in the jumble shop.'

Frankie turned briefly. ''Course I told 'em. But they only took the piss out of me – as usual. It wouldn't 'ave 'appened if Jeff 'adn't got me ter knock on that door.' It was at times like this that Frankie was grateful that out of the Merton Street gang, only he and Prof had places at Highbury Grammar School.

Prof decided to pursue the subject no more. All of a sudden he felt lonely. Frankie was his best pal, probably his only real pal, and he hated it when Frankie snapped at him.

Frankie was more and more aware that the girl sitting opposite was sneaking more and more sly looks at him and on one occasion, he accidentally caught her glance, and she actually tried to smile at him. Frankie immediately panicked and quickly lowered his eyes to the stone floor. Girls didn't really mean much to Frankie, except his sister Helen of course. But she was different. Helen was more like a mate to him, like any boy. This girl was odd though. Her looking at him all the time gave him a funny feeling, something he hadn't felt before.

'Are you comin' on the trip on Sunday, then?' The Prof was aware of the girl opposite, and was irritated that she was attracting Frankie's attention.

Frankie turned with a start. 'Trip? What trip?'

'We're all biking over to Hackney Marshes – depending on the weather, of course. Didn't Jeff tell you?'

'No. Nobody told me.' Frankie felt a dull ache in his stomach. Once again the Merton Street gang were going off on a Sunday bike ride – and because he was the only one without a bike, he couldn't go. 'Anyway, yer know I couldn't come,' he snapped irritably.

'Well, maybe you can persuade your old man to buy you that Raleigh. It's still in Pascall's window. I saw it over the weekend.'

Frankie didn't answer. How could he tell Prof that there wasn't a chance in hell that his father could afford to buy that Raleigh Sports bike for him. Frankie firmly believed that dreams never came true.

Prof sensed Frankie's depression. 'If you want, I could ask the man downstairs at my place if you could borrow his bike. He doesn't use it much. He's far too fat.'

Frankie looked up, his eyes were shining with excitement. 'Yer mean it, Prof? Yer really mean it?'

'Why not? It's a bit of an old clanger, though. Only one speed. But it'd get you there. We could have a good time, Frankie. How about it? Will you come?'

Before Frankie had the chance to answer, 'Boggy' Marsh's voice echoed out from the other end of the corridor. 'Keep the chatter down, you two!' In a flash he was upon Frankie and the Prof, his schoolmaster's gown trailing around his short, stubby legs as he walked. 'If you concentrated a little more on your maths, Lewis, perhaps you wouldn't have quite so much to say!'

Frankie lowered his head, and mumbled 'Sir'

apologetically. Ever since he started at the school, Frankie had loathed 'Boggy'. To Frankie, he was a headmaster straight out of a horror film but in reality Mr Marsh was simply a strict disciplinarian, whose obsessions were religion and mathematics. Fingering his horn-rimmed spectacles, 'Boggy' turned and floated back down the corridor and, as soon as he was out of range, Frankie made a rude sign at him with two fingers. This immediately caused the girls sitting opposite to snigger.

'Boggy' was hardly out of sight when a sudden distant explosion shook the entire building. Frankie and the Prof immediately threw themselves face down onto the stone floor, and everyone else, including the girls from 'the Hill' did likewise. Nobody panicked, but as small bits of ceiling plaster fluttered down onto them, Frankie yelled out, 'We've been hit!'

'No! We're all right!'

In the eerie silence that followed, Frankie looked up to see who had spoken. The hall, corridors, and cells were full of young faces, some half-giggling, others fraught with anxiety.

'We're all right,' called the voice again. It was the young girl from 'the Hill' sitting opposite Frankie, smiling reassuringly at him. 'I think it was quite a way off.'

Frankie didn't know how to react. Somehow he felt embarrassed that he had shown fear. 'I know that,' he snapped angrily. 'I'm not stupid!'

Half-an-hour later, the 'All Clear' siren had sounded, and the boys of Highbury Grammar were swarming out through the school gates. Soon the Highbury Grove and St Paul's Roads were seething with mauve school blazers and caps with black and mauve badges showing the school motto: '*Ne absiste*' – 'Never Surrender'. As Frankie made his way home down the Holloway Road, leather satchel thrown carelessly over one shoulder, the idea of surrendering to a girl from Highbury Hill Fields School was stubbornly far from his mind.

The untypically clear blue November sky above was streaked with a long white vapour trail, which gradually spread out and dispersed into a tiny white puff of cloud. It was as though a huge, mystical phoenix had passed by high over the roofs and chimneypots, leaving a spell of magic in its wake. But this had been no phoenix. It was the mark of something far more deadly, silent and ferocious.

The final destination of yet another of Hitler's new secret weapons, the hated V–2 rocket, was a row of terraced houses in a working-class district on the other side of war-torn London, where the 'magic' was certainly not felt by its unsuspecting victims.

Chapter Four

Gracie Lewis rarely went into her son and daughter's bedroom. As far as she was concerned, Frankie and Helen were old enough to keep their own room clean and tidy and, if they didn't, well, they could lump it. But on the Wednesday afternoon following the weekend that Helen had gone off on a trip to the Essex countryside with her friends, Ivy and Joyce, Gracie, hanging up her washing in the back yard, had noticed that the curtains were still drawn at Helen and Frankie's bedroom window.

When Gracie entered the room, a fag dangling from her lips as usual, the first thing she noticed was that the place smelt of dog. Despite the fact that time and time again she had told Frankie not to take Winston into his room at night, the mongrel continued to sleep on his master's bed. Gracie quickly drew back the curtains and opened the window. When she turned to look at the room, it was exactly as she had expected. Neither bed had been made, and clothes were strewn carelessly around the room. She shrugged; neither she nor Reg were exactly house-proud themselves.

Gracie turned back to the open window, staring down at the Anderson shelter that had completely engulfed the small back yard, once full of daffodils and marigolds. The war had changed Merton Street and the people who lived there. And not for the better. Before, people had kept themselves to themselves, but nowadays everybody stopped in the street and chatted. Not her, though. She still kept to herself. Stubbing her cigarette out on the window ledge, Gracie closed the window again. She glanced at the small wooden cabinet at the side of Frankie's bed, where she found a copy of his favourite Picture-goer film magazine, and, surprisingly, a book – *Treasure Island* by Robert Louis Stevenson. It was the first time she had ever seen a book amongst Frankie's possessions. Then she held back the curtain separating Frankie's side of the bedroom from Helen's. She deliberately avoided looking into the mirror of Helen's tiny dressing-table. Gracie always avoided mirrors. Her own image distressed and irritated her, for she never took any trouble with her appearance, with her straight cut hair which Frankie always thought made her look like a prison inmate. And her eyes were always doleful, always tired-looking though she had a good, clear complexion and, in her young days, had been pretty.

It was only as she was about to leave the room that Gracie suddenly noticed something sticking out from beneath Helen's crumpled pillow. She came back into the room and picked it up. It was the photograph of a young soldier . . .

Downstairs, the street door slammed, a sure sign that Frankie was home from school. Winston was first to greet him, barking excitedly, leaping up so that he very nearly knocked Frankie down. 'Down Winnie! Down boy!' Frankie was laughing wildly as he found himself pinned against the passage wall, his face being licked all over. But when they rushed up the stairs together, they found their way barred on the landing by Frankie's mother.

''Ow many times!' Gracie's voice was shrill and bad tempered. ''Ow many times to I have to tell yer not ter take that bleedin' animal into your room. It smells like a bog in there!'

Frankie's happy mood changed immediately. Even the sight of his mother depressed him. 'It's none 'er yer business! Winnie's my dog. I *like* 'im sleepin' wiv me. Nobody asked yer ter go pokin' 'round my room!'

Gracie's eyes blazed with anger. The only time she ever seemed to spring to life was when she was quarrelling with Frankie. 'Now you listen ter me, yer little sod! I'm the one that cleans up in this 'ouse. I'm the one that has ter clear up after *your* dog does 'is business anywhere 'e bleedin' chooses!'

Winston cowered behind Frankie. As usual, he knew he was the cause of all the rumpus.

'You're always pickin' on Winston! You're always blamin' 'im for everythin''! Frankie pushed his way past his mother and made straight for the tiny lavatory behind her. Winston followed him in. He quickly bolted the door, yelling, 'Why can't yer leave 'im alone? It's not fair!'

Frankie could clearly see the figure of his mother through the two smoked glass panels on the door. As she pressed her face forward she looked ghostly and menacing. 'If you don't get that bleedin' dog outa there, I swear ter God I'll 'ave 'im put down!' Frankie refused to answer, so his mother shouted louder, and banged on the lavatory door. 'Did you 'ear what I said!' she screeched.

'Leave him alone, Mum!' Frankie shouted back angrily. 'Leave 'im alone!'

'Right! If that's the way you want it!' Frankie could hear his mother hurrying down the stairs. 'Just wait 'til yer farver gets 'ome. "E'll 'ave yer guts fer garters!' By the time she had reached the bottom of the stairs, Gracie was in a blind rage. 'And don't fink I don't know about that book in your room!' Her voice was almost hysterical. 'If I find yer've nicked it, I'll get the narks 'round 'ere!'

Frankie pulled a face. It was obvious his mother had been having a good snoop around his room, and he hated her for it. Then he panicked. Suppose she'd taken *Treasure Island*? Elsa loved her books; what did she call them – her 'friends'? If anything had happened to that book, he'd never forgive himself. For the next few minutes, he sat on the lavatory seat, waiting for his mother to go back into her kitchen and forget all about him. As always, whenever he needed peace and quiet, Frankie used the lavatory as a sanctuary; many an evening he and Winston had spent time there, sometimes up to an hour. Usually, he just sat there looking at the four drab walls, which, if he stretched out with both his hands, he could reach easily. But, drab though it was, Frankie's imagination had turned this tiny room in the house into something completely different. Most times, he imagined he was sitting in the front row of the dress circle of his beloved Gaumont Cinema, a once-great, plush building in the Holloway Road, now devastated by the doodle-bug which gutted it just a few months before. If he closed his eyes he could still recall one of his favourite films with Tyrone Power or Alice Faye, or Basil Rathbone in some spooky *Sherlock Holmes* adventure. There were times when Frankie's father stopped on the landing outside the lavatory, thinking that his son had gone mad as he listened to the boy wailing like the sound of the Gaumont cinema organ being played by their much-loved resident organist, Edward O'Henry. As for Winston, well he just slept through it all, although his snores were not very conducive to Frankie's extravagant dreams.

It was not until he heard the kitchen door slam that he felt it safe to emerge from his sanctuary. Rushing up to his room, he collected Elsa's *Treasure Island* and, with Winston tagging close behind, quickly left the house. Although it was getting dark, there was still a slight red glow on the rooftops above Merton Street, for the sun had been shining miraculously from sunrise to sunset, a rare treat for a cold November day. Frankie had discarded his cap, but was still wearing his school blazer and scarf. His grey flannel shorts were no protection against the frosty night, and his legs were rapidly matching the colour of his blazer. Four-year-old Winston, a shaggy black and white cross between a labrador and a back-yard mongrel, had plenty of hair to keep him warm, and seemed impervious to the cold.

There were plenty of people around in the street, some of them gossiping with their neighbours, others hurrying back from late afternoon shopping in the Seven Sisters Road. Outside number 47 a group of young kids were still playing hopscotch on the pavement, encouraged by old Bert Gorman, who always tried to join in the kids' street games. As it was almost blackout time, people all along the street were drawing dark blinds or curtains at their front room windows and, as there had been no street gas lamps lit since the start of the war, total darkness would soon descend on the entire neighbourhood. But there was hardly a chimneypot anywhere that wasn't already hard at work, with palls of thick black smoke billowing up into the cloudless, deep red sky.

Frankie decided to make his way to Seven Sisters Road the long way round, which took him to the far end of Merton Street, and then into Herslet Road. After saying goodnight to Bert Gorman, Frankie made his way to the end of the street. On the way he ignored Mrs Robinson at number 22, who was, as usual, conspicuously arranging her new net curtains so that they draped like the curtains over the screen at the Gaumont cinema. 'All kippers and curtains,' thought most of her neighbours. And her husband was no better, for he seemed to encourage it. Winston showed no respect for number 22's shining white gate, and paused only long enough to raise his back paw and leave his mark. Then Frankie quickened his pace so that he could hurriedly pass number 78, where old Clancy lived – 'nancy Clancy' to the kids in the street, who teased him mercilessly every time he set foot outside his front door, to do his shopping, or to venture out for a pink gin at the Eaglet pub.

By the time Frankie and Winston reached the Seven Sisters Road, most of the blackout blinds were already in place. But the shops were still open, although the window displays could only be seen in whatever natural light was available from the road outside. One or two shopkeepers however – namely Ma Digby in the greengrocers' shop – were becoming somewhat careless of late. Since June, when the Allied forces had landed in France, people were beginning to sense that the war was coming to an end, despite the fact that Hitler's doodle-bugs and rockets were still a menace. On more than one occasion Ma Digby had been warned by a Special Constable to 'keep 'er lights to 'erself!'

At the junction of Seven Sisters Road and Hornsey Road, Frankie had only to say 'Wait!' to Winston for him to sit down obediently and wait with his master for the traffic to clear. Although everyone warned Frankie to keep Winston on a leash when they were out for their walk, he always insisted that Winston would never disobey him.

Once the traffic lights had changed, Frankie and Winston crossed the road, passed Stagnells the baker shop with its seductive smells of freshly baked bread, and continued their walk along Seven Sisters Road. It was just after five o'clock when they reached Pascall's bike shop on the corner of Hadleigh Villas. The sky above was now an inky black and the first stars of the evening where beginning to show themselves. This was the moment Winston dreaded, for he knew that once Frankie had reached the bike shop, it could be an endless wait while his master gazed at the one bike on prominent display in the window. Sure enough, this was to be no exception.

Frankie pressed his hands against the glass. There it was, hanging from a wire right in the centre of the window, the Raleigh Sports, with the dropped handle-bars and three speeds – the bike of Frankie's dreams. Every time he looked at it, he could hear the theme music of some big Hollywood love film echoing all around him, and Edward O'Henry at the organ of the Gaumont cinema building his dream to a crescendo. To Frankie, this was *the* bike of all time. He could just imagine himself gliding effotlessly along the road to Southend, way ahead of the Merton Street gang, the sun and wind caressing his face as he pedalled. But there was no hope that he would ever own this one – not at the incredible price of two pounds and ten shillings! Why, it was probably more than his old man earned in a month at the Hornsey Road Baths. But it cost nothing to dream, and, with his nose and face pressed against the window, he dreamed. But the condensation from his hot breath against the cold glass soon destroyed that dream and, much to Winston's relief, he eventually moved on.

Turning off Seven Sisters Road, Frankie and Winston made their way down Hadleigh Villas. Although Frankie was carrying Elsa's book with him, he didn't stop at number 19 because he had already found out that the shop she ran kept open most evenings until seven o'clock. The two of them made their way to Barclay's jumble shop on the corner of Hornsey Road. When they got there, the shutters were already down, but the shop was obviously still open for business, for a light could be seen beneath the door.

'Won't be long, Winnie.' Winston sat down obediently. His reward was a piece of bread which Frankie had saved from the cheese sandwich his mother had made him for his lunch. Then, retrieving Elsa's *Treasure Island* from underneath his pullover, Frankie took a deep, apprehensive breath, and went into the shop.

As Frankie's head peered around the door, the bell above shook and tinkled.

'Be with you in just one moment!' Elsa's voice called from the other side of the shop where she was attending to a woman who was buying a secondhand dress for her small child.

Frankie remained by the door, looking around. When people called this a jumble shop they were right. It was fairly spacious and part of it was for cheap, secondhand jewellery – brooches, rings, necklaces, cuff-links, bracelets, ear-rings – everything a woman or man needed for personal decoration. Then there was the bric-à-brac section where everything from a silver-plated picture-frame to a small-sized brass model elephant could be found. There was a mountain of different objects piled on top of each other, covering the shop counter, an old varnished table, and various travelling trunks. Tin-openers, delicate china cups and saucers, moth-eaten teddy bears and dolls of every shape and size, kitchen utensils, pots and pans, a paraffin stove, odd rolls of wallpaper, and even an ancient typewriter. And books! Whichever direction Frankie looked in – there were books, dozens and dozens of them, piled high. There was very little available space for moving around, for old furniture cluttered the place, with kitchen chairs piled on top of each other, and a wash-stand balanced on a chaise-longue looking as though one finger could topple the whole collection. And on one entire side of the shop were rows and rows of secondhand clothes: dresses and suits and raincoats, fake fur stoles and corsets; a vast collection of hats, some with feathers, some with wax fruit; men's flat, checked caps and sombre-looking bowler hats. It was an incredible sight. If this was a shop where anything was bought or sold as the claim above the shop door said, then Frankie reckoned more was bought by Elsa Barclay than was ever sold.

Elsa took some time to serve her customer. 'Charming!' she kept saying to the little girl who was trying a pretty, though somewhat faded floral-patterned dress. The mother was clearly thrilled to have such attention for her little girl and a few minutes later, Elsa was opening the door for her customers, beaming with delight that she had earnt the princely sum of one shilling and ninepence. After the customers had gone, Elsa turned to Frankie, who was hovering behind a brass elephant. 'So – Misster Frankie Lewis!'

Frankie looked sheepish. 'I've brought back yer book.' He held out *Treasure Island*.

'Ah!' Elsa quickly advanced on him and virtually snatched the book from him. 'But – did you read it?'

Frankie nodded.

Every single page?'

Frankie nodded again, firmly.

'Excellent! Excellent!' Elsa beamed with delight, and clutched the book to her breast in triumph.

The shop was much brighter than the parlour at 19 Hadleigh Villas, and Frankie could see that Elsa's hair was almost unnaturally ginger.

'So, now we must find you another book to read!' She made her way behind the shop counter. 'But first you must tell me all about *Treasure Island*!'

And for the next half-hour or so, Frankie did exactly that. Elsa sat on her high chair behind the counter and listened enraptured as Frankie recounted the adventures of Jim Hawkins and the bloodthirsty Long John Silver, of the good ship *Hispaniola*. The more excited Frankie became as he described what he had read, the more quickly Elsa sipped her tea. When he'd finished, Elsa yelled, 'Bravo!' and applauded rapturously.

The noise alarmed Winston, who started barking outside and scraping against the shop door.

To Frankie's amazement, Elsa told him not to leave the poor creature out in the cold, and when Winston was brought into the shop, Frankie was even more amazed to see her making a fuss of the dog, something Frankie's mother had never done. And when Elsa fed him a small piece of her home-made apple cake, it was clear that this was the start of a beautiful friendship.

It was almost eight o'clock when Helen Lewis got home from work. Although she quite enjoyed her job in the Dolcis shoe shop in the Holloway Road, it was very frustrating at times. Since the start of the war there had been a shortage of good footwear and, even when there was anything decent to buy, most people didn't have enough ration coupons. Her hours were from nine to six, but by the time she and her friend Ivy had met up for a cup of Camp coffee in the café next door, she was nearly always late home for her supper.

Tonight, as Helen put her key into the lock of the front door, she could feel the 'atmosphere' inside. Her heart sank. Gracie was a moody and ungiving person, and when she felt fed up, she made everyone else feel likewise. Reg wasn't much better. He got up in the morning, went to work at the Baths, and came home again. He didn't seem to have any friends; if he did, Helen never saw any of them. Many, many times she wished her mum and dad would do what other mums and dads did, go out together occasionally

– to the pictures, or for a drink in the pub. But her parents' lives seemed to consist of reading the *Daily Mirror* and listening to the wireless. It was so different to Helen herself. Helen loved the company of her friends and, unlike her mother, despite the austerity of wartime, really cared how she looked. She always made sure her light brown shoulder-length hair was combed, and whenever she could get her hands on some lipstick was careful never to over use it. But, although they were so different, Helen *did* love her mother, and did everything she could to understand her. But it wasn't easy.

'Who is 'e, then?' Gracie was ironing at one end of the kitchen table when Helen walked in. Reg was in his usual chair by the oven range, reading the *Daily Mirror* and listening to *Forces' Favourites* on the wireless.

'What d'yer mean?' Helen hadn't even put down her handbag.

'Don't give me none 'er that. You *know* what I mean!' Resting her iron upright on the kitchen table, Gracie nodded her head towards something on the kitchen table. 'Who is 'e?'

Helen looked at the snapshot of Eric and coloured immediately. 'Oh, Mum,' she said, quickly picking up the snapshot and putting it into her handbag. 'I wish you wouldn't take fings from my room. I'm entitled to a little privacy, yer know.'

'I asked you a question! Who *is* 'e?'

'Leave off, Grace.' Reg Lewis spoke without

emerging from behind his newspaper. 'It's none of our business.'

Gracie hated to be contradicted. 'If she comes 'ome at eight o'clock at night, it *is* our business!' Then she swung her anger back at Helen. 'What 'appens if yer get accosted by some man in the street? What 'appens if there's an air-raid?'

Helen sighed, and took off her coat. 'I won't get accosted in the street, Mum. And we don't get air-raids any more. The war's nearly over.'

'You tell that ter those people who got blown up in that rocket up near the Archway the uvver week. You mark my words, it ain't over yet – not by a long way.'

Helen knew it was no use arguing. She sat down at the other end of the table, which had been laid for her supper and when she took off the plate covering it, it hardly looked very appetising: cold spam fritters, pickle, and two chunks of bread thinly spread with margarine. Helen sighed, but hoping to put Gracie in a better mood, tucked in to it as though it was a feast. *Forces Favourites* was still bellowing out from the wireless on the dresser.

'You still 'aven't said.' Gracie, arms crossed, was glaring at her daughter. 'Who's this bloke then?'

'Don't be silly, Mum,' replied Helen, mouth full of spam fritter. 'I don't know anyfin' about 'im. ''E's a pal of Ivy's.'

'Oh yes? Then what's that pitture doin' under yer pillow?'

Helen tried not to sound flustered. 'I don't know 'ow it got there. It probably fell out of my dress pocket when I was makin' my bed. Is there any tea?'

Although she didn't believe a word of what Helen had said, Gracie was momentarily distracted. Using an iron-cloth, she picked up her old flat iron and took it out to the scullery for re-heating on the gas-stove. Just when Helen thought she was getting a moment's peace, her mother's shrill voice called: 'Are you sure yer didn't see this bloke over the weekend?'

Helen looked up with a start to find her father watching her carefully over the top of his newspaper.

''Elen! Did you 'ear what I said?' Gracie's voice could be heard above the sound of her filling the kettle at the scullery sink. 'Did you go off wiv this bloke at the weekend?'

Helen's frantic eyes were fixed on her father who was trying to say something to her, without actually saying it.

'Wot's the matter wiv yer!' Gracie, kettle in hand, was peering round the scullery door. 'Don't I speak the King's English or somefin'?'

Now Helen was really flustered. She just couldn't say *anything* to her mother. How could she tell Gracie that she had indeed spent the weekend away with a soldier she had only known for a few short weeks? How could she tell her that she was madly in love with Eric Sibley, and that her heart was breaking because he had already been called away on active duty, and he might be killed, and she might never see him again?

To her amazement, it was her father who came to her rescue.

'Leave the gel alone, Gracie!' he said, sharply.

Reg Lewis was dimly aware that he had not been a good father to his kids, mainly because he didn't know *how* to create a good family life. When he was eight his parents had split up and, as neither had wanted him, he was put into a Children's Home at Bethnal Green.

'She's already told yer,' he snapped, slamming down his newspaper. 'She went ter Essex with Ivy and Joyce and their people.'

On the wireless, Jean Metcalfe was playing a record for a girl in the East End of London from her sailor husband on active duty. It was Bing Crosby singing *Always*. Gracie had to shout to be heard. 'Oh yes? And 'ow do we know that?'

Suddenly, Reg got up from his seat, slammed down his newspaper on to his chair, and angrily turned off the wireless. 'Because Ivy's old man came inter the barfs last night, and *'e* told me. Ivy's old man and woman went wiv 'em. Is that good enuff for yer, Grace? Is it?'

Gracie was completely taken aback by Reg's

energetic vehemence. For a moment she could say nothing. So she quickly retreated back into the scullery.

Helen could hardly believe what she had just heard. Her father had lied for her! He had deliberately lied. As she watched him turn and leave the room without looking at her, she realised that he knew about her weekend away with Eric. She picked up a slice of bread, and took a bite of it, but it stuck in her throat. Someone had betrayed her. And the only other person who knew her secret was Frankie . . .

Frankie didn't know what had hit him. He had only gone to Elsa's shop to return her book, and now here he was helping her to move boxes and books. He had even been given the jobs of dusting the shelves, and sweeping behind the counter, and getting rid of the cobwebs around the lights. But for some reason he didn't mind. In fact, for the past hour he had been thoroughly enjoying himself. Winston, too, was having a whale of a time. Not only was he full of apple-cake and bread and cheese, he was allowed to stretch out on a moth-eaten Persian rug. Apart from him, the shop was a hive of activity, with Elsa very firmly at the helm.

'Winston is a good name to be given, my friend.' The way Elsa was talking made it clear to Frankie that Elsa thought he was far more important than a dog. 'After all, Winston Churchill is one of the greatest human beings this century. He is the defender of truth, the hope and inspiration of all mankind. We Jewish people have much to thank Mister Winston Churchill for.'

'Are *you* really a Jew?' called Frankie from the top of a stepladder.

Elsa's back straightened proudly. 'Yes, I am Jewish!' She eyed him warily. 'What makes you ask?'

'Nuffink, really. I just fawt you was a German, that's all.'

'One can be German *and* Jewish, and one can also be *English* and Jewish.' There was an air of indignation in Elsa's response.

Frankie was beginning to feel the effects of all the dust and he was now quite hoarse. 'But you ain't got a big nose. My dad says all Jews are greedy, an' they've got big noses.'

Elsa flinched. 'Then your father is either ignorant or stupid. I suspect he is both.' She glanced up quickly to see Frankie balancing precariously from the top of the ladder. 'Please come down from that ladder. You are making me and Winston very nervous.'

Frankie came down from the ladder and leant it against the wall. 'I've heard your old man got killed at Dunkirk. Is that right?'

Elsa shivered and went very quiet. She was taken aback by the boy's bluntness.

Frankie perched on a trunk in front of her. ''Ow'd he get it, then?'

Elsa turned on him and snapped, 'Mein Gott, it's none of your business!'

Frankie was shocked. Although Elsa had been bossy with him, he had actually started to like her. But this outburst was different. 'Sorry, miss.' His eyes widened with puzzlement, for he didn't understand what he'd done wrong.

Elsa glared at him for a moment, then realised how foolish she'd been. How could she expect a boy of Frankie's age to understand the pain of losing someone you love so much. Without saying anything, she slowly pulled a dust cover over the rail of secondhand dresses, then started a slow, methodical tour of the shop. Frankie and Winston watched her in awed fascination, for it was an extraordinary spectacle, as she appeared to glide from one display to another, as though in slow motion, touching objects with the tips of her fingers, caressing them as though they were living things. For a few fleeting moments Frankie thought Elsa looked quite beautiful, like an angel floating on air. Finally, she reached the electric light switch, and turned it off. For a brief moment there was total darkness but, before Frankie had had time to grow accustomed to the dark, Elsa had raised the blackout blind, to allow a great shaft of moonlight through the window, bathing everything within in a ghostly white colour.

Elsa sat on a stool by the window, staring up at the almost full moon, her voice low and gentle. 'Yes, Frankie. My husband *was* killed at

Dunkirk. His name was Robert. Major Robert Michael Barclay, Royal Parachute Regiment!'

There was an anguished smile on Elsa's face as she started to relive her life all over again. 'We met in 1923 when Robert was on holiday in Germany and we fell in love and married despite the differences in our race, our religion . . .' She smiled sadly. 'My parents were not happy – but they liked Robert and they knew that I would never give him up.' She laughed. 'I was always the strong-willed one of their children . . . Robert was a career officer and so we lived mostly abroad or in army accommodation. Then –' her voice faltered. 'Then Hitler came to power in Germany and suddenly Jewish people were outcasts in their own country. It all happened so quickly. One day, when I was holidaying with them and was spending the day with my dearest friend, I came home to find that my entire family had disappeared – my mother and father, two brothers and their wives and children, my sister . . . Even my dog, Greta, had gone. I – I never saw them again . . .' She swallowed hard, then continued. 'I knew that if I was to survive, even though I had a British passport, I had to get out of Germany at once. My friend Gertrude, also.'

She turned to look at Frankie. 'Do you know what we did?'

Frankie shook his head, enthralled. All he could see was a silhouette sitting at the window.

Elsa chuckled to herself. 'We dyed our hair blonde and we took all the money and jewellery we could, and made our way very slowly, very dangerously to England. We even got a lift from a Nazi officer at one point! I tell you, that was quite a ride!' She shook her head. She had almost forgotten about Frankie . . . 'The first time I saw Robert, you know, was in a Jewish restaurant in Berlin. All the tables were full, so he asked if he could join me and Gertrude. He told us that even though he wasn't a Jew, it was his favourite restaurant. The food he liked best in the whole world was veal stew with dumplings – and apple cake. Can you imagine it!' She chuckled to herself, and then sighed. 'I thought he was *so* handsome . . . Anyway, we got talking, and – well, six months later, we were married.'

Winston whimpered a little in his sleep.

'The closer this country came to war with Nazi Germany, the more I dreaded every time Robert went away. To give me something else to think about we moved into the house in Hadleigh Villas which had been his parents' and which he'd rented out for most of his army career, when he didn't need a base. And he bought me the shop.' Elsa was absolutely motionless, her eyes staring up through the window. In the eerie shaft of light her skin was fair and clear like that of a young girl. 'The last time I saw him alive was on the steps of number 19. He had a taxi waiting for him and he wouldn't let me go with him to

King's Cross Railway Station. As the taxi was leaving, I ran after it along the Seven Sisters Road – but there were so many other cars and it disappeared so very quickly . . .'

There was another long pause, but when she continued, her voice was calm and firm. 'They didn't tell me until the end of June 1940. The telegram just said . . . *We regret to inform you. . . . Captain Robert Michael Barclay, 2nd Division, Royal Parachute Regiment . . . killed in Action.*' She dabbed her lips with her handkerchief again, so that her words were slightly muffled. 'God forgive Adolf Hitler, Frankie, for *I* never shall.'

Frankie watched her in silence for a moment before speaking. 'I fink I'd better be gettin' 'ome.' He stood up, and patted Winston on the head. 'Come on Winnie.' The two of them slowly made their way to the door, but Frankie suddenly stopped at the side of a pile of old books. 'Please, miss. Could I take anuvver book?'

Elsa turned and, although Frankie couldn't quite see her, he thought there was a wisp of a smile on her face. 'Help yourself.'

Frankie couldn't see what he was taking, so he just picked up the first book he came to. Then he paused briefly and turned to Elsa, who was still standing at the window. 'Please? Could I come again termorrer?'

'I'll be expecting you,' she said quietly. 'Good night, Frankie.'

When Frankie got home his parents and Helen

were in the kitchen listening to *Appointment with Fear* on the wireless, so he sneaked in quietly and went straight to his room. The first thing he did when he got into bed was to look at the book he had just borrowed from Elsa. It wasn't quite what he had been expecting: *The History of the Steam Traction Engine.*

Nonetheless, he started to read it . . .

Chapter Five

Frankie was fast asleep when his sister Helen came into her part of the bedroom. He had managed five and a half pages of the *History of the Steam Traction Engine*, but by the time he'd got to the part about poppet-valves and coupling rods, his eyelids flickered and very soon he joined Winston in a chorus of snores. But not for long.

'Wake up, yer little tyke! Wake up!'

Winston woke in a panic and Frankie, still half asleep, leapt out of bed. 'Wot's up! Wot's goin' on!' His sister picked up one of his pillows and threw it at him. 'Stop it, 'Elen! Wot's up wiv yer!'

'I'll tell yer wot's up wiv me, yer treacherous little pig! Yer caved in on me, din yer? Din yer?' Helen, usually the most placid member of the family, was making no attempt to keep her voice down, for her parents had decided to sleep the night in the air-raid shelter.

'Wot yer talkin' about!' Frankie's back was pinned helplessly against the wall and the pocket of his old brown and white striped pyjama jacket was half ripped off. 'I dunno wot yer talkin' about!'

'You know wot I'm talkin' about, you stinkin' git!' Helen was now towering above her young brother, for she was standing on his bed. 'You told dad about my weekend away wiv Eric!'

'I din't!'

'You bloody did!'

This was the first time Frankie had ever heard his sister use a swear word. So he saw nothing wrong in doing the same. 'I bloody din't!'

As Helen got down from the bed, she trod directly onto *The History of the Steam Traction Engine*, which had fallen on to the floor. 'Then 'ow come dad knew all about it? 'E didn't say so, but 'e knows all right!'

'Well, *I* din't tell 'im!' Frankie was now yelling at Helen.

'Then *who* did?'

'Why don't you ask him, yer stupid cow!' Frankie was now so angry, he pushed his sister with both hands, sending her reeling back on to his bed.

Helen quickly pulled herself up and made a lunge at Frankie, dragging him back with her on to the bed. For the next moment or so they pushed and punched at each other in the kind of furious, wrestling match they'd often had since they were tiny. ''Ow could yer do such a fing! 'Ow could yer! Yer knew I didn't want mum and dad ter know. I'll never tell yer a secret again –

never!' And with that, Helen walloped him hard on the top of his head with the flat of her hand.

Frankie squealed and grabbed hold of Helen's hair. 'I din't tell him! I din't tell no one!' And with that, he grabbed hold of her shoulder-length hair and tugged hard.

The battle only came to an end when Winston decided to intervene. Leaping up on to the bed, he barked and barked at them both, and eventually, exhausted, both Helen and Frankie fell back on to their respective beds, having pulled the dividing curtain down in their furious antics. For a moment or so, both just lay without saying anything, trying to get their breath back. Winston made a brief yowling sound, settled down at the foot of Frankie's bed again, yawned, and fell asleep immediately.

Although she was still breathing heavily, Helen, lying flat on her bed staring up at the ceiling, was first to speak. 'Dad covered up fer me. 'E could only of done that if 'e knew.' She turned her head and looked at Frankie, who was staring up at the ceiling. 'Yer *must* 'ave told 'im, Frank.' Her voice had calmed down, and she was trying to sound more reasonable. 'You and Ivy were the only ones I told. It was you, wasn't it?'

Frankie turned his head and looked at her. 'No. I swear ter God, I never said a word.' Then he sat up, and propped himself up on his elbows. 'But you're right. 'E did know. When I went fer my barf on Friday night, 'e said 'e knew you'd gorn off fer a dirty weekend wiv some feller.'

Helen covered her face with both hands.

'If yer ask me, it was *'er* downstairs. Yer know wot that old cow's like.'

Helen uncovered her face. 'If mum had known she'd 'ave killed me stone dead by now. She only suspects because she found Eric's picture under my pillow.'

'She's an interferin' old cow!' Frankie said gloomily.

Helen sat up quickly, also propping herself on her elbows. 'No, Frank! That's not fair. Mum's a good woman—'

Frankie let out a sarcastic grunt.

'She *is*, underneath it all, and you treat 'er very badly at times.'

'An' wot about 'er?' he complained bitterly. ''Ow d'yer fink she treats me? She resents everyfin' I do. I only 'ave ter open my mouf, and she yells at me.'

'That' not true, Frank.'

'It is! Mum don't care if I live or die.'

Helen gasped. 'Frankie Lewis! 'Ow can you say such a thing? I know this is not easy, but old people always find it difficult ter get on wiv young people. Deep down inside, of course mum loves yer. She loves both 'er kids. But love is a two-way fing. If yer don't give 'er a chance ter love you, she'll always fink yer 'ate 'er.'

Frankie grunted and dropped his head down to the pillow again. He couldn't understand the way Helen kept defending their mother. It seemed to him that she was nothing like his pals' mums. They took notice of their kids, gave them a kiss when they went off to school and when they came back in the evening. But if he was to ever try and kiss *his* mum, she'd turn her cheek the other way as though he'd got leprosy or something. And as for his father – well, he wasn't much better. After Helen had turned the light off, Frankie lay in the dark for a long time pondering on just why he had to have a father who couldn't even buy his own son a Raleigh sports bike . . .

For Elsa, Thursday afternoon meant early closing day for Barclay's jumble shop. On the dot of 1 o'clock, she would take out the long wooden pole with the metal hook at the end, and pull the heavy wooden blinds down over the outside of the shop window. Then, after collecting her hat, usually the one with the veil and wax fruit, a black fur coat and a fox stole, she would lock up and make her way along Tollington Road, past the Astoria Cinema on the corner of Seven Sisters Road, and eventually on to Finsbury Park Underground Station, via the entrance just beneath the railway bridge. Usually, she had to wait no more than a few minutes for her train for, despite the war, the London Underground system was managed meticulously, with the trains nearly always punctual. Elsa loved the journey, for it gave her the chance to study the faces of the English people who sat so po-faced in their seats, nobody speaking or even acknowledging the other's presence. And she loved practising her English by reading advertisements like those for Zubes and Lyons Ointment, and also official Ministry of Defence warnings like: *'Careless Talk Costs Lives.'* Another favourite way of passing the journey was to sit in the rear compartment, usually quite empty, and to chat to the Guard. More than once the thought that she was an escaped lunatic from the Colney Hatch Asylum crossed his mind. Other times, she got so bored staring at the strips of bomb-blast protective tape across the windows that she fell asleep and went on to the next station.

Elsa's final weekly destination was always Gershners, the Jewish restaurant in North London's cosmopolitan Swiss Cottage. At three o'clock every Thursday afternoon she would meet her old friend Gertrude Rosenberg there, always at the same table in the corner by the window, and always ordering their customary afternoon tea and apple strudel. For an hour and a half they would indulge in their customary exchange of barbed one-upmanship, which occasionally ended in a tantrum from Elsa or floods of tears from Gertrude. Theirs was a real love-hate relationship, but at the heart of their friendship was their childhood together in Germany and the risks they had taken when escaping from Adolf Hitler's persecution of the Jewish people.

'If you come at zis time, why bother to come at all?' Gertrude, dressed almost identically to Elsa, was at her most spiky. She always hated to be the first one to arrive. 'Vot happened zis time?'

Elsa was still peeling off her gloves. 'They say a woman threw herself on to the railway track. Somewhere along the Piccadilly Line.'

Unlike Elsa, Gertrude's English accent was totally fractured, and she was furious that her friend refused to speak German when they were together. However, she could never resist the odd relapse into her mother tongue.'*Dumm frau*!' she snapped. 'She must have felt guilty about keeping her friend waiting!'

'Oh shut up, Gertrude!' snapped Elsa firmly. 'It's only two minutes past three!'

While the elderly waiter came to accept their order, Gertrude, raising her hat veil, and for a brief moment getting it caught up in her spectacles, suppressed her irritation by powdering her face. Once Elsa had ordered the usual tea and strudel, Gertrude was ready to pursue her weekly antagonism of her old friend. 'Zo, how are things in zat terrible shop of yours?'

'It's not a terrible shop, Gertrude. It gives me a lot of pleasure.'

'Does it make money?'

'Money isn't everything.'

Gertrude peered over the top of her compact mirror. Her face was shaped a bit like the fox on the fur stole she was wearing, and her cheeks, like Elsa's, were heavily rouged. She also had a large mole on the right hand side of her chin, which she had painted, like her eyelashes, with black mascara. 'It's a terrible shop,' she insisted, as always wanting the last word.

Gertrude had never liked the shop Robert Barclay had bought for his wife. To her, it was common to sell secondhand goods, and she felt Elsa was demeaning herself by running it. Gertrude had never approved of Elsa marrying an Englishman, especially a Christian Englishman and she had resented Robert Barclay taking her friend away from her. Gertrude herself had never married, though since arriving in England she had had a succession of gentleman friends, most of them mid-European exiles, and most of them very well-off.

'Do you know,' she said, 'if now you vere to sell zat shop, you could buy a very nice flat up here in Swiss Cottage.' She closed her powder compact, and slipped it into her handbag. 'Zere are some beautiful places in Goldhurst Terrace.' What she really meant was that it was in an area where there were plenty of their own sort, refugees from Hitler's invasion of Europe.

Elsa sighed and started aimlessly to rearrange her cutlery. 'I've told you before, Gertrude – I don't want to live in Swiss Cottage. I like it very much in Holloway. They are honest and hard-working people, there.'

Gertrude sniffed haughtily. 'How can you like zem vhen they paint your door viz swaztikas, and call you *dumm* vords in ze street?'

'Some people only see what they want to see, Gertrude. We mustn't forget that we are not the only ones to suffer. The people of this country have suffered, too and, to them, all Germans are the same – even if they are *Jewish* Germans.' Elsa stared out at the main road through the windows criss-crossed with protective bomb-blast tape, her mind on her own beloved part of London. 'I've grown very fond of those funny little streets where I live probably because they're so different to the old country. And you know, sometimes when I walk along the Seven Sisters Road, I can see my Robert as a young boy there, holding his mother's hand as they went out shopping together. It's strange, isn't it? I mean, I never knew him as a little boy, but I *can* see him.'

The elderly waiter brought their order, and Gertrude immediately complained about the sogginess of the apple strudels. But then Gertrude always complained about most things when she came to the restaurant; it was her way of trying to show how important she was. However, the elderly waiter, who was also an exile, knew her well, and snapped back with a dismissive, 'Zo vot do you vant me to do, make the pastry myself?' As the waiter waddled back to the kitchens, Gertrude glared at him and quickly used her fork to tuck into her strudel. 'You know your trouble, Elsa?' she muttered. 'You have no idea how to use your money.'

Elsa ignored her friend's remark, and used a knife and fork to cut her strudel. So many times she had listened to this same nagging from Gertrude, mainly because Gertrude was convinced that Elsa had a large amount of money stacked away somewhere. When they escaped to England in 1933, Elsa knew that her friend had sewn plenty of jewellery in her clothes – but how much it was all worth, Elsa had no idea. In return, Gertrude had always suspected that Elsa's family had managed to smuggle money out of Germany into a Swiss bank. But there was no way she could prove it without actually asking Elsa – and that she couldn't do. 'I always say, unless you invest for your old age, vot's ze use of having money. Zat is – ' Gertrude was taking a sly look at Elsa over her strudel, 'depending on how much you have to invest.'

Elsa clattered down her fork. 'Oh, do stop talking about money, Gertrude! I've told you so many times, money doesn't interest me. As long as I have a roof over my head and enough food to eat, who cares? Robert left me more than comfortable, and I'm a very lucky woman.'

'But vot happens if you die?'

'So I die. It happens to everyone in time.'

Gertrude's false eyelashes quivered with

irritation. '*Dumm frau*! You know vot I mean!'

Else put her knife and fork down, and wiped her lips on a paper napkin. 'I may be a stupid woman, Gertrude, but at least I'm not obsessed with money like you.'

Gertrude was outraged. 'Obsessed! You call *me* – obsessed!'

'Yes, I do.' Elsa was completely calm. 'Yes, Gertrude, I do.'

'Just because I like to buy nice things, and not all zat secondhand junk you sell in zat – zat shop of yours!

'I *like* secondhand junk!'

'Of course you do! It suits your position in life!'

The elderly waiter, hearing the two women's raised voices, recognised all the signs of yet another Thursday battlefield and shrugging, scuffled off back into the kitchen.

Now Elsa's hackles were rising. 'If it is my position in life to buy only things that *I* can afford, so be it!'

'Ha!' Gertrude let out a loud dismissive laugh. 'Vhen you die, Elsa Lieberman, ve shall see how much you you have *never* been able to afford!'

'When *I* die, Gertrude Rosenburg,' Elsa snapped back, 'at least no one can accuse *me* of being mean!'

This final remark was like a dagger to Gertrude's heart. Her lips started to quiver, her face crumpled, and she began a self-indulgent little sob. Then she rose to her feet, saying that she never wanted to see Elsa again as long as she lived, and a moment later she stormed out of the place, leaving Elsa to pay the bill. On the way, however, she managed to smile sweetly at a handsome, middle-aged man sitting by the door. Once outside, she lowered her hat veil, and swept quickly past the window, pointedly ignoring Elsa who was waving to her from inside, smiling.

The following Thursday, at three o'clock in the afternoon precisely, Elsa returned to the restaurant, where Gertrude was waiting at their usual table, in the corner, by the window, waiting for her tea, apple strudel, and, of course, her dearest and most cherished friend, Elsa Lieberman . . .

Chapter Six

The symphony orchestra was playing a Hollywood love theme at full blast and, in the middle of it all, was Frankie, resplendent in cycling shorts and school cap, gliding his way along the cycling path alongside the great Southend Road, the sun in his eyes, the wind on his cheeks, his blue and white Raleigh Sports bike the envy of all the other cyclists on the path . . .

'Who, I wonder, would ever want to ride on a thing like that?'

Frankie, nose pressed up against the window of Pascall's bike shop, turned with a start to find Elsa standing just behind him. 'Miss! What are you doin' 'ere?' As he spoke Winston leapt up, grateful that someone had at last interrupted his master's dream, and delighted to see his new friend.

'Winston! Good boy!' Elsa patted him on the head and made a great fuss of him, and his tail nearly fell off it wagged so much. 'It's terrible the way your master keeps you waiting so long every night. And all because of a silly old bicycle machine.'

Frankie looked puzzled. ''Ow d'you know I come 'ere every night?'

Elsa grinned mischievously. 'Because a good spy must always keep her eyes open. Tell me,' she said, looking at the dream bike in Pascall's window. 'What's so special about such a dreadful machine?'

Frankie answered as quick as a flash. 'It 'ain't a dreadful machine!' Then he turned to look back in the shop window. 'It's the most t'rrific bike in the 'ole wide world!'

'Then why not get your father to buy it for you?'

Frankie fell silent and suddenly he felt depressed. 'My 'ole man in't got that sorta money – an' never will 'ave.'

Elsa didn't look at Frankie, but she understood immediately. 'Oh – I see.' She allowed a respectable pause before continuing. 'Then, I suppose you must save all your pennies until you can afford to buy it for yourself.'

'Yeah,' groaned Frankie. 'And by then it'll be long gone.' Dejected, he turned away from the shop window. 'Anyway, I don't get any pennies ter save.'

'Then it's time you found yourself a part-time job.' They moved away from Pascall's shop window, and strolled off down Hadleigh Villas. They walked very slowly, for it was now dark and a thick frost was settling on the pavements. Elsa was a little unsure on her feet in such conditions, so, to Frankie's surprise, she took hold of his arm for support. Winston followed on behind, and all three of them made slow progress across the road to Elsa's house.

While she was opening the front door, Elsa said that she wanted a cup of tea before going to do some tidying up in the jumble shop. Frankie accepted her invitation to join her and was told to go into the kitchen and put the kettle on.

Elsa's kitchen fascinated Frankie. Situated at the back of the house overlooking the garden, it was bigger than the front room in his own family's house and it was full of interesting things like a coffee grinder, a dresser lined with blue-and-white willow-patterned dinner plates. The kettle was huge and made of copper, so it took a long time to boil on the smart-looking gas stove.

Elsa came into the kitchen and, to his horror, insisted that Frankie make the tea, something he had never done in his whole life. But, under Elsa's supervision, the job was accomplished most successfully.

Triumphantly, Frankie carried the tea-tray into the sitting-room, where Winston had already curled up on the rug in front of the fireplace and within a few minutes all three were relaxing with tea and petit-beurre biscuits, which Elsa had bought with her ration coupons just a few days before at Woolworth's in the Holloway Road.

The room was chilly, so Elsa lit the paraffin stove, which immediately emitted its own particular pungent smell.

As soon as tea was over, Elsa went upstairs to change into work clothes. While she was gone, Frankie wandered across to the fireplace to look at the collection of old snapshots that were scattered all along the mantelpiece. One or two were merely torn pieces of sepia photos, of people Frankie imagined were friends or relatives of Elsa from pre-war Germany. But nearly all the others were of Elsa and a man whom Frankie presumed to have been Elsa's late husband, Major Robert Barclay. The centrepiece of the collection was a large, framed photograph of Robert in army uniform, a full-length studio portrait which revealed on the back that it had been taken at Jerome's photographer's studio in the Seven Sisters Road. Robert Barclay had been a good-looking bloke, Frankie thought, tall, with strong features and a friendly face. Just as he was studying it closely, there was a loud banging on the front door. Winston immediately leapt up and rushed out into the hall, barking loudly. Quickly replacing the picture, Frankie followed him and yelled up the stairs, 'Miss!'

There was no response from Elsa, and when the knocking on the front door started again, this time more aggressively, Frankie yelled again, louder, 'Miss! Someone at the door.'

At last, Elsa called out from a room at the top

of the stairs. 'Then open it!'

Frankie went to the street door. It was now blackout time, so he turned off the hall light. Then, after grabbing hold of Winston's collar, he timidly opened the door. Standing there were two figures, only visible as silhouettes.

'Elsa? Is that you?' It was a man's voice, deep, and to Frankie's mind, hoity-toity.

Frankie said nervously. 'Who is it, please?' as Winston barked frantically.

As soon as Frankie spoke, a torch beam shone directly into his eyes. 'Who the devil are *you*? and where did this dog come from?' asked the intruder.

Before Frankie had a chance to answer, the two figures pushed past him, and strode into the hall. Struggling to hold on to Winston's collar, Frankie was too startled to know what to do.

This time a woman's voice called out, 'Elsa? Are you there?'

Suddenly, the man turned on the hall light, and Frankie got the shock of his life. 'Shut the door!' commanded the man. 'Don't you know there's a war on!'

Frankie obeyed, but his eyes never left the man's face. Standing before him was the man in the photograph on Elsa's mantelpiece.

'He must be a neighbour or something,' said the woman, who had a high-pitched voice, and a nose that was plum-coloured from the cold.

'Who is it?' Elsa yelled down.

'It's us, Elsa,' called the woman, looking up the stairs. 'Jack and Celia.'

'Jack and Celia?' Elsa, wearing light blue slacks and high-heeled, clog-like shoes, came down the stairs. 'What are you doing here at this time of night?' Then she patted Winston who was still barking. 'It's all right, Winston. Down boy! Down!' Winston duly obeyed.

'It's only six o'clock, Elsa!' The woman, who was almost the same height as her husband, had to bend down to greet Elsa. 'It's so good to see you, dear.'

Elsa turned her cheek, reluctantly allowing the woman to kiss it. 'You can't have any tea,' said Elsa, meanly. 'We've just finished ours.'

The man stepped forward. He was tall, and wore a dark overcoat with a velvet collar, and his trilby hat had been steamed into a very cocky shape. 'We don't need tea, Elsa. We were just passing, and wanted to know how you're keeping.' He bent down to peck her on the cheek, but even as he was doing it, Elsa strode off to the sitting-room.

'You live in Hertfordshire, and you're just passing Seven Sisters Road?' She grunted dismissively. 'What kind of a map do *you* read?' When they had all entered the sitting room, she sat in her usual armchair. 'You don't have long. We're on our way to the shop.'

The woman sat on a straight-backed chair, body upright. Her husband remained standing.

'Isn't it about time you got rid of that shop, Elsa?' he said. 'It can't bring you much of an income.'

From her sitting position, Elsa's feet didn't quite reach the floor, and they dangled as she talked. 'How interesting. You're the second person to ask me that question today, Jack Barclay. The answer is no. I am not going to sell the shop. As a matter of fact, it is about to make me quite a lot of money.'

'Oh really?' The woman crossed her legs, adjusted her top coat and headscarf, and smiled. 'How nice.'

The man Elsa had called Jack Barclay, had taken off his trilby, and was holding it in both hands, behind him. 'I'm all for your making yourself a lot of money, Elsa, but I'll be darned if I know how you'll ever make it running a jumble shop single-handed!' As he talked he seemed to rock himself back and forward, which irritated Elsa enormously.

'Who said I am single-handed?' she replied immediately? 'I have plenty of help from my assistant.'

'Your assistant?' The woman's curiosity got the better of her. 'What assistant?'

'Frankie!' called Elsa, but as she turned to introduce him, she found the boy in the hall outside, peering round the sitting-room door, thunderstruck by what Elsa had just said. 'What are you doing out there, boy? Come in and meet my brother and sister-in-law.'

So that was it, thought Frankie, as he entered the room with great trepidation. A twin brother! No wonder he was the living image of Elsa's husband.

'Frankie. This is Mr and Mrs Jack and Celia Barclay.' Then with a look of immense satisfaction, Elsa turned back to her obviously unwelcome visitors. 'And *this* is my friend – *Misster* Frank Lewis!'

Barclay paused only briefly, refusing to acknowledge the boy's presence. 'Where does this dog come from?' he asked, none too sure of the beast who was glaring at him.

''E's mine, sir. 'Is name's Winston. But 'e's quite 'armless. 'E don't bite.'

Celia Barclay smiled. 'My husband's not afraid of dogs, young man,' she said confidently. 'They always respond very well to him.'

Barclay put his hand out to stroke Winston. But he quickly withdrew it when, accompanied by an angry growl, Winston's lip started to quiver. Quickly turning to Frankie to hide his embarrassment, Barclay curtly asked, 'Are you a neighbour of my sister-in-law?'

'No, sir. I live in number 1 Merton Street.'

Barclay and Celia exchanged a puzzled look. 'Merton Street?' asked Celia casually. 'Is that local?'

Elsa, a smug grin on her face, was happy to answer. 'Quite local.'

By now, curiosity was practically killing Celia.

'Then – how did you two get to know each other?'

Jack Barclay was eager to hear Elsa's reply, and she knew it. But Elsa was savouring this moment too much to let it pass quickly. To keep her brother-in-law guessing gave her a wonderful feeling of power, for there had never been any love lost between them. As Barclay waited for her reply, Elsa's mind went back to the time when Robert, who was the younger of the twin brothers by one minute, first announced that he was going to marry a German Jewish woman. Jack had done everything in his power to talk his brother out of the marriage. Robert had often told Elsa about his childhood days with Jack, who had been the bully of the family. How different the brothers were, thought Elsa. How extraordinary to think of those two identical Englishmen who had nothing in common whatsoever . . .

'Misster Frankie works for me in the shop.' Elsa was beaming at Frankie, who was standing in the middle of the room, looking very awkward indeed. 'I don't know how I could manage without him.' She pursed her lips and, glancing straight at Frankie, hoped that he would give the right reply. 'Isn't that so, Frankie?'

For a brief moment, Frankie was nonplussed. But he suddenly understood what she was asking. 'Yes, miss – I mean, Mrs Barclay.'

Celia was shuffling uneasily on her seat, but

Elsa was thoroughly enjoying the mystery she was creating.

'Elsa.' Barclay suddenly became very business-like. He crossed the room, picked up a chair, and placed it very close to his sister-in-law, and sat facing her. 'I hadn't meant to discuss this matter today, but—' He was suddenly aware that Frankie was still standing in the middle of the room. 'I wonder if you would be good enough to leave us for a moment?' he snapped irritably. 'I have some private business to talk over with my sister-in-law.'

Frankie turned to leave.

'No!' Elsa's voice was strong and firm. 'Stay where you are, pleass, Frankie.' Then she turned to Barclay. 'You can speak quite freely in front of Misster Lewis. We have no secrets from each other.'

'Sit over there by the books, Frankie,' suggested Elsa. Then, turning to her brother-in-law she said quite pointedly, 'This won't take very long.'

Barclay waited for Frankie to sit down by the book shelves on the far side of the room. For a rare moment in his life he felt at a disadvantage, and he didn't like it one bit. 'Elsa,' he said, feeling ill-at-ease, 'for some time, I – that is, Celia and I – have been very worried about what would happen to you if – well, if you were taken ill or something.'

'Oh yes?' Elsa, her elbow resting on the arm of her chair, and her chin resting on the palm of her hand, was staring very sceptically straight into Barclay's eyes.

'What I mean is, if you were unwell or something, there'd be no one to – to look after you, and take care of – this house, the shop – everything. D'you follow my meaning, Elsa?'

'Yes, Jack. I follow your meaning very well.'

Elsa didn't have to look at Jack Barclay to know what he was leading up to.

'So I was thinking – what Celia and I were thinking – well, if there's anything we can do to help . . . After all, I do feel responsible for you. Robert would turn in his grave if he thought I'd just left you to cope all on your own.'

Elsa was feeling sick. The hypocrite! She knew only too well that ever since Robert died it had riled Jack that only a wretched German Jewess stood between him and his brother's share of the family inheritance. But it was in Jack Barclay's interest to retain as good a relationship as possible with his sister-in-law, for Elsa had absolutely no relatives of her own.

'That's very considerate of you, Jack.' Elsa, still staring straight at Barclay, briefly flicked her eyes across to Celia, who smiled nervously. 'So, what do you suggest?'

Before Barclay answered, everyone was distracted by the loud voice of a man calling from outside, 'Lights!' It was the street Air Raid

Warden who had noticed that one of Elsa's black-out blinds had not been fully lowered. Elsa got up immediately, went to the window, and yelled back, 'Sorry!' while quickly attending to the offending blind.

'The thing is, Elsa,' continued Jack immediately, 'the war's coming to an end. In my opinion, you should start thinking about what you're going to do with the shop, and . . .' At this point, his eyes were scanning the room. 'Well – this house, for instance.'

Elsa was still standing by the window with the drawn blind. 'This house?'

'I'll be perfectly honest with you, Elsa. I don't want to interfere in your private affairs, but – both Celia and I think it's about time you made a will.'

Celia was nodding eagerly in agreement. 'Not that anything is likely to happen to you for a very long time, my dear. But it does leave things . . . tidy.'

'I'm sure it does.' So now it was the house he was after! 'But what makes you think I *haven't* made a will?'

Jack and Celia swung a panicked glance at each other. 'Well, of course, I don't know,' said Jack, tensely. 'I just presumed . . .' By this time, he had, unwittingly, almost squeezed the shape out of his trilby hat. 'Why?' he tried to ask, casually. 'Have you?'

Elsa smiled, and began putting on her hat,

which she had left with her fur coat on the settee. 'I don't remember,' she said sweetly.

'Don't remember?' Jack was getting irritated. 'You don't remember if you've made a will or not?'

'I don't remember, because it's not important.'

'Oh but it *is* important, my dear,' said Celia, trying to sound as though she was Elsa's closest confidante. 'In wartime, one has to be prepared. One never knows what each day will bring. I mean, let's face it, it would be *criminal* for the Tax Man to get his hands on all your assets.'

Frankie was moving from one foot to another, doing his best to appear deaf to the extraordinary conversation.

By this time, Elsa was putting on her fur coat. 'So I should make a Will? Is that what you're suggesting?'

'At least talk it over with a solicitor,' said Barclay in his most reasonable voice. 'I could help you with that.'

'Our chap is a real gem,' assured Celia. 'He'll do *anything* to help.'

'Oh, I'm sure he would,' replied Elsa, in her most acid voice.

Barclay exchanged another look with his wife. 'So would you like us to speak to him on your behalf?'

'I'll think about it. Now, if you'll excuse us, we have some business to attend to in the shop.' Without another word, Elsa picked up her handbag and strode out into the hall.

Barclay and his wife watched Elsa go in disbelief. Then, with Winston tagging on behind, followed her out, ignoring Frankie as they went.

Elsa was standing near the front door, holding her huge leather handbag in both hands, as though it were a weapon. 'It was so good of you both to call, Jack. I'm very grateful.'

Barclay kissed Elsa on the cheek. As he did so, Elsa looked into his eyes. For one fleeting moment she could see her Robert there, warm, loving, caring . . . The brothers were so alike, – and yet, although they were physically identical, there was only coldness in her brother-in-law's eyes. Jack wasn't a bad man, she knew. But he was foolish and greedy . . . 'Keep in touch Elsa,' he whispered in her ear. 'If you'd like to talk to our man, just drop us a line.' Then he put on his trilby hat, which was now quite shapeless.

Celia also kissed Elsa on the cheek and, as she did so, whispered in her ear. 'He really is very good, my dear. Worth a try.'

Elsa smiled sweetly, turned off the hall light, then opened the door. As he left, Barclay glared briefly at Frankie without saying a word to him. Then he and Celia made their way down the steps to their small car. Elsa watched them go, and called out, 'Next time you're passing by from Hertfordshire, please call in!'

In a moment, Barclay and his wife were gone, the sound of their car quickly disappearing into the Seven Sisters Road and narrowly missing a number 653 trolley-bus as they went. Elsa closed the door. 'So!' she said. 'And what do you think of my brother and sister-in-law?'

Frankie looked flustered. 'They're – peculiar, in't they?'

Elsa roared with laughter. 'Very perceptive of you, Frankie!' He and Winston followed her back into the sitting-room. 'Turn off the paraffin stove, please. We don't want to waste the heat!'

Frankie duly obeyed. 'Wot's all this about me bein' your assistant? I didn't know I was supposed ter be workin' for yer.'

Elsa turned off the sitting-room light, leaving only the hall light to guide them out. 'I thought you wanted to buy that terrible machine in Pascall's window?'

'I do!'

'Then you have to work for it, don't you? Come to the shop after school in the evenings. Three shillings a week – and by next summer you can save enough for your machine. Yes – or no?'

Frankie's excitement suddenly turned the blood in his body red hot. 'Yes, miss!'

Elsa reached the front door, paused, and turned slowly. There was a warm smile on her face. 'Then if we are going to work together, don't you think it's about time you called me – Elsa?'

Frankie looked at her for a moment, then he, too, broke into a wide smile. 'Yes, miss – I mean – Elsa.'

'Well, let's get going!' said Elsa, with a flourish.

'It's getting near Christmas. We have a lot of work to do!'

Elsa turned out the light, and within a few moments she, Frankie, and Winston were making their way slowly down Hadleigh Villas, then into Tollington Road, and on towards the jumble shop in Hornsey Road. There weren't too many people around, for the evening had all the signs of being one of the coldest of the winter so far.

As they strolled together, arm in arm, with Winston padding not so far behind, Elsa and Frankie made an odd couple, two tiny silhouettes leaving their footprints behind them on the white frosty pavements.

Chapter Seven

The closing weeks of 1944 were anxious ones. After the great surge of public optimism generated by the June D-Day landings in France, September had seen the tragic massacre of British and American airborne troops at Arnhem in Holland, and then, on December 16th, General von Rundstedt launched an aggressive and well-plan ned offensive against Allied forces in the Ardennes region of Belgium. This was a bitter blow to Winston Churchill, for the German onslaught had the effect of delaying the deployment of General Eisenhower's great assault on Hitler's own Nazi fatherland.

In London, the earlier expectations of a swift Allied victory were giving way to depression – and fear. Each day the Germans' deadly V2 rockets were being fired across the English Channel from Holland, and landing in and around the London area. They arrived without warning, causing havoc, massive destruction – and the greatest number of fatal casualties since the great London blitz in 1940. Islington had been one of the early victims of the bombardment, with the Guy Fawkes night rocket attack on a residential street in Upper Holloway. The smoke from the explosion had been seen easily from Merton Street, where once again windows were shattered and ceilings collapsed. Day by day the skies above the street were regularly streaked with the long white vapour trails of the Nazis' most vicious weapon.

By the last week before Christmas, however, Merton Street was looking like its old self again. Although the blackout regulations were still in force, small Christmas trees had appeared in the front room windows of practically every house, and the coloured lights on them could be seen quite clearly during the day until dusk. By popular consensus, it was the Gorman brothers who had the best Christmas decorations. Every window in their house had the words, Merry Xmas, stuck on in cotton wool, colourful home-made paper chains could be seen dangling across the front room ceiling, and the street door itself was beautifully adorned with cotton wool 'frost' and a home-made wreath of holly leaves. The Robinsons at number 22 had quite a good show too, but theirs was much more tasteful, with decorations bought from Gamages Department Store in Holborn. Even old Clancy in number 78 made an effort. Each year he put up the same small Father Christmas doll he had bought in

Woolworths before the war. It always hung in the same place, the window of the front room parlour. As the curtains were permanently drawn, day and night, it was the only view of the inside of his house that any of the passing residents could ever see. Clancy himself usually spent Christmas alone, and only went out for a quick pink gin at the Eaglet pub on Boxing Day. Occasionally, one of his 'gentleman friends' would visit but he spent most of the time listening to his favourite ballet music on gramophone records.

Without doubt, the most disappointing house in the street was number 1. Gracie Lewis had always considered that spending money on Christmas decorations was a terrible waste. However, Frankie and Helen had tried to make something of their bedroom. Helen had stuck cotton wool 'frost' around her dressing-table mirror and Frankie had painted an old piece of cardboard with the words, 'Merry Xmas to all' and stuck it in the window. Unfortunately, as their bedroom window overlooked the back yard, no one could really see it except the occasional passing cat.

For Frankie, the last few weeks before Christmas turned out to be hectic. Each afternoon he rushed home from school, quickly did his homework, and, with Winston at his side, made his way to Elsa's jumble shop on the corner of Hornsey Road. Once there, he really earned the three shillings a week Elsa was paying him, for he dusted, polished, swept, moved boxes, tidied up, wrote out price tickets for the jumble stock on sale, and did things that he had never done in his whole life before. And he loved it! By Christmas Eve, Barclays jumble shop had never looked so organised.

Helen was also in great spirits. During the previous three weeks she had received two letters from Eric, both heavily censored, but full of hope about their future together. On their last secret weekend together in Bognor Regis, Helen had been convinced that she was deeply in love with her soldier boyfriend, and all she wanted to do was to be his wife and bear his children. That dream came nearer to reality just a week before Christmas Day, when she received a third letter, in which Eric proposed to her. From that moment on, Helen's whole attitude to life changed. For the first time ever, she had real hope, not just dreams and wishes, and it didn't matter how difficult life was at number 1 Merton Street, now. But for the time being, the only two people Helen confided in were her friend Ivy, and Frankie. Frankie was delighted to see his sister so happy, but he reckoned that if he heard Corporal Eric Sibley's name mentioned just once more, he'd go bonkers!

After helping in the shop for a month, Frankie had earned himself twelve shillings, which he carefully tucked away in a jam jar underneath his pullovers in the chest of drawers and although he remained one of 'Boggy' Marsh's few mathematical failures at school, Frankie estimated that by the summer of the following year he could be well on the way to buying his dream bike in Pascalls' window. But he earned a great deal more than just money during his evening job. For one thing, he read seven more books from Elsa's collection at 19 Hadleigh Villas and, although he had to admit failure with the *History of the Steam Traction Engine*, Elsa's choice of *Tom Brown's Schooldays, Wuthering Heights*, and *Huckleberry Finn* made compelling reading for him.

In those final weeks leading up to Christmas, Frankie's work in the jumble shop transformed the place. Cardboard boxes were emptied of their contents which were then stacked on the proper shelves; silver and gold plate items were polished, furniture was gathered into its own corner, books were dusted and indexed, and all the secondhand clothes received clear price-tags.

Winston added his own contribution by catching a rat in the back yard, for which he was rewarded with a huge piece of apple cake. Frankie also revealed a hidden talent for shop design, and his Christmas window display was a triumph, with passers-by constantly stopping to peer in at the wondrous selection of secondhand goodies and Elsa gradually built up a collection of new customers. For the first time ever, it seemed she was actually beginning to make a profit. Elsa, however remained the boss, ordering Frankie to sweep this and dust that, orders which Frankie was always willing to carry out. But Elsa occasionally allowed him to serve customers, which meant that he could use the cash till. Such a responsibility made him feel very important and responsible and, Elsa noted, most important of all, he was starting to act more like a boy of his own age.

Ever since the night when he was first hauled into Elsa's front hall, Frankie had hardly set eyes on his pals in the Merton Street gang. They knew, of course, that he was working in the jumble shop, but because they still thought of Elsa as 'the old Kraut' and some kind of Nazi monster, none of them ever attempted to pursue him there. However, the Prof was eventually invited by Frankie to meet Elsa, and when he saw the shop for the first time, he was terribly excited by all the secondhand electrical equipment on show.

Elsa, too, was enjoying her new lease of life. Something was happening to her, but she didn't quite know what. There were times when Frankie thought that Elsa bought more goods than she actually sold, and he told her so. At first Elsa objected to the boy's interference in things that he didn't understand, but after she had shouted at him a couple of times, she accepted that he was probably right, and invariably took his advice. Frankie soon got used to her little fits of rage, and even enjoyed them, especially her colourful, incomprehensible German curse whenever she dropped something or was forced to fumble. In fact, Elsa made him laugh a great deal, for her tantrums were always short-lived and often very funny. And Elsa loved to see Frankie laugh, for laughter was something she had not experienced since Robert's death.

And so, with Christmas Day only a few days away, and Highbury Grammar School closed for the holidays, Barclays jumble shop on the corner of Hornsey Road, full of paper chains, tinsel, and cotton wool decorations, looked like a veritable Aladdin's Cave!

The Emmanuel Church Hall wasn't very big, but it was very convenient for the residents of Merton Street and their neighbours. Situated snugly between the playground of Pakeman Street School and Hornsey Road, it was used throughout the year for Sunday school classes, Boy Scout and Girl Guide meetings, and, most important of all, the annual local residents' Christmas get-together. This took the form of a cold buffet with crates of beer, R. Whites lemonade and Tizer, but as there was still a war on, everyone had to pool their ration coupons to provide the spam and cheese sandwiches, home-made sausage-rolls, tea, biscuits, and iced Christmas cake (usually made by old Winnie Brackell, who lived just around the corner in number 9 Roden Street). But the highlight of the evening was the traditional residents' Concert Party. This, of course, was always organised by Merton Street's very own ex-professional Music Hall double-act, the Gorman brothers. The programme was meticulously planned and usually included such celebrated and well-loved acts as Doris Simmons from number 37 ('*the harmonica virtuoso*'); Fred and Gertie Potts from number 11 ('*tap dancing wizards*'); Mr Mickey Saunders from number 43 ('*uncanny bird sounds*'); recitations from eight-year-old Ruby Penfold and her young brother 'the Spiv' from Herslet Road; an annual rendition of *Come into the Garden, Maud* by the Reverend Monty Marshall (accompanied by Florrie, the pianist from the Globe pub in Tollington Road) and Stan Grout from number 29 doing his 'amazing' impersonation of the stars of film and radio such as Tommy Handley, Arthur Askey, George Formby, and Gracie Fields. But the star attraction of the evening was, of course, always the Gorman brothers from number 47. After all, who could resist their quick-fire jokes ('*I say! I say! I say! Who was that woman I saw you with last night? Answer: That was no woman. That was my wife!*') delivered like the pros they were. The residents of Merton Street and their neighbours adored them.

Frankie's mum and dad never attended the Christmas party in the church hall, preferring to sit at home in the Anderson shelter listening to special Christmas editions of their favourite wireless shows such as *ITMA*, *Forces Favourites*, *Music Hall*, and *Happidrome*, and *Hi Gang!* For Frankie however the residents' Concert Party was the event he looked forward to all year. But when he arrived at the church hall on this Christmas Eve, he did not expect the reception that was waiting for him.

'So 'ow's our Nazi sympafizer, then?' It was Jeff Murray, who, despite the fact that he was underage, was swigging back a pint glass of brown ale. 'Don't tell me yer old Kraut friend's given yer the brush off?' Patty, who had her arm around his neck, roared with laughter. But Alan Downs looked uncomfortable with this baiting.

Only a few weeks before, Frankie would have flushed with embarrassment at such a remark. But tonight he just took it in his stride. 'Elsa's not a Nazi sympafizer, Jeff. She's a nice lady. I *like* 'er.'

'Oh? Did yer 'ear that, Pat?' Jeff leaned over and kissed Patty firmly on the lips. ''Er name's not Kraut. It's *El-sa*.'

Patty repeated Jeff's pronounciation, '*El-sa*,' then roared with laughter again.

Alan quickly changed the subject. 'Any sign of your gettin' that bike in Pascall's yet, Frankie?'

'I'm savin for it,' Frankie replied, lowering his eyes. He was still upset that when he was last asked to go out for a bike ride with the Gang to Hackney Marshes, the bike the Prof managed to borrow for him had a puncture, and he'd had to turn back after less than a mile.

'Wot's up?' asked Patty, mischievously. 'Don't your Kraut friend pay yer enough?'

Frankie looked up. 'Wot d'yer mean?'

Jeff had a knowing grin on his face. 'Come off it, Frank! Everyone knows yer work for the old geezer. 'Ow much she payin' yer, then?'

Frankie glared at Jeff. Despite the older boy's athletic build he looked as though he was prepared to challenge Jeff to a scrap. 'It's none of yer bloody business, Jeff!'

'Oh, but it is, Frank. It's *everyone's* business.' Jeff looked round, pretending that he didn't want to be overheard. 'Tell me somefin'?' He leaned towards Frankie, his voice only barely audible above the excited chatter of the party guests. 'Wot do yer ma and pa say about you workin' in the Kraut's shop every night?'

Frankie lunged at Jeff, but before he could raise his fist, Prof restrained him. 'Don't, Frankie! It isn't worth it.'

'Ladies and gentlemen!' The Rev. Marshall was on the tiny stage tapping the microphone to see if it was working properly. 'Please take your seats. The Variety Show is about to commence!'

There was a great cheer from everybody as Florrie from the Globe pub struck up a welcoming chord at the upright piano, which hadn't been tuned in years. One by one the party guests took their seats around the sides of the hall and, as Mr Ridley from number 16 turned off the hall lights, the stage was floodlit. Almost immediately, Bert Gorman appeared from behind the curtains. He was greeted with another great cheer and burst of applause. 'Thank you! Thank you very much, my friends! And a very Merry Christmas to one and all!' As he spoke, Florrie straightened herself on the piano stool – which was a little difficult, for she was all of fourteen stone – and quickly launched into *I'm Dreaming of a White Christmas*. Everyone in the Hall, joined in, including Frankie and the Merton Street gang, and very soon the community singing was so robust poor Florrie's trills could hardly be heard.

A few minutes later, while the merriment was in full swing, a young girl sneaked in at the back of the hall, and started to look around for someone. She was wearing a heavy winter coat and headscarf, and her cheeks were flushed red from the cold air outside. When she finally caught sight of Frankie, who was squatting on the floor near the stage, she carefully made her way among the guests to him and knelt down to avoid obstructing everyone's view of the stage. 'Frankie!' She had to raise her voice to be heard above the sounds of *White Christmas*.

Frankie turned with a start. ''Allo, Ivy.'

Ivy Villiers, Helen's best friend, was looking

very distraught. ''Ave yer seen, 'Elen? I've gotta speak to 'er.'

Frankie also had to shout. 'Why, wot's up?'

'Where is she, Frankie?'

Frankie pointed to his sister, who was on the opposite side of the Hall, singing her head off with a group of Merton Street neighbours. Ivy said nothing more, but picked her way through the half-singing, half-shouting audience, many of whom were squatting on the floor, rocking to and fro to Florrie's heavy-handed piano playing. Frankie, still singing, but a little concerned by Ivy's anxiety, watched her go, and waited to see what was going to happen when she eventually reached Helen. Ivy spoke quickly and Helen stopped singing immediately and got up. Then she and Ivy left the Hall.

The community singing was followed by Bert Gorman introducing the first of the evening's acts, Stan Grout doing his impersonation of the stars of film and radio. Frankie recognised them all, and applauded wildly, but was convinced that he himself could impersonate James Stewart and George Sanders better than Mr Grout. Despite his enjoyment, however, he kept looking to the entrance door to see when Helen was coming back. But she hadn't returned by the time Mrs Simmons was giving a rousing interpretation of *The Blue Danube* on the harmonica and he started to become anxious. He decided to go and look for his sister.

During the concert party, there had been a light fall of snow outside, and when Frankie came out of the warm church hall, the biting cold immediately attacked his face, and soon his eyes were watering. In the garden, which led from the vicarage and church itself, Frankie could just see two or three young couples snogging in the shadows, including Jeff and Patty. But he could see no sign of either Helen or Ivy, so he decided to go back into the Hall.

'Frankie!'

Frankie turned to see Ivy hurrying through the garden from the direction of the church. 'Ivy! Wot's goin' on? Where's 'Elen?'

Ivy, shivering, tried to keep her voice as low as possible. 'She's in the church, Frankie. Go and look after 'er – please.' There was a tone of desperation in her plea. 'She's in a terrible state.'

Frankie was alarmed. 'Wot's up wiv er?'

Ivy was clearly upset herself, for her eyes were red from crying. 'It's Eric. Eric Sibley. 'E's missin' in action.'

'Wot!'

''Is bruvver Gary came round and told me and Joyce. 'Is mum and dad are in a terrible state.' Ivy used her already very wet handkerchief to dab the tears filling her eyes. 'Eric was such a nice bloke. We all liked 'im. It's terrible fer 'Elen! Terrible!'

Frankie was shocked and embarrassed. He wanted to comfort Ivy, but he didn't quite know what to do. 'But missin' in action – that don't mean 'e's dead or anyfin'?'

'That's not wot 'Elen finks. She knew Eric was goin' to the front line. She knew he was goin ter be in danger. It was somefin' about the way he wrote 'is last letter to 'er.' Ivy suddenly put her arm around Frankie's neck and, sobbing and speaking at the same time, whispered in his ear, 'I've gotta go, Frankie. Mum and dad are takin' us to our Auntie Polly fer Christmas. Go an' see, 'Elen – please! She needs yer!'

Frankie and Ivy walked back through the vicarage garden. The branches of the big oak tree were stark and bare, and, for one brief moment, Frankie thought it looked sinister and overpowering. But the light sprinkling of snow had softened the bleak winter look of the rose bushes, although it didn't help what was left of the chrysanthemums, whose dead blooms drooped down pitifully.

As they passed through the iron gate which led into Hornsey Road, Ivy said goodbye to Frankie and made her way home while he climbed up the few stone steps of the red-bricked Emmanuel Church. Before going in, he paused for a moment. What was he going to say to his sister? How could he, of all people, comfort her? In those few seconds he thought of the many times Helen had helped him out of trouble at home, how she had always defended him when their mother went for him. Now it was his turn to do something for

Helen. But Frankie didn't know anything about being in love, so how could he assure his big sister that everything would be all right? It *wasn't* going to be all right and there was nothing he could do or say that would make it so. Oh, if only Elsa was here now, thought Frankie. *She'd* know what to do.

No one would claim that the Emmanuel Church was the most beautiful building in the world, but it did have a special atmosphere of its own. It wasn't particularly old – it had been built sometime during the latter part of the nineteenth century – with pews set out each side of the central aisle. If there was any sun during the day, it would stream through the windows on the right-hand side of the building in the morning. After dusk, it was poorly lit, mainly by a few overhead chandeliers, and during Evening Service it was difficult to know how the Rev. Marshall was able to read the lesson.

It was the first time Frankie had been inside the church since he was a small boy, and he immediately felt conspicuous, though he didn't know why; the first thing he did was look around for Helen, but there was no sign of her. As he moved down the centre aisle, his shoes, with their metal-tipped heels and toes, echoed on the marble tiles. When he reached the front he stopped briefly to look up at the Christmas tree near the altar. On the top of it was a small figure of Jesus, and not the traditional fairy. But not far away was a manger designed and constructed by the children of Pakeman Street School, whose playground was overlooked by the church itself.

'Elen?' Frankie summoned up enough courage to call his sister's name. But the silence unnerved him, so he kept his voice very low. 'You in 'ere, 'Elen?'

There was a pause, during which time Frankie felt comforted by the sudden distant sound of the Rev. Monty Marshall giving his annual rendition of *Come into the garden, Maud* at the Concert Party. He called again, this time a little louder. ''Elen?'

Only then did Helen call back. 'Over 'ere, Frank.'

Frankie turned, and finally spotted his sister sitting in a pew on the edge of the left-hand aisle. She was sitting in partial darkness, for she had chosen a pew beneath a chandelier which had only one electric light bulb working. 'Wot yer doin' 'ere then?'

'I just wanna few minutes quiet, that's all.' To Frankie's surprise, Helen was perfectly calm, sitting upright in the pew with her hands tucked into her coat pocket.

Frankie sat at her side. 'Ivy told me about – about Eric. I'm sorry. I'm really sorry.'

Helen half glanced at him and smiled gratefully. 'Fanks.'

'It could be a mistake, yer know.' Although

Frankie felt decidedly awkward, he was making an effort to be reassuring. 'I've 'eard it's 'appened before. They report someone missin' in action, then find they've made a mistake.'

'It's no mistake, Frank.' Helen was staring at her lap. 'It's all over. I always knew somefin' like this would 'appen. Everyfin' was going too well for me. It's all over. Eric's dead.'

'Don't talk like that!' Frankie was suddenly and uncharacteristically firm. 'People in't dead 'til you see them fer yerself, stretched out in their coffin.' In his desperation to be objective, Frankie had been unwittingly tactless.

Helen quickly turned and snapped back at him. 'You stupid little nit! Eric won't *be* in no coffin. He's probably lyin' out there in a field somewhere, waitin' ter be picked up and frown down an 'ole in the ground!'

'No, 'Elen!'

'Yes! Yes! Yes!' For the first time, Helen was showing emotion, biting her lip to try and hold back tears. 'We was goin' ter set up 'ome tergevver. We 'ad all sorts of plans. As soon as 'e was demobbed, Eric was gonna go and see mum and dad, and tell them 'e wanted ter marry me, an' if they didn't say yes we'd run away from 'ome and do it anyway.' Helen was talking faster and faster, as if she was living through that final conversation she had had with Eric before he went away. And while she was talking, the tears were beginning to trickle down her cheeks. 'I loved 'im, Frank. I loved 'im so much!'

Frankie let his sister talk on, for he felt that this was the only real way he could help her.

'We 'ad such good times tergevver – me and Eric. An' I could tell 'e loved me by the way 'e used ter tease me all the time.' She turned to face Frankie. There was such eagerness – and desperation – in her eyes. 'D'yer know wot 'e once told me?'

Frankie shook his head.

''E said, 'Elen – if you wasn't such a good looker, I'd fancy you!' She roared with laughter, which echoed right across the church ceiling. The laugh mixed with her sobbing and the tears which were rolling freely down her cheeks. ''E was always doin' it, Frank. 'E was always teasin' me.'

While she talked, Frankie never stopped looking straight at her. To him, Helen had always been more like a brother – the way they'd fought together as kids, the way they both spoke about their 'pals', the way Helen could talk to him as an equal when it came to disagreements over football matches. But as he studied her face, with the solitary light bulb from the ceiling above reflecting in her eyes, Frankie gradually realised that this wasn't a brother who was talking to him. Helen was his *sister*. She was a girl – and she was beautiful, really beautiful. 'You'll find anuvver feller, 'Elen. You're bound to.'

'I don't want anuvver feller! I want *Eric*.' She

rubbed her eyes with her fingers, and the little make-up she was wearing immediately smudged. 'Don't you understand, Frankie? 'E was the only one who meant anyfin' ter me, the only one who cared what I fawt or wot I looked like. There are some people yer just can't replace. Yer just can't!'

Frankie could bear it no more. In the most spontaneous act of his life, he threw his arms around her and hugged her tight. 'It'll be all right, 'Elen, you'll see. I'll take care of yer – I promise I will.'

Helen's voice was muffled, her face pressed tightly into Frankie's shoulder. 'I wanted to 'ave 'is kid, Frankie. I wanted so bad ter 'ave 'is kid . . .'

'You'll 'ave uvver kids, 'Elen,' whispered Frankie reassuringly. 'When the war's over, you'll find some uvver nice feller, an' you'll 'ave lots an' lots of kids.'

Helen took her hands out of her coat pockets, threw them around Frankie, and squeezed him tight. 'I don't want somebody else's kid, Frank. Don't you understand?' She looked up at him, anguished, and said, 'I'm pregnant. I'm gonna 'ave Eric's baby.'

A couple of hours later, the Concert Party in the Church Hall was over, and most of the residents of Merton Street and their neighbours filed into the Emmanuel Church for the Midnight Service. Frankie had always convinced himself that he didn't really believe in religion, and since his mum and dad never went to Church he never saw any reason why he should. But, with Helen at his side, he stayed for this one.

Chapter Eight

Christmas Day at number 1 Merton Street was always a non-event, and this year was no exception. Reg and Gracie had bought Frankie his first pair of long trousers, and for Helen a frilled white blouse which she'd asked for after seeing it in *Jones Brothers* shop window. The presents had been quite a sacrifice for Gracie and Reg who had had to forfeit quite a few of their own clothes' ration coupons to buy them. Helen's present to her parents was a thoughtful one, though: new cushion covers for the tatty three-piece suite in the front parlour room, which she herself had been secretly crochetting for the last five months. Frankie, who was saving every penny he was earning to put towards his new bike, kept enough aside to buy an ounce of tobacco for his father, who rolled his own Rizla cigarettes. For his mother he bought a penny bar of her favourite Lux toilet soap together with a dark brown hairnet and a packet of hairpins. Frankie's present to his sister was a blue leather-covered pocket diary for 1945, for he knew that she recorded all sorts of boring details about her daily life. But Helen's present to her brother not only took him completely by surprise, but absolutely delighted him. It was a gramophone record of Bing Crosby and the Andrews sisters singing *Don't Fence Me In* and for the rest of the day Frankie drove everyone mad by playing it at least a dozen times.

The Lewis Christmas lunch was traditional, and for Frankie – boring. His mother was a lousy cook, and even though she managed to get a small chicken every year, she always over-cooked it so that by the time it reached the kitchen table it, and the roast potatoes, were shrivelled up to half their size. And the vegetables – greens and brussel sprouts – were boiled soggy and absolutely tasteless. But the family always adored the Christmas pudding – and that was because Gracie Lewis never made it. It was 'commissioned' from the Gorman brothers, who were excellent cooks, on the understanding that they didn't have to provide the necessary ingredients from their own ration book. They also made succulent mince pies, which Frankie and his father soon polished off, usually smothered in Gracie's thick, lumpy custard made with powdered milk. Thanks to Frankie, Winston had his own Christmas lunch too, a couple of slices of chicken and some vegetables all mixed up with some hot Bisto gravy.

By the time lunch was over, Reg Lewis had drunk so much Guinness and brown ale that he had to retire to the front parlour where he soon fell asleep on the settee, snoring loudly. While Helen helped her mother to wash up, Frankie took Winston out for an afternoon walk. He had offered to call on Elsa, but she said that she never liked to see anyone on Christmas Day. What she meant was that she didn't want anyone to see her crying to herself as she reflected on the Christmasses she and Robert spent together. Frankie couldn't understand why people had to get so weepy and sentimental at Christmas. To him it was just like any other day.

The previous night, Helen had been weepy, too. In fact, Frankie was up half the night trying to comfort her, but without success. Her eyes red raw with crying, all she could say over and over again was, 'What am I going to do, Frankie? What am I going to do?' Frankie had no idea what his sister was going to do. The only thing he did know was that when their mother found out that Helen was going to have a baby, she would either kill her or order her out of the house . . .

As he and Winston strolled around the deserted back streets, Frankie could hear the sound of laughter coming from many houses. Why, he wondered, couldn't it be like that in *his* house? For most people, Christmas was a time for all the family and their relatives to get together and have a good blow-out and a knees-up. But not the Lewises. His grandparents had abandoned his dad and his mother had quarrelled with her own parents and didn't know whether they were alive or dead. But, thought Frankie, people should have friends, friends who want to get together and enjoy each other's company. Christmas wasn't Christmas without company.

Frankie and Winston took the short cut to Hornsey Road by crossing the Pakeman Street School playground. The sky was now very overcast and, although it was still only half-past three in the afternoon, it was getting dark. Despite the fact that this was supposed to be Winston's Christmas treat, he knew exactly where he was being dragged off to, and the moment they reached *Pascall's* bike shop, he flopped down on to the pavement and, with a huge sigh, rested his chin on the shop step. The window itself was already in partial darkness, so Frankie took out his pocket torch and directed the beam straight at his dream bike. Relieved to see that it was still there, he could see his own broad, excited smile reflected in the glass. To Winston's delight, however, Frankie moved on very quickly and headed off down Hadleigh Villas. As they approached number 19, Frankie could hear the sound of a record being played on Elsa's gramophone. He recognised the tune immediately, for he had heard it requested many times on *Forces' Favourites*. It was called, *Till We Meet Again*, and was sung by a man called Sam Browne. Frankie didn't like the song because it was too sloppy and sentimental and he decided to leave Elsa alone so that she could have a good cry all to herself.

A few minutes later, Frankie and Winston headed back down the Seven Sisters Road, so that Frankie could call on Prof.

Prof lived with his Auntie Hilda in a small maisonette above a ladies' handbag shop in the Seven Sisters Road, just opposite the North London Drapery Stores. Auntie Hilda was a treasure, and Prof was very fond of her. By taking him in she'd saved him from life in a children's home after his parents were killed in an air-raid on the Angel, Islington, in the early years of the war.

'Frankie!' Prof beamed with delight when he opened the door and saw his pal there. 'Winston! Merry Christmas, boy!' He made a great fuss of Frankie's dog, and was rewarded with licks and a lot of excited tail-wagging.

'Merry Christmas, Prof!' Frankie and Winston followed their pal up the narrow staircase and as they climbed, there was a strong smell of leather from the handbag shop, mixed with the more seductive smells of Auntie Hilda's cooking. As they reached the first floor, Frankie could hear Auntie's voice coming from her parlour, where she was entertaining several of her friends and relatives, all laughing and joking in excited chatter.

Prof's room was on the top floor and was quite big, with sloping ceilings. Frankie never ceased to be amazed at the endless array of weird contraptions that Prof had built. In one corner, dangling from the ceiling, was an enormous cardboard model of an RAF Mosquito fighter bomber, complete with markings and wing-mounted machine guns. On his chest of drawers was a model of a four-mast sailing ship, complete with sails, designed and constructed by Prof himself. Elsewhere, there were extraordinary electrical contraptions made out of bits and pieces of discarded household goods, and the place was littered with over-hanging electrical wires which, to Frankie, looked absolutely lethal. As Prof's heroes were neither film or sporting stars, his walls were plastered with photographs and newspaper cuttings of inventors, astronomers, and great adventurers. But Prof's great pride and joy was the model train system which completely covered the floor of the bedroom. It was a replica of the London North Eastern Railways' *Flying Scot* Express train, and Prof had made it entirely himself, complete with railway track, bridges, stations, and signal boxes. It was, in Frankie's opinion, a work of pure genius.

'Is it finished?' asked Frankie, immediately dropping to his knees eagerly to inspect the sleek model railway engine.

Prof crouched down beside him. 'I put the last electric circuit in last night. Watch.' He flicked a switch and the engine, which had been waiting patiently with its carriages at '*Seven Sisters Road Railway Station*', burst into life and, after waiting for the signal baton to rise, rushed off on its journey of discovery around Prof's bedroom. Frankie roared and cheered with delight, and Winston barked and barked as it sped at enormous speed to the far corner of the room, disappearing beneath a chair, reappearing from behind the settee, and taking every corner as smoothly as the *Flying Scot* engine itself, speeding around the hills and lochs of Scotland.

As Prof brought his wonderful creation to a halt at the same platform that it had left from, Frankie broke out into wild applause. 'Fantastic, Prof!' he yelled. 'It's fantastic! You're a genius!'

Prof beamed with delight. 'D'you think so, Frankie? D'you really think so?'

'It's magnificent!' Frankie assured his pal, patting him triumphantly on the back. 'I in't never seen anyfin' like it! Wot say you, Winnie?' Winston barked and barked at the model engine, and his tail very nearly wagged off.

The noise brought Auntie Hilda into the room. 'What's going on up here, then? Oh – it's you, Frankie.' She was greeted by Winston who immediately tried to get a sniff of the hot mince pies and bottle of Tizer she was carrying on a tray. 'Hallo Winston – lovely boy!' As usual there was a greal smile on Auntie Hilda's chubby face who, with her hair neatly brushed into a bun at the back of her head, and her spotless floral-patterned pinafore, gave no indication that she'd been cooking all morning. 'Have you had a good Christmas Day, then?'

Frankie lowered his head, almost guiltily. 'Yes, fank you, Auntie.'

'That's good.' Auntie Hilda beamed. She insisted on her nephew's friends calling her Auntie because it made her feel as though she had a family of her own. Prof took the tray from her, and placed it on the floor between him and Frankie. 'And how's your mum and dad these days?' said Auntie, as she watched the two boys, helped by Winston, devour her newly baked mince pies. 'Have they got visitors this Christmas?'

Frankie, mouth full of mince pie, shook his head. 'Mum and dad never have visitors. They like ter keep themselves ter themselves.'

Auntie's happy smile briefly faded. 'Really? Well, that's a pity now. I'd hate to spend Christmas without my loved ones around me.' She trotted back to the door; a plump little woman, she was very light on her tiny feet. 'You two boys enjoy yourselves. Don't drink too much Tizer.'

When she reached the door, Frankie, swallowing a particularly hot last piece of mince pie called to her. 'Fanks fer the mince pies, Auntie. They're smashin'.'

Auntie turned at the door, a mischievous twinkle in her eyes. 'So they should be. Those currants took a whole week of my ration coupons!' With a little chuckle, she closed the door and returned to her own visitors downstairs.

'You're lucky ter 'ave Auntie,' said Frankie, ruefully. 'I wish my mum was like 'er.'

Prof was collecting two beakers from a cupboard at the side of the fireplace. 'Auntie's not like other women. She let's me do what I want.' He came back with the beakers, filled them with Tizer and handed one to Frankie. 'I saw that girlfriend of yours the other day.' There was a touch of scorn in his voice.

Frankie took a swift gulp of his Tizer. 'Girlfriend? Wot yer talkin' about?'

Prof sat down beside Frankie again. 'That one from the Girls' School at Highbury Hill – you were eyeing her up in the air-raid shelter.'

Frankie coloured. He knew exactly who Prof was talking about. 'I don't remember.'

'Well, she remembers *you*. She was in Marks and Spencers with her mum and she had the cheek to come up and ask if I knew whether you were going to our school concert in January.'

'Wot d'yer tell 'er?' Frankie was trying to sound disinterested.

'I said I wouldn't know, I'm not your secretary.' Prof took a quick swig of his Tizer, which almost half-emptied the beaker. Frankie was the only real pal Prof had ever had. In fact, no other member of the Merton Street gang would ever have bothered with him if it wasn't for Frankie because Prof was a real one-off. He dressed peculiarly, sometimes putting on odd socks, his trousers hoisted so high by his braces that they were invariably at half-mast, and, to the despair of Auntie, he often wore plimsolls out in the street in the dead of winter. He would do anything for Frankie, because Frankie treated him like a human being. The idea that Frankie should have a girl-friend upset him. It wasn't that Prof didn't like girls; he just didn't trust them, especially after the way Patty in the gang had teased and taunted him so many times.

Frankie shuffled awkwardly, then quickly changed the subject. 'Yer know somefin', Prof.' You oughta sell this train set. I bet yer'd make a fortune out of it.'

Prof replaced the model train engine on the track beside the station platform. 'I don't want to sell it. There's no point.'

Frankie looked puzzled. 'Wot yer gonna do wiv it, then?'

Prof hesitated, then turned to look straight at Frankie. 'It's yours, Frankie. At least it will be – one of these days.'

Frankie was thunderstruck. 'Mine!'

'What good is it to me when I'm dead?'

'Come off it, Prof! Yer only fifteen. Yer've got donkey's years left yet.'

Prof flopped back on to the floor. 'Not

necessarily.' He tucked his hands behind his head, staring up at the ceiling. 'I went to the Royal Northern hospital in Holloway Road last week. They did a whole lot of tests on me.' He was speaking quite naturally, with no trace of self-pity. The specialist said I've got to be careful, I could drop down dead any time.'

Frankie felt the blood drain from his body. 'Whose leg are yer pullin', Prof?'

Prof sat up and propped himself on his elbows. 'I'm not pullin' anyone's leg, Frankie. It's true. It's all to do with this rheumatic fever I had when I was a kid. I haven't told anyone except you about it. Auntie knows, of course. She says she's not worried, as long as I take care of myself and wants me to get rid of my bike. But I'll never do that.'

For once, Frankie was at a loss for words.

Prof grinned broadly. 'Don't look so worried. I'm not going to pop off yet. At least – I hope not.' But his expression became just a little more intense as he sat upright and stared straight at Frankie. 'But when it does happen, I want you to have all this – the train set, and all the rest of the stuff. You can sell it if you want. I want you to have it, Frankie. You won't forget, will you?'

Frankie suddenly stood up. He was feeling angry, which was his way of expressing how upset he was. 'I'm not gonna listen to this crap, Prof. Ye're only fifteen years old. Only *old* people die. I'm tellin' yer, Prof. Yer'll be around when most of us are dead and gone.'

Prof roared with laughter. 'Don't be a nit, Frankie. I mean, let's face it – nobody lives forever.' And with that, he poured them both another beaker of Tizer.

All the way home, Frankie couldn't get the Prof off his mind. It was something about the cool and calm way that his own best pal had told him that he was going to die. It was impossible, thought Frankie. He looked so well, so alive! Surely there must be doctors around who could put him right? After all, since the war started thousands of people had been pulled from the bombed wreckage of their homes and saved from death, so why could'nt they do the same for the Prof? Churning over in his mind what his friend had told him, Frankie said to himself that he didn't want the stupid old train set, or the 'Mosquito' fighter bomber model or the four-mast sailing ship model. He just wanted the Prof to stay alive! As he and Winston turned into Merton Street from Hornsey Road, Frankie wished this miserable Christmas would hurry up and end.

It was after nine o'clock when Frankie and Winston arrived back home at number 1. But just as he was about to put his key in the street door, someone called to him.

'Frankie!' It was Helen, approaching from the

other side of the street. 'Don't go in yet.'

''Elen?' Frankie was surprised to see her outside, wrapped up in her coat and headscarf. He expected her to be down in the shelter, listening to the wireless with Mum and Dad. 'Wot yer doin' out 'ere?'

Helen beckoned to him silently, and he came back out into the street to join her. 'Dad's been gettin' stroppy,' she said, keeping her voice low. ''E's 'ad too much ter drink.'

'Oh no,' groaned Frankie. His father seemed to think that every high day and holiday was an excuse to get as much booze down him as possible. That was fair enough, but Reg Lewis couldn't hold his drink and it transformed him from a fairly placid, hard-working man into an uncontrollable monster. 'Where's Mum?'

Helen turned, and indicated the other side of the street. Their mother was wrapped up in her warm clothes, sitting on the coping-stone of a front garden wall opposite.

'Wot's she doin' over there?'

''E went for 'er. So we came out for a walk – ter give 'im time ter go off an' kip.'

Frankie had just about had his fill of this Christmas. 'One of these days someone's gonna give 'im a wop! 'E's a menace when 'e's on the booze!'

'Don't make fings worse, Frankie!' Helen was trying to pull him away from the gate. 'Come over and sit wiv me and Mum.'

Frankie refused to budge. 'No I won't! I'm tired. I'm goin' upstairs to read my book.'

'Well, make sure yer do,' sighed Helen, only too aware of how stubborn and obstinate her brother could be. 'Just ignore 'im and go straight upstairs. I'll see yer later.'

Frankie watched Helen return to their mother, who looked pathetic sitting disconsolately in the freezing cold, hands tucked into her coat pockets. Then he and Winston made their way back to the street door, and went in.

Frankie was determined not to creep quietly into his own house, so as soon as he followed Winston in, he closed the door quite normally. But he had got no further than the bottom of the stairs when he heard his father's voice yelling from the front parlour room.

'Grace! Is that you?'

Frankie took no notice, and started to push Winston gently up the stairs. 'Go on, boy!'

Suddenly, the parlour door was flung open and Reg was there, hardly able to stand up. 'Did you 'ear wot I – ?' On seeing Frankie there, he stopped dead. 'Oh – so it's you, is it?'

Frankie couldn't bear to see his father in this state, his hair all over his bloated, blood-red, drunken face, his shirt half-hanging out of his trousers. As usual, he had the last remnants of a fag dangling from his lips and a dog-end tucked behind one ear. 'I'm goin' up ter bed, Dad. G'night.' He turned, but his father yelled after him.

'You get back 'ere! I wanna word wiv yer!'

'I'm goin' ter bed, Dad! I'm tired!'

Now Reg was really angry, and he staggered out of the parlour doorway, and yelled up at his son. 'You get down 'ere, yer toffee-nosed little git, or I'll cuff the bleedin' daylights outa yer!'

Frankie hesitated for a moment then, in a fit of rage, stormed back down the stairs, and fearlessly swept past his father into the parlour. What he saw made him feel physically sick. Chairs were tossed on their side and the settee was stained with beer. The floor was littered with newspapers, half-eaten sandwiches, and countless quart bottles of brown ale. And the stench! It was that same terrible smell of stale beer and home-rolled Rizzla fags which nauseated Frankie every time he passed a pub at throwing-out time.

'So – yer fink you're so high-and-bleedin' mighty, don't yer!' Reg had just managed to stagger back into the room, but he had to hold on to the door. ''Specially now you're so well bleedin' 'eeled.'

Frankie, his arms crossed defiantly, didn't like the sound of this. 'Wot're yer goin' on about?'

'I'll tell yer wot I'm goin' on about, young clever-arse!' Reg moved towards Frankie, waggling his finger menacingly at him, his eyes glazed with drink. 'You an' your fancy lady pal in the jumble shop. Yer fought I din't know about 'er, din't yer?' And he yelled, 'Din't yer!'

Reg's raised voice caused Winston to growl in the passage outside.

'I don't care wot yer know or don't know!' Frankie yelled back. 'Wot I do is none of yer business!'

'It is my bleedin' business! If you go out and take money off a bleedin' Kraut, then it's *my* business!' Reg was wavering dangerously on his feet. 'I'm not 'avin my own son make *me* a laughin' stock down the 'ole bleedin' street!'

'I'm not the one that's makin' yer a laughin' stock!' Frankie yelled. 'And since yer're so concerned about me bein' yer son, then why don't yer treat me *like* a son!'

''Ow much is she payin' yer?'

'I told yer, it's none of yer business!'

Reg staggered menacingly closer. 'I'm warnin' you!'

'It's none of yer business! I work fer wot I earn, and you got no right to ask me questions!'

Reg was now brandishing his fist at Frankie. 'If I go round to that bleedin' shop, I swear to God I'll cut that bleedin' Kraut bitch down ter size!'

'Don't you call 'er fings like that!' Frankie was now eyeball to eyeball with his father. 'Elsa's a kind and wonderful lady. I work 'ard for 'er, and she pays me for it. Wot's wrong wiv that?'

'Ha! Kind an' wonderful my arse!'

Now Frankie was really rattled, so he yelled back in a high-pitched shriek. 'At least she *does* somefin' for me. Which is more than *you've* ever done!'

This was too much for Reg. He had always felt vaguely guilty about his inadequacies as a father, about never being able to give his son any pocket money. His clenched fist suddenly launched at Frankie and struck the boy straight in one eye. Frankie tumbled back on to the floor and, as he did so, Winston, with teeth bared, leapt through the open door and grabbed hold of Reg's ankle. The sounds of shouts and dog snarls were horrifying.

'No, Winnie! Down boy!' Frankie, holding his wounded, weeping eye, was trying to get up from the floor.

Reg tried to pull his ankle away from Winston, and in desperation, suddenly kicked out at the dog with his other foot, sending Winston reeling across the other side of the room, squealing in pain.

Frankie leapt up, yelling hysterically at his father. 'Yer pig! I hate yer! I hate yer!' and he pushed Reg hard with both hands, sending him sprawling on to the settee, scattering bottles, glasses, and plates as he fell. 'I hope yer *die*!' Then he grabbed hold of Winston's collar and dragged him out of the room. 'Come, Winnie! Come boy!' he begged. 'Let's get out of 'ere!'

As soon as he and Winston had reached the safety of their bedroom, Frankie locked the door.

Within a few moments, his father was outside, banging wildly and yelling, 'Open this door, yer little sod! Open it!' Frankie was now sobbing hard and all he could do as he listened to his father's drunken rantings on the landing outside was to hug Winston as tight as he possibly could.

It was some minutes before Frankie heard the sound of his father's footsteps thumping back down the stairs. Then, with a last yell of, 'Don't worry, I can wait! I'll get yer, yer little bleeder!' the parlour door was slammed, shaking the very foundations of the entire house.

Frankie, his eye stinging from the savage blow he had just received, got up very quietly and unlocked the door, then lay on his bed, clutching Winston. Eventually, the huge tears rolling down his cheeks sent him off to sleep, but not before thinking to himself that it had been a hell of a way to spend Christmas.

The following morning was Boxing Day and, when Frankie got up, Helen was still asleep in her own bed. He got a shock when he looked in Helen's dressing-table mirror, for his eye was hugely swollen and was a deep mauve colour. It was still quite early, so he and Winston crept downstairs very quietly, making sure they didn't wake Reg, who was more than likely sprawled out on the settee, dead to the world. But when Frankie got down the stairs, he noticed that the parlour door was open and, when he looked inside, there was no sign of his father. There was no one in the kitchen either, but something did catch Frankie's eye on the table. There was something scrawled almost incomprehensibly on the top of the front page of an old *Daily Mirror.* It just said: *For Frankie.* With it was a solitary shilling piece.

It was the only way Reg Lewis knew how to say sorry.

Chapter Nine

Elsa spent the few days of the Christmas holidays preparing for a rather special occasion and when Frankie returned to work in the jumble shop on the day after Boxing Day, she invited him, subject to his parents' permission, to join her and her friend, Gertrude, for a New Year's Eve dinner at Hadleigh Villas. Frankie was overjoyed and accepted at once, saying that there would be no problem with his parents because they always went to bed early every New Year's Eve.

The following Sunday, as soon as lunch at home was over, Frankie got spruced up in his new long grey flannel trousers, a clean white shirt and school tie, and a woollen pullover which Elsa had given him as a Christmas present. By four o'clock with Winston at his side, Frankie was knocking on Elsa's door.

She was in an ebullient mood, complaining about everything from the bad plumbing in the house to the feeble gas pressure on her gas stove.

'You British can never get anything right!' she kept telling Frankie, over and over again.

Frankie was very amused to see Elsa in such a state, but fascinated to see all the weird and wonderful things she was preparing in the kitchen, and in particular the pancakes (which she said were called *kartoffel-puffel* in German, or something like that). Anyway, they were made out of mashed potato and covered with bread-crumbs, and Frankie couldn't wait to taste them. During the last frenzied hour before Gertrude was due to arrive, Frankie helped Elsa lay the table in her dining-room. For him this was an absolute revelation. It was just like in the pictures. To have a separate room to have dinner in was smart enough, but to have silver cutlery, crystal glasses, and lace napkins was what Frankie had always imagined only people like the King and Queen had at Buckingham Palace. Despite her panic to get everything finished in time, Elsa was meticulous in the way she showed Frankie how to lay the table. She was determined that this was to be an evening which he would not only enjoy, but one in which he would also learn a great deal.

At a quarter to seven, Elsa went upstairs to have her bath and get dressed. She was away for ages and while she was gone, Frankie, worn-out with over-excitement, fell asleep in her armchair in the sitting-room. He was awoken by Winston who was barking and wagging his tail briskly.

'Well? What do you think of old Elsa?'

Frankie opened his eyes to find Elsa standing in the open doorway, posing with arms outstretched, as though she were the lady on the opening of every Columbia Pictures film. Both Frankie and Winston were staggered by her appearance, for she had changed into the most elegant full-length black velvet evening gown, which set off her carefully arranged gingery-coloured hair to the most stunning effect. She was also wearing two gold bangles on one wrist, a gold wristwatch on the other, diamond drop earrings and, tastefully pinned to the black velvet near her right shoulder was a glittering brooch in the shape of a scorpion.

'Yer look – t'rriffic, Elsa!' was all Frankie could say, 'just like – like Hedy Lamarr in *Boom Town*!'

Elsa threw her head back and roared with laugher and, as she did so, Frankie thought she looked really beautiful. Winston also approved, for he immediately rushed up to her and started sniffing the black velvet. 'Thank you, Winston!' said the vivacious Hedy Lamarr of Hadleigh Villas. 'I'm glad you approve!' Then, quickly glancing at her watch, she suddenly disappeared out of the room, calling back to Frankie as she went, 'Follow me, Frankie! We have work to do!'

Frankie obediently followed Elsa to the door beneath the stairs, then down some narrow steps to the cellar. When Elsa turned on the light, Frankie found that they were in a wine cellar, but the shelves were almost entirely empty but for a few dusty-looking bottles which occupied one small corner.

'Before the war these shelves were full of the finest wine you could buy. Robert always had it sent from France – that is, until the Nazis took it all.' She found a bottle of wine and gave it to Frankie to take back upstairs.

Gertrude Rosenberg arrived on the dot of eight o'clock. Unlike Elsa, she was always punctual, which she considered to be polite.

'Zo! Ziz iss the famous Misster Frankie Lewis!' Having paid off the taxi driver who had brought her from Swiss Cottage, Gertrude was now at the street door which Frankie had opened. As ever, she was a vision of over-dressing, wearing the most flamboyant creation paid for by one of her pre-war boyfriends. Like Elsa, she was in a long evening dress, but it was bright scarlet and she also wore heavy make-up including false eyelashes that were so long they curved up at the ends. 'Zo, do I com in, or do I stand on der doorstep all night?'

'Oh – sorry, miss.' Frankie stood back to let Gertrude enter. As she did so, she handed him her small overnight suitcase, as if he were a servant. Frankie took the case, then quickly closed the street door. Winston greeted Gertrude's arrival with total indifference, for he only sniffed her dress twice before returning to the rug in front of the sitting-room fire.

'Gertrude! Mein lieber Freund!' Elsa came hurrying out from the kitchen to greet her old friend. Frankie thought they would never stop kissing each other's cheeks. 'Come, Frankie! Say hallo to my dear friend, Miss Rosenberg.'

Frankie transferred the overnight suitcase to his left hand, and offered the other hand to Gertrude. ''Allo, miss.'

Gertrude held her hand out as though she were Queen Mary. When Frankie shook it heartily, she withdrew it quickly and put it into her coat pocket. 'He's much smaller zan I imagined.'

The two women were now both looking at Frankie. 'Nonsense!' Elsa said, with a dismissive wave of the hand. 'English boys always take a little longer to grow tall. It's the terrible food they eat.'

As the two women continued to talk about him as though he wasn't even there, Frankie knew why he had been invited. Elsa was putting him on show to Gertrude, who was clearly irritated that Elsa had found a friend other than herself. It was going to be quite an evening!

Before dinner, Frankie sat on a pouffe by the sitting-room fireplace, watching Elsa and Gertrude as they sipped sherry and talked about 'the old days' and he learned more about Elsa than he had since they first met. He heard how, at the beginning of the war, because of a bureaucratic mix-up, Elsa had been interned in an Alien's Camp on the Isle of Man, but when Robert, eventually contacted by the hopelessly misinformed Home Office, produced their marriage certificate, she was immediately released.

Dinner was nothing like the food served up by Frankie's mother. For starters there were Elsa's little home-made tartlets filled with fish roe, and that was followed by veal stew with small suet dumplings, the meat provided by Mr Dorner, the butcher in Hornsey Road, whose own family, although he would never dare admit it, had German origins, hot shredded white cabbage cooked in vinegar called sauerkraut (which Frankie hated), and the *kartoffel-puffel* potato pancakes, which Frankie thought were tasty, but not as good as chips. The 'afters' consisted of extra-special apple-cake (the apples cooked in brandy), accompanied by a very curious cold semolina pudding mixed with home-made gooseberry jam. But when Frankie was offered a quarter of a glass of Elsa's precious sweet white wine, Gertrude was somewhat astonished when he declined. When he was asked his reasons, Frankie explained that his dad would not allow him to drink alcohol until he was eighteen as it was against the law.

Gertrude scoffed indignantly at this. 'So typical of ze British. Ven I vos your age, young man, I had already been drinking for at least five or six years.' Then, turning to Elsa with a shrug of the shoulders, added, 'No vonder British children are so behind children on ze Continent. Zeir parents vont to keep zem young until zey are too old to know any better!'

Frankie didn't quite know what Gertrude meant by this, but he felt he couldn't take it lying down. So he changed his mind and tasted the wine. He only sipped it but, as he did so, he tried to give the impression that he was enjoying it, which he wasn't. To him it was sickly, and even as he smelt it, he felt like sneezing. But in a funny way Gertrude was right. It did make him feel grown up.

As the evening wore on and 1945 loomed closer, the party really got into its stride. They pulled the Christmas crackers that Elsa had brought along from the shop to decorate the dining-table and suddenly they were all helpless with giggly laughter at the silly, different coloured paper hats they were wearing. Then Gertrude, who had consumed three glasses of sherry before dinner and more than half the bottle of Elsa's white wine during it, yelled out at the top of her voice, 'Musik! Ich wunsche die Musik!'

'Ah!' Elsa immediately responded by leaping up from the dining-table and going to the huge oak dresser, where she collected something from one of the lower cupboards. 'Die Musik!' With a triumphant flourish she held up a small concertina. To vigorous applause from Gertrude, Elsa launched into a lively German song, swaying to and fro as she pressed the bellows and sang for all she was worth. Gertrude clapped her hands and joined in the song, urging Frankie to do the same. Frankie was absolutely staggered by this instant display of entertainment and, even though he hadn't the faintest idea what he was singing, he la-di-da'd and clapped in time with tremendous gusto. The next moment he was being dragged up from his seat to follow Elsa and Gertrude in what was presumably a German folk dance. With Elsa singing and playing her concertina, then Gertrude waving her hands and arms and displaying the most awful singing voice, Frankie jigged excitedly behind, singing and laughing, deliriously happy, winding around the dining-table, then out across the hall, and into the dining-room. During all this, Winston cowered behind the settee, convinced that everyone had gone quite mad. Finally, Gertrude flopped down exhausted on to the settee, Elsa into her own armchair, and Frankie on to the pouffe by the fireplace.

A little later, when Elsa had brought in coffee, Frankie listened to her and Gertrude talking about the war, and how soon it would end. Then they told him fascinating stories about their escape from Germany and Frankie learnt how courageous Gertrude had been when she saved Elsa from a Nazi supporter who had wanted to hand her over to the military police. Frankie also contributed his own story of terror, a vivid account of how, in 1940, he and his friend Alan Downs had been machine-gunned in Annette

Road by a stray German Messerschmitt fighter plane, before it crashed into nearby Finsbury Park. Elsa and Gertrude listened, enthralled.

With barely half-an-hour to midnight, the evening began to look just a little uneasy. It started with Gertrude insisting that she be given a brandy and Elsa duly obliged. The danger sign came when Gertrude started to slur her words.

'Tell me somesing, Frankie.' Gertrude's dark, piercing eyes were watching him carefully over the brim of her large brandy glass. 'Vhy do you come to see Elsa so much?'

Elsa intervened immediately. 'Don't be silly, Gertrude. Why shouldn't Frankie come to see me?'

'Because he's a young boy, and you are an old voman! He should be out viz boys and girls his own age.'

Frankie didn't like this. Gertrude was reminding him of the way his father behaved when he started to drink and Frankie's eye was still a dark red after the beating he had taken on Christmas night. It had not been easy to lie to Elsa by saying he got the bad eye in a friendly fight with one of his pals in the Merton Street gang. 'I like ter work wiv Elsa,' said Frankie, feeling a little unsure of himself. 'She's very good ter me.'

'But vot about your mudder? Isn't *she* good to you?'

Elsa was getting irritated. 'Gertrude!'

Gertrude would not be fobbed off, and kept her eyes glued to Frankie. 'Vot does your mudder think zat you see Elsa so much?'

Frankie shrugged his shoulders. 'She don't mind.'

'She's not jealous perhaps?'

Elsa thumped her fist on the arm of her chair. 'You are being *dumm*, Gertrude. *Dumm*!'

Winston, who had his chin resting on Frankie's lap, flinched when Frankie patted his head a little too hard. 'My mum in't jealous. She don't care *who* I see.'

'Ah!' Gertrude gulped down the last of her brandy, convinced that she had stumbled on to something. 'Zo maybe you prefer to be viz Elsa more zan your mudder?'

'Dumm! Dumm! Dumm!' Elsa got up from her seat, and grabbed the empty brandy glass from Gertrude. She was clearly embarrassed by her friend's tactless questions. 'The cognac has made your tongue loose, Gertrude! It happens every time!' Clearly irritated, she very nearly snapped the stem of the brandy glass as she slammed it down on to a small side table. Then she returned to her own chair again.

Gertrude shrugged her shoulders smugly. 'All I am saying is zat it's not possible for a person to haf two mudders. It's not natural.'

Without looking up, Frankie answered quite casually. 'Elsa's my friend, miss – not my mum.

And, let's face it – she's not your mum either – is she?'

Elsa swung around with a start and stared at Frankie, delighted. After a brief moment Frankie looked up, and they both exchanged a mischievous grin, which soon turned into a giggle.

'I'm going to bed!' With supreme effort, Gertrude eased herself up from the settee. She was very wobbly on her feet.

Elsa rose quickly from her seat. 'But Gertrude, dear, it's nearly time for the New Year.'

'Ze New Year . . .' Her words were now more slurred than ever '. . . vill soon be . . . not so new. And it is not *our* New Year . . .' As she staggered towards the door, Frankie leapt up and rushed across to help. But Gertrude shrugged him off and, as she disappeared into the hall, the last thing she was heard to mutter was, 'Sank God anozzer year is over!'

Elsa rushed to the door and called after her. '*Gute nacht wunschen, Gertrud!* Happy New Year!' She closed the door, and turned round triumphantly to Frankie. 'I'm having a wonderful time!'

'Me too!' beamed Frankie.

At one minute to midnight Elsa turned on the wireless to listen to the chimes of Big Ben ushering in the New Year. As Gertrude had drained the last few drops of wine from the bottle, Elsa and Frankie had to toast the New Year in with

R. W. White's lemonade and Winston wasn't left out. Frankie dipped his finger into his own glass, and dropped some of the lemonade into the dog's mouth.

When the chimes of Big Ben had finally greeted the first day of the new year, Elsa and Frankie listened for a while to the rest of the festivities on the wireless, and joined in with the crowds singing *Auld Lang Syne*. Then, before he went home, Frankie asked Elsa if she would play just one more song for him. So Elsa turned off the wireless and picked up her concertina. She sat down in her own armchair, settled her head back, closed her eyes, and accompanied herself on the concertina as she sang. This time, however, it was a very different song: *Till We Meet Again*.

It was a sad little tune, and for the first time, Frankie realised why it meant so much to Elsa. Her voice was not perfect, but it was sweet and pure. But, most important of all, there was no doubt that she and her husband Robert had learnt the words together, for Elsa had just sung the song in the most impeccable English accent. As he watched her dab away her tears with her lace handkerchief, he got up from the pouffe he had been sitting on and, without a second thought, kissed her lightly on the cheek. Elsa's eyes immediately lit up.

'I'm sorry ye're not my muvver, Elsa,' Frankie whispered into her ear. 'But I'm very proud ter 'ave you as my friend.' Then he kissed her on the other cheek. 'Happy New Year, Elsa!' Winston added his greeting by barking just once, and licking Elsa's hand.

Frankie and Winston made their way home along darkened streets. There were still a few revellers around, but on the whole, most people had already gone to bed. When they reached Merton Street, Frankie sat for a few moments on the coping-stone of the garden wall opposite number 1. The house was not only in darkness, but also absolutely still and quiet. But Frankie thought the street itself seemed to be generating a very special atmosphere, totally different from anything he had known before. It was as though the roofs and chimney-pots were all trying to tell him something – maybe something about the New Year that was now only an hour old. Would life in Merton Street be any different next year, he wondered? Would he pass his Matriculation Certificate at school? Would he get on better with his family? Would he be able to save up enough for his new bike! And would the war finally come to an end?

The New Year had a lot to offer. Frankie just hoped that 1945 would live up to all its promises.

Chapter Ten

The Thursday after New Year's Eve, Frankie received an offer he couldn't resist. It was his sister Helen's afternoon off from the shoe shop, and she asked her brother if he would like to go to the pictures with her. Frankie jumped at the chance, especially as he wasn't paying. The last time they'd gone to the pictures together was way back in 1940, to see Tod Slaughter in a really spooky horror film called *The Face at the Window.* The film had an H Certificate, so no children were allowed anywhere near the place. But Frankie and Helen had sneaked into the cinema through an Exit door, and concealed themselves on the floor at the back of the Circle. However, when the film was half-way through, the sudden wail of an air-raid siren was immediately followed by a flash on the screen:

The Air Raid alert has sounded.
Will those patrons who wish to leave,
please do so quietly.

For those patrons who wish to remain,
the programme will continue.

To their immense frustration, Frankie and Helen were forced to leave, not because they were afraid, but because the attendants were moving through the auditorium with their torches, showing the few people who wanted to leave the way out, and they'd been afraid of being discovered. Once outside, the anti-aircraft gunfire was already shattering the buildings along the Holloway Road, so Frankie and Helen had had to hurry back to Merton Street, dodging the red-hot pieces of shrapnel that were falling out of the sky as they ran.

This afternoon, as Frankie and Helen settled down in their seats in the circle, for which Helen had paid one and threepence each, all the horrors of those nightly air-raids seemed like a bygone nightmare and the double bill playing that week was well worth the money. The picture Frankie wanted to see most was the 'B' feature – Laurel and Hardy in *The Dancing Masters*, his favourite screen comics. But he was also eager to see *Down Argentina Way*, a colour musical with Betty Grable and Carmen Miranda. Although he laughed a great deal at 'the Brazilian bombshell' as Carmen Miranda was called, Frankie always cringed with embarrassment every time he saw her, for it reminded him of the time when, at the age of seven, he had been forced to impersonate her at the annual Christmas party in the church hall.

Helen didn't seem particularly excited by the thought of seeing any of the programme. There was, as Frankie suspected, an ulterior motive in his sister's sudden generosity but Helen waited until the interval before revealing it. Frankie had already consumed the Mars bar Helen had donated with her ration coupons, and now he was joining in the chorus of *Shine on Harvest Moon*, which was being played with skilled bravado by Mr Rupert Hufpepper, who was in the spotlight, his back to the audience, smiling and nodding his head at them in the mirror of the cinema's Compton organ.

'Got somefin' ter tell yer, Frank,' Helen said, turning to Frankie, as Mr Hufpepper and his 'musical wonder machine' sank into the bowels of the Marlborough pit. 'I need yer 'elp.'

Frankie turned to look at her. 'Wot's up?'

Helen looked carefully around to make sure no one was listening. 'I'm gettin' rid o' the baby.'

Frankie practically leapt out of his seat. 'Wot!'

Helen quickly put a hand to Frankie's mouth and lowered her voice even further. 'Ssh, Frank! I don't want the 'ole cinema ter 'ear.'

Frankie was utterly flabbergasted. 'Wot d'yer mean – gettin' rid of it?'

'I'm 'avin' an abortion. Ivy knows some woman up in Hornsey Rise who'll do it.'

Frankie started biting his fingernails hard. As

he listened to Helen, he found he couldn't look at her. The cinema house lights had already darkened, and the projectionist was showing some local advertisements on the screen.

'I've thought very 'ard about it. In fact, I've 'ad 'ardly any sleep since – since I 'eard about Eric.'

'But why d'yer 'ave ter get rid of it?' Frankie was watching the cinema screen without taking anything in. 'Why can't yet just 'ave it, and look after it?'

'Are yer jokin'!' Helen leant across the arm of her seat so that she was almost whispering straight into Frankie's left ear. ''Ave yer any idea wot Mum'd do ter me if she knew? Dad, too, most like. They just couldn't take it, Frank. They wouldn't know 'ow.' She stopped speaking abruptly when two small children passed along the empty row of seats just in front of them, clearly heading for the toilets. Helen waited for the two kids to disappear, then leant across to Frankie again. 'At first, I thought I'd take a chance and just sit it out. But then I decided, well – it wouldn't be fair on the kid. I mean, wot's the point if I'm kicked out of 'ouse and 'ome, wiv nowhere ter go, and a small baby wiv only a muvver ter bring it up. It wouldn't be right, Frank. It just wouldn't be right.'

Frankie had chewed his thumbnail down to the quick, and he was now moving on to his forefinger. As the last advertisement was coming to an end on the screen, he thought he saw the dim figure of a man flickering hurriedly across the projection beam. He swung around with a start, half expecting to see the ghost of the Edwardian actor who, it was alleged, had haunted the circle seats area since the turn of the century, when the old Marlborough cinema had been an elegant variety theatre.

'So wot d'yer say, Frank. Are yer wiv me?'

Frankie forgot all about the 'ghost', and turned back to his sister. ''Course I'm wiv yer. But I don't see 'ow I can 'elp yer?'

Helen waited for the usherette to show an excited family party of four kids and three adults to their seats on the other side of the gangway. Once they had settled she drew close to Frankie again. 'I need some money, Frank. It's gonna cost five quid ter get rid of the baby.'

'Five quid!' Frankie swung a horrified look at her.

Helen shushed him. 'She's doin' it cheap 'cos she knows Ivy. I've got nearly four quid of me own. I was savin' it fer . . .' She stopped speaking for a moment, for there was a huge lump in her throat. 'I was savin' it for when Eric came 'ome. Did yer know 'e'd asked me ter marry 'im? We'd only known each uvver a few weeks. ''E loved me, Frank. I swear ter God, he did love me!'

Frankie suddenly stopped chewing his fingernail, grabbed hold of his sister's hands and squeezed them hard though he'd never done such a thing before. Knowing Elsa was changing him in lots of ways . . . 'I'll give yer the rest of the money, ''Elen. I can take it out of my money jar.'

Helen, whose eyes were glistening with tears in the light from the cinema projection, stared at her brother with a look of anguish and astonishment. 'But you can't, Frank. You're savin' that money for yer bike.'

'There's no rush,' said Frankie, taking a deep breath and straightening up in his seat. 'I've waited so long, I can wait a bit longer. Anyway, you'd do the same fer me.'

Helen threw her arms around her brother and hugged him. 'Oh fank you, Frank!' she whispered. She wanted to cry, but somehow felt that it would probably embarrass him. 'I'll never forget this, I promise. Never!'

They quickly straightened up again as the two small kids returned from their visit to the toilets, giggling at the two funny people who were cuddling each other.

The lights in the great chandelier on the ceiling above gradually started to dim and, within seconds, the fading red plush seats and peeling gold leaf stucco were plunged into total darkness. But then that magic, flickering light beamed down from the projection booth behind and, as the dusty old quilted curtains drew back across the screen, it was only moments before the Marlborough cinema in the Holloway Road was transported into the glamour of technicoloured Argentina.

This was always the moment that Frankie loved the most. To him, the lights dimming at the start of a film was the most exciting thing in the world. But not today. At this precise moment, all he could feel was a sense of overwhelming depression . . .

On Saturday morning, Elsa woke up to find that there had been a heavy fall of snow overnight. But, as she had never failed to open her shop promptly at nine o'clock every morning, she left number 19 Hadleigh Villas half-an-hour earlier than usual. It was a slow and perilous journey, for although most people were already clearing the snow from the pavement in front of their gates, others were clearly taking advantage of a Saturday morning lie-in. As she plodded her way along Hadleigh Villas, she couldn't tell where the pavement finished and the road began, for the snow was way up past her ankles. Luckily, because of the appalling conditions, there wasn't much traffic on the road, so she didn't feel too threatened if she occasionally wandered off the kerb.

Once in the Tollington Road, Elsa stopped briefly at the small newsagents shop where she bought her usual copy of the *News Chronicle*. However, it wasn't until she was making her way out again that she suddenly noticed a large front-page photograph that sent a chill down her spine. '*DEATH CAMP HORROR*' read the headline above it, and below, it told the terrifying story: '*Allied forces advancing on a small town in north-western France, came upon this scene of human carnage and destruction . . .*' Elsa could read no more, for she immediately realised that the photograph was of a group of French men, women, and children, their heads shaven and marked with the word: *JUDE*. All were riddled with machine-gun holes and had been thrown into a muddy trench grave in some quiet country woods. It was a horrifying picture, and Elsa couldn't look at it. She quickly folded up the newspaper and tucked it in her shopping bag, hurrying out of the shop.

As she made her way slowly down the Tollington Road, Elsa felt sick in her stomach. She was overwhelemed by the deep, merciless cruelty of the Nazis. How could one human being do this to another human being, she kept asking herself? And her mind went back to those early days in Germany, to her family and friends, and what had happened to them during those brutal, soul-destroying times. She and Gertrude too might have ended up in a pile of death like those poor, tragic creatures in the newspaper photograph. As she walked, her hand felt for the Star of David brooch she was wearing on a chain around her neck. And, as she rubbed it gently in her fingers, she prayed that the human slaughter would soon end . . .

As she reached sight of Hornsey Road, Elsa

was in a deep depression. But, as she drew closer to the jumble shop on the corner, her face lit up. Winston was bouncing in and out of the snow towards her. 'Winston!' she yelled, half-laughing, but doing her best to keep her balance. 'You young rascal! What are you doing out so early?'

''Allo, Elsa.' Frankie suddenly appeared from around the corner. He was wrapped up against the cold, with a woollen scarf tied around his head and ears, and Wellington boots which were covered with snow. What could be seen of his face was very flushed, for he had been toiling away at clearing the snow from the pavement outside the shop, using a small coal shovel lent to him by Mr Jones in the dairy yard just down the road.

Elsa was astonished to see what Frankie had been doing. 'Frankie! You excellent chap! This is wonderful, wonderful!'

Elsa quickly took the shop key from her pocket and opened up. Winston followed her in, then Frankie, who immediately lit the paraffin stove. The shop was at once filled with the sour smell of burning oil. In no time at all, Elsa had boiled a kettle on top of the stove, and, after putting two teaspoonfuls of tea into her small brown china teapot, poured piping hot water on to it. During this, Winston took up his usual place as close to the stove as possible, where he was kept quiet with a couple of Jacobs cracker biscuits covered with Marmite. Frankie took off his scarf, but kept his raincoat on, then set about trying to unfreeze his fingers over the stove.

'You're a good boy, Frankie. I'm very lucky to have you help me.' Elsa poured hot tea into two mugs which immediately gave off a fresh smelling aroma, dispelling the sour vapour from the stove. While she waited for the tea to brew, she went to the window and raised the blackout blinds. It was only when she turned that she noticed how tired and miserable Frankie was looking. 'Frankie? Is something wrong?'

A shaft of early morning winter light was piercing through the window, which caused Frankie to shield his eyes. It also made him look even paler than he was already. 'I'm all right. Just tired, that's all.'

Frankie's response was almost surly, so Elsa knew something was wrong. 'Are you worried about your examinations? I think maybe you shouldn't come here so often. You need time for your homework.'

'It's got nuffin' ter do wiv me exams, Elsa. I don't take them 'til the summer.'

Elsa decided not to push it. She knew Frankie well enough to know that he wanted to tell her something, but didn't know how. But she wouldn't force him. Shrugging her shoulders, she made her way back behind the counter again. 'Would you like some ginger in your tea today?'

'No, fanks.'

Elsa took some fresh ginger from a small jar

underneath the counter, cut off a piece, popped it into her mug, and stirred it. She put a flat teaspoonful of sugar into Frankie's mug and left the spoon there. Then she picked up both mugs and took them over to the paraffin stove where Frankie was still thawing his hands. 'Here.'

'Thanks.' Frankie took his mug, stirred it, and took a sip. It was piping hot and it burnt his lips.

For a moment or so, neither said a word as they stared down almost mesmerically at the flickering flame on the burning wick of the stove. Sooner or later, thought Elsa, Frankie wouldn't be able to resist speaking. During the months since she had got to know him, she had grown used to her young friend's little mannerisms, his moods, and anxieties. And if there was one thing she had learnt, it was that he could not resist the temptation to share his anxieties with someone. And she was always flattered when it was she whom he confided in. So Elsa waited, sipping tea, and warming herself by the stove. For her, there was no drink in the world like a good cup of tea. It reminded her so much of her young days in Germany, when, during the cold winter months, after the long walk home from Synagogue on Saturday afternoons, the whole family would sit down to lemon and ginger tea, cinnamon biscuits, and apple strudel.

'Elsa . . .'

Elsa smiled gently to herself as Frankie finally spoke.

'If yer were goin' to 'ave a baby, would yer ever get rid of it?'

Elsa's smile immediately collapsed. 'What's that you say?'

'Wot I mean is, if you was goin' ter 'ave a baby that yer didn't want, would yer get rid of it?'

'Get rid of it? A baby?' Elsa was staring hard at him, unable to believe what he was asking.

'If a bloke gives a gel a puddin', and she don't want it, d'yer fink it's best – well – that she goes ter someone?'

For a brief moment, Elsa felt her heart thumping harder than she had ever known. Frankie had always seemed such an innocent boy, not at all worldly. She had never even heard him talk about girl-friends, let alone sex. As she stared down at the flickering wick inside the stove, all sorts of things were going through her mind. What was Frankie trying to tell her? Could it be that he himself had got a girl into some kind of trouble? 'I'm not sure what you are asking me, Frankie,' she said, still not raising her eyes from the stove. 'Are you talking about – an abortion?'

'Yeah! That's it! An abortion!' As Frankie turned to look up at Elsa, he felt no awkwardness in speaking so frankly with her, yet it was something he had never been able to do with his own parents.

Elsa sat down on her usual stool by the stove. Both her hands were wrapped around her mug as she sipped her tea. She was totally unprepared for this kind of conversation with Frankie and, for a brief moment, could say nothing. But something inside her told her that she was duty bound to treat the boy as an adult. After all, that's what he was now – more or less, and he had a right to be treated as such. Even so, Elsa felt she was taking on a great deal of responsibility by offering him any kind of advice. After all, Frankie was not her son, and she had no right to talk to him as though she was his mother. But then, she thought, if his own parents were incapable of sitting down and talking to the boy, who *could* he turn to? 'Frankie.' Suddenly, her mind was made up, and she turned to look straight at him. 'Are you in some kind of trouble?'

'Me?' He laughed weakly. 'No, it's nuffin' ter to wiv me – well, not really. It's this girl I know. Some feller she went out wiv – 'e put 'er in the puddin' club.' At this point, he turned his look away from Elsa, unable to meet her eyes while he explained. 'Er mum and dad'll kill 'er stone dead if they find out.' The heat from the paraffin stove was now reflecting a warm glow on to his anguished face. 'That's why this gel wants ter get rid of the baby. Not that she wants to, but because, because – well, she *has* to.'

Winston now grunting at rival dogs in his sleep, was curled up as close as he possibly could around the paraffin stove. Elsa bent down and calmed his nightmare by gently stroking him behind one ear. She felt quite sick. What they were talking about was a human *life*. And Elsa could not forget what she had seen just a short while ago, in that photograph on the front page of the *News Chronicle*, the men, women, and small children who had been massacred by sadistic murderers. And now, she and Frankie were talking about the extinguishing of another young life, one that was being given no chance to see the light of day. What could Elsa say? What could anyone say that could possibly justify such a decision? 'And what about the father of this child?' she asked cautiously. 'How does *he* feel about – the situation?'

Frankie thought long and hard before answering. There was a great sadness in his voice. ''E was in the Army. 'E got killed.'

Elsa's face crumpled. 'That's terrible, Frankie,' she said, in a barely audible voice. 'It's so terrible!'

'The lousy thing is,' said Frankie with a huge sigh, 'my sis – I mean – this gel – well, she still loves this feller – even though 'e's dead. It don't make no sense ter me.' He was looking at Elsa again, hoping that she would, as usual, say the right thing. 'What do you fink, Elsa? Wot would you do if you was this gel?'

Elsa was staring so hard into the glow from the paraffin stove that her eyes were beginning to water. 'You know, Frankie,' she said, her voice soft and low, 'to have a child must be a wonderful experience for a woman. Unfortunately, it's an experience I never had, something I regret every single day of my life. If I had borne his child, today I would still have something left of the person I loved more than anyone or anything else in the whole world. I would have someone who was mine. In a way it would be as if Robert were still alive, because it would be him I was listening to, him who was caring for me, loving me, just like he always used to.' She slowly turned to look at Frankie, and their eyes met in the glow of the stove. 'Oh, Frankie! If God had given me Robert's child, I would *never* have parted with it. How could I, when I loved Robert so much?'

For a moment, there was silence between them. Over Elsa's shoulder, Frankie could see through the shop window, where snowflakes were just beginning to flutter down again. He knew exactly what Elsa had been trying to say to him, and she was absolutely right. All he could think about was Helen. He was perceptive enough to know how much she still loved Eric Sibley despite the fact that he was probably dead. So why get rid of Eric's kid just because of the row it would cause with Reg and Gracie Lewis? Helen was *wrong* to do what she was doing. Helen loved Eric, she had to have his baby – *their* baby! She had to stand up to their mum and dad.

The silence was suddenly broken by the sound of a large oak wall clock chiming nine-thirty. Before it had finished, two other small clocks which were also waiting to be sold, joined in.

Frankie immediately panicked. 'It's 'alf-past! It can't be – not already!'

Winston leapt up out of his sleep with a startled bark as Frankie rushed across to the shop counter, left his mug there, and quickly made for the door. 'I didn't know it was that time! I didn't know!'

'What is it, Frankie?' said Elsa, anxiously rising from her stool. 'What's wrong?'

'I've gotta stop 'er, Elsa! I've gotta go!'

'Stop who? What are you talking about?'

Frankie was at the open door, already wrapping his scarf around his neck. 'I can't tell yer now, Elsa. I'll tell yer later. I'm sorry, Elsa! I'm sorry!' He opened the door wide. 'Winnie! Hurry boy! Hurry!'

Winston, tail wagging excitedly, rushed out into the street, leaving his master to close the shop door behind him.

Elsa quickly made her way to the window, where she watched Frankie and Winston struggling to reach the other side of Hornsey Road. It was becoming difficult to see much, for the wind had come up and huge snowflakes were already turning into a blizzard which was blowing straight against the shop window itself. But before she was completely sealed in, Elsa could just see Frankie and Winston disappearing up Arthur Road.

Soon they looked like nothing more than two tiny specs on an artist's huge, white canvas.

Chapter Eleven

Finsbury Park was looking like a Hollywood film set. After the heavy falls of snow the night before, the branches of the huge oak, elm and sycamore trees were bending with the weight, especially as the snow had frozen the moment it had settled. Ever since first light, the sun had tried desperately to tear a hole in the heavy wintry clouds, but without success, and now the twisting winds had turned into a blizzard, which scattered the massive snowflakes in every direction.

Saturday mornings were always the most popular time for strollers in the park, but today was definitely for the kids. By the time Helen Lewis reached the gates at the Seven Sisters Road entrance, it seemed that every kid in Islington was there and, even though the wind was howling, she could hear their excited laughter and cheers which were competing with a passing train on the adjoining railway line. On the snow-covered football pitch, harassed fathers and elder brothers were toiling away, pulling and pushing small children along in toboggans made out of old wooden boxes. High above them all, fluttering helplessly in and out of the clouds, two giant silver barrage balloons were being buffetted by the high winds, held only by the steel cable attached to their RAF trucks on the ground below. It was a timely reminder that, despite the joy and excitement this dramatic winter's day was causing in the park, the war was not yet over.

Helen trudged along a winding narrow path which led to the boating lake. It was hard going, for the snow was deep enough to drop into the top of her rubber bootees. Luckily, she was wearing a pair of ATS slacks which Eric had given her after bribing one of his mates in the Stores Unit back at his barracks, so her feet were still quite protected. But her camel-coloured winter's coat was flimsy and not nearly warm enough for such Arctic conditions, and her yellow headscarf was totally inadequate to protect her from the snow which was covering it. During the summer months, the path she was now using was flanked on either side by flower-beds bulging with stocks, marigolds, lupins and English roses of every colour. It was one of Helen's favourite walks, one which she always took when she was feeling miserable. Today was just such a day . . .

The park café was closed when Helen got there, so there wasn't even the chance of a cup of hot tea to warm her up. With her handbag strapped across her shoulder, she dug her hands deeper into her coat pockets and made her way down to the lake.

As she trudged along, Helen was completely oblivious to the blizzard which was bombarding her with huge snowflakes. It was very difficult to see more than a few yards ahead, so she kept her head down, staring as she went at the deep fresh snow in which she was leaving her own footprints. Even so, her eyebrows looked as though they were made of cotton wool, and her face was blood-red with the intense cold. But none of this seemed to matter. Helen's thoughts were on a tall, terraced house in Wilmington Road where, in a short time, she would abandon forever her unborn child – Eric's child. It was a prospect that chilled her far more than the weather. It was all that was left of Eric, and she never wanted to part with it – never. But what could she do? If she had the baby, her mother would never accept it and how could she possibly support it on her own?

When she reached the lake, Helen found it almost completely frozen over, and covered with a thick layer of snow. From the distance, she could hear the angry chorus of cackling from the duck colony on the tiny island in the middle of the lake. Some of the inhabitants had ventured out on to the ice, but they became even more cross when their search for pieces of discarded bread proved a hazardous, sliding waddle across the newly formed skating rink.

After a few minutes, the blizzard eased off a little, so Helen plodded through the snow to the edge of the lake, and, stepping carefully over the low metal fence, found herself within a few inches of the frozen surface of the water. Her coat and headscarf were now covered with snow, but she made no effort to brush it off. Her eyes were mesmerised by the wintry scene around her. Everything was white – the lake, grass, trees, park seats, the roof of the park café – everything. But suddenly, Helen's eyes flicked across to the far side of the lake, where a group of children were snow-balling each other. One of them was wearing a red scarf. It seemed to be such a striking fleck of colour against so stark a background, as though the whole scene had been painted. Standing there, hands deep inside her coat pockets, Helen could hear sounds filtering through her mind – the sound of coins being rattled inside a money-box. She was thinking back to just a few days before, when she had watched her brother Frankie counting out the money he had saved, handing over the pile of threepenny bits, shillings, and sixpences that added up to the one pound and two shillings Helen needed to make up the five pounds' fee for her abortion. There were tears in her eyes as she thought about it. Frankie was such a good brother. Although she had several good friends of her own, in her heart of hearts Helen knew that Frankie was the one person she could truly rely on. Without being conscious of what she was doing, Helen took one hand out of her pocket and gently placed it on her stomach. She could feel the start of that tiny new life inside her, a life that within just a few hours would be snuffed out forever. Tears were trickling down her cheeks and melting the few puffs of snow that had settled there. 'Oh Eric!' she sobbed, over and over again. 'Why? Why!'

'Missus!'

Helen's private moment of grief was suddenly broken by a chorus of kids' voices. As she turned, she could see at least five or six of them leaping through the deep snow towards her.

'You're on the lake, missus!'

'Get off – quick!'

'It in't safe! It's cracking!'

Helen panicked. She had stepped without realising on to the frozen surface of the lake, and suddenly felt her feet beginning to give way beneath her and water covering her rubber bootees. The next few seconds seemed totally unreal, for just as she was struggling to step back on to the snow-covered grass verge at the lakeside, she found herself being grabbed at by the kids who had rushed towards her. With a mighty heave and a tug, Helen was yanked off the ice to end up sprawled out face down on the snow.

'That was a near fing, missus!'

Helen looked up, to see a sea of young faces staring down in breathless astonishment at her. The voice who had spoken belonged to a small girl, aged no more than about six or seven. She was wearing a bright red scarf.

On the lake behind them the ice had now cracked to reveal a surface no more than an inch or so thick. And in the place where, only a few seconds before, Helen had been standing, a huge hole had appeared, to reveal the dark and murky water below . . .

Despite the blizzard, it took Frankie and Winston no more than a few minutes to get back home from the jumble shop. When they got there, Frankie's mother told him that Helen had left for work as usual at a quarter to nine. Now Frankie was really panicking, for although he didn't let on that his sister had taken the day off sick from the shoe shop where she worked, he knew she was now on her way to keep her appointment in Wilmington Road.

When Frankie and Winston reached the junction of Hornsey and Seven Sisters Roads, the clock on the top of the Public Baths building showed ten minutes to ten. There were now drifts of snow piled up on the pavements, and although the main roads were gradually turning to slush, there was hardly any traffic at all. Frankie looked along Seven Sisters Road towards the Nag's Head, hoping that, by some miracle, a

Number 14 bus would appear and take him and Winston up to Hornsey Rise. But after waiting for five minutes at the bus stop outside the North London Drapery Stores, he realised that the buses were clearly having a tough time keeping to schedule, so without another thought he and Winston headed off on foot towards Hornsey Rise.

It was a grim walk up Hornsey Road, for 'the Rise' was well over a mile away, uphill all the way, and a constant struggle to make progress in the deep snow and slush. There were times when Winston almost disappeared completely in the middle of a drift, and only the tip of his tail could be seen, but eventually he would reappear, shaking himself free of the snow that had gathered on his fur.

It was well over an hour later when Frankie and Winston reached the first road at the bottom of 'the Rise'. On the way they had passed the Star Cinema, a real bug-hutch of a place where Frankie and Helen had often gone to Saturday morning Tom Mix cowboy serials, and, just behind that, poor old Mitford Road which had been practically devastated by one of Hitler's bombs early in the war.

It was only when they reached Hazelville Road that Frankie suddenly realised that he had no idea where Wilmington Road was and, even worse, nor did any passer-by whom he asked. Eventually, however, he did get some sort of garbled directions from a girl in a newspaper shop, who clearly fancied him like mad. Blushing profusely, he rushed out of the shop, thanking her far more than he needed to.

Wilmington Road turned out to be completely different to how Frankie had imagined. It wasn't in the least sordid-looking, in fact it was quite 'select', as Frankie's mother would say. It was a long terraced road, with tall houses arranged on three or four floors. They looked a bit like the houses around where Elsa lived, and it gave him a funny feeling inside. Another nice feature was the trees which lined the road, on each side. On one corner was a sweet shop, which also doubled as a sub-Post Office, and the vivid red post-box outside was practically submerged in the snow that had blown against it during the blizzard.

For a few moments, Frankie stood outside and gazed down Wilmington Road. There wasn't a soul around and the bleak atmosphere only increased his sense of doom. What time was it Helen was due to go to this – this person who was going to do the 'operation'? Was it eleven o'clock? Or was it ten? Panic was swelling up inside Frankie again and his stomach was churning. Over and over again he kept blaming himself for his stupidity. Not only did he not remember what time Helen was due there, but he hadn't even asked her what number she was going to.

Frankie's ears were now so cold they felt like blocks of ice, so he quickly pulled out the woollen scarf from around his neck, and placed it over his head, covering his ears. Then he cupped his hands together and blew into them. They were red with cold. Gradually, he started to make his way down the street, peering at the front of every house as he went. To him, they all looked exactly the same: especially most of them had clearly not seen a coat of paint since the start of the war. He stopped outside Number 6, with its small front garden and stone gnomes on a raised plinth, all covered with snow. They reminded Frankie of *Snow White and the Seven Dwarfs*. He spotted a middle-aged woman staring out of a first-floor window, she looked just like the sort of person who would perform such a terrible 'operation', he thought, full of suspicion. But when he stared back at her, he changed his mind, for the woman was joined at the window by a man wearing a dog-collar, and Frankie didn't think a Vicar would be the sort of person who would approve of the kind of 'operation' Helen was going to have.

Moving on, Frankie desperately searched the front windows of practically every house in the street, imagining that Helen was behind each and every one of them. As the minutes passed by he became more and more depressed, convinced that he was too late, and that by now Helen's baby had been taken away from her. In desperation, he trudged his way back towards the sweet shop. He peered through the window.

The time on the Post Office clock on the wall showed twenty-five minutes to twelve. Frankie gulped hard. There was now no doubt that he had missed Helen. He turned away and clearing the snow from a coping stone in front of the house next door, sat there disconsolately. Winston squatted beside him, and pushed his heavy body against Frankie's leg, always a sign that he knew his master was feeling fed up with himself. There was a huge lump in Frankie's throat, which, no matter how hard he tried, he was unable to swallow.

'Come on, boy.' Frankie finally stood up. 'No point in 'angin 'round 'ere.'

As they crossed the road to make their way back to 'the Rise', Frankie took a casual look back over his shoulder. The blizzard had stopped, so people were beginning to emerge from their houses and, in no time at all, the whole area was buzzing with activity as residents, brandishing shovels, started to clear the snow from the pavement in front of their own houses. Frankie took very little notice, but just as they were about to turn the corner, he caught sight of someone in the distance at the far end of the road. It was a girl, her head down, wearing a headscarf and a camel-coloured coat. Frankie's eyes widened. ''Elen?' Shouting and waving madly, Frankie struggled through the snow to reach his sister at the end of the road.

Unfortunately, Helen could neither see nor

hear Frankie hurrying towards her and, to his horror, she suddenly stopped outside a house at the end of the road, paused a moment while she looked up at the windows, then opened the front garden gate.

''Elen!' Frankie was now shouting and waving frantically. At the same time, Winston joined in, barking for all he was worth, his tail wagging so hard it was in danger of falling off.

Helen reached the front door of 82 Wilmington Road and raised her hand to the knocker – but before she could reach it, Winston leapt over the front hedge, barking and barking, and nearly knocking her down as he jumped up at her. 'Winston!' She was taken completely by surprise. 'What are *you* doing here?'

''Elen!' Now Frankie appeared at the front gate, breathless and red-faced. ''Elen – wait! Wait!'

Helen, closely tailed by Winston, hurried back to the gate. 'Frank! What are you doing?' She quickly glanced over her shoulder to see if anyone was watching them from inside the house. 'You shouldn't be 'ere, Frank.' She was trying to keep her voice low, particularly as there were now so many people clearing snow from their front gardens. 'Yer shouldn't 'ave followed me!'

'Don't do it, 'Elen! Don't go through wiv this. It in't right! Yer *mustn't* do it!' he said, passionately.

'Stop it, Frank! I've made up my mind. I'm

gettin' rid of the kid. I don't want it!'

'You're lyin', yer know you are! Yer can't go through wiv it, 'Elen. If yer love Eric Sibley, you won't get rid of 'is kid. It's not right, 'Elen. If you get rid of the kid, you'd be losin' *both* of 'em. Don't you understand?'

For a moment, Helen stared in disbelief at her young brother. It hardly seemed possible that it was he who was talking. What did he know about love, about having a child? 'I've made up me mind, Frank,' she said, finally, determinedly. 'There's no way I could 'ave a baby, not without it 'avin' a farver. I couldn't face up to it on me own.'

'Yer wouldn't 'ave to.' Although Frankie's voice was still breathless, it was firm and commanding. 'You'd 'ave me ter 'elp yer.'

Helen couldn't believe what she was hearing. She and Frankie had always had the best brother and sister relationship that anyone could ever wish to have, but this – this was a Frankie she had never known before. He wasn't talking like a kid. He was talking to her like a grown-up man. 'You can't 'elp me, Frank. No one can. What I've done is me own fault, and I've got to pay for it.' She suddenly noticed that they were being watched by an elderly man and woman who were shovelling snow away in their front garden just a couple of houses along. She lowered her voice again. 'I couldn't face up to it, Frank. I couldn't face up ter mum and dad, and all the people in our street. Every time I looked at them I'd feel – dirty.'

'Tell me somefin', 'Elen.' Frankie took a firm hold of her arms and forced her to look him straight in the eyes. 'D'yer love Eric?'

'Of course I love 'im!' Helen's face crumpled, for she was now close to tears. 'But 'e's gone, Frank! Don't you understand? I've lost 'im. 'E's gone!'

As Helen dissolved into tears, Frankie, quite instinctively put his arms around her and held her close to him. 'Listen, 'Elen,' he said quietly in her ear. 'Mum an' Dad 'ave got nuffin' ter do wiv this. They've made a muck-up of their own lives, and they in't got no right ter interfere wiv yours. You're goin' ter 'ave yer kid – yours an' Eric's kid. An' d'yer know why? 'Cos if yer don't, as the years go on, yer'll never forgive yerself.'

Helen, her eyes full of tears, looked up at Frankie. It was incredible that this was the only person that she could trust, someone who was firm and decisive, who was prepared to help her stand up against the condemnation that would surely come, and not just from her mother and father. For the first time, someone had given her the strength to stand up to what she faced, had given her the determination to see it through with her head held high. And this someone was her own kid brother.

'Keep the kid, 'Elen. Let it grow up. *See* it grow up.' Frankie was now holding his sister firmly by both arms, and staring straight into her eyes. 'Keep the kid, 'Elen – fer yourself – and fer Eric.'

As he spoke, a loud explosion was heard in the distance. Automatically, everyone in the street fell flat on to their stomachs into the snow. Everyone, that is, except Helen and Frankie. The explosion from yet another V–2 rocket was far enough away to cause no damage whatsoever in Wilmington Road. But, as Frankie held his sister close in his arms, a row of long, pointed icicles suddenly dropped from the windowledge of a second-floor window of number 82 just behind them.

At the window itself, the face of a middle-aged woman appeared. She looked quite ordinary and, when she saw Helen, Frankie, and a large, floppy dog strolling off together in the snow, she simply drew the curtains and carried on with her own business . . .

Chapter Twelve

The Reverend Monty Marshall was not blessed with a very striking personality. In fact, just a few minutes in his company was enough to drive the most dedicated churchgoer into a state of total boredom. Even his appearance was a hindrance. According to most of his parishioners he always 'looked as though he could do with a damned good meal'. And he was rarely seen in public without his black trilby hat, his dog-collar and his dull grey jacket.

The main trouble with the Rev. Marshall, however, was that he seemed completely incapable of offering to his parishioners any kind of comfort when they needed it. He conducted funerals in the Emmanuel Church with a bland detachment that seemed to ignore the spirit of the poor soul lying in the coffin before him, and weddings were not much better – the happy couple were often left with the feeling that their marriage hadn't a hope of lasting more than a few days. Even during the early years of the war, when the

Luftwaffe had dropped a bomb and devastated several shops in the Seven Sisters Road, he was quite unable to cope with the human scale of the tragedy. It wasn't that he didn't try, simply that he became too emotionally involved to be of any real help to the victims. However, he was greatly liked by the Boy Scouts and Girl Guides, but even they found his Sunday School afternoons crushingly boring as they were forced to read endlessly from the Bible. But there was one person whom the Vicar could talk to, and that was Elsa. Despite her different faith whenever the Rev. Marshall visited her shop, he was always offered a cup of tea – and words of advice and comfort.

On the day that Helen and Frankie had called on him at the Vicarage, to tell him about Helen being pregnant, the Rev. Marshall had delivered them a stern lecture about how God frowned on sinners who made love before marriage. As Rev. Marshall had never married himself, Helen thought it a bit hypocritical of him to talk in such a way. But, surprisingly, he was sympathetic to her, especially when he realised that the child's father had been killed in action. Without hesitation, he offered to be with her when she broke the news to her parents, and assured her that he was perfectly capable of dealing with Gracie Lewis's response . . .

'Call yerself a man of God! You ought ter be ashamed ter wear that collar round yer neck!' In the front parlour of number 1 Merton Street, Gracie Lewis's eyes were blazing with temper. She was appalled to hear that her daughter was going to have a fatherless baby, and nothing the Vicar told her would change her opinion. 'You dirty little bitch!' she screamed at Helen. 'I don't want any part of yer! Yer can pack yer bags and sling yer bleedin' 'ook out of my 'ouse! I don't want yer here! I don't want yer!'

The Rev. Marshall was taken aback. All he could say was, 'Now then, Mrs Lewis, you *must* be reasonable. I know Helen has done wrong, but we must have compassion. After all, she *is* your daughter – and the poor child she is bearing will have no father.'

'That's 'er bleedin' fault! Don't blame me!' By now, Gracie's voice could be heard outside in the street, and Winston decided it was time to retire to his basket in the scullery.

By this time, Helen had dissolved into tears, Frankie was gnashing his teeth in anger, and Reg Lewis was already rolling his fourth Rizla fag.

'Please, Mrs Lewis, be reasonable.' The Rev. Marshall was sitting beside Helen on the mock-velour sofa, his arm around the girl, trying his best to console her. 'Helen is one of God's children like all the rest of us and she has a hard time ahead of her. The least we can do is to be merciful. Remember, both Helen and Frankie *were* baptised in my church.'

'Why don't yer shut up, Vicar. This's got nuffin' ter do wiv you!' Apart from Frankie, Gracie Lewis was the only one in the room who was standing. ''Ow would you like to 'ave a daughter who goes sleepin' around wiv any Tom, Dick, or 'Arry she meets in the street?'

'Don't talk about 'Elen like that!' Frankie, standing in the open doorway, could hold his tongue no longer, and he virtually exploded at his mother. 'She's better than you! She's better than you could *ever* be!'

Gracie immediately turned on the boy. 'You mind yer own soddin' business, or you can sling yer 'ook wiv 'er!'

The Rev. Marshall looked absolutely crushed. 'I know this is a difficult time for you, Mrs Lewis . . .'

''Ow do yer know?' screamed Gracie, eyes glaring at him. 'You don't 'ave ter walk down that street, knowin' that all the neighbours are talkin' about the goin's on at number 1.'

'Who cares about the bloody neighbours?' yelled Frankie, daringly.

'I care!' Gracie yelled back at the boy, and gave the impression that she was going to hit him. But she just stopped herself from doing so. 'An' you use that kind of language in my 'ouse once more, and I'll 'ave yer bleedin' guts fer garters!'

At this point, the Rev. Marshall quickly rose from the sofa. 'This is really no help at all, Mrs Lewis. Helen needs help. In a few months' time she'll be having a child, and having to care for it all on her own. Now we *must* be practical. What can we do to see her through this traumatic time?'

Gracie swung around with a start and ignoring the Vicar, pointed a menacing finger straight at Helen. ' I'll tell yer what *she* can do. She can get out of my 'ouse as quick as she likes. I want 'er out of 'ere by first fing termorrer mornin'! Right?'

'Wrong!' Reg Lewis spoke for the first time. 'If she goes, I go wiv 'er!'

Everyone turned to look at Reg, as he stood up and tossed his fag butt into the fire.

Although she was clearly taken aback by her husband's intervention, Gracie Lewis remained defiant. 'I want 'er out of my 'ouse!'

Reg turned on his wife. He didn't raise his voice, but he made it clear that he was just as determined as she was. 'Grace, this is *my* 'ouse just as much as yours. I pay the rent – not you. I say that if 'Elen wants ter stay, she can stay – baby or no baby.'

Frankie exchanged a startled look with his sister and Gracie found herself standing face to face with her husband in front of the fire. 'You *knew* about this, din't yer? You knew about it all the time.'

'Yes, Gracie, I did.'

Once again, Helen and Frankie exchanged an astonished look.

'That's lovely, in't it?' Gracie crossed her arms angrily . 'Yer own daughter gets laid by a bloody soldier, an' yer quite 'appy to let 'er get away wiv it!'

'Everyone makes mistakes, Grace. Even you and me.'

Reg immediately regretted what he had said. As Gracie lowered her eyes, he knew that he had hurt her. And it wasn't the first time it had happened, though he never intended it. Over the years it had become obvious to both of them that their marriage had been a disastrous mistake. When they first met, they'd got on so well together that as both had come from unhappy family backgrounds, getting married seemed an easy escape. But getting on well wasn't being in love and their existence as man and wife had turned into a daily grind at best, a war of vicious slanging matches at worst. On the other hand, Reg Lewis loved kids and, although he would never admit it to anyone, Helen was his favourite.

For a brief moment, Gracie seemed stung by Reg's remark and she tried to disguise it by running her fingers through her hair which hadn't been combed since she got up that morning. 'If yer knew she was pregnant, why didn't yer tell me?' she said. 'I *am* supposed ter be 'er muvver, yer know.'

Frank took a box of matches from the mantelpiece over the fireplace, and lit his fag. 'I didn't know 'Elen was pregnant.'

Suddenly, the room was plunged into a tense silence.

Reg took a deep draw of his rolled fag, but took time to exhale it. A few seconds later the room was filled with the foul stench of the raw tobacco. 'If you're a muvver, Grace,' he said, without raising his voice, 'if yer bring a kid inter this world, there are some fings yer get ter know *wivout* bein' told. 'Elen's our daughter, Grace. If she gets inter trouble, it's our duty ter stand by 'er. The same goes fer Frankie.'

The Reverend Marshall was almost mesmerised by Reg Lewis's calm reasoning, and only wished that he had thought of saying the same thing.

Helen was too surprised and upset to say anything. Throughout the last terrible half-hour she had kept her head low, her eyes streaming with tears.

Frankie was utterly amazed by his father's intervention. He had never heard him talk like that before, never realised that this meek and mild man even had the ability to stand up for his kids against their mother. In fact, it had never once occurred to Frankie that his father had any feelings at all for either Helen or himself. As he watched his father calmly draw on his fag, he thought back to all the times when he was growing up, of how Reg had never seemed to show any interest in anything his son was doing. He remembered a time when he was still at Pakeman Street Junior school; he had got into a fight with another kid and been whacked on the forehead with a cricket bat. Streaming with blood, Frankie had been rushed off to the Royal Northern Hospital where the gash had needed five stitches. But when one of the teachers brought him home, all Reg Lewis could say was that the boy had probably asked for what he got, and that, in the future, it might teach him to stand up for himself.

Gracie Lewis, more subdued but still angry, watched her husband with quiet disdain as he stared into the fire, puffing away at his newly lit fag. 'And 'ow's she goin' ter look after this baby, may I ask?'

Reg didn't even bother to look up at her. 'We'll find a way.'

'Oh yes? Well, if you fink I'm goin' ter sit at 'ome and look after some bleedin' soldier's kid whilst she goes off ter work, yer've got anuvver fink comin'!'

'Don't worry, Grace.' Reg inhaled deeply, and blew smoke into the fireplace. 'No one expects *you* ter do *anyfin'*.'

Once again, there was a deathly silence. Then, without another word, Gracie swept out of the room.

As usual, the Rev. Marshall was at a loss for

words, so he took out a handkerchief from his jacket pocket and wiped his eyes with it. Whenever he was anxious or ill-at-ease, his eyes always seemed to water.

Frankie was absolutely riveted to his father as he watched him turn towards Helen, whose head was still lowered.

''Elen. 'Ave yer seen a doctor about this?'

'Not since – since I found out,' she replied, her voice barely audible.

'I want yer ter go round and see Dr McWhirter as soon as possible. Right?'

Still without looking up, Helen nodded.

Then Reg went across and stooped over her. 'It's goin' ter be all right, gel – you'll see.' His voice was quiet, warm and sympathetic. 'Anyway, a baby in the 'ouse might brighten the place up a bit – eh?'

Helen looked up, managed a weak smile, and threw her arms around her father's neck.

Frankie looked on. Suddenly, he was seeing his father for the first time . . .

On a Sunday morning a few weeks later, Frankie and Winston went with Elsa to visit the grave of her husband in the Islington Cemetery. It was a straightforward route, which involved taking a 609 trolleybus from the Nags Head in Holloway Road to East Finchley, a journey of about forty-five minutes. Luckily, the bus was reasonably warm, for although most of the snow had now thawed, the air was still very cold.

Elsa insisted on finding two seats on the upper deck of the bus, which suited Frankie, for it gave him the chance to take in the views of North London that he had never seen before. The only trouble was that the upper deck of the bus was reserved for smokers and, because no one ever wanted to open a window, the air was thick with grey cigarette smoke, which aggravated Frankie's asthma, causing him to cough frequently. However, dogs were only allowed to travel on the top deck of the bus, and Winston soon settled down without any fuss beneath Frankie's seat.

As the bus passed the majestic Gaumont cinema on the other side of the Nags Head, Frankie couldn't help feeling a sense of loss. Until one of Hitler's doodle-bugs had gutted the building in August of the previous year, the Gaumont had been one of his favourite cinemas. He remembered the opening of the cinema just before the war, where, before the big feature film, *The Hurricane* had started, all sorts of famous people like Jessie Matthews and Will Hay had appeared on the stage. Frankie himself didn't have the ninepence it cost to get in but, after seeing all the famous stars arriving for the opening, he had rushed home and heard it broadcast on the wireless by the BBC. The Gaumont on the wireless, – and it was coming from just around the corner near his own street! A week later his father had taken him and Helen to see a comedy called *Tov-*

arich on the screen, and *Gert and Daisy* on the stage in the same bill as *Old Mother Riley and her daughter Kitty*. Now, all that remained of that exciting stage, with its 'mighty Wurlitzer' organ, huge dome, and a richly ornamental proscenium, was the burnt-out shell of a building, with the rubble of former grandeur strewn everywhere.

In one of his propaganda broadcasts for the Nazis, the hated 'Lord Haw-Haw' had promised that, as the Gaumont Cinema in the Holloway Road was built and run by the Jews, the building would be a prime target for the Luftwaffe. He had certainly kept his promise.

The 609 purred its way effortlessly towards Upper Holloway and, as it started the climb up Archway Road, Frankie couldn't help turning back to look at the Central Hall, which only a few months before, on Guy Fawkes night, had been used as a makeshift mortuary for the victims of the V–2 rocket explosion in nearby Grovedale Road. Frankie remembered that evening well, for, despite the fact that the bomb had come down two or three miles away, lots of the windows in Merton Street had been shattered, and chimney-stacks everywhere had collapsed on to the rooftops. Mr Mitcheson, the caretaker of Pakeman Street School, had been blown off his feet by the blast and Rita Robinson at number 22 had a terrible experience – when she took her leftovers to the pig swill bin on the corner, it all blew back at her. Neighbours said she'd gone quite hysterical and had smelt like a pig herself. Frankie smiled to himself. It was funny how, even in times of tragedy, there was always something to laugh at. But Frankie hated the V–2's. They gave no one the chance to escape, because there was no warning. Just a white streak of vapour across the sky, then a swishing sound, followed by the most devastating explosion.

For most of the journey Elsa never stopped talking. But when they passed beneath the infamous Archway Bridge, spread out high across the busy main road, she suddenly went very silent and, with a sigh, recalled to herself the number of poor souls who had leapt to their death from that footpath so high above them.

It was only when the 609 reached a bus stop in East Finchley Road that it showed its vulnerability. Operated from electric lines hanging above the road, its connecting rods suddenly became detached and started to dance out of control. Frankie had seen this happen before, and loved the hassle that was involved to get the bus moving again, so he poked his head out of the window and watched the harassed bus conductor while he removed the long wooden pole from beneath the floor base of the bus, and started the precarious business of trying to replace each of the unruly flapping poles back on to their respective electric line. After cheers from some of the passengers, the 609 purred its way on again.

Elsa, Frankie, and Winston got off just outside the gates of the cemetery, and Elsa immediately bought a bunch of daffodils from an elderly woman flower-seller who was squatted on a wooden vegetable box by the wall. For the first part of the long trek down the main cemetery road, Winston was put on a leash, and as they walked, Elsa grumbled about the price of the flowers, saying that as soon as she had the time she was going to start growing daffodils in her own back garden.

Frankie had never been to a cemetery before. To him, it seemed a cold, remote sort of place, where dead people were thrown down holes, covered with earth, and a stone erected above them to mark their last resting place. And, as he and Elsa walked, he could see plenty of those stones. Hundreds of them, probably thousands and thousands. All shapes and sizes, most of them either white or black or grey, some made out of granite, some with a large cross at the head, others with just a plain block and a simple inscription. Frankie soon gave up trying to read all the inscriptions. What he did discover, however, were the number of bomb victims who were buried there. Men, women, children – some of them babies of no more than a few months. As he passed all those endless rows of mysterious head-stones, he couldn't help wondering how many of those hapless victims he might have seen somewhere in the street, or the cinema, or in a shop in the Seven Sisters Road. Frankie felt himself becoming consumed with anger. This war should never have happened, he said to himself. Hitler had a lot to answer for.

'Hallo, my dearest one!'

Hearing Elsa's voice, Frankie came to a halt and turned to look back. Elsa had stopped by a graveside, tucked away in a corner beneath a huge chestnut tree. It was quite a simple grave, in dark grey stone, with a gold-coloured inscription which read: *Captain Robert Barclay. Born 16th April 1896. Died 3rd May 1940. A brave soldier and a loving husband.* The headstone was completed with an ornamental cross, which was also outlined in a shining gold colour.

'Looks as though you could do with a little bit of a clean up, Bobby.'

Frankie felt a little awkward standing there, listening to Elsa talk to the grave as though her husband could talk back to her. Winston also wondered what was going on, and despite being scolded by Frankie, he sniffed all around the grave.

'Let's see what we can do!' Elsa put down the bunch of daffodils she had just bought, then took some things out of the small brown paper bag she was carrying – a pair of scissors and a garden trowel. 'Be a good boy, Frankie,' she said, taking up the empty green metal vase from the grave. 'Go and fill this with water. You'll find a tap just over there on the side of the road.'

Frankie took the vase without saying a word. Then Winston followed him back to the road, where he duly washed out the dirty vase and filled it with water. When he got back to Elsa, she was crouched over the grave, freshening up the frost-covered earth with her trowel.

'You know something,' said Elsa, taking the vase from Frankie and replacing it in its position just beneath the headstone. 'His brother thinks he knows everything. But he doesn't. Jack Barclay knows nothing. Nothing at all!' There was a twinkle in her eye as she grinned at Frankie and cut the daffodil stalks down to size with her pair of scissors.

Frankie didn't know what Elsa was talking about – but it was often like that. Elsa loved saying things to him that she really meant for herself. It was her way of sharing her thoughts out loud.

'We have one or two secrets that Jack Barclay won't like, don't we, my dear?' Again Elsa was talking to the grave and not to Frankie. Then, with a little chuckle to herself, she said, 'One of these days, Bobby. One of these days . . .'

Frankie now felt really awkward and, when Elsa looked up at him, the only response he had was to scratch his nose.

'Give me ten minutes,' Elsa said, flashing a warm smile at her young friend. 'We have things to talk over.'

Frankie was relieved to leave the graveside

and have a stroll around the cemetery with Winston.

There was only a sprinkling of people – attending to graves or, like him, just taking a stroll. He imagined that this was either because it was a very cold March day, or that a lot of people were at Sunday morning church service. It didn't seem much like a Sunday, for since the start of the war the Government had stopped the pealing of church bells, only allowing them to be used in an emergency, such as an enemy invasion. Frankie had always liked the Sunday bells and hoped that it wouldn't be too long before they would be heard again, next time in celebration of the end of the war. With his hands tucked deep inside his trouser pockets, he moved in and out of the grave-stones, stopping only briefly to pick up a few old conkers which had fallen off many chestnut trees last autumn.

Winston had no respect whatsoever for the sacred stones he was constantly desecrating. Every few yards he raised his back leg to leave his mark, despite Frankie's scoldings.

It was only when Frankie stopped to peer inside what looked like an old soldier's mausoleum that he suddenly realised Winston was missing. He immediately panicked, for the dog hardly ever went off on his own, not unless he had a good reason for doing so. 'Winnie!' He called in as loud a voice as he dared in such surroundings. But there was no sign of Winston among the gravestones that stretched out for as far as the eye could see. Frankie turned to look back at Robert Barclay's grave in the distance, where Elsa still looked to be in animated conversation with her last husband, but there was no sign of Winston.

Suddenly he heard a dog barking just beyond the First World War Memorial statue about a hundred yards ahead of him, and the noise was interspersed with the sound of a girl calling back excitedly.

Frankie started running. Although he knew Winston wouldn't hurt anyone, he was big enough to scare someone who wasn't used to dogs – especially in a cemetery! After jumping over endless graves covered with frozen leaves, Frankie finally caught up with Winston. He was leaping up on all fours at a young girl who, with her back to Frankie, was collecting water in a glass vase at a tap just behind the memorial statue.

'Winnie! Down boy, down!' Frankie tried to keep his voice down as much as he could. But it wasn't easy, for Winston was clearly thoroughly enjoying himself. 'Stop that, will yer! Get down!'

As Frankie spoke, the girl turned around. To his relief, she had a broad smile on her face and had clearly been thoroughly enjoying the encounter. 'It's all right,' she said, her bright, violet-coloured eyes gleaming happily in the cold frost of the morning. 'He's not doing any – Oh – hallo!'

Her bright smile suddenly turned into a rather shy one.

Frankie immediately recognised her from the day in that school air-raid shelter, when she seemed to smile an awful lot at him, and he scowled an awful lot at her. After grabbing Winston by his collar, Frankie plucked up enough courage to respond.

''Allo.' He only found it difficult to answer her because he was embarrassed. 'Din't expect ter see *you* up 'ere.'

'I didn't expect to see you, either.' The girl's voice was soft, almost husky. She pulled back her long, blonde hair, which had got caught up inside the knitted white woollen scarf around her neck, and quickly rearranged her black woollen bobble hat.

For a brief second their eyes met and, for the first time, Frankie thought what a good-looker she was. Feeling a bit awkward with the thought, he ducked his head and pulled Winston away. 'Sorry about this. 'E wouldn't 'urt yer. 'E don't bite.'

'Oh, I'm not scared of him. I love dogs.' The girl stooped down and patted Winston on his head. 'He helped me finish off my cheese sandwich. Didn't you boy?'

Winston panted and rolled on his back to allow the girl to rub his stomach.

'Trust you, Winston!' Frankie shook his head. 'Old cadger!'

'Winston? That's a good name.' The girl was now crouched down, stroking the shamelessly abandoned Winston under the chin. 'I bet Mr Churchill would approve.'

Frankie was watching the girl. He liked her a lot . . . 'Wot are yer doin' 'ere then?'

The girl looked up. 'I came with my mother.' Frankie thought she had quite a posh voice. 'My grandma and grandad are buried just over there.'

Frankie turned to look, and in the distance could see a smartly dressed woman arranging flowers on a rather grand, well-kept family grave.

'What about you?'

'I'm wiv a friend. 'Er 'usband got killed at Dunkirk.'

The girl's radiant smile became a sympathetic one. 'Oh, I see. It's so *horrible* this war.' Her eyes looked all around her. 'Everyone seems to have lost *someone*.' Much to Winston's disappointment she stood up. 'How's school?'

'Not bad. Got me matric in July.'

'Me too. I'm *dreading* it. I haven't got a chance.'

'Don't believe yer. I bet yer'll get frough wiv flyin' colours.'

The girl removed a strand of blonde hair from her lips. 'How can you say that? You don't know me.'

Suddenly, Frankie felt embarrassed, and he blushed. 'I can tell, that's all. You're the brainy type.'

The girl laughed. 'If only you knew!'

Frankie loved the way she laughed. Her eyes seemed to sparkle in the bright sunshine and, as she threw back her head, her teeth seemed almost as white as the last remnants of snow on the tarmac road.

'Are you going to your school's concert?' All of a sudden her eyes briefly met Frankie's, and she immediately became shy again.

'I dunno.' Frankie found himself looking straight into the girl's eyes. 'When is it?'

'Friday evening, next week.'

Frankie shrugged his shoulders. 'I might. It depends.'

'On what?'

Without realising it, Frankie was shrugging his shoulders again. It was his way of trying not to show too much interest. 'Oh – lots of things. It was lousy, last year. Too much chat, not enough songs. Old Lincoln always loses his place on the song sheet when 'e plays the piano.'

This time they both laughed. Then they both shuffled about on their feet, trying not to catch each other's glance again.

After a brief silence, a woman's voice called from the distance. 'Maggs! What are you doing over there? Where's that vase?'

The girl called back: 'Coming, Mother!' Then she picked up the glass vase and smiled at Frankie again. 'Sorry, Frankie. I've got to go.'

Frankie did a double-take. ''Ow do you know my name?'

This time, it was the girl's turn to blush. 'Got to go! We're going on to see my godmother at Swiss Cottage.' She turned. ''Bye, Winston! See you, boy!'

The girl started to hurry off, but she had gone no more than a few yards when she turned to look back at Frankie. 'See you, then. Maybe at the concert?'

'Yeah. Maybe.' Frankie suddenly came out of his trance. As the girl rushed off, he found himself calling after her eagerly. 'See you there – Maggs!'

The girl ran off back towards her mother and Frankie watched her go. He could hardly believe how much he had enjoyed those few, fleeting moments. She knew his name and he knew hers. It was quite extraordinary for Frankie – Frankie, who had never had any time for girls. But in those few short moments he had been convinced that Maggs was not like other girls – especially girls like Patty. As she rejoined her mother, Maggs turned and waved.

For the first time ever, Frankie couldn't wait to go to the annual School Concert.

Chapter Thirteen

When Prof got home from school at half-past four, Aunty Hilda had his tea waiting for him, and, after tucking into a plate of hot spam cooked in batter, mashed potatoes, peas, and his favourite pickled onions, he immediately disappeared up into his room to do a bit of swotting for his forthcoming geography mock exams. He finished at about six o'clock, which was pretty good even by his standards. But geography was one of Prof's favourite subjects; it gave him the chance to imagine himself travelling to the most exotic parts of the world, places like the Sahara Desert or the Himalayas, or the Grand Canyon, or Tahiti. Most of all, however, Prof dreamed of going to Switzerland. He loved the idea of being a passenger in a pony and sleigh, gliding effortlessly along snow-covered roads beneath the shadow of the Alps.

Prof thought mountains were the most incredible things in the world. Not that he'd ever *seen* a mountain, except when he and Frankie went to see a Sonja Henie film. But oh how he would love to climb one! So many times he had seen himself trudging in the snow, climbing up steep rock-faces, feeling his way bit by bit to the summit. And then the exhilaration of standing there at the top of the world – the freedom, the danger, the excitement! But people with dicky hearts don't climb mountains . . .

'Don't be nervous tonight now, dearie,' said Auntie Hilda, sipping her Camp coffee and chicory while her nephew washed himself at the kitchen sink. 'You don't have to worry, 'cos me and Gladys'll cheer you on.'

'Thanks, Auntie.' Prof dried his face with a towel and rubbed the soap out of his eyes. When he turned to look at his Auntie, she was only a blur, because he was very short-sighted and didn't have his specs on.

As usual, Auntie Hilda was being a tower of strength. She knew how her nephew hated the thought of taking part in the school concert, but she also knew that no one could play a mouth-organ like him and she was very proud that she and her friend Gladys were going to be in the audience to hear her nephew's performance. 'Have you decided what you're going to play yet?'

'Yes, Auntie.'

'No! Don't tell me. I want it to be a surprise.' The old lady's chubby cheeks were glistening in the light from the 100 watt bulb that dangled from the middle of the ceiling, and seemed almost naked despite the tassled yellow shade that only partially covered it. 'I've put out your clean shirt and, before you go on, don't forget to make sure your tie's straight.'

'Yes, Auntie.' Prof knew that Auntie was fussing, but he didn't mind, because she was obviously excited and only wanted him to do well. To Prof, Auntie was a saint. She had brought him up single-handed and wanted nothing from him, but gave everything in return. Most of her weekly food ration was spent on her nephew, even if it meant she had to go without. In return, Prof loved her without reservation and, as the years went by, had grown to think of her as his one and only mother. He never stopped telling himself how lucky he was.

After quickly putting on his freshly ironed white shirt and black-and-mauve-striped school tie, Prof combed his hair neatly, kissed Auntie Hilda on her cheek, and made his way down the stairs. A few minutes later he was out in the Seven Sisters Road, his stomach churning at the thought of the ordeal he was about to endure. Despite what Auntie had said, he was furious with Charlie Garratt, the school's history master, who had talked him into playing his mouth-organ. He was sure he was going to make an ass of himself in front of all his classmates. Still, at least there was one person who wouldn't make fun of him – one person who meant as much to

Prof as Auntie. Frankie Lewis was the best friend anyone could have and to Prof Frankie was not just a friend. He was a hero.

As he made his way to meet his hero in Merton Street, Prof's stomach wasn't churning any more . . .

Frankie used so much of his father's Brylcreem that, when he plastered his hair down with it, it made his face look fat and bloated. So, after looking at himself in Helen's dressing-table mirror, he wiped some of it off. Then, after polishing his shoes with one of his old socks, he finished dressing by putting on his school blazer.

When Frankie went downstairs, Helen was helping their mother to clear away the tea things. As it was Friday evening, they had all had fish and chips from Anderson's in Hornsey Road, which Frankie had loved because it gave him a welcome break from his mother's lazy cooking. Reg Lewis didn't get his until he got home from work after nine o'clock, so it was kept in the oven for him, to be warmed up later.

Helen was the first to notice how clean and tidy Frankie was looking, but she didn't say anything. Since that awful half-an-hour with her mother and the Vicar a few weeks before, Helen said very little at any time and her mother clearly didn't want to speak to her unless she had to. So, on the evenings when she didn't go round to see her friends, she spent most of her time in her bedroom reading old magazines and knitting baby socks.

Frankie found the atmosphere at home so much more depressing than usual that he got out whenever he had the opportunity. He hated the way his mother had reacted to the news of Helen's pregnancy, and hated even more the way she made her daughter feel so unwelcome in her own house. But their father had come up trumps. When he was home he would often sit and talk with Helen about Eric and about how she should cope in the future. This invariably led to more tension with Gracie, who usually reacted by turning on the wireless full blast, and listening to programmes that she obviously didn't like.

Helen waited for her mother to disappear into the scullery before she spoke. 'Must be a pretty special school concert ternight, eh Frank?'

Frankie turned with a start. 'What d'yer mean?'

'Come off it,' she said with a sly grin. 'I've never seen you tog yerself up so much ter go ter school!'

Frankie immediately loosened his black-and-mauve-striped tie, doing his best to look untidy. 'I'm not togged up! We 'ave ter look decent fer the concert. If yer don't, "Boggy" Marsh kicks up a rumpus.'

Helen smiled knowingly. She didn't believe a word of it.

Frankie was saved by someone knocking on the front street door. 'That's Prof. Gotta go!' Frankie grabbed his raincoat and rushed to the kitchen door. 'See yer later, 'Elen.'

Helen got up, and followed him out into the passage. 'Frank!'

Frankie stopped and turned.

'If you're in late ternight, try not ter wake me up. I've not been feelin' too special terday. I'm goin' ter pack in early.'

Frankie was immediately concerned and came back to her. 'Wot's up? You gonna be all right? I mean . . .' He felt a bit awkward and didn't quite know what to say. 'Is it anyfin' ter do wiv the baby?'

Helen smiled. 'No. Everythin's perfectly all right. I just feel a bit tired, that's all.'

Frankie took her by the shoulders, and held her firmly. The light bulb and tatty shade hanging above them were swinging to and fro, casting flickering shadows across their faces. 'Listen ter me, 'Elen. If *she* gives yer any trouble ternight, just lemme know. OK?'

Helen smiled fondly. 'I'll be fine. Nuffin' ter worry about.' Then she leant forward and gave him a quick hug. 'Go and enjoy yerself.'

Frankie hugged her back, then rushed out, slamming the street door behind him as usual. Helen watched him go and immediately heard the Prof chattering excitedly as they met up on the door step outside. Helen stood there for a brief moment, listening to them, a broad smile on her face. But the smile faded immediately when she heard the wireless turned on full blast in the kitchen.

Helen turned, and wearily climbed the stairs up to her bedroom.

Frankie and Prof made their way along Annette Road to catch the number 38 tram outside Jones Brothers Department Store in the Holloway Road. As it was already twenty-five to seven and the school concert was due to start at seven-thirty, they had very little time to spare and had to walk briskly. Although Annette Road was only a couple of streets away from Merton Street, Frankie always thought the people who lived there were a bit on the posh side but the only reason he had for such a conclusion was that one or two of the houses had a car parked outside. By the time they crossed over the main Tollington Road, Prof was feeling a bit fed up. He didn't understand why, but it certainly had nothing to do with the school concert.

'She's really nice, Prof.' Frankie, hands tucked deep inside his jacket pockets, was walking, as usual, with his eyes fixed firmly on the pavement. 'I didn't fink so the first time I saw 'er. D'yer remember? When we was down the air-raid shelter at school?' He was talking with such enthusiasm, he didn't bother to wait for any response from Prof. ''Er name's Maggs. That's short for Margaret, I reckon. She didn't *tell* me 'er name, though. I 'eard 'er mum calling for 'er.'

Prof remained stony-faced, and never once turned to look at Frankie whilst he was speaking.

They made a dash across the main road, just in time to miss an oncoming truck that was in danger of losing some of its cabbages as it rushed off towards the Holloway Road. Then, as they passed by Sherbourne Road Elementary School to make a short cut to the tram stop, they heard a rumpus coming from Jones Brothers back yard. At first they couldn't see anything, but what they heard was several people shouting at each other. As they drew closer, they found two teenage boys locked together in an angry brawl, shoving and kicking and punching at each other for all they were worth. And then, out of the darkness, a girl's voice yelled out: 'Cut it out you two! I'm not 'angin' round 'ere much longer!'

Frankie and Prof couldn't believe their ears. What they could hear was the shrill voice of Patty Jackson from the Merton Street gang.

'Patty! Wot's goin' on?'

Patty turned with a start as she heard Frankie's voice. 'Frank? Is that you?'

Even though they were now standing right in front of each other, all they could see were dim outlines.

'Wot is it, Pat? Wot's goin' on?'

'Wot d'yer fink's goin' on! It's Al and Jeff – the stupid gits!'

'Oh no – not again!' Frankie sighed despairingly. Of recent, the sight of Alan and Jeff brawling in the street was becoming a nasty habit. 'Wot's it about this time?'

Although there was a note of irritation in her voice, Patty was concealing the fact that she was really enjoying the ugly scene going on before her. 'Alan asked me to the concert up at your school. We was just comin' through 'ere ter get the tram, when that stupid bloody Jeff jumps up from nowhere and starts bashin' out wiv 'is fists.'

Frankie felt sick. Jeff Murray was such a bighead. Because of his athletic build and good looks he strutted around the streets as though he owned them and his mother and father doted on him. Jeff took advantage of their no-questions-asked loving support of him, but he was not only spoilt, his was dishonest and a downright bully, using his brawn as a substitute for brains.

'Jeff! Alan!' Frankie's voice pierced the darkness. 'Cut it out you two!'

But Frankie's pleas were ignored, and Jones Brothers echoed to the futile sounds of 'I'll teach yer, yer sod!' and 'Oh no you don't!'

In desperation, Frankie rushed straight at the fighting silhouettes and struggled to separate them. 'Stop it – both of yer! It's stupid! Stupid!' But no matter how hard he tried, the two fighters refused to budge and held each other in a tight, aggressive clinch.

'Oy! You lot!' A man's voice suddenly boomed

out from a back door of the department store. 'What the bloody 'ell's goin' on out 'ere?'

As the man spoke, the beam of his torch landed straight on Frankie's startled face. But it did the trick, for the brawl came to an immediate halt. 'Sorry, mister!' Why Frankie had to be the one to offer excuses, he didn't know. 'Just larkin' around, that's all.'

'Well, you lark around somewhere else, or I'll 'ave the 'bottles on yer!' Although the body behind the torch did not advance, the voice was angry and menacing. 'Sling yer 'ook – the bleedin' lot of yer!'

The last thing Frankie wanted was for the bluebottles to be called out from Hornsey Road Police Station. 'Goin' mister! Goin'!' he yelled desperately, as he quickly grabbed both Jeff and Alan by the arm and started to lead them out of the yard towards the Holloway Road entrance. Patty and Prof followed discreetly behind, making sure they used the darkness to conceal their identity.

'If I catch yer back 'ere again, I'll 'ave yer guts fer bleedin' garters!' The torch beam followed the beleaguered Merton Street lot until they had disappeared out of the yard.

'Wot's up wiv you two?' Frankie waited until they had reached the safety of the main Holloway Road. 'Wot's the point of scrappin'? Don't yer know there's a war on?'

Yes, there was still a war on all right, for there

was no street or shop window lighting, and even the traffic had to use dipped half-headlights.

Jeff and Alan were out of breath from their brawl and, in the dark, sounded like a couple of dogs on heat.

'When I want your advice, Lewis, I'll ask for it! Right?' Jeff's reply was, inevitably, hostile.

'You're the one that started it, Jeff.' Patty tried to sound like an innocent, hurt female. 'Alan wasn't doin' you no 'arm. We was mindin' our own business when you 'ave ter poke yer nose in.'

'Let's forget it, Pat.' Alan used the back of his hand to wipe away a small flow of blood streaming down from one side of his nostrils. 'If we're goin' to get to that concert, let's go.' He grabbed hold of Patty's hand and started to lead her off towards the tram stop.

Jeff wasn't going to take that, so he quickly followed them, yelling, 'If you think you can kick *me* up the arse like that, Patty Jackson, yer've got anuvver fink comin'! I'll get yer fer this! I promise yer – I'll get yer!'

At this point, Prof, who had said absolutely nothing during the entire rumpus, went after Jeff and, grabbing him by the arm, snapped, 'Why don't you leave them alone, Jeff? Stop being such a bully.'

Jeff, as usual, reacted on impulse. Swinging around angrily, he clenched his fist tight and punched it straight into Prof's face, sending his glasses whirling up into the air.

'Prof!' In the restricted glare from a passing car's headlights, Frankie saw his friend collapse to his knees, where he was given another upper punch beneath his jaw by the frenzied Jeff. 'Leave him alone, you sod!' Frankie yelled and rushed at Jeff, waving his own fist angrily. 'Leave him alone!'

Frankie's shouts brought Alan and Patty hurrying back, but by the time they got there, Jeff broke away and sprinted down the road, heading off in the direction of the Nags Head.

'I'll get yer, Jeff!' yelled Frankie. 'I swear ter God I'll get yer!'

By this time Prof was spreadeagled on his face on the wet pavement. As Frankie and Alan helped him to his feet, he was swaying a little dizzily, and, in the passing car headlights, blood could be seen trickling down his face from a cut above his right eye.

'Prof! Are you all right?' Frankie was desperately concerned for his friend. ''As he 'urt yer bad?'

'It's OK, OK.' Prof seemed uncannily calm. 'Jeff's the one with the problem, not me.' He tried to brush off his raincoat, which was covered in wet dirt from the pavement. 'But can you find my glasses for me?'

Everyone searched for the Prof's tortoiseshell spectacles, one arm of which was held together with sticky paper taken from the edge of postage stamps. But, after ten minutes, they could not be found anywhere.

The stage of Highbury Grove Grammar School was draped in so many Union Jacks that one indiscreet member of the audience (a father who had clearly just topped up in a local pub) remarked that this is how he imagined it must look like in Churchill's bedroom in Downing Street. The fact was, however, flags were the cheapest way to dress the stage, and the only props used were the odd chair, a card table (for Charlie Garrett's conjuring act), and a stand microphone which had a nasty habit of causing a deafening humming sound on the Tannoy speakers.

There were over five hundred people in the audience, most of them pupils from the school itself, together with a sprinkling of adoring parents who applauded every act with rapturous excitement.

Also in the audience was a representative selection of pupils and teachers from Highbury Fields Girls' School. The girls, enjoying themselves, spent most of the evening either taking the mickey out of the performers on stage, or flirting with some of the older boys in the seats at the back of the Assembly Hall.

As soon as Frankie had been satisfied that Prof was recovered enough to take part in the concert, he left him with the other performers assembled in Classroom 6A, who were awaiting their turn to go on. Then Frankie made his way to the hall where, after scanning the audience eagerly, he spotted Maggs sitting in a row of seats with some of her own school friends and a rather stern-looking teacher who was supposed to make sure there was no hanky-panky between the pupils of both schools. Maggs was clearly looking out for Frankie, for when she caught sight of him she indicated a spare seat at the side of her. Frankie dashed so hard to reach her that he trod on the stern lady teacher's toes, which earned him an immediate glare.

The concert itself proceeded in its predictable way. One of the 'star' performers, as always, was of course, Mrs Goulding, the rather rotund and full-bossomed Highbury Grove music teacher who wore the same revealing black evening dress year after year, mainly to tantalize her fellow physics and chemistry teacher Mr Lincoln, who once again accompanied everyone at the upright piano, dressed immaculately in full white tie and tails, a long sleek cigarette holder protruding from his lips, from which smoke constantly curled up from the many lighted cigarettes he was never without.

Mrs Goulding's musical rendition of Lord Tennyson's '*Come into the garden, Maud*' was always a firm favourite with the parents in the audience, but despite the fact that Headmaster 'Boggy' Marsh, wearing his school gown, was assiduously watching his pupils from the side of the auditorium, some of the boys covered their mouths and either jeered, booed, or whistled. The real 'star' of the evening, however, was the professional BBC singer, Alfred Swain, a baritone of great intensity, whose 'performance' of a little ditty entitled, *The Song of the Flea*, complete with the singer's rolling eyeballs, was judged to be a triumph, especially by his young son, a pupil at Highbury Grove.

And so the performance continued, with varied acts ranging from sixth-form recitations from Shakespeare, a piano solo from Mr Lincoln – who gamely ploughed on despite the fact that all his music had scattered on to the floor when one of the Highbury Grove boys mischievously opened a nearby window – more patriotic songs from Mrs Goulding, and an absolutely ingenious conjuring act from the history teacher, Charlie Garrett. But the moment Frankie and Prof's Auntie Hilda was waiting for came immediately after Mr Wood's highly dramatic reading from Milton's *Paradise Lost*. As Mr Woods left the stage to thunderous applause, the stage lights dimmed, and into a solitary spotlight stepped the fragile figure of Prof.

There was a gasp from Frankie, Auntie Hilda, and even Alan and Patty, as Prof appeared, for his lips were swollen and there was a huge bruise on his left cheek and a nasty-looking gash just above his right eye. But despite his physical appearance, he was neat and combed just as Auntie Hilda had wanted.

Suddenly, there was a deathly hush in the Hall. Frankie didn't know how his friend was going to manage to do his 'act', and felt himself tense up inside.

Prof, however, was completely calm and relaxed, or at least that's how he seemed as he took a slow bow. The only problem was that he had to squint to see his audience, for, as he had no glasses, they were nothing more than a vast, out-of-focus mass. Undeterred by that, he raised the mouth-organ to his poor swollen lips, and started to puff into it.

The sounds that drifted around the hall for the next five minutes were the most beautiful that Frankie had ever heard in his whole life. In his opinion, *Shine on Harvest Moon* had never sounded so good, not even when it was sung by Bing Crosby on the wireless. Soon, the audience was swaying to and fro, joining together in a unanimous hum, sounding almost as though they were just one person. Despite his heavily swollen face, Prof had certainly captured the mood of his audience. As Auntie Hilda and Gladys swayed to and fro in time to the music, joining in the words, tears were streaming down their eyes, and even Mrs Goulding, who in her own act had used her black chiffon scarf to devastating theatrical effect, now used it to dab the tears in her own eyes.

As soon as he had finished the last bars of his song, Prof's performance was greeted by a split second of total silence. So he bowed briskly, hoping to make a quick exit from the stage. But suddenly the Hall erupted into thunderous applause, and there were repeated yells of '*Core*! '*Core*! Then everyone seemed to be on their feet. Maggs joined Frankie clapping wildly and cheering; Alan whistled, Patty applauded; Auntie Hilda was no longer crying, she was sobbing. She and Gladys were on their feet, clapping so hard the palms of their hands were blood red. Even Alfred Swain and Mrs Goulding joined in the frenzied reception for the brave young artist and his mouth-organ, and when Mr Lincoln started thumping the top of his piano lid in appreciation, this set off a chorus of feet stamping which threatened to shake the very foundations of the entire school.

As he stood in the solitary spotlight, a frail, poignant little figure, bowing awkwardly, Prof gazed out at his audience with a mixture of astonishment and bewilderment. He couldn't see anything but a vast, fuzzed mass of people waving and leaping up and down.

The cheering seemed to go on forever, and it only came to an end when there was a sudden explosion in the distance. Obviously a V–2 had come down somewhere, yet another reminder that the war was not yet over. Although it was far enough away not to cause any damage to the school itself, everyone, including Prof, dropped to the floor. Simultaneously, the lights went out, but there was no panic and, in the few minutes of darkness that followed, Maggs felt someone take hold of her hand and squeeze it. The lights came on much sooner than Frankie had thought, for when they did, he had to quickly let go of Maggs's hand. Even though she was blushing, Maggs felt good inside, and turned to give Frankie a warm, shy smile.

When the concert was over and everyone was filing out of the Hall, Prof was overwhelmed by the number of people who congratulated him on his performance. Flushed by his triumph, he made his way through the audience trying to reach Frankie. On the way, Auntie Hilda, tears still swelling up in her eyes, hugged her nephew and told him over and over again how proud she was of him.

'That was terrific, Prof!' Frankie took his friend's hand and shook it up and down so hard it nearly fell off. 'You was clearly the best fing in the 'ole show!'

Prof beamed with delight. This, coming from his pal, Frankie, was worth more than anything anyone else had to say. 'D'you think so, Frankie?' he said, eagerly. 'D'you really think so?'

''Course I do!' Frankie was now patting his friend on the back. 'Everyone says so – ' Then he turned to Maggs, who was standing at this side, smiling broadly. 'Don't they, Maggs?'

'Oh, yes!' Maggs grabbed Prof's hand and shook it vigorously. 'It was a lovely song. You played it beautifully!'

As he took it in that Frankie was *with* the girl he had been going on so much about, Prof's eager smile faded immediately. 'Oh – thanks', he said, awkwardly. 'Thanks very much.'

'We'll talk about it termorrer – right, Prof?' Frankie put his arm around his friend's shoulder and hugged him. 'You're a star! Yer know that, don't yer? It'll cost us fifty quid ter talk to yer!'

Suddenly, Prof wasn't interested in praise any more. 'Are we takin' the tram home?' he asked, weakly.

Now it was Frankie's turn to feel awkward. 'Er – no – wot I mean, Prof, is . . . Well, yer see – I've offered to walk Maggs 'ome. She only lives up at Canonbury and she oughta 'ave someone to . . .'

'It's all right. I've gotta see Auntie Hilda home anyway.' Prof tried not to look hurt, but it wasn't easy. 'Might see you over the weekend. If not – well, see you in class on Monday.'

'See yer, Prof!'

'Goodnight,' Maggs called gently as Prof made his way off through the departing audience.

''Night!' Prof called back to Maggs over his shoulder without looking, then quickly went to look for Auntie Hilda.

Auntie Hilda and Gladys travelled back home to Seven Sisters Road on the number 38 tram.

Her nephew wasn't with them.

Prof had decided to walk.

Chapter Fourteen

Jack Barclay hadn't been in touch with his sister-in-law since before Christmas when he had written to ask her if she would let him make an appointment for her to see his solicitor about making her will. To Barclay's frustration, Elsa had written back to say that while she was very grateful for her brother-in-law's interest, she had made 'other arrangements' regarding her will. Barclay, however, didn't give up easily, though it was not until the middle of April that he decided to call on Elsa again, this time without his wife.

'Sell the shop? Why should I sell the shop? It makes me money.' Elsa was behind the shop counter, half-way up a ladder using a feather duster to clean off some bookshelves. 'I don't understand you, Jack Barclay,' she called, without bothering to look back at him. 'I thought you were supposed to be a good businessman?'

'I *am* a good businessman, Elsa.' Barclay was perched uncomfortably on one of Elsa's favourite high stools, warming his hands over the flickering flame of the paraffin stove. 'That's why I think someone of your age shouldn't be bothering herself with – well, with a place like this.'

Elsa swung round indignantly. 'What do you mean someone of my age? Just remember, I'm younger than you.'

Barclay could have kicked himself. The last thing he wanted to do was to offend his sister-in-law. 'Oh no, Elsa,' he said very quickly, as he watched her come down the stepladder. 'What I meant was, this shop is too much for you to cope with all on your own. If you sold it, you'd be able to invest the money and retire. You could move up to Golders Green or Swiss Cottage. I know how much you like it up there.'

Elsa slammed her feather duster on to the counter, sending up a huge cloud of dust as she did so. 'I don't want to live in Golders Green or Swiss Cottage. I want to live *here* – Islington – in Robert's home – in *my* home!' She crossed her arms defiantly and glared at her brother-in-law. 'And in any case, I have all the help I need to run the shop.'

Barclay's moustache twitched nervously. 'Help? You mean that scruffy local boy?'

Elsa immediately came out from behind the counter and, with clenched fists resting firmly on her hips, confronted Barclay face to face. 'His name is *Mister* Frankie Lewis. And he is not scruffy. He is my friend!'

'This is a tough neighbourhood, Elsa,' he

blustered. 'You must be careful about trusting a boy like that.'

This raised Elsa's hackles even more. 'What do you mean – a boy like that? Mister Lewis is not a boy, he's a *man*. And I trust him more than anyone else I know – *anyone*!'

Barclay didn't take kindly to this remark. In his mind he was convinced that he knew only too well what the young ruffian was after, but he decided to change tack. 'You see, my dear,' he said, tucking the handkerchief back into his top pocket and trying to sound as reasonable as possible, 'it's only your welfare I'm thinking of.

'The war is almost over, Elsa. Once rationing comes to an end, there'll be no demand for places like this.' Surrounded by rails of secondhand clothes, Barclay was scanning the jumble shop as though it was a public lavatory. 'The Government will want to start rebuilding London, especially areas that have been damaged by the Blitz.' Before he continued, he made quite sure Elsa had no eye contact with him. 'Chances are, places like this will be the first to go. It'll be worth nothing. Nothing at all.'

Elsa went to the window, and started to rearrange the second-hand china tea service display there. 'So it seems things are not looking too good for me, eh Jack?' Her comment was wry and not anxious. 'Even if I wanted to sell the shop, no one would want to buy it. Is that what you're saying?'

'Not exactly, Elsa.' Barclay was watching her carefully. 'As a matter of fact – *I'd* be prepared to make you an offer.'

Elsa looked back over her shoulder. '*You*? You want to buy this shop?'

'Oh, I couldn't offer very much, Elsa. But you *are* Robert's widow, and you know how close he and I were. I feel I owe it to him to help you out in any way I can.'

Barclay's lies made Elsa feel quite sick. 'How considerate of you, Jack.' Her voice was like ice. She turned around, perched herself on the window-ledge, crossed her arms, and fixed him with a look that totally summed up what she thought of him. As she watched his pale face, Elsa remembered all the times when her 'caring' brother-in-law had done everything in his power to drive a wedge between her and Robert. And she couldn't help resenting the fact that Jack Barclay had used the war years to make money out of other people's misery. For Barclay bought at very low prices, the land on which various properties had been bombed, land that would inevitably increase in value once the war was over. 'And what would you do with an old jumble shop like this?' she asked.

Barclay, detecting what he thought was some interest in Elsa's response, said eagerly, 'Oh I wouldn't keep it as a shop. Goodness no! I'd pull the place down. Demolition job. No value in the place. None at all.' His confidence growing, he made his way across to Elsa and stood in front of her. 'I couldn't afford to offer much, Elsa. I just don't have the capital.'

'How much, Jack?'

Barclay felt the blood rushing through his veins with excitement. 'I'm sure you realise how much it would cost me to get all this junk cleared out. More than likely we'd have to throw the whole lot away.'

'How much?' Elsa was sick of his double-talk.

'Difficult to put an actual figure on it without – '

'How much!'

Carefully avoiding any eye contact with her, Barclay swallowed hard before answering. 'No more than a couple of hundred – at the very most. That's generous, Elsa – I promise.'

Suddenly, the total silence that had fallen was pierced by Elsa's laughter, which was so forceful it threatened to scatter dust from every bookshelf in the shop. 'Generous!' Still roaring with laughter, she made her way back behind the counter. 'So your *generous* offer is to give me two hundred pounds, take the place off my hands, and get rid of all this – "junk". Is that it, Jack?'

Barclay was rubbing his chin uneasily. 'It's the best I can do, Elsa, it really is. I can assure you, you wouldn't get an offer like this from anyone else.'

'Oh, I'm quite sure of that!' Elsa said, silkily.

She put on her reading glasses and started to

search for a particular book, one that she wanted to give to Frankie the next time she saw him. 'Let me tell you something, Jack,' she called, her back towards him. 'I don't need you or anyone else to take this place off my hands. And do you know why?' She found the book she was looking for and removed it from the shelf. 'Because this dusty old shop never stops reminding me why I loved Robert so much.' She turned around and took off her glasses. 'When he bought the shop, he knew exactly what he was doing for me. Every piece of "junk", as you call it, is special. It has a story to tell – *someone's* story. Sometimes, when I'm alone here, I can hear them all telling me their different stories.' Still holding the book in one hand, she moved slowly around the shop, touching each object with her fingertips as she talked about it. 'An old umbrella that is too stubborn to open out . . . a teapot with a chipped spout that once belonged to grandma . . . a camera that took all the family snapshots . . . or a little girl's Sunday dress that was only worn once.' She finished up in front of Barclay, now clutching the book to her chest. 'You know, Jack, it makes me very sad to sell any piece of this "junk". To me, it's like losing a part of Robert all over again.' She smiled wryly to herself. 'It's ridiculous, isn't it? But, you know, money doesn't mean a thing to me.'

Barclay was now really irritated. 'You're not getting any younger, Elsa. This place is a lot to handle on your own. I mean – what are you going to do if you get ill or something?'

'I've told you, I have all the help I need!'

'You really can't be serious about that – that ragamuffin?'

'*Misster* Frankie Lewis is not a ragamuffin. He is my *friend*.'

Barclay's back stiffened. He wasn't getting anywhere with this stubborn hag, and he had another element to contend with, one that he hadn't bargained for. 'Well, I hope you know what you're doing,' he said, pulling out the pocket watch that was tucked into his waistcoat pocket. 'I'd better be on my way.' He leaned forward to kiss Elsa on the cheek. 'Goodbye, Elsa.' His voice was cold and distant. 'If you change your mind, let me know.'

Elsa smiled sweetly again. 'Goodbye, Jack. Give my regards to Celia – *and* to Hertfordshire.'

A moment later, Barclay had gone. Elsa didn't bother to go to the window to see him leave. Instead she looked at the cover of the book which she intended to give to Frankie.

The book was by Charles Dickens, and it was called *The Old Curiosity Shop*.

Winston looked fed up. His master had been home from school for over an hour, and yet he was still sitting on the edge of his bed, scribbling into his notebook.

Frankie's homework for the evening was his

worst subject – mathematics. Thanks to Elsa, Frankie had certainly discovered the joys of literature, but quite how pi-squared contributed to the quality of life remained, to him, a total mystery.

Finally, he put down his pencil. 'Come on Winnie,' he said thankfully, 'let's go round the shop.'

Even before Frankie had put on his jacket, Winston had leapt to his feet, nudged open the door with his nose, and was half-way down the stairs.

'Frankie? Is that you?'

Gracie Lewis's shrill voice calling from the kitchen brought Frankie to a halt. He had no time to answer before his mother suddenly appeared in the hall passage.

'I fawt yer was suppose ter be doin' yer 'ome-work? Where yer goin'?'

Much to Winston's frustration, Frankie closed the street door again. 'We're goin' for a walk.'

'Don't gimme that!' Gracie had a fag dangling from her lips and the smoke was causing her right eye to squint. 'You're goin' 'round to that bleedin shop again, in't yer? Well, yer farver an' me don't want yer ter keep seein' that old bitch. The 'ole street's talking about it.'

If looks could only kill, Frankie's would have struck his mother stone dead there and then. He thought it was really rich for his mother to talk about the whole street, when he knew only too well she never even passed the time of the day with any of them. 'I don't know what you're goin' on about,' he said contemptuously.

'You know what I'm talkin' about!' Gracie took the fag out of her mouth and ash flicked down the front of her cardigan. 'I've told yer ter keep away from that bleedin' kraut. In case you 'aven't realised, we've been fightin' the likes of 'er for the past five years!'

Frankie was fed up to the teeth with hearing people talk like this. First it was Jeff, now his own mother. 'Give over, Mum! Elsa's British – just like you and me!'

'She's no more British than 'Itler!' Gracie took a deep puff of her fag and shrieked at him. 'That woman oughta been locked up years ago!'

'You know nothin' Mum – absolutely nothin'!' Frankie was grinding his teeth so hard in his enraged frustration that they felt as though they were wearing away. 'D'yer know what they did to Elsa at the beginnin' of the war? They put 'er in an Internment Camp on the Isle of Man. And d'yer know 'ow long they kept 'er there? Exactly six weeks! Six weeks, Mum – that's all! And d'yer know why they let 'er out after such a short time?' Frankie wasn't aware that he had advanced on his mother, and was now face to face with her half-way down the hall passage. 'Because they didn't take the trouble to find out that she was a British subject. A *British* subject, Mum – married to a *British* army officer!'

With a dismissive wave of the hand, Gracie threw her fag butt down on to the lino and stamped her foot on it.

'Elsa's husband was killed at Dunkirk, Mum. He was killed fightin' the people you're talkin' about – not people like Elsa. She's a good, fine lady, Mum – one of the best I know. She's kind, and thoughtful, and . . . and . . . Elsa wouldn't 'urt no one, Mum – no one in the whole wide world!'

Gracie turned to go back into the kitchen.

'You don't believe me do yer, Mum? You don't believe me – because you don't *want* to believe me! Why, Mum, why?'

Gracie turned swiftly, her eyes piercing him through the yellow glare of the hall passage light. 'Because *she* ain't yer muvver – that's why!'

Frankie watched his mother disappear back into the kitchen and slam the door behind her. For a moment he just stood there, staring at the blank door, totally unable to believe what she had just said. Oh, God, if only Gracie Lewis had given birth to someone else and not him!

Frankie made his way down Pakeman Street. It was very cold, so he tucked his hands deep into his jacket pockets. When he reached the school gates, the caretaker, Mr Mitchison, was just locking up for the night.

'That you, Frankie?'

'Hallo, Mr Mitchison.'

'Bit late for the shop tonight, aren't yer? It's nearly six o'clock.'

This remark took Frankie by surprise, for he had no idea his movements were followed so closely. However, Mr Mitchison was known to be a bit of a nosey-parker, so he didn't take too much notice. 'I'm just taking Winston out for a walk, that's all.'

Mitchison grinned and carried on locking the school gate. 'Well, don't work too hard, son. The wife says she often sees you through the shop window. I 'ope that old girl's givin' you a good wage.'

Frankie didn't know why, but he deeply resented Mr Mitchison's remarks. After all, his wife had no right to go nosing through shop windows spying on him. Why couldn't people just mind their own business!

'G'night, Mr Mitchison,'

Frankie hurried on and, as he reached the corner of Roden Street, he saw old Mr Kendrew, 'the dummy' smiling and waving at him. Frankie hated himself for thinking of Mr Kendrew as 'the dummy' just because the poor man had been deaf and dumb since he was a child. But every kid in the neighbourhood had always called him that, and through the years the name had stuck. It was a pity, for Mr Kendrew and his wife were two of the nicest people in the street, always smiling and waving at their neighbours as they passed by, and often fetching out a biscuit or a barley sugar if a mother came along with her child. Their house was not only the best kept on the outside, but those who had been invited inside for a cup of tea were full of stories of how clean and tidy the place was kept. Yet in most people's mind, the house in Roden Street beside the school would always be 'the dummy's house.

It was just beginning to drizzle as Frankie made his way along the first terrace of houses in Roden Street. As he looked up into the dark evening sky there wasn't a star to be seen, and the light raindrops that were falling felt like tiny particles of ice that quickly melted on his glowing red cheeks.

'Still helping out in the shop, Frankie?'

Frankie looked down with a start to see Letty Hobbs just hurrying into number 13. From the inviting smells that were coming from the newspaper-wrapped parcel in her string carrier bag, it was obvious that she had been round to collect the family's supper from Anderson's fish and chip shop in Hornsey Road. 'I don't go round every night, Mrs Hobbs.' Frankie liked Letty Hobbs. She was never too busy to stop and have a little chat with him, despite the fact that she had a family of her own to look after, and a husband, Oliver, who had lost a leg in the last war.

'What's she like?' Letty called as she opened her front door. 'That woman who runs the shop. She looks very nice – never stops working. Is she really a German like they say?'

Frankie bit his lip hard and pulled up his jacket collar. 'She's very nice, Mrs Hobbs. She was only born in Germany, that's all.'

'Oh well, as long as she treats people nice, what's it matter? She's very lucky to have you and Winnie working for her. I bet you're both a great help.'

Frankie was about to answer, but Letty and her sweet-smelling fish and chips quickly disappeared into number 13.

''Night, Mrs Hobbs.'

''Night, Frankie.'

As soon as Letty closed her front door, a nagging feeling crossed Frankie's mind. Letty Hobbs was the second person to mention his working in the shop. Maybe his mother was right. Maybe everyone in the street *was* talking about his working for someone who, in their eyes was part of the enemy they'd been fighting for the past five years.

The drizzle had now turned to sleet and, as Frankie hurried on his way, it was getting very slippery underfoot and he had to shuffle along rather than walk. Hell! How he hated the winter months with their endlessly long, dark evenings. On a night like this it seemed impossible to believe that the start of spring was only a couple of days away. He only hoped that the first yellow-head daffodils of the year he had seen appearing in the Robinson's window box at number 16 Merton Street would survive such a frozen onslaught. By the time he had turned into Annette Road and passed the timber cutting factory, Frankie's hair and jacket were covered with a thin film of white which made him look ghostlike as he glided along in the eerie, unlit street.

At the corner of Annette Road a sudden gust of wind hurtled furiously along Arthur Road and caught Frankie completely off-balance. The sleet engulfed him, leaving him to struggle helplessly to protect himself from the surging wall of freezing white rain.

'Winnie!'

Frankie's cry for help was to no avail, for the sound of his voice was lost in the howling wind. And he could no longer keep his balance. His foot slipped on the sleet beneath him, which sent him crashing on to his rump on the ice-cold pavement.

'Winnie!'

A moment later, the rush of wind disappeared as suddenly as it had arrived. But the sleet continued to flutter down mercilessly and, as he sat there Frankie's stomach started to churn. Where was Winnie? Ever since Winston had been a puppy, he had hardly ever failed to come when Frankie called out for him.

'Winnie!'

Frankie struggled to his feet.

'Winnie! Here boy! Here!' But in whichever direction he turned to look, there was no sign of Winston anywhere.

Ignoring the slippery pavements, Frankie started to hurry down Arthur Road, whistling and yelling and making just about every sound he could think of that Winston would react to. But it was only when he was within a few yards of the front door of Dr McWhirter's surgery that Winston finally made his presence known.

The barking sounds were coming from Hornsey Road and they were unlike anything Frankie had heard from Winston before – angry, aggressive, and relentless. It was only then that Frankie realised that during the past few months that he and Winston had been taking this same route to the jumble shop, Winston had got into the habit of rushing ahead, eager to get to the apple cake that Elsa always had waiting for him. But he had never crossed the main Hornsey Road on his own until this evening. Frankie didn't know what was different, but something had clearly aggravated Winston causing him to ignore every call Frankie was making.

'Winnie!'

The moment of horror came just as Frankie struggled his way to the corner of Arthur and Hornsey Roads.

'Winston! No, Winnie! No . . .!'

But it was too late. Through the blinding swirl of sleet, Frankie could just see Winston charging down the middle of the main Hornsey Road, barking and howling at a small motor car that was just pulling away from the kerbside outside the jumble shop. Winston was frantic, angrily trying to get at the car, slipping and sliding all over the road as traffic raced by all around him in the blinding sleet storm.

'Winnie!' Oblivious to the danger he was putting himself into, Frankie rushed out into the road and tried to get to Winston, who by now was half-way towards the junction with Seven Sisters Road. 'No, Winnie! Come back! Come back . . .!'

As Frankie spoke, a large furniture van, travelling far too fast for the appalling road conditions, hit Winston sideways on, which tossed him into the air and left him slumped against the kerb at the side of the road.

'Winnie . . .!'

Frankie's cry of anguish echoed above the roar of passing traffic and eerie, half-dipped headlights. No one stopped to let him cross the road, so he rushed in and out of the cars and vans, yelling, sobbing, tears streaming down his ice-cold cheeks. By the time he reached the kerbside and dropped to his knees, Winston's eyes were closed and he was quite motionless.

As he held Winston tightly in his arms, Frankie realised with horror that his cold hands were covered with blood . . .

Chapter Fifteen

Frankie woke with a start. For a moment or so he was completely disoriented, for as his eyes began to focus all he could see was a bare electric light bulb dangling from the ceiling above and the sound of a gentle voice calling to him.

'Frank. Wake up, Frank. It's time.'

Frankie sat bolt upright in bed. His sister Helen had drawn the curtains and, although the room was as chilly as usual, the early morning sunshine was streaming straight down on to his face.

'It's quarter-to-nine, Frank.' Helen's voice was quiet and sympathetic. 'The Vet told you to call at nine.'

Frankie didn't need any more reminding. He was out of bed in a flash and, after throwing on his clothes, leapt down the stairs two by two and dashed straight out the front door.

As he hurried off towards Herslet Road, the whole nightmare experience of the previous evening came tumbling back to him. The sound of

Winston's squeal as the furniture van hit him, without even bothering to stop. And then the horror of holding the poor, lifeless creature in his arms, blood seeping from Winnie's mouth on to Frankie's arms and hands. It had been horrible, just horrible . . . As he rushed along the frost-covered pavements, Frankie blamed himself over and over again. It should never have happened. *He* should never have allowed it to happen. How many times had people warned him about letting Winston roam without his lead? He shouldn't have taken the chance – it wouldn't happen again – not ever! But then, harsh reality dawned on him. Suppose there *wasn't* a next time? It was true that Winnie was still alive when he took him to the Vet. But that was last night. Suppose – suppose something had happened to him during the night, when Frankie wasn't with him? It was almost too unbearable to think about. He couldn't remember a time when he and Winnie weren't together. They were a team! He should never have left Winnie with the Vet on his own. He should have stayed with him. Tears were swelling up in Frankie's already sore eyes as he imagined Winnie dying without him being there.

When he reached the public telephone box in Bovay Place, Frankie found someone already using it. Despite glaring at her, and pacing up and down so that she could not help noticing he was there, the woman carried on relentlessly with her telephone conversation. Gab! Gab! Gab! Why can't people say what they have to say and push off, thought Frankie, whose ears were now quite numb with the cold.

The waiting seemed interminable. All he could think of was how, if it hadn't been for Elsa, Winnie would probably have died, because when she came running out from the shop to find out what had happened, she immediately called a taxi and took Frankie and Winnie to the vet in Fonthill Road. That was more than his own mother or father would ever have done.

Gab! Gab! Gab! How much longer?

It was five minutes before the woman finally left the telephone box and, when she did, Frankie nearly knocked her down in his desperation to make his call. When he put the two pennies into the coin box, it seemed an eternity before anyone answered. It was two minutes past nine o'clock. Surely he couldn't be too late already?

'Fonthill Road Veterinary Surgery.'

Frankie pushed Button A, which allowed him to speak. 'Could you tell me how my dog is, please? His name's Winnie – that's short for Winston. I brought him in last night. He had an accident, in Hornsey Road . . .'

'One moment, please,' answered the brusque-voiced woman at the other end. 'I'll ask the vet for you.'

Suddenly, Frankie didn't feel cold any more. In fact, his hands were sweating and he found it difficult to hold the cumbersome black telephone receiver. 'Please, God,' he said to himself at least three times, 'Don't let Winnie be dead.'

'Are you there?'

'Yes! I'm here!'

'The vet says your dog has woken up . . .'

Frankie practically yelled with joy in the woman's ear. 'Can I come and collect him?'

'I'm afraid not. He's had a very bad haemorrhage and he's broken one of his back paws. He's still quite groggy. He's not well enough to leave the surgery just yet. Mr Purvis would like to keep him under observation for the next day or so. Please call again the day after tomorrow. Goodbye.'

Frankie heard the line go dead at the other end, and the dialling tone returned. For a moment he just stood there, just staring into the telephone receiver as though he could see the woman who he had just been speaking to. Groggy? *'He's still quite groggy,'* she'd said. What was that supposed to mean? All his fears returned. Were they trying to keep something from him? Was Winnie much worse than they were saying? He felt sick. If Winnie was awake, he'd want Frankie to be with him. It wasn't right that he should be left alone with people he didn't know and who probably didn't care whether he lived or died. Without realising it, Frankie was running rather than walking home.

By the time he got there, he was so worked

up, he forgot that he should have been at school nearly half-an-hour before . . .

As usual, Charlie Brend's sweet shop was full of kids from Pakeman Street School. But, as it was Friday and the end of the week, most of the kids didn't have any ration coupons left to buy sweets, so the roaring trade was a glass of one of Charlie's legendary fizzy drinks. The counter was dominated by five large glass bulb-shaped containers, each containing a different flavour cordial. The cordial was fed into a highly complicated soda-making machine which looked like one of the army's secret war weapons. The favourite flavour always seemed to be sarsparilla and, as he pulled handles and turned knobs, a sea of fascinated young faces watched in awe and expectation for the rapturous moment when, after a great deal of hissing and bubbling, a magical single glass of highly coloured fizzy drink was produced. When the price of one penny was finally handed over, the drink inevitably disappeared faster than it took to make.

Gracie Lewis wandered into the shop to buy her daily packet of ten Players fags. She pushed her way to the counter, for the kids gathered there always irritated her.

Although he was a jovial little man, utterly adored by the kids, Charlie took Gracie's half-crown, handed over the cigarettes and gave Gracie her change without passing a single word of greeting. For, although Gracie had been coming into his shop for years, she had never exchanged any form of greeting with Charlie, and when once he asked her how the family was, she replied with cold indifference that if he wanted to know then he should ask them himself.

Once outside, Gracie quickly ripped open her fag packet, took one out, pushed it into her lips, and immediately lit it with a match from her box of Swan Vestas. Gracie never inhaled deeply, but she produced plenty of smoke, which, on a cold day like this, curled up into the air and practically froze into a twisted shape.

She moved on at a slow pace, strolling rather than walking, past Mitchell's newspaper shop and then the dairy. When she reached Barclay's jumble shop, she came to a halt and, uncharacteristically, took a deep puff of her fag. She stopped to look in the window and glanced casually at the display of a rather tatty looking secondhand china tea-set. She lingered just long enough to take a sly look through the window into the shop. There was no sign of anyone inside. She moved on a few paces until she reached the shop door. After another quick puff of her fag, Gracie turned the door handle and went inside.

When Gracie entered, Elsa was sewing the hem of a torn dress. At first Gracie didn't notice her, for she was sitting among the hordes of old suits and dresses that took up at least one half of the shop.

'Can I help you, please?'

Gracie stopped dead as Elsa's head peered from behind a pin-stripe suit. Elsa came out to greet her customer. 'Are you looking for anything in particular, my dear?'

Gracie was stony-faced. 'I'm lookin' for the woman who runs this place.'

Elsa's smile became rather fixed. 'Yes? What can I do for you?'

'You can't do nuffin' fer me.' Gracie puffed her fag, and blew out a funnel of grey smoke. 'Wot's more, I don't want yer to.'

Elsa became a little uneasy, but remained quite calm. 'I'm sorry, I don't quite understand?'

'My name's Lewis. I'm Frankie's muvver.'

Elsa felt her face tighten. 'Oh – I see.' She smiled again and held out her hand. 'How nice to meet you at last, Mrs Lewis. Frankie has told me so much about you.'

Gracie declined to shake hands. 'Yeah. I bet 'e 'as!'

'Can I make you a cup of tea?' As she made her way back to the counter, Elsa did her best to appear hospitable. 'It won't take a second to boil the kettle.'

'No! I don't want no tea.'

For a moment, Elsa stood with her back turned towards Gracie. Then, after patting the bun she had combed her hair into at the back, she turned around. 'Then what can I do for you, Mrs Lewis?'

Gracie peered around the shop. Although she

would never admit it, she had always adored junk shops like this. 'Me and 'is farvver don't approve of Frankie workin' 'ere. We don't like it, OK?'

'Oh, I see. And what does Frankie say about that?'

'It's got nuffin' ter do wiv 'im. 'E's under age, and we don't want 'im workin' 'ere.'

'I quite understand.'

Even in the poor light of the shop, it was easy to see the difference in the two women. Elsa, small and diminutive, but looking so elegant in the most simple floral cotton printed dress, and Gracie, at least a head taller, wearing a smudged and dowdy grey winter coat flecked with cigarette ash, a tatty-looking woollen scarf tied around her head.

Elsa clasped her hands together in front of her and leaned back slightly to rest her back against the counter. 'Tell me. Is there any particular reason why you object to Frankie coming here?'

'It's not 'ealthy!'

Elsa squinted at her, quizzically. 'I'm sorry? I don't understand.'

'When Frankie leaves school 'e'll get a real job. 'E don't need ter take money from people like you.'

Elsa lowered her eyes. The remark had hurt, but she was determined not to show it. 'I don't force him to come, you know. He comes because he wants to. At least it gives him some pocket money. I gather he's saving up to buy his own bicycle.'

Gracie made a dismissive, scoffing sound, then, without thinking, flicked ash on the floor.

'Has he not told you about it?' Elsa picked up an ashtray from the counter and took it across to Gracie. 'It's a way of his doing something on his own.'

''E's always doin' fings on 'is own.' Gracie stubbed her cigarette out in the ashtray that Elsa was still holding. 'For my mind, 'e's *too* independent.'

'You think that's a bad thing?'

''E should tell *me* what 'e's doin'.'

'Do you ever ask?'

Gracie fixed her with a stony glare. 'I don't want my boy workin' in this shop! It's givin' me and my family a bad name. Everyone in our street's talkin' about it.'

Elsa smiled wryly. 'People talk about me, too, Mrs Lewis. But does it really matter?'

'It matters ter me!'

'In the end, it will be Frankie's decision to do what *he* wants to do. There's nothing we can do about it, Mrs Lewis, neither me – nor you.'

'*I'm* 'is muvver. 'E'll do what *I* tell 'im.'

Elsa shrugged her shoulders. 'Frankie is no longer a child, Mrs Lewis.'

Without answering, Gracie turned, and made her way to the door.

'You're very lucky to have a son like Frankie,'

Elsa said quietly. 'One of these days you're going to be very proud of him.'

Gracie, about to open the shop door, stopped briefly, without turning.

'I'm sure you know that he's a very intelligent young man.'

In the road outside a particularly noisy lorry was thundering past. Until it had, Gracie remained absolutely motionless, her back still turned towards Elsa.

'You know, Mrs Lewis, Frankie is like a flower that needs the sunshine to open him up. Sometimes, when he talks to me, I can hear him – so full of wonderful, creative ideas. He *inspires* me. But those who inspire need to be inspired, too. Flowers not only need sunshine and water, they also need to be noticed. After all, what's the point of them being there if you *don't* notice them. And, when you do, it's amazing how much pleasure they can give you.'

Gracie slowly turned to look at Elsa. Although she didn't quite understand her analogy, the feeling of what she had said sank in. And, as she stood there, a tuft of prematurely greying hair just dangling down from beneath her headscarf, Gracie could see her whole life behind her – the life she had had, and the life that she could have had . . .

When she was a child, someone had told her mother how intelligent Gracie was and, for a time, Gracie believed it. So what happened to her over the years? Why had she allowed herself to disintegrate into the pathetic, difficult creature that she had become? If she thought about it, Gracie Lewis could see Frankie in herself – the rebel, determined not to conform to anything or anybody. Gracie had never had a guiding hand to draw her out and, for a long time, she had known that Frankie was different, that if he was given the chance he could be all the things that she never was. And yet, inside her a voice kept telling her that she had to prevent Frankie from thinking for himself . . .

Gracie blinked her eyes. Elsa was still standing there. She was real. She was a fact. She was a different, sane voice begging her to listen. And, to Gracie's astonishment, she found that she actually *liked* this woman. And that scared Gracie. For some reason, it scared her half to death.

Without saying another word Gracie opened the shop door and was gone.

Chapter Sixteen

Ever since he moved into number 78 Merton Street twenty years before, Clancy had kept himself to himself. Not that he wanted to, but most of his neighbours had instantly decided that he was not the type to associate with and he was almost totally ignored. The clothes he wore didn't help. Most days he did his shopping in a yellow beret and polka dot kerchief (yellow was his favourite colour), a loose fitting shirt and heavy knitted pullover, tan-coloured corduroy trousers, bright pink socks and open-toed sandals. His real name was Clarence Dudley Porritt, but since the people of Merton Street had long since accepted that he was a 'pansy', the kids had given him their own nickname, and there was hardly a time when he left his house without being hounded by a bunch of kids calling after him. '*Clancy nancy – don't let him tickle yer fancy*!'

Early on Saturday morning, Clancy left his house and did his shopping in Seven Sisters Road. In the greengrocer's shop, Ma Digby served him with his usual two pounds of King Edward potatoes, pound of brussel sprouts, pound of carrots, lettuce and bunch of celery, and salad. 'How are yer today, dearie?' To Clancy's delight, Ma Digby always stopped to have a little chat with him, for she had no problems about who or what he was. In fact she loved the way he dressed, for he looked so different to some of the dreary customers who were always grumbling and complaining in the shop. They weren't so nice in Liptons the grocers, though. Every time he went in just like today, the silly young girl assistants behind the counter stopped to giggle amongst themselves.

With his string bag full of vegetables and his minute weekly ration of sugar, margarine, flour, and his favourite liquorice allsorts, Clancy waddled his way back home.

At number 1 Merton Street, Frankie was just leaving home to go to the shop. It was three days since Winston's accident, but the latest news from the Vet still left him anxious about how serious the dog's injuries really were so his mind was still preoccupied when he came out of the house and, for the first moment or so, he didn't take in the noise that was coming from down the street.

'*Clancy! Nancy!*' The chorus of kids' voices yelling, singing, chanting cat-calling, and whistling, suddenly impinged on Frankie. He and the rest of the Merton Street gang had been part of the same merciless teasing of poor old Clancy many times over the years so at first he decided to ignore the rumpus. But when he saw that the crowd of kids gathered at the end of the street was larger than usual, he decided to investigate.

Once he had managed to push his way through the crowd of yelling, jeering kids, Frankie was horrified to find Clancy spreadeagled on the pavement, the contents of his shopping bag strewn all over the road.

'Get back all of yer!' Frankie had to shout at the top of his voice to be heard above the din. 'Leave 'im alone!'

Frankie had to battle with some of the older kids, who were having too good a time to stop. It was only when he threatened to have a punch-up with some of them that they turned tail and ran off. And, on the other side of the street, just outside number 27, someone quickly started up their motorcycle and roared off at speed. Although he hadn't seen Jeff Murray since the evening he beat up the Prof, Frankie was in no doubt as to who the rider was, or who was responsible for whipping up the kids' frenzy.

'Give us yer 'and, mister.'

Frankie bent down and held out his hand to Clancy, who was trying to raise himself up to his knees. It was the first time he had seen the resident of number 78 close to and it came as a surprise to see that the old man's face had been powdered, and that he was wearing a trace of lipstick.

Clancy took hold of Frankie's hand and allowed him to help him stand up. 'Thank you, young man. It's very kind of you.'

Despite the cold morning, Frankie was amazed at how warm the old man's hand was. 'Are you all right, mister?'

'Oh yes. Nothing to worry about.' Clancy quickly tucked his white hair back underneath his beret and straightened his kerchief. 'It's very good of you. Very good indeed.'

Frankie had never heard Clancy speak before. It was a funny sort of voice, high-pitched, and a bit like a woman's. And he couldn't help noticing how shaky the poor man was, for although he was trying to appear unaffected by what had happened, he was clearly very upset and agitated. 'Did they push yer? Which one of 'em did it?'

Clancy was quick to reply. 'Oh no. Nobody pushed me. It was my own fault. I'm not very good on my feet these days. Getting old, I suppose. No. No one pushed me.'

Frankie didn't believe him, but he admired the old man's courage. 'Let me give yer a hand.' He picked up the remains of Clancy's string shopping bag, and started to collect the contents which were scattered around the pavement.

Clancy tried to help, but not only was he too

shaky to stoop down, it was not easy for someone who was quite so tubby.

Why do kids have to pick on people who can't fight back? Frankie thought, suddenly ashamed at the way he'd hounded Clancy when he was younger. Just because this old biddy was different to them was no reason to mock and jeer him. After all, he seemed nice enough, and he was no harm to anybody, for he always kept himself to himself. But it would have been Jeff who pushed the kids to going much farther than usual. It was just the sort of vicious fun he'd get a kick out of.

'There you are, mister.' Frankie handed over the string bag, complete with its shopping again. 'Can I give yer a hand inside.'

'Oh no. I shall be perfectly all right now, thank you very much. You've been admirable. Quite admirable . . .' Before he had finished speaking, Clancy wobbled and seemed as if he was about to lose his balance again.

Frankie grabbed at the old man's hand and supported him. 'Just 'ang on ter me.'

Clancy held tightly on to Frankie's arm and allowed himself to be led back towards his own house at number 78.

'Oy, you! Frank!'

The voice calling out along the street caused Frankie to stop dead. As he turned, he was startled to see his father, Reg Lewis, hurrying towards him.

Lewis, his flat cap pulled tightly on to his head,

was only too aware that eyes were watching their every movement from behind curtains all along the street. So, although he was clearly angry, he tried to keep his voice as low as possible. 'What the bloody 'ell d'yer think yer doin'?'

Frankie couldn't understand why his father was so angry. 'What's the matter? What 'ave I done?'

Reg, desperately awkward and uneasy, was looking up and down at the street windows. 'You *know* what's wrong!' he snarled through clenched teeth. 'Bloody get out of 'ere!'

Clancy started to panic and immediately pulled away from Frankie. 'It's all right, young man. I'll be quite all right.'

'No!' Frankie tried to slam the front garden gate behind him and old Clancy. 'What's the matter wiv yer, Dad? Can't yer see 'e's 'ad an accident?'

'I really can manage, I promise.' Clancy grabbed his shopping and rushed off toward his front door.

'Get out of there!' Reg Lewis, now absolutely furious with his son, grabbed hold of Frankie by his jacket collar, tugged open the garden gate, and virtually hoisted the boy back out on to the pavement.

'Stop it, Dad! What're yer doin'?'

Frankie's yells of protest were ignored by his father, who started to frog-march him as discreetly as he could to the end of the street. As they went, curtains fluttered and the eyes peering from behind them gradually retreated into the safety of their own back parlours.

As soon as Lewis had got Frankie away from the prying eyes of his neighbours in Merton Street and into the relative obscurity of Herslet Road, he gave his son an almighty push, which sent him reeling. 'Yer bloody little sod!' he spluttered, his face blood-red with anger. 'If I catch you 'round that 'ouse again, I'll 'ave yer bleedin' guts fer garters!'

'What's the matter wiv yer, Dad!' Frankie was in a state of total anguish. 'What's wrong wiv Clancy? Why does everyone keep pickin' on 'im? You're a bully, Dad! Just like all the people in Merton Street. You're nothin' but a rotten bully!'

Lewis's temper exploded and Frankie flinched as his father lashed out with a hard slap across the boy's face with the back of his hand. 'It's the last time I tell yer! The last time, d'yer 'ear!'

Frankie, tears streaming down his cheeks, watched his father stride off back down Merton Street. As he went, he called after him. 'I 'ate yer, Dad! I've *always* 'ated yer!' Then he walked right back into Merton Street and into the middle of the road and yelled at the top of his voice: 'I 'ate the 'ole bloody lot of yer!'

At number 78, Clancy peered nervously out of

his ground floor window and quickly drew the curtains.

Frankie didn't go home for the rest of the day. Nor did he go to see Elsa in the shop. After the way his father had treated him he just wanted to get away. Over and over again he kept asking himself how anyone could bring themselves to bully someone like old Clancy. Even if he was different and behaved more like a woman than a man, he was a human being, just like anyone else. How could it be so wrong just to talk to someone, to help them when they were in trouble?

Feeling thoroughly fed up, Frankie wandered up Seven Sisters Road. When he reached the Astoria Cinema he crossed over the road and made his way under the Railway Bridge by the entrance to Finsbury Park Tube Station. The whole area was congested with football crowds on their way to a game at the nearby Arsenal Stadium. Frankie was in no mood to share the high spirits of the 'Gunners' supporters. He thought of all the times his father had tried to get him interested in the game, and how he had said that it was 'nancy' not to behave like other *normal* youngsters by taking up 'a man's game.'

Frankie stopped briefly to look at the posters for the current week's films at the Rink Cinema, then quickly slipped through the gates of the park and made his way past the children's playground. But in the park where the football pitch was being used by local youngsters, he noticed Jeff Murray's old Triumph motorcycle parked at the kerb nearby and a quick glance revealed that some of the Merton Street gang were playing in the teams, watched from among the thin line of spectators by Patty Jackson. Making sure that none of the gang had seen him, Frankie hurriedly crossed the road then doubled back towards the bridge over the railway line which ran alongside the western fringe of the park.

As he climbed the steps leading up to the heavy iron bridge, three figures came down towards him, emerging from the steam of a passing train. Frankie recognised Letty Hobbs's husband, Oliver, a regular visitor to the bridge, despite the fact that he only had one leg and had to walk with the aid of an artificial limb. As usual, Oliver had his two young sons with him. Frankie liked the eldest boy best, for he had once heard him sing in a talent contest at the Star Cinema in Upper Hornsey Road, and it was so awful it made everyone laugh. But he didn't care for the youngest boy, Mick. Frankie thought he was snooty and too big for his boots. Once Frankie had exchanged a casual greeting with them all, the Hobbs trio left, and Frankie took up their former position in the middle of the bridge. But much as he always liked to watch the trains go by, today Frankie's mind was preoccupied with other matters.

Ever since that humiliating scene with his father in Merton Street, Frankie had been plunged into a deep depression. The dreary grey sky of the March afternoon didn't help and, as he stood there on the bridge, staring through a gap in the high metal fence, the railway line below gradually seemed to disappear into a distant haze. Frankie felt as though he was drowning, with his whole life floating before him. He could see number 1 Merton Street, the house he had been born and brought up in, dark and dingy and totally without love. There had never been any love at all in the Lewis family, he thought. A family which existed with no hope, no ambition, and no future. He could see his mother, a lost soul who, for some reason, had relinquished any chance she might have had to get the best out of life. Gracie, Frankie thought, didn't care what her children did, whether they lived or died. She wasn't even really aware that in just a few months' time her son would be taking important exams at school and then going out into the world to earn his own living. And what difference would it make even if she was aware? What difference would it make to his mother *or* his father? His father! How could he have behaved the way he did?

And then he thought of poor Helen. Although Frankie had persuaded her not to get rid of her baby, what would happen when it arrived?

How would she cope on her own without a

husband to support her? He thought about Merton Street, that long straight street, just like any other in London, with the same shaped houses on each side, and heartless creatures who peered out from behind their curtains to watch an old man being spat on and jeered at by their own precious kids. How would they treat Helen and *her* kids. Were these really the same people who had helped each other during the dark days of the blitz, no matter who they were or where they came from? 'Our street is the best in London,' he had once heard Bert Gorman say. Frankie had never before doubted that comment. But he did now.

The distant, shrill whistle of an approaching train brought Frankie out of his trance. But his mind continued to race. This time, however, there was more hope in his reasoning, for he was thinking how Elsa had changed his life. Thanks to her he was reading books to improve his knowledge – but he was also reading them for enjoyment. Ever since that foggy night in November, when he and the gang had teased her with their childish game of 'Knock Down Ginger', Frankie had grown as a person. He didn't exactly know how or why, but he could feel it happening inside him, as though a seed had been sown and was growing throughout his entire mind and body. Elsa was an inspiration, a person who had known prejudice of one kind or another almost all her life and yet she had survived, and survived with the most extraordinary dignity.

The approaching train made its presence known again. And as it did so, Frankie's heart started to beat faster and faster. Suddenly, all the anger and frustration came swelling up again. His mother! His father! The gang! And Winston! Winston was going to die and there was nothing he could do about it! Oh God! Frankie was now screaming inside. What am I doing on this earth? I'm nearly sixteen years old and I have no meaning – no meaning at all! He looked down at the railway line below and, as the approaching train rushed faster and faster towards the bridge, there was a split second when Frankie thought that this would be the way to solve all his problems. Yes! Now! This is it . . .! But as the train whistle shrieked and the steam from its engine engulfed Frankie in a massive grey cloud, he found the only release that made any sense to him.

He just yelled and yelled and yelled at the top of his voice. A yell that seemed to go on for ever.

Ten minutes later Frankie was ringing the front door bell at the Fonthill Road Veterinary Surgery. The door was answered by a middle-aged woman in a white coat, whom Frankie imagined had been the snooty voice at the end of his telephone calls. She had a much kinder face than he had imagined.

'I'm sorry. The surgery is closed until six o'clock,' she said.

'You've got my dog. His name's Winston.' There was a tone of desperation in Frankie's voice. 'You said – well, the vet said, I could see him some time.'

The white-coated lady was smiling firmly. 'I told you, young man. The surgery is closed.'

Frankie was more anxious than ever. 'But I've got money to pay the vet's bill. Well – not all of it. If it's all right, I could give you some now and a bit each week?'

The white-coated lady suddenly felt rather guilty. 'The bill is not a problem. Mrs Barclay has already taken care of it.'

Frankie was taken aback. 'She has?'

'Who is it, Mary?'

The voice that called from behind the partly open door was that of a young man. Frankie bit his lip nervously and waited anxiously while the two voices conversed inside.

After a moment, the white-coated lady opened the door again. 'Mr Purvis says you may come inside.'

Frankie's heart was thumping hard as he entered. To his surprise he found this Mr Purvis was a young man, the vet's son.

'You've come to see Winston?'

'Yes, sir.' Frankie felt a bit silly calling the vet '*sir*', because he didn't seem all that much older than himself. 'Is he all right?'

It was difficult to see the colour of Mr Purvis's eyes because, rather worryingly, he kept them lowered. 'He's as well as can be expected.'

'Is he going to die?' This was a question Frankie had been dreading to ask, but he just had to know.

'We're doing our best,' was all the vet would reply, 'but he has had a very bad haemorrhage. Anyway, come and say hello to him.'

Frankie felt sick in his stomach, for it was obvious that Winston's life was in danger. With tremendous trepidation, he followed the vet through a door and along a stark white corridor. The place smelt of ether and all sorts of other ghastly smells . . .

Before they reached the end of the corridor, dogs could be heard whimpering and barking in the distance. But Frankie knew Winston's bark too well to know that his was not one of them.

As Mr Purvis opened the door, a deafening chorus of howling dogs and cats rose from their cages. The young vet yelled at them to be quiet, and, in a quiet, adjoining room there were just two cages. Frankie's heart missed a beat when he saw Winston in one, stretched out fast asleep. One of his back legs was bound up in plaster and, although an effort had been made to clean him up, there were still patches of dried blood on his shaggy black and white fur.

'Is he – all right?' he asked anxiously.

'He's been like that ever since the accident.' Although he was clearly concerned, the young vet tried hard not to show it. 'After the anaesthetic had worn off, he opened his eyes for a few moments. But he's been like that ever since. I'm afraid he's still in a semi-coma.'

'Will he come out of it?'

The vet shrugged his shoulders. 'Hard to say.'

Frankie felt the anxiety swell up inside him. 'Please – could I talk to him?'

Mr Purvis tried to give Frankie a comforting smile. 'It won't do much good, I'm afraid.'

'Please! Let me try.'

The young vet shrugged. There was no harm in the boy trying. He undid the latch on the cage, opened the door, and stood back.

Frankie leaned into the cage and gently put his hand on to Winston's head. 'Winnie. . . . ' His voice was clear, but low. 'Winnie, it's me.'

There was no response from Winston and, if Frankie hadn't seen a slight breathing movement, he would have been convinced that the dog was dead.

'Come on now, Winnie. Don't lark around. There's nothin' wrong wiv yer.' Frankie stroked Winston's head, then gently removed the fur covering his eyes. 'Shall I tell yer somefin', boy?' He leaned as close as he could to the dog's ear, and whispered, 'We ain't finished yet, yer know. Not by a long chalk. We got fings ter do, Winnie – you and me tergevver.' Without realising it, tears were rolling down Frankie's cheeks. 'I can't do it on me own, Winnie. Not wivout you. I need yer. Yer need *me* too!'

The young vet leaned forward. 'I should leave him now.'

'But I can't leave 'im! Not on 'is own! Me and 'im are always tergevver. Ain't we, Winn? Please, Winnie! Wake up, boy! *Please* wake up!'

'Come on now.' Although he had been through this kind of scene many times before, it gave young Mr Purvis no pleasure to go through it again. 'There's nothing more we can do for him.' The vet closed the cage and led the sobbing Frankie back to the door. But before he opened it, they were both distracted by a whispering sound coming from Winston's cage.

'Winnie!'

Frankie turned and rushed back to the cage. To his near disbelief he could see Winston trying to raise his head, his eyes half-open. In a mad, excited frenzy, Frankie, watched by the astonished young vet, undid the latch, opened the door, and squeezed his shoulders back into the cage. 'Winnie.' As he gently stroked Winston's head, Frankie was half-sobbing half-laughing. 'I knew you could do it boy! I *knew* it!'

Mr Purvis looked on, grinning very broadly indeed.

As soon as he had left the vet's surgery, Frankie practically ran down Isledon Road to the jumble shop, where Elsa was just locking up for the evening. She was overjoyed to hear about the recovery Winston was beginning to make and suggested that they go back to Hadleigh Villas and have a bit of a celebration. That meant cheese and gherkin sandwiches with a glass of white wine for Elsa and a glass of cider for Frankie. It was the first time the two of them had felt their spirits rise since before Winston had had his accident . . .

That night, Frankie didn't get home until well after ten o'clock. By the time he got there, the house was in darkness, so he crept quietly up to his room where Helen was already fast asleep in bed. He quickly undressed and put on his pyjamas. For a few minutes he lay awake just thinking of Winston, and how different things would be once he came home again . . .

In the room next door, Reg Lewis was alone in his own double bed, wide awake, and smoking a fag. He hadn't enjoyed the day much, either, and kept asking himself why . . . and, in the lower bunk in the Anderson shelter, Gracie opened her eyes. The shelter was in total darkness, and yet she felt as though she could see its cold, unfriendly, curved aluminium walls. Her mind churned with thoughts and it was the early hours of the morning before she finally went to sleep . . .

Chapter Seventeen

By March 1945, the residents of Merton Street were convinced that the Second World War was finally coming to an end. Day after day their newspapers were full of stories about British and American armies crossing the River Rhine in Nazi Germany and on 25th April they listened in awe to graphic descriptions on the BBC Home Service of how Russian troops had met up with American forces on the River Elbe at Torgau. However, it wasn't until 7th May, a week after Adolf Hitler's suicide, when General Jodl made the final capitulation of Germany to General Eisenhower near Rheims, that practically everyone in the street was able to tune in to the impeccable voice of Alvar Liddell on their wireless sets, reading out the words they had waited for nearly six long years to hear: '*The War in Europe is over.*'

Even before Prime Minister Winston Churchill had finished his dramatic address to the nation, the front doors of every house in Merton Street and the entire neighbourhood were thrown open in a frenzy of unrestrained joy. People streamed out into the street, hugged whoever they saw, danced, sang, yelled, cheered, and copied, en masse, Mr Churchill's victorious 'V' sign. Wherever one looked, a sea of two fingers were pointing into the air.

As 8th May had been declared VE Day, the residents of Merton Street had very little time to prepare for the celebrations. But by midday flags of all the Allied nations were draped across the street, trestle tables and chairs provided by Pakeman Street School were set up down the middle of the road, and hordes of sandwiches and cakes and buns were ready for an immediate feast. And that was only for the kids! By evening, a bonfire had been lit on every street corner, and the adults had brought out endless bottles of brown ale. Laughter mingled with tears, for no one could forget the sacrifices that had been made over the past six years, the bomb damage on their own doorsteps, the sons and husbands who had been taken away, some never to return. But now it was over, and a new life was about to begin.

For the first time in five and a half years, Gracie Lewis decided it was safe to abandon her nightly sleep in the Anderson shelter. It was an odd experience for her, returning to the double bed upstairs, especially as it meant sharing it again with her husband, Reg. To their surprise, however, they soon became used to the idea, and got into a routine of having a little chat with each other before turning in. Over the past few weeks there had been a change in both of them. Frankie couldn't quite make out how or why, but he did notice something – especially when his mother helped make sandwiches for the VE Day party, and his father actually organised putting up the trestle-tables!

But not everyone could feel overjoyed by the celebrations. On the evening of the street party, Frankie found Helen sitting on a wooden kitchen chair in the back yard of number 1. Her eyes were glistening with tears as she stared up into the sky, the evening sun casting a deep red glow across her sad face.

'It'll be all right, 'Elen,' Frankie said, putting his arm around his sister's shoulder. 'Now it's all over, you'll find someone else – someone who'll take care of you and the baby.'

'I don't want no one else, Frank,' she said, wistfully. Her hands were resting on her stomach. 'This baby belongs ter Eric. I couldn't let anyone else be its farver.'

'That's not fair, 'Elen.' Frankie had to speak above the din coming from the street party outside. 'Yer can't bring someone back who's – well, who can't come back. So yer 'ave ter fink of the kid now – an' yerself.'

'I *am* finkin' of the kid, Frank. That's why, as

soon as I've 'ad it, I'm goin' ter find a place of me own.'

'What d'yer mean?'

'I'm goin' ter move out, away from 'ere. I've got to stand on me own two feet and I don't want Mum glarin' at me every time the baby bawls its 'ead off.'

Frankie crouched beside her. 'You can't leave 'ere, 'Elen! How're yer goin' ter support yerself?'

'I don't know, yet. But I've got plans. Ivy says she knows someone in Tottenham who might let me 'ave a room in 'er 'ouse. If I can get someone to keep an eye on the baby durin' the day, I could carry on workin' at the shoe shop and pay the rent.'

Frankie took hold of Helen's hands, and squeezed them tight. 'Don't do anyfin' rash, 'Elen. But if yer *really* wanna get out of 'ere, I'll do me best ter 'elp yer. Once I've taken my Matric in July, I'm goin' ter get a job. I promise yer, I'll 'elp yer out.'

Frankie meant what he said. Because of the war, he and quite a few of the other kids had been late starters at Highbury Grammar, so he was having to stay on a bit past the official school-leaving age. But despite his mum and dad's objections, he was determined to have a go at his Matric, thanks mainly to Elsa's encouragement.

Helen felt like bursting into tears. As she

looked at Frankie's wide-open face, she felt such trust in him. He made up for all the loveless years she had suffered from their mother and father. 'You're – marvellous, Frank,' she said, kissing him gently on the forehead. 'I wish you'd have had the chance to meet Eric. You and 'im would've got on so well tergevver.'

There was a street party going on in Hadleigh Villas, too, but Elsa contented herself with watching it from an upstairs window. Earlier in the day, Frankie had turned up to help her drape a large Union Jack flag from the same window and, as she peered out, there was a certain irony in the image she presented.

Like Helen, Elsa was feeling the loss of her husband Robert deeply. In her mind she could see him walking up the street where people were now joining hands to dance around a bonfire. Oh, if only he had lived to see this day, she thought! And, as the early summer evening gave way to a dark night sky, and fireworks skimmed the rooftops to sparkle amongst the stars, she thought back to what it must have been like on that similar night in May just five years before, when the beach at Dunkirk echoed to the sound of tracer bullets and anti-aircraft fire. Yes, she thought, it must have been a night just like this that claimed her Robert, and took him away from her forever . . .

'What yer doin' up 'ere then?'

Elsa, her eyes misty from her lonely vigil at the landing window, turned with a start to find Frankie calling up the stairs to her. He hadn't bothered to knock on the street door, for Elsa now trusted him with his own key to the house.

'Frankie!' Elsa's eyes lit up immediately. 'Why aren't you at the party with everyone else?'

'I could ask you the same question.'

Elsa came down to meet him. 'It's not for me, Frankie. This night is for the British people.'

'So? You're British in't yer?'

Elsa's smile did not reveal that she had been crying. 'In my heart – yes. But not to the people of Hadleigh Villas.'

'That's OK, then.' Frankie waited for her to reach him, then stood aside to let her pass. 'So you can come to *our* party.'

Elsa stopped dead. 'Me? Go to – Merton Street?'

'Why not?'

Elsa paused briefly, then chuckled as she made her way down the last flight of stairs. 'Can you see the look on your neighbours' faces when they see the defeated enemy joining in their victory celebrations?'

'You in't the enemy, Elsa,' said Frankie, as he followed her down the stairs. 'You're one of us. You've always said so, and you are!'

They made their way into the sitting-room, where Elsa went to the fireplace and poked the fire. 'You're a good boy, Frankie. But I couldn't do it. This is a night your family and friends and neighbours have been waiting for. I wouldn't want to spoil it for them.'

'But you wouldn't spoil it for them, Elsa.' Frankie took the poker from her, and replaced it on the companion set. Then he took her by the shoulders. 'Listen to me, Elsa. I've listened ter you a lot of times – and I'm glad I've listened, 'cos' you make more sense than anyone I know. But about this, you've got to listen ter *me*. This is your night just as much as any of that lot out there – in Hadleigh Terrace, Seven Sisters Road, Merton Street, Hornsey Road – anywhere! People have got a lot of fings to put right with you, Elsa. They've got a lot of time ter make up for. Because you gave up somefin important for them, for all of us. You gave up yer husband . . .'

It took all Elsa's strength not to cry. She looked at Frankie. Was this the same boy who had first come knocking at her door to play a silly street game? Was this the boy who, only a few months before, could hardly put two or three sensible words together? But how had it happened? Yes, it was true that she had tried to open his mind by giving him books to read, and to talk to him as her equal. But it was Mister Frankie Lewis himself who had *allowed* his mind to grow. What he was saying not only made sense, but it also made Elsa more aware of herself.

'Tell me just one thing, Frankie,' Elsa said, moving away from the fireplace. 'Are you saying that, if I come to Merton Street, you will be with me?'

To her surprise, Frankie suddenly left the room. He returned immediately, holding her top coat and hat which he had collected from the hall stand. 'I'll be more than wiv you, Elsa,' he said, holding up her coat for her to slip into. 'I won't leave your side for one single second.'

For a brief moment, Elsa stared in awe at him. Then, quickly brushing the tears from her eyes, she smiled broadly and rushed towards him to put on her coat and hat. 'Let's go!'

As she spoke, a cacophony of noisy fireworks exploded in unison high above the Hadleigh Villas' street party outside.

Not far away, the Merton Street party was in full swing. The Gorman brothers, Mike and Bert, were leading a boisterous Conga, which formed outside their house at number 47, then snaked deliriously along Merton, Herslet, Roden, and Pakeman Streets until it reached fever pitch back where it had started. Although it was getting near midnight, the street bonfire was still burning fiercely, for everyone in the street had raided their back yards for anything they could lay their hands on that would burn.

Small groups of residents were sitting around everywhere, chatting, laughing, joining in the sing-song together, and the most unlikely neighbours found themselves dancing with one another. It was, of course, no surprise to see Mike and Bert Gorman dancing with practically every woman in the street, or every man, woman, and child joining in *Knees up Mother Brown*, but to see snooty Mrs Robinson from number 22 doing a cheek-to-cheek pastiche of the tango with Ma Digby the greengrocer was something no resident of Merton Street had ever expected to see. But this was the end of nearly six years of war and nobody cared what they did as long as they enjoyed themselves.

Another surprise was Gracie and Reg Lewis. Not only had they both taken the trouble to spruce themselves up a bit, but, once they had got through a few glasses of blackmarket gin and brown ale, they even joined in the spirit of the occasion by dancing a waltz with each other. At one time, Prof's Auntie Hilda tried to get him to partner her in the waltz. But Prof hated dancing. He felt very out of it all, especially as Frankie seemed to have deserted the party. Patty Jackson was there, too, with Alan Downs. But she was in a furious mood. Earlier in the evening Jeff Murray had tried to force her to take her knickers down in the secluded darkness of his family's back yard.

It was about twenty-past eleven when Helen's friend, Ivy Villiers, turned up at Merton Street. With her was a good-looking young man in an ill-fitting suit. He looked as though he hadn't had a decent meal in months and he smoked his cigarette in the side of his lips, clearly to give the impression that he was more grown up than he really was. All the partygoers were delighted that Ivy had at last found herself a boyfriend and, as the two of them made their way through the crowds, they were constantly dragged into one of the endless knees-ups that were destined to carry on throughout the night. When they finally managed to break loose, Ivy caught sight of Gracie and Reg Lewis who were sitting on one of the front garden coping-stones. She left her young man for a moment, and went across to talk to them.

''Allo, Mrs Lewis,' she said, expecting a frosty response. 'I'm Helen's friend, Ivy.'

''Course you are, dear.' Even by the light of the bonfire, Ivy could see that Gracie had been drinking, for her cheeks were red, her hair was dishevelled, and perspiration was trickling down from her forehead. Ivy was both surprised and relieved to get a smile from her. ''Ow are yer, Ivy? Long time no see.'

'I'm very well, thank you, Mrs Lewis.'

''Ow about a drink, gel?' Reg Lewis got up. In his hand was a quart bottle of brown ale which was almost empty. By the way he swayed unsteadily on his feet, it was not the first bottle he had consumed that evening. 'What ya say we douse those bleedin' German gits once an' fer all? OK?'

Ivy laughed with him, but shook her head. 'No, fanks all the same Mr Lewis. I just come in ter see if 'Elen's around?'

Gracie downed the last of her gin. 'Last I saw of 'er, she was sittin' out in the back yard. I tried ter get 'er out 'ere, but she don't feel up to it.'

'Would you mind if I go in and see er then?'

''Course not, dear. 'Elp yourself. The front door's open.'

'Fank yer, Mrs Lewis! Fank you!'

Gracie watched Ivy rush off, not really knowing why the girl was so grateful, or so excited. She was even more curious when the young man who was waiting for Ivy nearby, smiled across at her. Gracie smiled back, and raised her empty glass at him. She had no idea why she did it.

Ivy made her way down the dark hall passage of number 1, and out into the back yard. Although there was a hard wooden chair out there, Helen was nowhere to be seen. ''Elen! You out 'ere?' There was no response, so she turned back into the house. But, just as she was about to make her way along the dark passage again, Helen's voice called to her from the Anderson shelter.

'Ivy? Is that you?'

''Elen!'

'I'm down 'ere – in the shelter.'

For the past half-hour or so, Helen had been sitting in the dark. Although she felt guilty that she was not joining in the celebrations, the end of the war only meant to her that Eric would not be among those who would return to enjoy the peace.

''Ang on a minute 'Elen!' Helen could hear Ivy's voice competing with the distant festivities and fireworks from the street outside. 'I'll be right wiv yer!'

Helen pulled herself up in the uncomfortable old armchair that her mother always sat in. Then she waited for Ivy to pull back the blanket that covered the entrance. She couldn't understand why she was taking so long to come down.

'Ivy?' she called tentatively. 'Are yer there?'

Just a little concerned, Helen levered herself up and stood in front of the entrance. However, just as she did so, the blanket was pulled apart, although all she could see was a silhouette against the distant kitchen light.

'Ivy?'

The silhouette came down into the shelter and drew the blanket across the entrance again. Then Helen heard a soft, gentle voice calling to her. But it wasn't Ivy's.

''Ow's my gel, then?'

Helen felt a chill go down her spine as she heard the voice – a voice that, night after night, she had heard in her dreams. A voice she'd never expected to hear again in her waking hours. 'Eric!' She wanted to yell, but all she could do was to croak. And then, suddenly, she felt arms around her, holding her tightly, clasping her and their coming child against a firm, warm body. 'Eric!'

For the next few minutes, no more words were spoken. But Helen's tears of joy were quickly smothered in kisses, her hair pushed away from her face.

Outside, Ivy cried so much she had to blow her nose at least three times. By then she thought it was about time she went back to the party to find herself a boyfriend of her own.

It was almost midnight when Frankie got back to Merton Street with Elsa. The celebrations were still going strong and, for the first few moments nobody noticed their arrival. The Gorman brothers had organised a mass sing-song, and as the Merton Street roof-tops echoed to the sound of *Don't Fence Me In* and *She'll Be Coming Round the Mountain*, Frankie and Elsa made their way to number 1, where Gracie and Reg were still sitting on the front coping-stone, singing their hearts out with everyone else. Just as they got there, several people caught sight of them and immediately stopped singing. Doris Simmons from number 37 stopped playing her harmonica, which caused the Gorman brothers to turn and, by the time Frankie and Elsa had reached Gracie and Reg, all heads were turned to look at them.

'Mum. Dad. I want you to meet a friend of mine.' Frankie was completely composed as he stood before his mother and father.

Gracie remained sitting, but Reg, his eyes glaring hard through a haze of brown ale, slowly raised himself up.

'This is Elsa,' Frankie said. 'Mrs Elsa Barclay.'

Gracie and Reg just stared at Elsa, without replying. Suddenly the air was charged with tension.

Then Gracie put her glass down and stood up and held her hand out to Elsa. ''Allo, Mrs Barclay,' she said, making a surpeme effort to smile. 'We've met before – in't we?'

Frankie was shocked, and swung a startled look back at Elsa.

'Yes, Mrs Lewis.' Elsa also smiled, and held out her hand. 'It's so nice to meet you again.'

Most people seemed absolutely astonished as they watched the two women shake hands with great warmth.

'Reg,' said Gracie. 'In't yer goin' ter get Mrs Barclay a drink, then?'

Reg Lewis didn't reply. Swaying, he turned tail, and walked off without saying a word.

It was Bert Gorman who lightened the atmosphere. Stepping forward from the crowd of subdued people who had been watching the whole exchange, he went straight to Elsa and said with a smile, ''Ere, Mrs Barclay. Yer wouldn't care ter buy an old lavatory seat, would yer? Me and my bruvver 'ave got one goin' cheap!'

Laughing, Elsa replied. 'You have a deal, Mr Gorman. There is always a good sale for one of those!'

One or two people in the crowd chuckled, and then everyone erupted into laughter. Then Elsa, Frankie, and Gracie joined in and, within a few minutes, the party had resumed with gusto.

The revelry went on until nearly daybreak, and did not come to an end until everyone had sung a rousing and emotional chorus of *Land of Hope and Glory*, followed closely by *God Save the King*, which echoed around the rooftops of not only Merton Street, but was heard as far away as the main Holloway Road itself.

Elsa joined in the final rendition of the National Anthem. And why shouldn't she? thought Frankie. After all, she was as British as anyone there . . .

Chapter Eighteen

A few days after VE Day, Winston was finally allowed home. His back leg was still encased in plaster, so he made it quite clear to everyone he met that he required a great deal of attention and from his reclining position at the foot of Frankie's bed he graciously accepted any left-overs from meal times that anyone cared to offer. Frankie was his main supplier, but Helen was also good for the odd boiled potato or half a sava-loy. Winston's big surprise, however, was when Gracie Lewis started coming up the stairs to give him the odd tit-bit. At first he growled and bared his teeth at her, for Gracie had never been any-thing but hostile to him. But he very quickly accepted her peace offerings of shepherd's pie and tinned peas with gratitude.

There was no doubt that, since the VE night street party, Helen's reunion with Eric Sibley had been the main topic of conversation among the residents of Merton Street. It was, they said, nothing short of a miracle that Eric had been released from a prisoner-of-war camp in Germany and sent back home just in time for the VE Day celebrations. For Helen, of course, Eric's return home was a gift from God and, although she wasn't a religious person, the first thing she did after the VE night street party was to go to church. At last her life seemed to be taking a turn for the better, for Eric had immediately asked her to marry him.

Frankie was thrilled that his sister would now have a husband to look after her and their baby, but he couldn't help feeling just a little sad when the couple announced that they had found a couple of rooms to rent in Tottenham, and would be moving there as soon as they could make the arrangements. Luckily, Frankie and Eric immediately got on like a house on fire, and when Eric asked his future brother-in-law to be best man at the Registry Office wedding, Frankie was over the moon – although scared to death at what his 'duties' would entail. To everyone's astonishment, Eric's introduction to Reg and Gracie Lewis turned out to be far less agonising than had been thought. In fact, Gracie asked him over to Sunday lunch and Eric and his future father-in-law got through at least two quart bottles of brown ale, followed by nearly half a bottle of whisky.

Frankie watched his mother and father's open-armed behaviour with incredulity. Times were indeed changing at number 1 Merton Street!

Winston, though, was not happy about the new contender for his master's affections. Frankie had been seeing Maggs Fletcher for some time now and referred to her as 'my girl-friend', but though it was quite obvious that Maggs was a dog-lover who not only stroked him a great deal and had once given him a pork bone she had saved from her dinner, Winston did not take too kindly to the arrangement.

Although it hadn't yet occurred to him, there was no doubt that Maggs Fletcher was beginning to mean something to Frankie. She was after all a lovely girl with bright, violet-coloured eyes, a fresh complexion with just a few freckles on her cheeks, and honey-blonde hair that tumbled down over her shoulders. Frankie loved to listen to her, for she had a velvet soft voice, although her laugh sounded really quite infectious. The only other slight problem for Frankie was that Maggs came from a fairly posh family. Her father was a bank manager and her mother helped out at the WVS and held afternoon bridge parties at their home in smart Canonbury Square, just behind Highbury Corner.

About a week before his birthday at the end of May, Frankie took Maggs to the pictures. They decided on the old Rink Cinema at Finsbury Park for there was a spooky ghost film playing there called, *A Place of One's Own* with James Mason and Margaret Lockwood, and although it had an A Certificate, both Frankie and Maggs could now easily pass for sixteen year olds.

For their first visit to the 'flicks' together, Frankie lashed out on the top-priced one shilling seats which took them to the exclusive but limited seating area in the circle. As the Rink used to be exactly what its name implied, a roller skating rink, the cinema still resembled exactly that. It was an oval-shaped barn of a place, with the narrowest of circle seats which seemed miles away from the very distant screen. But it was a great favourite for courting couples, and, very self-consciously, Frankie and Maggs chose two seats in the dark and secluded back row.

When they arrived, the *March of Time* magazine film was still playing, so they paid very little attention to it. The B feature was one of the *Dagwood Bumpstead* films, but all through it both Frankie and Maggs sat absolutely upright in their seats, almost nervous to say anything to each other. When the house lights went up, Frankie bought two tubs of ice-cream which lasted until the main feature started. For some time, however, there continued to be no real communication between the two, even though neither of them was really concentrating on the film.

Luckily, the spirit world came to the rescue. During a particularly spooky moment when ghostly goings-on were emerging on to the Rink's distant cinema screen, someone in the audience screamed. To Frankie's absolute astonishment, Maggs was so shocked she threw herself straight into his arms and buried her face in his chest. It took both of them a moment or so to take in what had happened, but when it did they both enjoyed the outcome. Their hearts thumping with an excitement which neither could understand, Frankie put both his arms around Maggs and held her as tightly as he could right to the end of the film. All the way through, Frankie found himself either squeezing Maggs' hand or brushing the hair from her face. Both of them felt a warm glow surging through their blood, but it was only just before the film came to an end that Frankie gathered all his courage, raised Maggs' head, and kissed her lightly on the forehead. In the darkness, Maggs could feel herself blushing, but she wanted Frankie to do this, and returned his kiss with a full one on his lips. They were still locked in this position when the lights went up, and an impatient usherette yelled: 'Show's over!'

Frankie and Maggs strolled down Seven Sisters Road as though there was no one else in the whole wide world. With his arm around Maggs' shoulder, and her arm around his waist, Frankie compared the kiss he had given Maggs to the way Errol Flynn had kissed Olivia de Havilland in *The Adventures of Robin Hood*. But he reckoned that Maggs kissed far better than Olivia de Havilland. As for Maggs, well, though she had had a couple of casual boyfriends before Frankie, her feelings for him were different from anything she had known before . . .

Frankie's birthday turned out far better than he expected. Not only did his mother and father buy him a new Bing Crosby record, the first birthday present he had ever had from them, they also gave him ten shillings towards the bicycle he was saving up for. And Helen and Eric, who had now moved into their rented rooms in Tottenham, sent him a birthday card with a postal order for five shillings enclosed.

Soon after school, Frankie collected the money he had saved in his money-box and called on Prof. They made their way to Pascall's Bicycle Shop. On the way, all Frankie could talk about was the great bike rally to Southend that was taking place on the following Sunday week to celebrate VE Day, and the fact that by then he would be able to raise the last five shillings to buy the bike of his dreams and join the Merton Street gang on the best day's outing they had ever known.

By the time they reached the corner of Hadleigh Villas, Frankie's heart was thumping so hard with excitement he felt his legs would collapse beneath him. As they waited on the corner to cross the road, Pascall's was in clear view, just waiting for Frankie to get there and put a deposit on the Raleigh sports bike that had been gathering dust in the shop window for at least the past six months.

It was only when they reached the entrance to the shop itself that Frankie felt as though his stomach had dropped out.

'It's gone!'

The bike was no longer suspended on a wire display and, even though Frankie and Prof were pressing their noses hard against the shop window, they could see no sign of the bike anywhere.

'It's around somewhere.' Prof did his best to sound reassuring. 'It's been in the window a hell of a time. Perhaps they've put it round the back of the shop or something?'

Crazed with anxiety, Frankie didn't wait another minute before rushing into the shop.

The shopkeeper was a huge, rotund man, who looked as though there was no bicycle in the world that could hold his weight. 'Yes, young man,' he called, emerging from the counter at the back of the shop, a pipe smoking in his mouth. 'What can I do for you?'

'The Raleigh,' Frankie was spluttering out his words. 'The one in the window. It was there for ages.'

'The blue Sports, you mean?'

'Yes! Yes! I want ter buy it.'

'Ah!' The man raised his head just enough to blow out a puff of pungent pipe smoke. 'Took 'er out a couple of days ago. 'Ad a good run for 'er money'.

'But where is it?' There was a note of sheer

desperation in Frankie's voice. 'It is still 'ere, in't it?'

The man shook his head. 'Sorry, son. Sold it to a customer. Paid ready cash for it.'

Frankie's heart missed a beat. 'But yer can't! Yer can't 'ave sold it! 'I've 'ad my eyes on it for ages, ever since yer first put it in the window.'

'Well that's not my fault, son. If yer wanted it so badly, why din't yer buy it before now? If yer'd asked me nicely, I'd 'ave knocked off five bob or so just ter get rid of it. This is a shop, yer know. We 'ave ter sell when we get the chance.'

Frankie felt as though his whole world had collapsed around him. It was gone. After all his hard efforts it had gone, and he would *never* get the chance to join the Merton Street gang on the VE Bike Rally.

'It's not the only bike in the shop, yer know. 'There's a coupla nice secondhand BSA's out the back. If yer like I'll go an' bring 'em out?'

By the time the man had finished speaking, Frankie and Prof had already left the shop.

Frankie slouched his way back along the Seven Sisters Road, totally dejected. He had dreamt about owning that bike, of being part of the great throng of cyclists who would be gathering together on the great Victory Rally to Southend. And now, instead, he would be a laughing stock among the likes of Jeff Murray and Patty Jackson. Frankie could think about nothing but the hateful person who had robbed him of that bike, of the one thing he had set his heart on.

'Look, Frankie,' said Prof. 'I know how much going to the Rally means to you. So you can take my bike. I don't care if I go or not and anyway, the doctor says I'm not supposed to do too much cycling. Not good for my heart, he says.'

'I don't want yer bike,' Frankie grunted, his hands sunk deep into his pockets.

'But you'd only be borrowing it for the day.'

Without thinking, Frankie, eyes blazing, suddenly turned on his friend. ''Ow many times do I 'ave ter tell yer! I don't want yer bike. I don't want no one's bike. I saved up fer *this* one. It should'a bin mine! Mine!'

'But you'll get another one, Frankie, far better than that one, you'll see. And you could take mine just for the Rally.'

Frankie's response was snarling and ugly. 'You stupid little ponce! Don't you understand that when yer've set yer 'eart on somefin', yer don't want nuffin' else! Nuffin'! That's the trouble wiv you – yer in't got a brain between yer ears!'

To Prof's absolute horror, Frankie suddenly turned away from him, and ran off down the Seven Sisters Road.

Prof had never known Frankie behave like this before and he went home, his thoughts bleak. Frankie clearly hated the sight of him, so from now on it would be best if he kept away from him . . .

* * *

All Frankie could think about was the Raleigh Sports that had disappeared from Pascall's shop window. The thought that some spoilt rich kid was at this moment riding around the streets of Islington on *his* bike was killing him.

At half-past six he got washed and changed into a clean shirt and a new Tootal tie which Eric had given him. Tonight, as it was his sixteenth birthday, Elsa had invited him and Maggs to come round for supper. Even though Frankie had told her quite a lot about Maggs, Elsa had never met her before. The least he could do was to look clean and tidy, which meant borrowing some his father's Brylcreem to make his unruly hair look a little more cared for.

At seven o'clock, Frankie collected Maggs from the bus stop just outside the Marlborough Cinema. It was quite a warm evening and Maggs was wearing a pretty plain blue cotton dress and a short navy-blue jacket. She was disappointed when Frankie didn't make any comment about the way she looked, for she had deliberately tried to make herself look nice for his birthday supper.

As they crossed the Holloway Road and walked down Tollington Road together, Frankie was in a sullen mood, and when he told Maggs why, she got quite irritated by the fact that he was more interested in a bicycle than herself.

When they got to number 19, Elsa gave them such a welcome that Maggs adored her straight away.

'People shouldn't have long faces on their birthday,' said Elsa, pulling up Frankie's chin and staring straight into his face. But when Frankie told her about the bike that had disappeared from Pascall's shop window, she shook her head sadly and gave him no comfort at all by saying that one just had to accept the disappointments that come in life.

Over dinner, Maggs gave Frankie her birthday present to him. But it only caused Frankie more despair, for it turned out to be an illustrated book about bicycling through the ages.

Maggs and Elsa spent a great deal of time talking to each other and Elsa was astonished how much Maggs knew about Germany before the war. Furthermore, Maggs could speak a few words of German, which sent her high in Elsa's estimation.

'Now comes the highlight of the evening,' announced Elsa, as she disappeared from the dining-room. 'Eyes should be closed tight,' she called.

'No cheating!' warned Maggs, for Elsa had confided to her what was to come.

After a moment, the kitchen door opened to a blaze of flickering light. 'Happy Birthday to you,' sang Elsa, with Maggs joining in.

Frankie quickly opened his eyes to see a huge birthday cake with sixteen lighted candles illuminating the room.

'Elsa!' Frankie's eyes lit up with excitement. It

was the first time in his whole life that anyone had taken any trouble at all over his birthday and suddenly he felt he was no longer a child, but a man.

'It's my own special recipe,' proclaimed Elsa, 'with sultanas and apples. I'm not so good at the icing, but I guarantee it tastes good!'

Frankie and Maggs stared in awe at the cake. The white icing had blue writing on it which read: '*Happy Birthday – my good friend Mister Frankie.*' Frankie felt like crying, for it was the most beautiful thing he had ever seen.

'Well – don't just sit there you foolish boy!' Elsa handed Frankie the cake knife. 'If we're going to get poisoned, let's get it over with.' And she added, with a wry smile, 'And please don't forget to take a piece for my friend, Winston!'

Frankie took the cake-knife, and positioned it on the cake.

'Blow out the candles, Frank,' whispered Maggs. 'But close your eyes first and make a wish.'

Frankie closed his eyes and wished. But, even though he didn't tell Elsa and Maggs what he was wishing for, they didn't have to guess very hard. Then he took a deep breath and blew for all he was worth and every candle was immediately extinguished.

Elsa and Maggs cheered and applauded energetically.

'So what did you wish for, Frank?' asked Maggs.

'Wishes are supposed to be secret,' he said suddenly deflated. 'But they never come true, so what difference does it make?'

At this point, Elsa, who had had a private conversation with Maggs before they ate, exchanged a pointed glance with the girl. 'Wishes are like everything else, Frankie. They don't come for nothing. They have to be worked for.'

Frankie cut three slices of cake. 'We need plates.'

'I'm feeling just a little worn out, Frankie,' replied Elsa. 'Be a good fellow and get some. They're in the kitchen.'

Frankie put down the cake knife and went off to the kitchen. But he had hardly entered the room when Elsa and Maggs heard the loudest yell of delight they had been expecting.

'No! It's not possible!' Frankie bellowed.

Elsa and Maggs, with wide grins, got up from the dining-table and made their way into the kitchen. When they got there, they found Frankie sitting on the saddle of the bicycle that had disappeared from Pascall's window. Frankie was in such a state of ecstasy and excitement that he could hardly breathe.

'Happy Birthday, Frankie!' chorused Elsa and Maggs, hugging each other.

'But how . . . when . . .?' Eagerly inspecting the

five-speed gear on the shining bike and impatiently trying out the pedals and bell, Frankie spluttered excitedly, 'It was you, Elsa! *You* bought it.'

'I was sick to death of seeing the thing stuck in that shop window.' Elsa was beaming. 'After all, you were going to get it sooner or later – so why not now?'

Frankie leapt off the saddle and threw his arms around her. 'Elsa, you're the most wonderful woman in the whole wide world!'

'Oh yes!' said Elsa. 'I bet you tell that to all the young ladies!'

That night, Frankie didn't sleep a wink. Now he really would be able to hold his own with the Merton Street gang on the Victory Rally to Southend the following Sunday. He had got what he wanted and the dream-bike was his. No one would take it away from him – no one. But at what sacrifice had he got it?

At nine o'clock next morning, he hurried along the Seven Sisters Road and stopped outside the door beside the Ladies Handbag shop, and rang the bell. After a moment he heard Prof's familiar footsteps coming down the stairs, and when he opened the door they just stared at each other.

Prof looked bewildered, until Frankie said, 'I'm sorry, Prof. I'm really sorry. Forgive me?' Then he held out his hand.

Prof paused for only a brief moment, and then

his solemn look turned into a radiant smile. 'Nothing to forgive!' he beamed, and shook his old pal firmly by the hand.

Half an hour later they were making arrangements for their entry in the great Victory Day Rally to Southend . . .

Chapter Nineteen

On Sunday, 2nd June, Finsbury Park echoed to the yells and laughter of nearly three hundred exuberant pedal cyclists. Although it was only six o'clock in the morning, there was already a good deal of warmth in the rising sun and, as the sky and trees and playing fields gradually became bathed in a spectacular red glow, the intrepid entrants in the great VE Day rally completed the last checks on their tyres, handlebars, saddles, and wheel-chains. Hopes were high that the weather would provide them with a radiant day, and even though war was still raging against the Japanese enemy on the other side of the world, this magical Sunday in June would be the first opportunity to celebrate, in style, the long-awaited peace in Europe.

Frankie and Prof were amongst the first batch of entrants to gather on the old playing fields on the Seven Sisters Road side of the park, Frankie astride his brand new Raleigh Sports and Prof on his old-fashioned 'banger' with the rusty straight handlebars. It was an odd feeling for everyone, for during the war those same fields had been taken over by the RAF who used them to operate their huge, silver-coloured barrage balloons, which had helped to save a great deal of Islington from aerial attack by low-flying enemy aircraft. Frankie was wearing his school football shorts and vest for the ride, but when Jeff Murray turned up, his old man had rigged him out in a flashy outfit that made him look as though he was about to compete in the Olympic Games. Patty also wore shorts, folded up as far as they would go, clearly hoping that she would prove a great attraction to the young male riders. Alan Downs turned up in an old pair of army trousers that had once belonged to his elder brother.

'So – who's in the money then?' Jeff strolled around Frankie's new cycle, inspecting it condescendingly as though it was kids' stuff. 'Yer don't reckon you're gonna make it all the way to Southend on that ole heap, do yer? Yer'll be lucky ter get ter the uvver side of the park!'

As usual, Jeff played to the crowds, who duly roared with laughter at his pathetic joke.

'At least I won't need an engine ter get there,' quipped Frankie, referring to Jeff's motorcycle. 'Not like some people.'

To everyone's delight, except Jeff's, Frankie's quick repartee got just as big a jeering laugh.

A few minutes later a great cheer heralded the start of the rally, and the mass of bicycles and their enthusiastic riders poured along the inner park road, and gradually headed out through the Manor House entrance. Jeff, Alan, and Patty immediately crept up into the advance group, but Frankie and Prof decided to take their time and enjoy every bit of the long journey.

Helen Lewis had set her alarm clock for six-thirty. It was a bit on the early side for a Sunday morning, but she and Eric had decided that they would go down to the High Street and wave Frankie on as he cycled by on the Rally to Southend.

The two rooms they had rented in St Anne's Road, Tottenham, weren't exactly paradise, but to Helen they represented the kind of home she had always dreamt of sharing with the man she loved. And since he came home from his days as a POW in Germany, Helen had confirmed to herself that she was indeed hopelessly in love with him. It wasn't just that the father of her child had returned from the dead, or even that she was able to set up her own home. What she really cherished was just being with him, to sit and talk with him, to feel his arms around her in bed at night. Helen was now nearly six months pregnant and, when her baby arrived during the coming August, she was determined to show Eric that he would not regret having put her in 'the family way'.

The only problem in Helen's life now were her

parents. It wasn't her father she worried about so much, but her mother. Although Gracie Lewis had more or less accepted Eric as a future son-in-law, the prospect of being a grandmother was clearly upsetting her. Helen felt totally depressed about her mother's persistent refusal even to discuss her future grandchild. But Eric had ideas of his own how to deal with that little problem.

Which was why Gracie and Reg Lewis were being invited to tea that Sunday evening.

A few miles away, in posh Canonbury Square, Maggs Fletcher was also having a few problems with her parents. Sidney and Jennifer Fletcher were nice people, and Maggs loved them very much. But, because she was an only child, they were very possessive of her. Whatever she did, they had to know about.

Although they had never actually met Frankie Lewis, the Fletchers were very apprehensive about their daughter having regular dates with someone from 'the other part of Islington'. To them, Holloway might have been the slums of Calcutta, and the people who lived there – especially around the Nags Head – were – well, 'different'. So when she was told on Sunday morning that she could not go to Finsbury Park to see Frankie off on the Rally to Southend, Maggs threw the type of tantrum that she had never shown to Frankie.

'You're just doing it because you're prejudiced!'

Maggs yelled at her father, as he and her mother packed some picnic things in the back of their Rover. 'I'll be seventeen years old this year, yet you're treating me like a kid in nursery school!'

'Then stop behaving like a kid in nursery school!' her father snapped back. 'You're going out for the day with your mother and me – and that's final!'

Jennifer Fletcher was more conciliatory. She looked a lot like her daughter, with the same violet-coloured eyes and fresh complexion, although her honey-blonde hair was just showing the first signs of grey beneath her headscarf. 'It'll be a lovely day, Maggs dear. There's some beautiful countryside down in Surrey, and while your father goes off to play his silly old golf, you and I can go for a stroll.'

'I don't want to go to Surrey, and I don't want to go for a stroll!' Maggs' voice was now raised far beyond the accepted norm in Canonbury Square. 'You know very well you're just trying to get me away from Frankie. You object to him, even though you haven't met him!'

Maggs' father was becoming very irritated with his daughter 'Now you listen to me, young lady . . .'

As always, Jennifer Fletcher acted quickly to avoid a scene. 'It's all right, Sidney, dear,' she said, doing her best to soothe her husband's rising temper. 'Maggs is just a little tired that's all. After all, she's got her exams in a few weeks' time, and it's very early in the morning to get her out of bed.'

Sidney Fletcher sighed in exasperation. Once again his wife was giving in to their daughter's tantrums. He gave a dismissive wave of the hand and started cleaning the front windscreen of his car.

Jennifer put her arm around Maggs' shoulder, and whispered in her ear. 'Come inside and help me finish making the sandwiches.'

Reluctantly, Maggs followed her mother back into the house. Their feet echoed on the black and white marble tiled floor of the front hall as they made their way into the ornate kitchen at the back of the house.

'You mustn't keep upsetting your father like that, Maggs.' Jennifer was at the kitchen table, cutting in half fish paste sandwiches that she had already made. 'He loves you very much, you know. He just doesn't want to see you get hurt, that's all.'

Maggs crossed her arms and watched her mother. 'Then why does he object to my seeing Frankie?'

'He doesn't object! It's just that – well, he's a little nervous about who you're seeing. After all, you're the only daughter we have.'

'It's because he lives in the wrong part of Islington, isn't it?'

'That's silly, Maggs. I won't have you talking like that!'

'Then why don't you let me do the things *I* want to do – meet the people *I* want to meet?'

'Now you're being selfish.'

'I *like* Frankie. In fact – I'm in love with him.'

Jennifer turned with a start. 'Love? At your age!'

'Stop being so pompous, Mother. This is 1945. Everything is different to your day.'

Now it was Jennifer's turn to get angry with her daughter. 'Love is not the prerogative of young people!' Then, slamming down the knife she was using to cut the sandwiches, she snapped, 'Going out with this boy has got nothing to do with love. Love is something that has to grow. And before that happens you have to get to know someone awfully well.'

Suddenly, Jennifer felt guilty for having spoken so sharply to the girl. She turned to her and tried to smile sympathetically. 'All I'm saying Maggs is that you're too young to be talking about such things. In time you'll get to know lots of boys. Eventually, you'll find the right one.'

'As long as he doesn't come from the wrong part of Islington!' Maggs' otherwise pretty jaw was fixed stubbornly as she glared back defiantly. 'Isn't that what you mean, Mother?'

Jennifer sighed deeply. She was clearly making no impression on her daughter. 'All I'm saying, dear, is: be careful. If you get too involved, well – I think you're old enough now to know what *could* happen.'

As she turned back to her sandwiches, Jennifer was totally unprepared for her daughter's response.

'I'm sorry, Mother. It's a little too late for that now.'

Jennifer Fletcher dropped her sandwich knife on the floor and turned back to Maggs with a look of horror.

Behind them, Maggs' father was standing in the open kitchen doorway. What he had just heard made him feel as if he had just been hit by a doodle-bug.

Despite the early hour, the people of Tottenham turned out in force to cheer the three hundred or so cyclists who were huffing and puffing their way along the Seven Sisters Road. By the time they reached the cinema on the corner of Broad Lane, there was a sizeable crowd which included Helen and Eric.

Frankie and Prof were almost lost amongst the great mass of Raleighs and other bikes that were being clicked into gear. When Helen finally caught a glimpse of Frankie near the tail end of the winding procession, she rushed into the road and yelled out for all she was worth. Eric joined her and pushed something into Frankie's hand. As the cyclists had to keep on the move, it wasn't until he had left Helen and Eric behind that he was able to see what his future brother-in-law had passed on to him. It was a ten shilling note.

In great excitement, Frankie turned back and yelled at the top of his voice: 'Eric! Fanks . . .!' Helen and Eric waved back, waited for the last of the procession to disappear down Bruce Grove, then slowly made their way back home.

Within an hour or so the Rally had thinned out considerably. The route planned had taken them via Walthamstow and then out on to the Southend Road, where the bike lanes alongside the main road itself were already jammed with cyclists riding single file for miles out into the Essex countryside. It was very nearly forty miles from Finsbury Park to Southend-on-sea, and those who were not used to peddling such long and arduous journeys soon found it hard going. Frankie was one of them, and despite the joy of at last owning his long-cherished bike, even in top gear he had to work hard to get up some of those hills. On the whole, however, most of the cycle-paths were quite long and straight and Frankie had the opportunity to savour for the first time the English countryside in early summer, lush green fields dotted with an explosion of flirting yellow buttercups, and rows upon rows of bungalows and little terraced houses that all looked the same. He adored the ecstasy of the wind rushing against his face, and the hot June sun beating down on to his head and bare arms. All along the route small groups of cheering people had gathered to wave flags or hold up encouraging 'V' signs and, in some of the smaller villages, trestle-tables were set up with bottles of free lemonade and slices of home-made bread. The Southend Rally had provided everyone with the chance to show their joy at the end of a long and ugly war.

However, by the time Frankie and Prof reached Laindon, which was a little over half way, it became hotter than they had bargained for and they stopped for a brief drink of water from a public roadside tap. Then, after knotting their handkerchiefs around their heads to protect themselves from the burning sun, they set off on the remaining part of the journey. Once or twice Frankie became a little nervous about Prof who quite often trailed far behind him. Frankie didn't believe his pal's story that the doctors had approved of his taking part in the Rally, that they'd decided the exercise would do his heart condition a lot of good. But, surprisingly, Prof's stamina held out. After a time he managed to catch up and, in a sudden burst of energy, even overtook Frankie.

The long journey also gave Frankie the opportunity to turn things over in his mind. He thought about the last time he had come along this road, before the war, with dozens of kids from his Pakeman Street Junior School. Frankie remembered the old double-decker bus the kids had travelled on, with the top deck and curved staircase open to the weather, and the horrified look of passers-by as they heard the yells and whistles of hordes of London kids on their way to their first glimpse of the seaside. Frankie also thought a lot about Elsa, and how he would never have been able to make this trip without her help. Elsa, too, had given him so much confidence, not only to do things that he had never done before, but also confidence in himself. She was the first person in Frankie's life who had actually taken the time and trouble to sit down and talk to him. Since he had met Elsa, he had somehow got to understand things. There was a time when he acted first and thought afterwards, but now he considered things carefully before taking action. Frankie thought back to the VE-night party in Merton Street, and how he had discovered that his mother had been to visit Elsa in the jumble shop. When he had heard about that meeting from Elsa he'd wanted to go back home and tell his mother that she had no right to go snooping on his friends, and that she was nothing but an interfering cow. But, as usual, Elsa had persuaded him that what his mother had done was no more than what any other mother would do, and that far from interfering, Gracie Lewis had been most responsible. Frankie thought an awful lot about Elsa on that rapturous journey along the cycle lanes of Essex. And he came to the conclusion that she was a remarkable woman.

He also thought a lot about Maggs. He was missing her more than he had ever thought possible . . .

It was after eleven o'clock before the Fletcher family left Canonbury Square for their picnic in Surrey.

Maggs could have kicked herself for suggesting to her mother that her friendship with Frankie had already 'gone too far'. It was not only untrue, but very cruel. For three hours she had sat in the family kitchen being interrogated by her father, while her mother paced the room in tears. However, when she eventually decided to tell her parents that she had only said it because they were being so horrible about her going out with a boy from the 'wrong part of Islington', they wouldn't believe her.

There were lots of tearful comments from Jennifer like 'Oh, when your poor grandmother hears about this, it's enough to kill her!' to 'Is this the way we brought you up? To behave like an animal!' from her father, who was, more than anything else, angry at the prospect of missing his day's golf.

In the end, Maggs felt thoroughly ashamed of herself, and said that she hadn't meant to hurt her parents. But before she agreed to go on the awful Sunday picnic, she at least got a promise from them that she could bring Frankie over to tea one day.

Sitting on her own in the back of her parents'

car, Maggs could think of no one else but Frankie. And despite the fact that she didn't much care for bicycle rides, she would have done anything in the world to have been with him on that trip to Southend . . .

Southend-on-sea was looking its absolute best. The sun was shining out of a clear blue sky, the sea was calm and thousands of holiday-makers were crowded on to the beach, where there was hardly an inch between mums and dads of all shapes and sizes, babies bawling their heads off, and kids trying to build sandcastles or leap in and out of the water. Nearly all of them were day-trippers, most of them Cockneys from the East End of London – hence the nickname Southend picked up over the years – 'London-by-the-sea'. But the locals were glad to see the old place thriving again after almost six sparse war years, and already the Kursaal Amusement Park was full to capacity, and the pubs, ice-cream bars, and bangers-and-mash shops were doing a roaring trade.

The VE Rally cyclists had been swarming into the town since before noon and cycles of every colour and design – some new, most of them old crocks – were padlocked up all along the seafront, and the queues at the jellied eel stalls seemed endless.

Frankie and Prof didn't catch up with the Merton Street lot until after noon, for, unlike Jeff

Murray, they had not considered the Rally to be a race. However, when they did meet up inside the Kursaal Park, Jeff was in his usual bombastic mood.

'What kept you?' Jeff called, as he, Patty, and Alan, all laughing hysterically, climbed out of the ghost train.

Frankie ignored the jibes – it was one of the things he'd learnt to do over the past few months and it took him very little time to realise that he didn't really enjoy their company any more, that he had simply outgrown them. 'Me and Prof are goin' off ter get some bangers,' he said. 'I'm starvin'!'

'Don't tell me you're too scared ter go on the Scenic Railway?' Now it was Patty Jackson's turn to be part of the comedy act.

'Yeah,' quipped Jeff. 'Yer might get sun-stroke if that 'anky blows off yer 'ead!'

He and Patty burst into hysterical laughter again but Alan Downs didn't join in. To him, it was all beginning to seem a bit silly.

'We'll maybe see yer later, then,' Frankie called back.

Frankie and Prof hurried off and disappeared amongst the crowds. Although she did her best not to show it, Patty was sorry to see Frankie go. During the past few months he had changed. She really quite fancied him now . . .

Making sure that their bicycles were safe and

secure amongst all the others huddled together on the seafront, Frankie and Prof headed as fast as they could to the bangers-and-mash café on the opposite side of the promenade. The Amusement Arcades were jammed to suffocation and, wherever they walked, families were strolling along in 'Kiss Me Quick' hats and stuffing themselves with candy floss, sticks of peppermint-flavoured Southend rock, and endless cornets of hand twisted Rossi's ice-cream.

After queuing for nearly twenty minutes, Frankie and Prof were back on the promenade tucking into their mouth-watering sausages which were smothered in fried onions, and embedded in a great lump of pease pudding – which to Frankie tasted so much better because it was served in newspaper.

With Eric's ten bob note practically burning a hole in his shorts pocket, Frankie decided to treat him and Prof to a couple of double cornets. But Frankie's legs were beginning to feel the strain of the long cycle trip they had just completed, so before contemplating the return journey, he and Prof made their way to the Westcliff side of the Pier and found a few feet of the beach that they could stretch out on. As soon as he had finished his cornet, Frankie took off his vest to soak up some of the sun. Prof kept his shirt on and both of them also kept their heads covered with their knotted handkerchiefs. Frankie was sporting a very red nose which looked as though it was going to be pretty sore on the way home.

For a few minutes, both boys just lay there, half-dozing, listening to the distant waves as the tide started to drift slowly in. Not far away they could hear the yells and laughter from the Crazy Car track just alongside the Pier and, when they opened their eyes, they could see the silhouettes of people strolling along the one and a quarter miles to the end of the Pier, where the matinee performance of the *GRAND SOUTHEND V.E. CONCERT PARTY* was about to begin. For Frankie it was all a magical experience . . .

'I'd like to be buried in the sea,' Prof said suddenly.

Frankie's eyes sprang open, but the sun immediately made him squint. 'Huh? What yer talkin' about?'

Prof was lying on his back, eyes closed, head resting on his hands. 'Well, wouldn't you? There's somethin' lovely about the sea. It's so quiet and peaceful.'

Frankie closed his eyes again. 'Not if you're out in a boat in the middle of a storm, it ain't!'

'Even so . . .' Although his eyes were still closed, Prof had a smile on his face. 'Just think of all those fish you'd see – all swimmin' around you, darting in and out of the rocks and seabed . . .'

'Yer stupid git! 'Ow could yer see them if yer dead!'

They both laughed. Then there was another silence between them.

Prof opened his eyes and turned to look at Frankie lying beside him. 'Frankie?'

Frankie only grunted because he was half-asleep.

'Thanks for being my pal.'

'Yeah – right.' Frankie wasn't really thinking.

'It means a lot to me, you know. I never liked Jeff and the others. I only knocked around with them because – well, because of you.' He turned over, leaned on one hand, and studied Frankie carefully. 'I've only ever cared for two people in my whole life, apart from my parents,' he said, almost as though he were talking to himself. 'Auntie Hilda – and you.'

Frankie started to snore and so, as he was clearly fast asleep, Prof thought it was quite safe for him to say all the things he had always wanted to.

'Just because I don't do the sort of things that people expect me to do, they think I'm a bit of a freak. Well – maybe I am. But *you* don't treat me like a freak, Frankie. You've always talked to me just like you talk to anyone else. That's been marvellous – really marvellous! But then you're that sort of person, Frankie. From the first time we used to play hopscotch down Merton Street, I knew you were someone special. There aren't many special people around, Frankie – there really aren't . . .'

Frankie suddenly groaned again. 'D'yer say somefin', Prof?'

Prof quickly lay down on his back again and looked up at the amazingly clear blue sky. 'Just thanks, that's all.'

'Fanks? Fer what?'

'Oh – for a lot of things.'

Prof closed his eyes again, secure in the knowledge that Frankie hadn't heard one single word he had said.

He was wrong . . .

It started clouding over about half-past four. By then Frankie and Prof were well on their way back home, having seen no sign of Jeff, Patty, or Alan since they left them behind in the Kursaal Amusement Park. As it would take most of the cyclists at least four hours to complete the return journey, the cycle path alongside the main Southend to London road was already filling up, and those energetic souls who wanted to get a move on were tearing ahead among the car traffic on the road itself. Frankie was really beginning to feel the strain on the back of his calves, so that he had to summon up all the effort he had left to peddle up even the most gradual of hills. Prof wasn't much better, and at times Frankie was quite concerned about him and insisted that they stop at regular intervals for a rest and a swig from their water-bottles.

By early evening the sky was not only grey but

very nearly black all over – and it was quite easy to see that a June thunderstorm was just waiting to show what it was made of.

The first drops of rain started to trickle down just as Frankie and Prof got on their yellow cycle-capes. Quite suddenly, the cycle path ahead seemed to have cleared, most of the other riders taking shelter in the nearest café or bus shelter or anything that would keep them dry until the storm passed. Frankie and Prof cycled on as far as they could, but when the rain began to pelt down they pulled over to the side to look for the nearest shelter. Unfortunately, they were in a fairly isolated rural area and, at first glance, the only protection they could find was beneath one of the many large elm trees alongside the road. But just as they got off their bikes and started to wheel them towards the largest tree they could find, a girl's voice suddenly yelled out through the first clap of thunder.

'Frankie! Frankie . . .!'

Frankie and Prof turned with a start to see Patty Jackson crouched beneath a white raincoat, with her bike laid out on the grass alongside the cycle-path. 'Patty! What yer doin'?' he called, then quickly looked around to see that Jeff and Alan were not with her.

Although she was yelling and waving, Patty could only just be heard above the rain which was now becoming torrential. 'Give us an 'and! I've got a puncture!'

Frankie immediately rushed over to her. Prof followed him, slowly and reluctantly.

'What yer doin' 'ere?' yelled Frankie, the rain running down from his head onto his cycle cape. 'Wot's 'appened ter Jeff and Alan?'

Although her raincoat had a hood, Patty's curly hair was so wet it was straggling down across her face. 'They don't know wot 'appened. I was miles behind 'em.'

Frankie tried to wipe away the rain which was now dribbling down his neck. 'So wot yer goin' ter do?'

'I can't go on wiv a puncture. Can yer mend it for me?'

Frankie's heart sank. He hadn't a clue how to mend a puncture. 'Not in this rain!' At least it gave him an excuse.

Patty turned and pointed across the field behind them. 'There's an old caff over there. It looks empty.'

Frankie turned to look. Through the rain he could just see what looked like a ramshackle old timber building. 'OK! I'll 'ave a go!' He put his hand down to help Patty up from her crouching position. 'Let's get a move on! Come on, Prof!'

While Patty picked up her bike and started to make her way across the field, Frankie and Prof went back to collect theirs from beneath the elm tree.

'I'm not coming with you, Frankie.' Rain was streaming down Prof's tortoiseshell spectacles and all he could see of Frankie was a blurred image.

Frankie was shocked. 'Wot're yer talkin' about? We can't just leave 'er!'

'I know that.' Prof picked up his bike and climbed on to it. 'But it doesn't need the two of us.'

'Don't be a twit, Prof! I 'aven't the faintest idea 'ow to mend a puncture, yer know I don't!'

Prof looked strange, unrelenting, and detached. 'You've got a brain on you, Frankie. You'll mend the puncture all right.'

Frankie had never seen Prof like this before, and it disturbed him. 'Wot's the matter wiv yer, Prof? Wot's up?'

'There's nothing wrong with me, Frankie. I just don't want to help Patty Jackson, that's all.' He pulled his cape closer over his head and shoulders and took his bike handlebars firmly in his hands. 'If you don't mind, I'll push on. We'll meet up down the road somewhere.'

'Frankie!' Patty, already half-way with her bike towards the old café, was yelling back through the rain.

Prof smiled briefly at Frankie. But it was an odd smile. 'See you, then.' And with that, he pedalled off.

Frankie watched him go in almost total disbelief. The last he saw of Prof was a solitary yellow-cloaked figure disappearing into the torrential rain of the Essex countryside.

'Frankie!' Patty was getting hysterical. ''Urry up!'

A few minutes later, Frankie helped Patty push open the broken door of the disused café. It wasn't very big, but there were still a few benches and one or two tables left behind.

Surprisingly there were no leaks in the roof.

'Wot 'appened to Prof then?' spluttered Patty, as she wheeled in her bike.

Frankie followed her in, ''E 'ad ter get back.'

Patty laid down her bike and quickly took off her white raincoat and hood. ''E don't like me – that's why. 'E never 'as.'

'Don't be stupid, Patty,' said Frankie, leaning his bike up against what was left of the serving counter.

'Oh, I don't care if 'e likes me or if 'e don't.' She took hold of her wet, straggling hair, and with both hands wrung out as much of the rain-water as she could. 'Still – *you* like me, don't yer, Frank?'

Frankie took off his cycling cape, and shook the rain off it. 'Let's 'ave a look at this puncture then.' He was very careful to avoid her question.

He knelt down and inspected the tyres of Patty's bike. The front one seemed firm enough, but when he used the tip of his fingers to feel the back tyre, there seemed to be very little air in it.

'It may just need pumping up.' Frankie unclip-ped the pump from the crossbar of Patty's bike, and unscrewed its valve.

'Wanna fag?'

Frankie turned to see Patty lighting a cigarette. 'No, fanks. 'Ow long 'ave yer been smokin', then?'

'Oh, I 'ave one when I feel like it.' As Patty glanced around she noticed an old black stove in a corner of what was once the café dining-room. Curling up from it was a chimney flu which went out through the roof. 'It's freezin' in 'ere. I wonder if we can light a fire.'

Frankie didn't even bother to look up as he struggled to fit the pump valve on to the wheel valve.

'I'll go and see if I can find some wood.'

Frankie didn't hear her go off into an adjoining room; he just started pumping up the flat tyre. While he was doing so, his mind kept pounding away at the thought of a lonely, solitary figure cycling off in the driving rain, and of the strange things that Prof had said while they were lying together on the beach at Southend. Although the two of them had been pals since they were small kids, Frankie had never known Prof to behave in such a way. What did he mean, for instance, when he said, *'You've always talked to me just like you talk to anyone else'*? Why was it Prof was such a loner, he wondered? Why was it he shrank from seeing Frankie when Frankie first started going out with Maggs?

'I couldn't find any wood.' Patty had re-entered

the room behind him. 'We'll have ter find anuvver way ter keep warm.'

Frankie had finished pumping up the tyre and was pressing it with his fingers. 'I don't fink it's a puncture. Anyway, wiv a bit of luck it'll get yer home all right . . .' As he turned to look at her, his blood suddenly turned to ice.

Patty was stark naked.

For a moment, Frankie couldn't say a word. Then he stood up. 'Bloody 'ell, Patty! Wot d'yer fink yer doing'?'

Patty smiled mischievously. 'Wot's up, Frankie? Ain't yer ever seen a gel like this before?'

Frankie said nothing. All he could do was stand and stare.

Patty slowly came across and stood in front of him. There was a moment of silence between them which was only broken by an angry clap of thunder and rain pelting down on to the tiled roof.

Frankie bit his lip nervously. He didn't know what to say or to do or how to react. All he could do was to stare up and down at Patty's naked flesh, her long neck, and slim shoulders. Her breasts seemed absolutely beautiful to him . . . Gradually, his gaze wandered down to that forbidden area where thighs were separated by no more than a wisp of young pubic hair. Frankie had seen many girls and women during his young lifetime, and had often lain awake at night fantasising about what lay beneath the clothes they wore. Even as a child he had never seen his mother without clothes, and this was arousing him in a way that he had so often dreamed about.

Patty waited a moment, then took hold of Frankie's hand and placed it on one of her breasts. It felt warm and inviting, and, as he started to feel her nipple, he was surprised to find it becoming firm in his fingers. While this was going on, Patty pulled Frankie's vest out of his shorts and tugged it off. But when she put her fingers into the top of his shorts and tried to pull them down, he resisted.

'Wot yer doing'?' His voice was barely audible.

Patty's eyes met his. 'I've done it before yer know. You're not the first.'

Frankie's heart was thumping fast. This was his chance to do something which he had fantasised about so often before. But as he looked at Patty, all he could think of was Maggs. If it was her, it would be so different. It wasn't Patty he wanted, it was Maggs. And yet – oh God, he thought – I *want* to do it. I want to know what it's like, so that when the same thing happens with Maggs, I won't look a fool . . . In those few seconds of agonising, Frankie's resistance ebbed away, and he allowed Patty to pull down first his shorts, and then his underpants.

Both of them were now completely naked. Frankie felt awkward; he knew he should be making the first move. But Patty saved his embarrassment by suddenly throwing her arms around him and kissing him fully on the lips. Their bodies were now pressed together, and Frankie felt the excitement pumping through his blood. He put his arms around her and returned her kiss – and as he did so, someone gave them a shrill wolf-whistle from behind.

Horrified, Frankie turned to find Jeff Murray standing in the doorway, rain running down his cycle-cape. 'Wow! So 'e *does* 'ave one, after all!' And as he spoke, he applauded, and roared with laughter.

At the same time, Patty pulled away from Frankie and she, too, threw her head back and shrieked with laughter.

Frankie felt sick in his stomach. He grabbed his pants, shorts, and vest from the floor, and put them on as fast as he could.

'Come on now, lover boy,' jeered Jeff, as he came across to Frankie making suggestive signs with one finger. 'Yer din't fink yer was goin' to get somewhere wiv *that*, did yer?'

To Jeff's absolute astonishment, Frankie turned on him in a flash and, with his clenched fist, landed the most devastating punch on Jeff's face, which sent him reeling across the room.

Patty trembled with fear as she watched Frankie. She had never seen him like this before, the fury and strength of his response boiling over into such a physical outburst. Now, looking faintly ridiculous without her clothes on, all she could do was to rush across to Jeff, who was bleeding heavily from the mouth. But he made no attempt to get up and challenge Frankie to a full-blooded fight.

'You're stupid! Both of yer! A coupla bloody, stupid kids!' Frankie put on his cycling cape, and picked up his bike. 'In't yer *ever* gonna grow up!'

Patty, crouched on the floor with Jeff's head cradled in her arms, watched Frankie go with a mixture of fear and admiration.

Frankie wheeled his bike to the door, but stopped briefly to call back to them. 'From now on, you bloody keep away from me – right? 'Cos if yer try ter set me up like this ever again, I'll tear yer bloody guts out!'

He wheeled his bike out of the café. It was still pouring with rain.

'I'm sorry, Frank.'

As Frankie was about to wheel his bike off, he found Alan Downs sheltering in the café porch.

'It 'ad nuffin ter do wiv me – honest. It was their idea – not mine. I'm sorry, Frank – really sorry.'

Frankie glared back at him. 'Piss off!' he yelled, and practically ran with his bike until he reached the main road.

A few minutes later, Frankie was cycling along the cycle-path, with driving rain pounding against his face and cycle cape. Although it was not yet dark, the storm had forced most car drivers to turn on their headlights, which dazzled

Frankie as he struggled to pedal on the glistening wet path.

So much was going through his head. How could he possibly have been so naïve? He should have known that Patty and Jeff would have tried to pull off a filthy trick like that. They were nothing but a pair of dirty, mindless gits who had nothing to do but think up things that could hurt people. And he thought about how he had betrayed Maggs by allowing himself to be drawn into such a situation. If she knew what he'd done, she'd never want to see him again. The whole episode was causing him to churn up inside, and riding along in the pouring rain he let out the most anguished yell at the top of his voice.

The sound Frankie made intermingled with that of another, quite different sound. It was the eerie clanging of an ambulance alarm. As he turned to look over his shoulder, a white, rain-splattered ambulance came speeding up behind him. It overtook him and came to a halt at the side of the main road just ahead of him.

Frankie had not intended to stop but he noticed something which suddenly sent a shiver down his spine. Lying on the grass at the side of the cycle-path was a bike that he recognised. It was old, with a tattered saddle-bag, and with straight, rusting handlebars . . .

In a blind panic Frankie got off his own bike and threw it down on to the grass. Then he pushed his way through the group of helpers calling, 'Let me through! Please! Let me through!' By the time he reached the ambulance, the back doors were open, and the driver and his assistant were already putting their victim on to a stretcher. When Frankie finally succeeded in reaching the ambulance, the small, slight figure, who was quite clearly unconscious, was being wrapped up in a red hospital blanket. But it was only when the stretcher was carried into the back of the ambulance that Frankie's worst fears were confirmed.

It was Prof . . .

Chapter Twenty

Peter Vernon Moosey, known simply as Prof, died at twenty-past seven on the evening of Sunday, 2nd June 1945. He was just one week short of his sixteenth birthday.

Although Prof was already unconscious when Frankie reached him at the roadside, Frankie was allowed to travel in the ambulance with his best pal, leaving the police to collect both their bicycles. For the thirty minutes or so it took the ambulance to get to the hospital, the driver's assistant tried to revive Prof with oxygen, but by the time they arrived, a doctor pronounced Prof dead. It was, he said, nothing more than a massive heart failure. 'Nothing more', thought Frankie. What a strange way to put it. And because Prof had died unexpectedly, there would have to be an autopsy. The doctor and nurses in the emergency unit were terribly sympathetic to Frankie but nothing could make up for the loss of his pal, who, only a few hours earlier, had called Frankie 'someone special.'

At about eight o'clock in the evening, Frankie was allowed in to see Prof for the last time. He was covered with a white sheet, and when the nurse pulled it down to reveal Prof's face, Frankie couldn't believe he was dead. If it hadn't been for the blue colour around his mouth Frankie would have thought he was asleep. His heart! Why did his heart have to fail, Frankie asked himself? Why couldn't it have gone on and on just like everyone else's? Why couldn't Prof have lived a long life, got married, had kids . . .? Damn his stupid heart! Damn it a hundred times over! Tears were trickling down Frankie's cheeks. He felt so stupid just standing there, so helpless. But then, quite suddenly, he leaned over and whispered close into his best pal's ear: 'See yer then, Prof! Fanks fer everyfin'.' It was an extraordinary, impulsive thing for Frankie to do. But he needed to do it.

Auntie Hilda arrived at about nine thirty. Two kindly police constables from Hornsey Road police station had called on her to tell her the news at her flat above the ladies' handbag shop in the Seven Sisters Road. When she heard what had happened, she was shocked, but not surprised. She had known how bad her nephew's condition really was for some time. The policemen took her in a patrol car all the way to Brentwood and, even though she was too late to see young Pete still alive, she was very grateful to everyone for all the trouble they had taken to help her. She didn't cry at all until she was taken in to see the last of the boy whom she had adopted at the beginning of the war. When she came out, she and Frankie hugged each other.

Suddenly, being together, they felt very close to Prof again . . .

Earlier in the afternoon, Grace and Reg Lewis had gone to tea with their daughter Helen and her husband-to-be, Eric Sibley. It was a highly unusual event for the Lewises, for they hadn't been visiting to anyone for years. But the two young people made them feel very welcome, and they had certainly made their two small furnished rooms on the first floor of a terraced house in St Anne's Road, Tottenham very comfortable. The only thing that Reg didn't approve of was that the walls were painted plain white instead of being covered with a nice patterned wallpaper. But Gracie was very impressed with the tea: Apart from a corn-beef salad, crumpets with margarine, and a strawberry jelly with custard, this included a good-sized fruit cake.

'Where d'yer buy a cake like this, then?' asked Gracie, her mouth crammed with as much as she could pile in. 'You got a good baker shop round 'ere? They don't 'ave none of these at Stagnell's.'

'I didn't buy it, Mum,' replied Helen, feeling rather pleased with herself as she poured more cups of tea from a large brown china teapot which Frankie had bought for her from the jumble shop. 'I made it meself.'

Gracie froze, a large lump of cake still unchewed in her mouth. '*You* made it?'

'Why not? We've got the use of a nice kitchen on the ground floor. I do all our cookin' down there.'

Reg coughed on the Woodbine Eric had just given him. 'Since when d'you know 'ow ter cook then?'

'Well, let's face it, it's only common sense, in't it, Dad?' Helen put down the heavy teapot.

Eric, clearly enjoying all this, drew hard on his fag, blew out the smoke, and grinned broadly. 'She's quite a gel, your daughter, Mr Lewis. She gets recipes from newspapers and fings.'

Gracie and Reg exchanged a glance, continued eating and drinking as much as they could, and didn't pursue the subject any further.

After tea, they all sat down by the open window and watched the kids from the downstairs flat playing in the back garden. It was a hot night, so Eric and Reg took off their shirts and sat there in their vest and braces while they quickly gulped the first quart bottle of brown ale. Helen and her mum sat side by side on the tiny sofa, but Gracie was irritated to see her daughter knitting baby's socks, mainly because she didn't know how to knit herself. However, she was allowed to listen to her Sunday evening ritual on the wireless, and soon they were all joining in the title song with 'Ramsbottom, and Enoch, and Me'.

When it was over, Helen went downstairs and made a pot of tea and when she came back, Eric and her father were talking politics.

'I can't believe you're really goin' to vote for Churchill though, are yer Mr Lewis?' The brown ale was beginning to make Eric quite lively. 'I mean – 'e's nuffin' but a bloody ole warmonger, 'e is.'

'Maybe so,' sniffed Reg indignantly, pouring himself another glass of brown. 'But at least 'e got us fru the war! If it 'adn't been for ole Winnie, bloody 'Itler would 'ave marched right past yer front door!'

'Well, I'm votin' for Attlee and the Labour Party. It's time this country did somefin' fer workin' class people, people who can't even afford ter go ter the doctor's.'

'Attlee!' This was the first Gracie had contributed to the conversation. 'That 'orrible little man. 'E's got slant eyes – like a Chinaman.'

'Don't matter wot 'e looks like, Mrs Lewis. We need someone who knows 'ow ter run the country in peacetime.'

Gracie came back, quick as a flash. ''Ow d'yer know 'e can run the country in peacetime? War's only been over fer a month.'

'Anyway,' said Reg, rolling up his vest sleeves, 'the war 'ain't over yet. We still got the Nips ter deal wiv.'

Eric lit another fag. 'That won't be long now, you mark my words. The Yanks've got somefin' up their sleeve, all right. Now we've got 'Itler and 'is lot out the way, you'll find the Japs'll give in at the drop of an 'at.'

'I dunno about the drop of an 'at,' retorted Reg. 'After the way they bin cuttin down our lads out in the jungles, they oughta bomb the bloody daylights out of 'em!'

'And Mr Clement so-called Attlee ain't the man ter do that!' asserted Gracie, dogmatically.

Helen was getting anxious that Eric was becoming too involved in a heated conversation with her parents. 'Well, I'm glad *I'm* not old enough ter vote in no General Election. They all sound the same ter me. Anyway, come July *we'll* be too busy wiv the weddin'.'

Gracie, stirring her tea, looked up with a start. 'Weddin'?

'Yeah,' said Eric. 'We've fixed the time, Mrs Lewis.'

'Yer mean *just* in time!' joked Eric.

Helen blushed, but Eric and her father laughed.

'So, when is it?' Gracie asked, rather nervously.

'Well, we're finkin' about the second week in July,' said Helen. 'It's goin' ter be in the Registry Office up at Islington Town 'All. Under present circumstances,' she said, feeling her now very enlarged stomach, 'I'd feel a bit embarrassed gettin' married in church.'

'Fair enough,' conceded Reg. 'But why wait 'til July?'

It was beginning to get dark, so Eric crossed the room and turned on the light switch by the door. 'It's really because of Frankie. As 'e's my best man, it's only fair ter give him time ter get over his school exams.'

Gracie's face hardened. 'Are yer sure Frankie's not too young ter be a best man?'

'Too young? Frankie?' Although it was getting late, the kids in the back garden were making a heck of a noise, so Eric went to the window and yelled out, 'Oy – you lot! Keep it down!' The noise cut out immediately, and Eric turned his back to the window. 'Frankie's not too young, Mrs Lewis. In fact, in my opinion there's no one in the whole world who'd be a best man as good as Frankie. 'E's got a good 'ead on 'im, I'm tellin' yer. One of these days, 'e'll do yer proud.'

Neither Gracie nor Reg quite knew how to answer that.

'So – 'ow many people you invitin' ter the weddin?' Reg asked, finally.

'Oh, no more than a couple of dozen at the most,' said Helen, picking up her knitting again. 'Some of Eric's family and a few of our friends.'

Reg seemed a bit put out. 'Well, wot about our side then?

'Our side?' asked Helen, surprised. ''Ave we got anybody?'

Gracie and Reg exchanged an uneasy glance.

'There's your Auntie Dot and Uncle 'Arry,' suggested Reg.

'We ain't seen 'em for years!'

The clicking of Helen's knitting needles was now beginning to irritate Gracie. 'That's not the point. If they're not asked, they'll be very hurt.'

'I quite agree,' Eric said, nodding in agreement. 'The last fing we want ter do is to offend any of your relations.'

'You speak fer yerself!' said Reg, wryly. 'Bloody awful lot!'

Eric did his best to conceal a chuckle. 'Mind you, as yer can see, it'll be quite a squeeze ter fit 'em all in.'

'Wot's that?' Gracie could no longer bear the clicking of Helen's knitting needles. She stretched out her hand and pulled the half-completed baby socks down on to Helen's lap. 'You're not goin' ter 'ave the reception 'ere?'

Eric shrugged his shoulders. 'Nowhere else, Mrs Lewis.'

'Blimey!' Reg quickly lit one of his own fags as he looked around the small room they were sitting in.

'But yer can't!' Gracie was turning around in every direction trying her best to imagine a crowd of wedding guests treading on each other's toes. 'There ain't enuff room ter swing a cat!'

Helen tried to give her mother a reassuring smile. Up until the past few months, she would never have thought that *any* contact would ever have been possible. 'Don't worry, Mum. We'll manage – some'ow.'

To which Eric added, artfully, 'Unless of course you've got a better idea, Mrs Lewis?'

There followed a pause, in which Gracie and Reg exchanged an anxious glance.

Eventually, after taking a deep drag of his fag, Reg said, 'There's always *our* place.'

'Oh no!' Eric said immediately, an earnest look on his face. 'We couldn't do that to yer, Mister Lewis – it wouldn't be fair. I mean, me an' 'Elen couldn't put yer to all that trouble, not wiv all the preparation and everythin'.'

'Well, we've got more room than you 'ave!' Reg started to pace the room nervously – which, given the size of the place, didn't take him long. 'We've got the front room, the back parlour and scullery, and now we've got rid of the Anderson we could get some of them out in the back yard.' Then he turned quickly to his wife. 'What d'yer fink, Grace?'

Gracie looked as though she wasn't far from a nervous breakdown. 'We couldn't afford to pay for it,' she said, very quickly.

'Well – not all of it,' Reg added.

'Oh, we wouldn't expect yer ter do anyfin' like that, Mr Lewis – oh no, no, no!' Eric was playing his own prearranged game, and was thoroughly enjoying it. 'I've got a good job on the trolleys, yer know. London Transport don't pay conductors a fortune, but once I've taken the driver's trainin' course I'll be on ter some real good money.'

Gracie sighed with relief.

'In any case,' Eric continued, 'I'm pretty sure my old man will chip in wiv a bob or two. 'E'll do anyfin' ter get me off 'is 'ands! And we'll get my ma ter 'elp. She can make some sausage rolls or somefin'.'

This last remark was greeted with stony silence by both Gracie and Reg, but especially by Gracie. 'That won't be necessary,' she said, haughtily. 'I'm sure 'Elen and I can manage on our own.'

Helen looked up with a start. 'Can we?' she asked in almost total disbelief.

'We'll 'ave to!' Gracie snapped grumpily. 'That's all there is to it!'

'Well, I'll tell yer this much, Mrs Lewis.' Ignoring Helen's reproachful look, Eric continued with his crafty buttering-up of his future mother-in-law. 'I tasted one of those spam sandwiches you made for the Merton Street VE night party. If the ones you make for our reception are anyfin' like that – we're in fer a real feast!'

Helen blushed with embarrassment and quickly continued with her knitting.

'Right!' said Reg, getting to his feet. 'That's decided then.'

Gracie could see that, after Eric had pumped nearly two quart bottles of brown ale down her husband's throat, he was none too steady on his feet. 'It's gettin' late,' she said, glaring at not only Reg, but at Helen's knitting needles which had almost driven her into a frenzy. 'We'd better be gettin' 'ome. Frankie should be back from his bike ride by now.'

Helen put down her knitting needles and eased herself up from the sofa. 'Good old Frank. I envy 'im goin' ter Soufend. I bet 'e's 'ad a lovely day.'

'Yeah,' said Eric. 'I just 'ope 'e didn't get caught in that rain.'

That night, Frankie got home from Brentwood Hospital soon after eleven o'clock. A friendly off-duty police constable had given him and Auntie Hilda a lift in a Police van, which was also able to carry Frankie's Raleigh Sports and the Prof's old straight-handlebar bike.

It had been an agonising trip home, so different to the one he and Prof had embarked upon when they set out with such exuberance from Finsbury Park that sunlit Sunday morning. Sitting in the dark in the back seat of the van, Frankie and Auntie Hilda hardly said a word to each other but as they sped along the main Southend-London road an occasional flash of light from passing cars would illuminate the van's interior and reflect in the tearful eyes of both the elderly lady and her nephew's best friend. Only once did Auntie Hilda lean across to Frankie. Taking hold of his hand and clenching it tightly she said, 'I'm glad you two were such good friends, Frankie. It helped him to live longer.'

Frankie was devastated by Auntie's remark, and it made him feel guilty – guilty because he thought of all the times when perhaps he could have been nicer to Prof. And guilty because friendship should always be two ways, and Frankie wasn't sure in his own mind whether he had been as good a friend to Prof as Prof had been to him.

When he eventually did get home, Frankie was surprised to find that his mother and father were still out. For that he was quite grateful; he didn't want to see or talk to anyone. When he went upstairs to his own room he didn't turn on the light, for he couldn't bear to see his own reflection in the dressing-table mirror as he passed it.

After undressing in the dark and stroking Winston, Frankie took a casual look out of the window. After the thunderous storm during the early part of the evening the sky was quite clear again, with the moon spreading a vast white glow over all the rooftops and tiny backyards along Merton Street. And as he and Winston stared up at the millions and millions of stars that flickered brightly out of that dark summer night sky, Frankie hoped that his pal Prof was out there somewhere.

In fact, he was certain he was.

Chapter Twenty-one

Most people who lived in Swiss Cottage had no idea why it was called that. Some thought it had once been owned by a rich Swiss banker; others were convinced it was named after a continental loaf of bread. But whatever the reason, this cosmopolitan area of north-west London contained an amazing selection of nationalities, of whom a great number were pre-war refugees from Nazi Germany.

On this Thursday afternoon, Swiss Cottage was sweltering in the intense humidity of a blazing hot June heatwave. From all the tall Edwardian terraced houses leading down to West Hampstead in the south, to the fashionable leafy suburbs of well-to-do Hampstead itself in the north, windows were flung open in the desperate search for even the slightest breeze and all along the main Finchley Road, hordes of shoppers were shuffling along at a snail's pace, wearing as few clothes as possible and doing their best to move in whatever shade was available. Amongst them was Gertrude Rosenberg who was making slow progress in her high-heeled shoes on her way to her Thursday afternoon tea and cakes with Elsa. Although her fox-fur had been replaced with a long chiffon scarf, her winter coat discarded in favour of a frilly printed silk summer dress, and her head now covered in a large-brimmed straw hat, Gertrude grunted and grumbled to herself as she was pushed and jostled by weary passers-by.

When she eventually reached Gershners Jewish Restaurant, the place was crowded, which irritated her hugely. But as she looked around for her usual waiter, the last person she expected to see was Elsa. It was only five minutes to three, and there she was, already sitting at their usual table by the window, sipping a glass of iced mineral water, dressed in white silk from head to foot, and looking as cool as a polar bear. To make things worse, Elsa hadn't even noticed her come in, which absolutely infuriated Gertrude. This wasn't good. She had never seen her old friend and sparring partner like this before.

There was definitely something on Elsa's mind . . .

Try as he might, Frankie couldn't bear 'Boggy' Marsh. There was something in his manner which was so lacking in humanity that Frankie felt that he had no mental contact with the man at all. 'Boggy' had been headmaster of Highbury

Grammar School all through the war years and yet not once had he ever sat down and had a friendly chat with any of his pupils and ever since he had joined the school after leaving Pakeman Street Juniors, Frankie had got it fixed in his mind that the old git had it in for him, for whenever they met – either in the corridor or the classroom – 'Boggy' had pulverised him with warnings about failing his matric exams if he didn't start concentrating more on mathematics. So, it was with some trepidation that he climbed the stone stairs to the headmaster's study after being summoned for an 'interview'.

The meeting, however, turned out somewhat different to what he had expected.

'Lewis. This has been a distressing experience for you. I am fully aware what good friends you and Peter Moosey were, and I want you to know that the entire school shares your sense of loss in this great tragedy.'

Frankie had never seen or heard his headmaster like this before. A short and tubby little man, with black horn-rimmed spectacles, he was sitting at his large oak desk with his back to the window.

'Moosey was a good pupil. He worked hard.' 'Boggy's' eyes only occasionally flicked up to actually look at Frankie. 'There is no doubt in my mind that he had tremendous potential.'

Frankie, standing in front of the desk with his head bowed, could say nothing.

Then 'Boggy' got up from his desk, and turned to look out of the window towards the indoor swimming-pool on the other side of the Recreation yard. Before he spoke again he straightened the gown, which, even on such a blistering hot day, he insisted on wearing over a formal pin-striped suit. 'I have, of course, written to Moosey's relative, and I have asked Mr Woods to represent our school at the funeral.' He paused briefly and turned from the window. He was now a silhouette. 'I have decided to hold a short service of Thanksgiving for Moosey during tomorrow morning's assembly. Mr Garrett has agreed to say a few words about him, and two of your form colleagues will be doing short readings from the Bible.' He paused again. 'However . . .'

The bright afternoon sun was shining directly into Frankie's eyes, so he could not see 'Boggy's' face.

'Under the circumstances, Lewis, I think it appropriate that you, also, should say something.'

Frankie stiffened. '*Me*, sir?'

'You were Moosey's best friend. It would be a generous farewell gesture.'

Frankie thought about it nervously for a brief moment. When he spoke again he could only just be heard. 'But – what should I say, sir?'

'That is entirely up to you. You probably knew him best in the entire school but it wouldn't have to be much. Just a few words.'

In the split second that followed, Frankie pondered on what 'Boggy' had just said: '*You probably knew him best in the entire school.*' Frankie was staring at his own feet, unconsciously shaking his head as he thought to himself that he didn't know his pal at all. In fact, it was impossible to ever really *know* Prof.

Frankie suddenly looked up, and his voice was firm and decisive.

'Yes, sir. I would like ter say somefin', sir.'

'Thank you, Lewis. I'm grateful to you.'

To Frankie's astonishment, 'Boggy' stretched out his hand and shook hands with him.

'And just one more thing.' 'Boggy' came out from behind his desk, stood beside Frankie and laid his hand on the boy's shoulder. 'I realise that, with your matric exams coming up in the next few weeks, this is a very difficult time for you. I've instructed the teaching staff to offer you any additional help you may require.'

Frankie was taken aback. 'Fank yer very much, sir.' He turned, made his way back to the door and opened it.

'Lewis.'

Frankie turned to look back at 'Boggy', who was once again a silhouette against the study window.

'I'm sure things will work out.'

'Fank yer, sir.'

Frankie left the Headmaster's study, and closed the door behind him. His footsteps echoed on the stone staircase as he went down to catch the start of Charlie Garrett's history lesson in a ground-floor classroom. As he went, his mind was pounding with the image of 'Boggy' Marsh standing with his back to that window. Funny, he thought, people aren't always what they seem.

Even headmasters . . .

At about the same time that Frankie was starting his history lesson, Elsa and Gertrude were tucking into iced tea, apple strudel, and a ration-book version of Black Forest gateau which contained powdered milk, dried eggs, and an awful lot of kirsch. There wasn't one table free in Gershners and the afternoon customers were being serenaded by a delicate selection of pre-war Central European love songs, played on the violin by an elderly Jewish gentleman who was togged up in full white tie and tails, with a red carnation in his buttonhole, and white gloves. It was the first time that this kind of musical treat had been provided by the management since before the war.

'You didn't get here five minutes early just to listen to *zis* rubbish!' Gertrude, trying to raise her voice above the violin solo, was in a spikey mood.

But Elsa loved the music. As she forked her strudel, she was swaying to and fro to the sound.

'Elsa!' Gertrude was in danger of breaking her

teacup as she slammed it down on to the saucer.

Elsa flinched, but refused to respond to her tetchy friend until she had joined in the genteel applause with the other customers at the conclusion of the violin serenade. 'Bravo!' she called over her shoulder, as the elderly soloist bowed low as though he had just performed at the Royal Albert Hall. Only when that was over did Elsa turn back to Gertrude. 'Now then, Gertrude. Where were we?'

'Vhere vere ve!' Gertrude practically exploded. '*Dumm frau*! One minute you say you have somesing important to tell me, and zen you turn avay and listen to all zat rubbish! Vot's it all about?'

Elsa refused to be provoked. So she put down her fork, wiped her lips on her white cotton table napkin, then leaned her elbows on the table and rested her chin on them. 'It's Barclay. Jack Barclay.'

'Who?'

'My brother-in-law. The one who lives in *Hertfordshire*.' There was a marked curl to her otherwise good English accent as she emphasised the county name. 'He promises to be big trouble.'

'In vot vay, big trouble?'

'You remember I told you – he wants to buy my shop?'

'So vot's new? Let him haf it,' spluttered Gertrude, as she tackled her first piece of gateau. 'Anything to get you avay from zat terrible place!'

'It's not as easy as that, my friend. It appears that Barclay has ambitions that not only include my shop.'

'And vot's zat supposed to mean?'

Elsa leaned across the table and lowered her voice. 'It means, Gertrude that this man is trying to buy up property in a certain part of the area in which I live.'

'So vot's wrong viz zat?'

Elsa leaned back in her chair. 'It's *where* and *what* he's trying to buy that concerns me.'

To Gertrude's intense irritation, the violinist approached their table, holding his violin and bow in one hand, and holding out his other hand for a tip. Gertrude, outraged, snapped at him, 'Do you expect us to pay for zat dreadful noise! My Persian cat vould haf made a better sound!'

The poor man was taken aback, and bowed humbly. But before he left the table, Elsa spoke to him. 'Please . . .' She dug into her purse, pulled out a half-crown, and dropped it into the palm of his hand. 'That was a beautiful performance,' she said, with a smile that showed she meant it. 'Thank you so much.'

The violinist's face lit up as his hand closed around the coin. 'Zank *you* so much, madame!' he said with a deep bow, suddenly feeling like the artist he used to be. And without even a glance at Gertrude, he left.

Gertrude tried to ignore the incident, but she felt a twinge of guilt. It was not the first time she had thought that Elsa was a much better person than herself. Returning to her gateau, she asked, 'Vot do you mean it's vhere and vot zis Barclay is trying to buy?'

Elsa leaned forward in her chair. 'I heard that's he's buying up houses in Merton Street.'

Gertrude shrugged her shoulders. Merton Street could have been in China for all she knew.

'Merton Street is where my Misster Frankie lives.'

For the first time, Gertrude took notice. She put her fork down. 'Vot's he up to?'

'I don't know, Gertrude. But I have a good idea.' Elsa leaned back in her chair again turning, briefly to look at the wonderful selection of faces around the crowded tables in the restaurant. The place was now thick with cigarette smoke – not Woodbines or Players or Gold Flake, but more exotic brands like Abdullahs and Craven A and scented Sobranies. And as she glanced around at the customers, many of whom she imagined had, like herself and Gertrude, taken refuge from Nazi persecution before the war, their lined faces were, in Elsa's mind, wiped out by one evil image – that of Jack Barclay. 'It's strange,' she said. 'When some people know you have something they want, they'll do anything to get it.'

Gertrude knew exactly what she meant. 'You know vot I zink,' she said, taking out a cigarette from her packet of Abdullahs. 'I zink you should invite zis man over to tea vun day, and poison him viz rat killer!'

Elsa laughed. 'No, Gertrude. Even for you that's a little extreme.'

'So vot are you going to do?' Gertrude fixed the cigarette into her holder. 'He vonts your shop. He vonts your house. He vonts your money. How can you stop him?'

'I think I know how.'

'How?'

As Gertrude lit her Abdullah, Elsa leaned across and said quite simply, 'I have a plan, Gertrude. But I need your help . . .'

At four o'clock that afternoon, Frankie walked up to Highbury Fields Girls' School to wait for Maggs. When she came out, they received a barrage of wolf-whistles from the other girls who were streaming out into Highbury Grove.

As the weather had turned so hot, Frankie and Maggs had arranged to bring their towels and swimming costumes so that they could go for a late afternoon swim at the Highbury open-air pool. But when they got there the air was filled with shrieks and laughter for the place was full of kids and excited teenagers who were leaping in and out of the pool, and queuing up to use the diving board. Maggs suggested that they go for a tram ride instead.

In Upper Street, the number 38 tram was just about to pull away as Frankie and Maggs leapt on to it. Luckily the back seat on the top deck was free and, after paying the conductor the fare for two tickets to the Victoria Embankment, they settled down to enjoy the journey, Maggs by the window, her head leaning on Frankie's shoulder.

For the first few minutes, as the old tram rattled its way along the main high street of Islington, neither Frankie nor Maggs said anything to each other. For most of the time, Maggs' eyes were closed, for she felt that she was never more in heaven than when she was with Frankie. But Frankie himself had a great deal on his mind, what with the Thanksgiving service at school first thing in the morning, followed by Prof's funeral in the afternoon. Then, on top of all that, there were things that he just had to tell Maggs, but didn't know how; things that could possibly pull them apart forever. Staring out of the window aimlessly, he hardly noticed the tram as it passed the ornate grey-stoned grandeur of the Town Hall, Collins' Music Hall on the Green, and the busy intersection of main roads at the Angel, Islington.

By the time the 38 bus turned into Rosebery Avenue and passed the Sadlers Wells Theatre, Frankie was in such anguish he felt that if he didn't say something to Maggs now, he would never be able to look with honesty into her lovely eyes again. His opportunity finally came when the tram made a lengthy stop to allow the conductor to help the driver of a horse-drawn coal cart, whose wheels had got stuck in the tram rails.

'Maggs?'

Maggs opened her eyes.

Although there was only one other passenger on the top deck, a rather large lady who was fast asleep in the front seat, Frankie leaned down close to talk into Maggs' ear.

'I've got ter tell yer somefin'.'

'I'm listening,' she said, snuggling up closer.

'In fact if I don't tell you, I'll go stark starin' mad!'

All of a sudden, Maggs was concerned. She turned, and looked up at him. 'What's wrong, Frank?'

'Somefin' 'appened. Last Sunday. The Bike Rally. On the way back from Soufend.'

Maggs was staring at him. But he was unable to meet her eyes.

'It's ter do wiv – wiv Patty Jackson.'

For a second or two, Maggs let his remark sink in, then she sat up straight. 'Yes?'

Frankie took his arm away from Maggs' shoulders, and sat with head bowed and both hands clasped together between his legs. 'She pulled a fast one on me, Maggs. I fell for it – like a stupid twit. I – I must've bin off me chump!'

Maggs took hold of his head, and turned it towards her. Although her speaking voice was so much more soft and cultivated than Frankie's, at this moment it was just as anxious. 'What do you mean, she pulled a fast one on you? *What* happened, Frank?'

Frankie slowly looked up into her eyes. They were warm, friendly, and so very beautiful that he was utterly tongue-tied.

'Tell me, Frank. Please.'

By the time the tram started moving again, Frankie had told her everything that had happened on the return journey from Southend. He kept nothing from her.

When he had finished, Maggs sat back in the seat, and stared out of the window. The streets of Islington and then Finsbury disappeared behind them as the tram grunted along its two rails, heading towards Southampton Row and Holborn. But neither Maggs nor Frankie saw any more of the journey. At Maggs' request, for the time being not another word was spoken between them.

The tram headed down into the depths of the Kingsway tunnel, stopping only briefly to pick up a few passengers at the underground tram stop. When it emerged again at the Victoria Embankment, the sudden glare of the sun was so blinding, it looked as though the clumsy old tram was about to plunge straight into the River Thames. But, with a back-aching jerk it immediately turned a sharp right-angle and continued on its journey, gliding majestically on its rails along the Embankment in the direction of Westminster Bridge. Frankie and Maggs had already decided to get off at the stop before that and take a leisurely, romantic stroll by the river in the opposite direction.

It was now after five in the evening, and office workers were already beginning to make their way home from the huge Government buildings in the area. As Frankie and Maggs strolled along, not holding hands or even exchanging a word, their heads were too glumly stooped towards the ground to notice the early evening sun reflecting a warm red glow on the surface of the river. They passed that magnificent obelisque, Cleopatra's Needle, without a glance, and were not even aware that on the other side of the river behind them, hundreds of LCC civil servants were streaming out of that Thames landmark, County Hall.

No contact was made between them until they were within sight of Captain Scott's old Antarctic vessel, *Discovery*. Maggs stopped strolling, and climbed up on to a stone parapet overlooking the river. She put down her school satchel and swimming towel and gazed out at the brand new, shining white Waterloo Bridge. And there she squatted, deep in contemplation, framed against the shimmering scarlet sun.

Frankie watched her. Having convinced himself that Maggs would now be finished with him, he had no idea what to do, no idea how he could possibly put things right with her again. To his surprise, however, she turned and called gently to him.

'Come and sit up here, Frank.'

Frankie's heart almost missed a beat. He quickly lifted himself up alongside her.

For a moment or two there was silence. They just sat there, looking out at the distant view of the dome of St Paul's Cathedral, which only a few years before had almost been destroyed by Hitler's aerial bombardment during the Battle of Britain, but was now drenched with the very different red glow of a summer's evening.

It was Frankie who spoke first. Taking a deep breath he said, 'It's a lovely view, in't it?'

There was a pause, then without turning to look at him, Maggs asked, 'Did you want to do it, Frankie?' Then she did turn to look at him. 'When Patty Jackson – when you both took your clothes off – did you *want* to do it with her?'

Frankie didn't know how to respond to so direct a question. Finally, all he could think of doing was to tell the truth. 'Yes,' he replied, turning his head away from her.

'Because you – like her?'

Frankie snapped back. 'No! I *'ate* 'er!'

'But you *wanted* to do it.'

Frankie rubbed his fingers through his hair in anguish. 'Only because – because – I was excited. Because I've never done it before. Because – I *'ad* ter find out what it was like.'

Maggs put her hand under his chin and raised it. His eyes remained lowered, but she was now looking straight at him. 'Frankie. Just tell me.

Are you in love with Patty Jackson?'

Frankie's eyes immediately looked up at her. 'In love wiv 'er! What're yer talkin' about, Maggs! I couldn't love anyone like Patty Jackson. I just couldn't!'

Maggs continued to watch him in silence.

Frankie felt desperate. 'Yer've gotta believe me, Maggs. Yer've just gotta! It's *you* I love. I swear ter God – I fell fer you the moment I set eyes on yer.'

For the first time Maggs smiled. All of a sudden she was not looking like a schoolgirl, but a lovely young woman. 'My mother says people of our age are too young to fall in love. D'you think that's true, Frankie?'

For a brief second, Frankie stared deep into her eyes. There was so much he wanted to say to her, to prove how he loved her more than anything or anybody in the whole wide world. But how could he convince her? How could he tell her that he would sooner be dead than live his life without her? Throwing caution to the wind, he grabbed hold of her shoulders, and kissed her full on the lips. To his immense relief, Maggs responded immediately. She threw her arms around him and pressed her lips against his for as long as they could breathe without coming up for air.

Down below on the river, a large coal-barge approached from beneath Waterloo Bridge and gradually made slow progress towards Hungerford Bridge and Westminster. As it passed by the parapet where two young people were locked together in a firm embrace, the skipper sounded the barge horn.

It seemed like a very approving sound.

Frankie got back to Merton Street at about half-past seven. The few hours he had spent with Maggs had raised his spirits more than he had dared hoped.

Even Merton Street itself looked better to Frankie. It was so uplifting to see so many of his neighbours sitting in chairs outside their front doors, basking in the warm evening sunshine. Since the end of the war only three weeks before, the residents of the street had started to freshen up the fronts of their houses, and even now some people were perched on ladders painting window frames or fixing gutters that had been neglected for so long.

However, he had noticed of late that the neighbours were beginning to keep themselves to themselves, so as he entered his own front gate it came as no real surprise when no one acknowledged him. So different to the war years, he thought, when everyone was in and out of each others' houses having cups of tea and a gossip. However, Bert Gorman and his next door neighbour, Edie Robson, did wave to him, so before disappearing into the house, he did likewise.

The first thing Frankie noticed as he entered

the front passage was that Winston had not come bounding down the stairs to meet him. As he closed the door behind him, he could hear the dog barking wildly from his bedroom upstairs.

'Winnie!' he called. 'Wot yer doin'? Come on boy!'

But as Winston continued to bark without appearing, it was obvious that for some reason or other the poor feller was locked up.

'Frankie! Is that you, son?' Gracie's voice called from the front room just as she herself opened the door and peered out into the passage. 'Ah – there yer are. Come in fer a minute. I want you ter meet somebody.'

Frankie was curious. He had no idea his mother and father were expecting any visitors. So he put his school haversack and swimming towel down on to the bottom stair, straightened his hair, and went into the front room. The moment he saw who was sitting there on the sofa, he froze.

'This is me son – Frankie.' Gracie was doing her best to be polite. 'Frankie. This gentleman has bought the 'ouse from Mr Jackson. 'E's our new landlord.'

'Don't worry, Mrs Lewis. Your son and I have already met.' The man got up from the sofa, smiled rather unctuously, and stretched out his hand to Frankie.

Frankie's blood turned to ice.

The man he was reluctantly shaking hands with was Elsa's brother-in-law, Jack Barclay.

Chapter Twenty-two

Friday 7th June 1945 was the first time for ages that nobody had come late for morning assembly at Highbury Grammar School. Whether it was out of respect or sympathy for Prof or because of 'Boggy' Marsh's warning of 'disciplinary measures' if anyone did arrive late, Frankie couldn't really tell. All he did know was that although it was only ten minutes to nine in the morning, the school hall was packed to suffocation. As usual, everyone had to stand, including the entire teaching staff who were gathered on the stage, all in very solemn mood.

Frankie had hardly slept all night. What with the horror of meeting up with Jack Barclay in his own home, and the prospect of having to face all his fellow pupils the following morning, it was little wonder he could now barely keep his eyes open.

'Boggy' Marsh arrived at one minute to nine and, at nine o'clock exactly, the short Thanksgiving service began. It wasn't really a religious service as in a church, but more of a chance for the pupils and teaching staff to pay their last respects to Prof. It started with 'Boggy' giving a short address about why this particular assembly was so special, and asking God and the school to give thanks for such a young life. Then everyone sang a hymn *The King of Love My Shepherd Is*, and that was followed by two of the pupils reading short extracts from the Bible. Frankie thought about the irony of these two particular boys being singled out to do such a thing, for Prof couldn't bear either of them. In a single row across the stage in the background stood the teachers and, once or twice, Frankie caught the eye of Mr Woods, the rather supercilious English master, who always seemed to Frankie to have a head too large for his body. Next to him was rotund Mrs Goulding, who spent most of the proceedings wiping tears away from her eyes, and alongside her was dear old Charlie Garrett, still sucking his loose tooth. Mr Lincoln, was, as usual, thumping away at the piano to accompany the hymn-singing.

By the time Charlie Garrett had finished his little speech about what a good pupil Prof was, Frankie's stomach was churning over so much he thought his legs would give way before it even came to his part in the proceedings. But after the next hymn had been sung, and he had been signalled by 'Boggy', he took a deep breath, clutched the book he was carrying firmly in his hands, and, climbing the steps on to the stage, took his place in front of the teaching staff.

The moment had finally come for him to look out at the mass of mauve school jackets. It was an awesome sight, and Frankie's mouth went so dry he didn't think he would be able to open it. It didn't help when one or two of the first term kids giggled in the front row, but one look from 'Boggy' sent a chill of terror through the culprits. In the few seconds that he stood there, trying desperately hard to summon up enough courage to speak, Frankie couldn't help thinking back to that night of the school concert, when Prof himself had been standing in exactly the same spot in the middle of the stage. In his mind's eye he could still see that frail little figure, who had just been beaten up so brutally by Jeff Murray, his lips swollen, a bruise on his cheek, and a gash over his eye. And in those few seconds he also remembered the magical sound Prof had made on his mouth-organ, and how he had got the entire audience to join in with a chorus of *Shine on Harvest Moon*. How they had loved him!

'As some of yer know, Pete Moosey was my best friend.' Without realising it, Frankie had started to speak. And his voice was so loud and clear it echoed around the Hall. 'Ter me, though, he was Prof. 'E'll always be that, 'cos that's 'ow I'll remember 'im – the one wiv the brains.'

'Boggy' Marsh was already beginning to wish he hadn't asked Frankie to speak. Shaking his head, the headmaster found it difficult to believe that despite Frankie Lewis's four years at Highbury Grammar School, he had stubbornly resisted losing his accent. The boy's vowel sounds were appalling!

'The fing is, sir,' he said, throwing a brief glance back at 'Boggy', 'there ain't much I can say about Prof – 'cos, ter be honest, 'e wouldn't want me to.' Then, turning back to the assembly, he continued, 'But if yer really wanna know somefin' about 'im . . .' at which point he raised the worn-looking book he was holding, 'it's all 'ere – in this book. I got it for 'im from this friend of mine who runs a shop. I reckon it was written by someone who was a bit like Prof.'

There was an air of curiosity throughout the Hall.

'It's about trains. Railway trains. 'E used ter go train spottin' over on Finsbury Park bridge – every Sunday mornin'. 'E must've collected 'undreds – no, *fousands* of train numbers. Yeah. That's what Prof cared about most of all. Not people – or fings – or knockin' around Merton Street where I live. It was trains. 'E worshipped 'em. Yeah. That was Prof all right.'

Mr Lincoln, who taught chemistry, was sitting at the upright piano, listening with great intensity to Frankie. He took off his metal-rimmed spectacles, and although Frankie was now only a blur, the boy's words were clearly having a marked effect on him.

'So if yer don't mind, sir,' continued Frankie, turning briefly again to 'Boggy', I'd like just ter read yer a bit from this book. 'Cos I know it's not only wot Prof himself would've liked, but I reckon it also tells yer quite a bit about 'im.'

There was a buzz of expectation around the Hall as Frankie opened the book and started to read:

'Wot is the attraction of the train, whose engine speeds yer fru the countryside at shatterin' speeds? Is it the smoke that billows out from the funnel of its coal-fired burner? Is it the convenience of gettin' ter yer destination in comfort an' on time an' wivout the trouble of 'avin ter ride yer 'orse or drive yer autermobile? Or is it because of the beauty of the creature itself, glidin' along the rails by day or night, defyin' the elements, tearin' against wind an' rain? As a regular passenger meself I know me journey well. I know every sound, every friendly jolt, an' every change in speed. I know where all the signals are, the junctions, an' the tunnels. Is there any more magical experience than ter sit in the comfort of a railway compartment as it disappears inter the darkness of a tunnel? Listen ter the sound! Yer can 'ear wot the engine's sayin' ter yer. An' when yer come out of the tunnel again, everythin' looks so much brighter. Yes, my friends, there is nothin' in this world like a journey by train, whevver it

be long – or whevver it be short.'

Frankie finished reading, closed the book, and walked off the stage.

Not a single sound could be heard in the Hall as he returned to his place in the front row of the Assembly.

Then everyone sang the school hymn: *To Be A Pilgrim*.

Frankie knew he would never forget this morning's Assembly at Highbury Grammar School.

As did his headmaster, 'Boggy' Marsh.

At three o'clock that afternoon, Prof's funeral took place in the Crematorium at Islington Cemetery. There were only two cars, sombre-looking black Daimler's. One of them was a hearse which carried Prof's body, and the other was for Auntie Hilda, her next door neighbour, Gladys, Mr and Mrs East who ran the ladies' handbag shop in Seven Sisters Road, and Frankie. The Vicar from the Emmanuel Church in Hornsey Road, the Rev. Monty Marshall travelled in the front seat with the driver.

When the tiny procession arrived at the entrance of the grey-stoned Crematorium Chapel, Frankie was surprised to see his sister Helen there with Eric. Helen knew Prof very well from all the times she had seen him with Frankie, and she also knew what a distressing experience

Prof's death had been for her young brother, so she wanted to be there to support him.

To Frankie's surprise, the service only lasted about fifteen minutes. The Reverend Marshall said a few words about Prof, and the sparse collection of people sang a hymn. Then Frankie's English teacher, Mr Woods, who had quietly entered from behind the procession when they came in, read from the Bible, and they finished with another hymn. Through it all, Frankie's eyes never left that coffin which was placed on a special plinth just in front of the altar. It seemed so small, both in length and width, with Auntie Hilda's single wreath of summer flowers placed on top.

Then the moment Frankie had been dreading finally came. In absolute silence, a huge pair of heavy curtains started to close solemnly across the altar. Frankie hated it. How different it was to what Prof had really wanted, he thought, as his mind flashed back to those strange few moments on the beach at Southend when Prof had talked about being buried at sea. He quickly shut his eyes and, in his mind, said, 'See yer, Prof!' When he opened them again, the coffin could no longer be seen.

Auntie Hilda was crying profusely and everyone filed out of the Chapel, with Frankie following last.

It was only as the procession reached the back of the small chapel that Frankie noticed three figures who had clearly crept in after the service had begun. It was Jeff Murray, Alan Downs, and Patty Jackson, all standing side by side in a back pew with their heads lowered.

Not one of Frankie's former friends in the Merton Street Gang raised their eyes to look up at him.

Everyone went straight to Auntie Hilda's flat above the ladies' handbag shop. Needless to say, she had made some cheese and fish-paste sandwiches, currant cakes, and a tinned fruit trifle. Once she had given the undertaker a cup of tea and paid him off, Auntie Hilda asked Frankie to come upstairs with her to Prof's bedroom.

'You're to take anything you want,' she said, her eyes were red from all the crying she had done. 'Peter left strict instructions. Whatever you like is yours.' She looked around the room with a warm, affectionate smile on her face. 'He said he particularly wanted you to have the train set, because you'd be the only one who'd appreciate it.' Auntie Hilda turned to look at Frankie. 'He was very fond of you, you know.'

Frankie felt numb inside. As he looked around his pal's bedroom, with all the gadgets and inventions Prof had worked on during his short lifetime, he just couldn't believe that he wouldn't be seeing him any more. 'I dunno wot ter say, Auntie,' said Frankie, feeling absolutely bewildered.

'Of course, whatever you don't want, I'll find a home for.' The rest I'll just have to put out for the dustman.' She made her way back to the door and turned. 'Anyway, you have a look round. Have a little think about it.'

After Auntie Hilda had gone, Frankie didn't know where to start. He wandered aimlessly around picking up pieces of Meccano and electrical wires. Then, with the tips of his fingers he gently touched Prof's enormous cardboard model of the RAF Mosquito fighter bomber which was dangling from the ceiling. It immediately started to swing to and fro as though it was actually in flight. Then he moved across to the chest of drawers and admired Prof's model of a four-masted sailing ship, which Frankie decided there and then that he would like to keep because in his mind it was absolutely brilliant. From the chest of drawers, he turned to look down at the floor. And there it was, Prof's pride and joy – the incredible model train system built entirely by Prof himself, complete with the replica of the *Flying Scot* train engine and carriages. Passenger station, signal boxes, bridges, and a railway track covered the entire floor. Frankie dropped to his knees, crouched alongside the minutely constructed track, and started to feel the engine and its colourful freight and passenger rolling stock. Then he turned on the switch. Suddenly, the *Flying Scot* started to pull away from the station marked, 'Seven Sisters

Road', and, as Frankie operated a lever outside the track, it gathered speed on its adventurous journey around its inventor's room. As it went, Frankie was telling himself that, as much as he would dearly love to have all this wonderful gadgetry for himself, he was growing up and would surely have no use for it. But as the mighty express train rattled effortlessly beneath Prof's bed, and headed off at high speed around the back of the chest of drawers, the *Flying Scot's* engine whistle shrieked out loud as if to remind Frankie that his own journey was only just beginning, and that one day maybe he himself would have a son of his own who would thrill to the sight and sound of Prof's great railway system. So, as tears flowed down his cheeks for the first and only time that day, he made an instant decision.

'I'll keep it, Prof!' he yelled out loud. 'I'll never part wiv it – not fer as long as I live!'

Chapter Twenty-three

During the first week in July, Frankie took his school exams. It was three days of sheer hell and he hated every minute of it. Despite the sympathetic extra tuition he had been given by the teaching staff, Frankie knew that he hadn't a hope in hell of getting the necessary number of passes, especially with subjects like mathematics, physics, and French. But for three days he sat there and sweated it out, dreading the time in September when the results – and his future – would be known. Before that, though, Frankie had another ordeal to endure . . .

Helen and Eric were married on the third Saturday in July. By then, of course, she was eight months gone, and, in the words of her father, 'only just made it.' The wedding took place in a rather stark oak-panelled room in the Islington Town Hall in Upper Street. Despite the fact that Helen had to have her friend Iris make her wedding dress, which was made up of rather a lot of plain blue taffeta, Eric thought she looked very nice in it. It was only a short dress, but luckily Helen was able to get a special ration coupon allowance for the material, otherwise it would have been a question of '*something borrowed*'. Helen had bought her close-fitting hat with its fashionable marine-look and blue veil from Jones Brothers in Holloway Road, pleased at how good a match it was for her dress. Eric didn't look too bad either, she reckoned proudly, in his navy-blue demob suit, white shirt, Tootal tie, and highly polished bull-shined shoes, a hangover from his army square-bashing days.

There were about two dozen guests. Apart from Gracie and Reg, on Helen's side there were Reg's sister and her husband, Auntie Dot and Uncle Harry (who hadn't seen Gracie and Reg for years, and only accepted the invitation out of curiosity), Lil' and Ed who worked with Reg at the Baths in Hornsey Road, and Joyce and Ivy, Helen's two best friends. Most of the remaining guests came from Eric's side – his parents, two widowed aunts, a grandmother from each side of his family and one grandfather, three cousins, two nieces, and two of his ex-army pals and their girlfriends.

And then, of course, there was Frankie, who arrived for the ceremony at the Town Hall far more nervous than both bride and groom and all the guests put together. First he was self-conscious in the new, double-breasted grey flannel suit Eric had bought him. Then, despite the fact that he had put the wedding ring on his own forefinger for safe keeping, he had convinced himself that when the time came he would have lost it. Tragedy did strike close, for when he was eventually asked to produce the ring he found it was stuck hard on his finger, and only some of his Auntie Dot's face cream solved the problem of releasing it.

The reception was held at number 1 Merton Street, and between them, Gracie and Helen had searched around for enough ration coupons to provide a very appetising buffet tea. This included a variety of sandwiches with fillings such as real ham and cods' roe, and among the many delicacies were two bowls of boiled pigs' trotters. There were also two enormous custard trifles but the pièce de résistance was the wedding cake, a gift from Auntie Hilda who had made it herself.

The problems did not start appearing until well into the evening . . .

It was obvious from the start that Gracie Lewis and Eric's mum, Phyllis Sibley were not going to get on. To Gracie, it seemed that the stupid cow of a woman had nothing better to do than to criticise. First it was about Frankie being a bit young to be a best man, and then barbed comments about how well turned-out her 'side' were. Gracie also couldn't bear Eric's father, a former semi-pro boxer who spoke as though he was punch-drunk, moaning about how tough the pigs' trotters were and complaining that the Guinness was too cold. The crunch came, luckily, after the bride and groom had left for their week's honeymoon in Bognor Regis and most of the guests had left.

'I must say, Gracie,' said Phyllis, 'I did feel so sorry for your poor 'Elen' – 'avin' ter stand up at the weddin' like that in 'er condition.' She was on her third gin and tonic, and clearly itching to get a dig at her hosts.

'Oh, I dunno,' Gracie said, icily. 'I fawt she looked really lovely.'

Phyllis popped a potato crisp in her mouth. 'It's such a pity they didn't get to know each other before they got – well, before they got so involved. I mean, I wonder wot would 'ave 'appened if Eric *'adn't* wanted ter marry 'er when he come back from the Army?'

Gracie didn't drink spirits, but she had already downed two bottles of stout, and the danger signals were there. 'I'm sure she'd 'ave done the same as any uvver girl – found someone else.'

'Oh, don't get me wrong, Gracie.' Phyllis was perfectly aware that she was being provocative. 'Eric's an 'onorable boy. Before 'e met your 'Elen, 'e'd 'ad lots of girls. Any one of 'em'd tell yer that 'e'd never leave 'em in the lurch.'

There was an uneasy silence as everyone in the room listened to the conversation between the two women and pretended not to.

Gracie slammed down her half-consumed glass

of stout, spilling some of it on to the tablecloth. 'Let me tell *you* somefin', *Mrs* Sibley. It takes two ter make a party, yer know. If your son 'ad taken precautions, they wouldn't've *'ad* ter get married.'

Phyllis's hackles rose immediately. 'Come off it! Your daughter knew exactly wot she wanted – and she got it all right!'

Gracie sat bolt upright in her chair. 'Are you tryin' ter make suggestions about my daughter?'

Reg, aware that his wife was rising too easily to Phyllis Sibley's bait, quickly interrupted. 'Forget it now, Grace.'

But Phyllis was determined to carry on with the scene. 'I'm not suggestin' anyfin',' she snapped. 'But your daughter only 'ad 'erself ter blame for gettin' 'erself inter this kind of situation.'

'Shut up will yer, Phyll!' This time it was Mick Sibley who interrupted.

But it was too late. The two women had now gone too far.

'Your son is just as guilty as my daughter!' Gracie yelled. 'Soldiers are all the same. They're only out fer one fing!'

'Don't you dare say that about my son!'

'Don't you say that about my daughter!'

Frankie leapt up. 'It's not true – none of it! Eric loves 'Elen, and she loves 'im. That's why they got married. *That's* why they're 'avin' a baby!'

This unexpected outburst from Frankie momentarily united both mothers.

'You mind yer own bleedin' business, Frank! This 'as got nothin' ter do wiv you!' Gracie's eyes were nearly popping out of their sockets with rage.

'Just keep yer tongue between yer teeth, young man! I told Eric you was too young to be a best man!'

'Don't you talk about my boy like that!' yelled Gracie, turning on Phyllis again. ''E was a wonderful best man!'

By now, Frankie was convinced they were both mad, so he quickly sat down again.

'Right! That's me lot fer one day.' Mick Sibley got up from the arm-chair. 'Come on, Phyll. Get yer arse out of 'ere!'

At which point, Reg Lewis got up from the other armchair. 'Come on now, everyone. This is supposed ter be our kids' weddin' day. If they 'eard us goin' on like this, they'd do their nuts!'

'I'm sorry, Reg.' Mick put on his jacket and made for the door. He looked fed-up with the whole set-to, for he actually got on quite well with his new daughter-in-law's father. 'I know my missus. She won't give up 'til she's got everyone pissin' in their pants!'

'Ha!' Gracie reacted in a flash. 'Well, she won't get me doin' any such fing!'

Last to get up was Phyllis. 'Don't worry, I've spent all the time in this 'ouse that I want!' She quickly straightened her dress and tried to look unruffled. 'I just 'ope that all the people who've tasted the muck that's bin served up 'ere terday will still be alive in the mornin'!'

'Well, p'rhaps they might've bin,' snarled Gracie, as she followed Phyllis to the door, 'if you'd given one hand or one penny ter 'elp!'

'Grace!' Reg yelled so loud that Winston leapt behind the sofa.

Reg followed Mick and Phyllis Sibley out into the hall passage, making quite sure he shut the front room door behind him. Gracie and Frankie remained behind, with Gracie, clenching her fists in anger. She found herself a fag and lit it.

After a moment, Reg came back into the room and slammed the door behind him. 'Yer stupid bitch!'

Gracie blew out an angry cloud of smoke, 'You leave me alone! I didn't start it!'

'No, you didn't start it! But yer couldn't resist 'avin' a go at yer, could yer?' He went straight to the ashtray where he had left a half-finished fag. 'She *wanted* yer ter take 'er on. She *wanted* ter make trouble. Yes – and yer let 'er, Grace. Yer bloody well let 'er! Yer own daughter's weddin' day, and you 'ad ter go and finish it off like this!'

'I did everfin' in my power ter make this a nice day for 'Elen!' yelled Gracie.

'So why ruin it by losin' yer temper! 'Ow d'yer fink 'Elen's goin' ter feel when she 'ears about all this?'

'That woman's a bloody bitch – and you know it!'

'Of course I know it. But that don't mean you 'ave ter be'ave like 'er. Don't yer understand, Grace? Wevver we like it or not, she's now 'Elen's muvver-in-law!'

Winston leapt up beside Frankie on the sofa, worried that the screaming match was something to do with him. Frankie himself found the whole incident deeply upsetting and disappointing. Over the past few weeks it had seemed that his mother and father were beginning to become better friends than they had ever been, but now they were fighting like cat and dog.

'It's no use, Grace!' Reg, his back turned towards the small, tiled-surround fireplace, took a deep draw on his fag. 'When I saw yer put so much effort inter – ' he looked towards the parlour table with the remains of the wedding buffet ' – inter all this, I felt proud of yer, really proud. But yer 'ad ter go an' spoil it all. Why, Grace? Why?'

'Let me tell yer somefin' – mate! *You* got me inter all this – you and that bloody son-in-law of ours! If I 'adn't 'ave listened to you, if I 'adn't 'ave been so bloody taken in by yer, I'd never 'ave agreed to 'ave the do in this 'ouse in the first place!'

'Don't be silly, Mum,' interrupted Frankie. 'It was marvellous . . .'

'You keep out of this!' Gracie shrieked back at him.

'Listen to 'er!' bawled Reg. 'You're like a ravin'

lunatic! Why can't yer see that it was our duty to give 'Elen a good send-off. We're 'er mum and dad, for Chrissake. Gord knows we've done little enough for our kids since they was born!'

'Speak for yerself!' Gracie pushed him out of the way, and threw her only partly finished fag into the empty fire-grate. 'P'raps if you'd given us a proper 'ome, we could've done more fer all of us!'

''Ang on, you!' Reg growled back angrily. 'Just wot's that supposed ter bloody mean?'

'You know wot I bloody mean! Pissin' yerself silly 'round the pub every night.'

'Well, I'd sooner piss myself 'round the pub than sit 'ere wiv you!' With his smoking fag gripped in his teeth and his finger wagging menacingly at Gracie. Reg was prepared to say anything that came into his head. 'Shall I tell yer somefin,' Grace? As a wife, you stink!'

Frankie was thunderstruck by his father's cutting attack. 'Dad!'

'Get out of 'ere, you!' yelled Reg at the boy.

''Ow could yer say such a fing!' Frankie was close to tears.

'Out!' Reg now seemed to have lost all control.

Frankie got up from the sofa and left the room with Winston. The rest of the conversation he heard by hanging around in the passage outside.

'Grace,' Reg said, no longer shouting. 'I've wanted ter tell yer this fer a long time, but I've always bin afraid of yer. Gord knows why I should be scared of me own wife, but that's 'ow it's been.'

Frankie could hear his father's voice clearly.

'We're not a 'usband and wife, Grace. We 'aven't bin fer years. Wot's 'appened to us? We don't talk, we don't listen to each uvver. Oh yeah, now the shelter's bin taken down, we sleep in the same bed tergevver agin. But we don't *do* anyfin', Grace. We don't do anyfin', 'cos – well, let's face, we don't know each uvver – do we?'

There was absolutely no response from Gracie at all.

'It comes ter somefin' when a 'usband and wife can't even talk ter each uvver about their problems, don't it? I mean, I go off ter the Baths in the mornin', do a day's work, and when I come 'ome, even if there is a meal waiting, we don't 'ave it tergevver, we don't talk about wot we've both done all day.' Gradually, the anger was leaving Reg's voice. 'Why is it like that, Grace? Why does it 'ave ter be like that? Why do yer 'ave ter shout and 'oller and go on all the time about 'ow much you 'ate everybody?' He paused just long enough to try to compose himself. 'Oh Grace. Why can't yer understand that I don't care *'ow* people like that woman be'ave. But I do care about you. About Gracie Lewis – *my* wife!'

In the passage outside, Frankie sat on the stairs and covered his face with his hands.

'Why do you 'ave ter treat me and 'Elen and Frank as if we were a big mistake in yer life?

Wot did I do wrong, Grace? Tell me? Wot did I do wrong?'

Suddenly, Frankie was startled by the sound of the parlour door being thrown open. As he looked up, his mother came hurrying out, and, without stopping for a single second, rushed straight out of the house and into the street.

'Mum!' Frankie got to his feet.

As he did so, Reg called from the front room. 'Let 'er go. She'll be back!'

In her sitting-room, Elsa was at her upright desk reading some documents which had arrived from her solicitor that morning. She hadn't been sleeping too well of late, so she delayed going to bed for as long as possible.

As he had now taken his school exams and had a few weeks to spare before the results were known, Frankie had been helping out in the shop on most days, for Elsa was trusting him more and more to take over the more strenuous duties in the running of the shop. But once or twice Frankie had noticed how tired she was looking, and he told her so. He put it down to the strain of working too hard, and also the pressure being put on her by her brother-in-law. Elsa feared that Barclay's purchase of the Lewises' house was going to be used as some kind of blackmail. Which is why she had been in touch with her solicitor.

As she read the documents, Elsa's mind

wandered to the events of the day at number 1 Merton Street. Her face broke into an affectionate smile as she tried to imagine Frankie, all togged up in his new double-breasted suit, acting as grown-up as he could as best man. But her smile quickly faded and she returned to the letter she was reading. How *could* she accept the solicitor's advice, she wondered? And how would she ever be able to tell Frankie?

She sighed and put down the letter, then she closed the desk and went to bed.

It was now after one o'clock in the morning.

An hour later, Gracie Lewis still hadn't arrived back home. When she rushed out of the house soon after ten o'clock that evening, she was only wearing the thin summer dress she had worn for Helen's wedding, but luckily it was a warm night so Frankie wasn't too worried that his mother would catch cold. What he was worried about, however, was that it was now four hours that she'd been gone, and despite his father's assurance of 'Don't worry, she'll be back', she *still* hadn't returned.

Frankie had gone outside several times to see if there was any sign of her, but Merton Street was totally deserted except for the odd scavenging cat. To make matters worse, soon after his mother had left the house, his father had gone up to bed, and hadn't reappeared since. Frankie couldn't believe anyone could be so heartless, and there were several times when he wanted to go upstairs and thump on his parents' bedroom door. It was so cruel of his father to just go off to sleep and ignore the fact that his mother was wandering the streets alone.

But Reg Lewis had not slept a wink. He hadn't even taken off his clothes or got into bed. For four hours, he had kept a lonely vigil at the upstairs bedroom window, peering out from behind the curtains at the street below. The effect of the large amount of brown ale that he had drunk was beginning to wear off, and, as his mind began to clear, he felt riddled with guilt and apprehension. He had belittled Gracie in front of Frankie, and robbed her of any dignity she might have had left. He lit fag after fag and kept asking himself how he could have talked to her like that. And why blame her, after all? A marriage was a partnership; it had to be worked at by two people, not just one. If Gracie had never been a good wife and mother to their children, he himself was just as much to blame.

'Dad!'

Reg turned from the window when he heard Frankie tapping on the bedroom door.

'Dad! Are yer there?'

Reg stubbed his fag end out in the lid of an old Zubes tin, went to the door and opened it. As there was no light on the landing outside, he could only see the dim outline of his son.

'Dad. She's bin gone fer over four hours. I'm goin' out ter look for 'er.'

Reg turned on the bedroom light. He could immediately see Frankie's tense and anxious face. 'Leave 'er alone, son. She'll come back when she's ready.'

Frankie stiffened. ''Ow can yer say that! She's all on 'er own out there. Suppose somefin's 'appened to 'er? Fer all we know someone might've coshed 'er or – or . . . Dad, we just can't leave 'er.'

Reg left the bedroom light on so that he could see his way back downstairs. 'We'll give 'er anuvver 'alf 'our or so.'

'If we wait anuvver 'alf 'our, we should call 'Ornsey Road Police Station!'

At the bottom of the stairs, where Winston was waiting patiently, Reg turned on the hall passage light, which immediately covered all three of them in a sickly yellow glow. 'Yer muvver's no fool, Frank. She knows wot she's doin'.'

'Does she, Dad? Do *eivver* of yer know wot yer're doin'?'

This piercing remark caused Reg to turn around and look at his son. Things had not been right between them since the day Reg had created the ugly scene outside poor old Clancy's house, so it was an odd feeling for both of them when they found themselves gazing straight into each other's eyes for the first time in several months.

'I'm just as worried about yer mum as you are, Frank.' There was anguish in Reg's voice.

'Then why did yer talk to 'er the way you did?'

Reg didn't know how to answer.

'Why?'

Frankie's naïve insistence sent a cold chill down Reg's spine. 'I don't know, son.' Reg's face began to tense, and his voice was cracking. 'It's one of the mysteries of lovin' someone.'

'I don't understand, Dad.' Frankie stared straight into his father's eyes. 'If yer love Mum, then why d'yer talk to 'er like yer did?'

Reg lowered his eyes. *Love* her, he asked himself. *Love* Gracie – after all these years? Surely their marriage had been nothing more than an escape from the depression of those turbulent years between the two great wars, and love had played no part at all, not then, not ever. Or *had* it? Had there been something lurking inside Reg Lewis that he had never recognised – or wanted to recognise? Without answering Frankie's question, he turned and made his way towards the front room.

Frankie followed him. 'Dad – tell me!' he said, raising his voice. 'Do yer love 'er – or don't yer?'

Reg stopped in the open doorway of the front room. He didn't turn. 'Yes,' he said, his voice cracking with emotion. 'I've always loved her.'

For a moment, Frankie remained quite still. It was not difficult for him to guess how much it had meant for his father to say such a thing.

'Then why don't yer tell 'er so?'

The strain of trying to understand his emotions finally took its toll on Reg. Without saying another word he burst into tears, ran into the front room, and shut the door behind him.

Frankie waited a moment, then he collected Winston's leash and fixed it to the dog's collar. 'Come on boy,' he said. 'Let's go and find 'er.'

Frankie and Winston's route took them into Seven Sisters Road, where Frankie knew his mother spent much of her time window shopping. But this was the middle of the night, and there was no sign of Gracie now, only the boxes of rotten fruit and veg waiting to be collected by the dustmen outside Ma Digby's greengrocer's shop, and the smell of winkles, whelks, and crabs drifting out through the door of the fresh fish shop. Winston got very excited by all the inviting smells.

As he reached the traffic lights at the junction with Hornsey Road, Frankie's stomach was churning. There was no sign of his mother anywhere, and he was in two minds about whether to go and report her missing at Hornsey Road Police Station, but he was temporarily distracted by the overpowering smell of bread-baking coming from Stagnell's shop, where the basement lights were on.

Winston suddenly became very agitated and tugged hard on his leash, pulling himself free and running off. Remembering what had happened the last time the dog was loose on a main road, Frankie panicked. 'Winnie!' he called, chasing after the dog. 'Winnie! Come back 'ere, yer stupid git . . .!' But Winston didn't stop until he had reached the front gate of number 1 and when Frankie finally caught up with him he was already being made a fuss of by Gracie Lewis, who was sitting on the coping-stone.

'Mum!' Wheezing badly from the start of one of his now less frequent asthma attacks, Frankie was desperately relieved to find his mother safe and sound. 'Wot 'appened ter yer? Me and Winnie . . . we've lookin' all over fer yer! I fawt – I fawt – ' He suddenly realised that he was babbling, but his relief was so intense that he did something that he had never done in all his life before. He threw his arms around Gracie and hugged her as tight as he could. 'Oh Mum! Don't ever do fings like that again!'

Gracie found herself hugging him back and holding on to him. For her, also, it was a new and rewarding experience, and for the first time it gave her hope. During the past few hours she had walked the dark and lonely streets, with only one horrifying thought tearing away at her mind: *'As a wife, you stink!'* Reg's words had been devastating and had made her look back over their whole life together. And it hadn't been the remark itself that had sent her rushing out into the night, but the fact that it was the truth.

Gracie knew that she had *not* been a good wife to Reg Lewis. She knew she had not been a good mother to their kids. But it wasn't true that she didn't love them. The trouble was, and had always been, that she didn't know how to *show* that love.

Not wanting to be left out of anything, Winston, tail wagging wildly, leapt up, and tried to lick them both. For a little while Gracie held on to Frankie, as if she wanted to savour this moment for as long as possible, then she kissed the top of his head. Finally, she spoke.

'Come on, son. It's past our bedtime.'

With that, she got up, put her arm around Frankie, and, with Winston leading them, they all went back into the house.

The following Monday morning, Frankie turned up at the shop to start work full-time until the results of his exams were known in a few weeks' time. When he arrived, Elsa was already there, brewing up her kettle of hot water for a mug of tea, despite the fact that it was yet another blisteringly hot July morning. But she was not in the best of moods, which was unlike her, for even when she was feeling depressed Elsa had a way of pretending that everything was perfectly all right.

Apart from a casual morning greeting, Elsa said very little to Frankie until he had finished stacking a pile of wooden boxes containing secondhand baby's clothing. Finally, she said 'Sit down for a minute, Frankie. I want to talk to you.'

The moment she spoke, Frankie knew that something was badly wrong. He sat on his usual high-stool by the counter, and Elsa sat on hers behind it.

'We have a problem, Frankie.' She tried to smile. 'What would you say if I told you that – I have to sell the shop?'

Frankie felt as though he had been nailed to the stool he was sitting on . . .

Chapter Twenty-four

On Thursday 26th July everyone got very excited by the results of the previous day's General Election, in which Mr Attlee's Labour Party was swept in by a landslide vote. Frankie thought it was marvellous news, for since he had become such a close friend of Eric, he was convinced that getting rid of the Tories would mean that ordinary people would be treated fairer, like having a National Health Service and all sorts of other benefits. Even so, he did feel a little uneasy that Winston Churchill had been kicked out of office after leading the country so triumphantly through a long and dangerous war.

Just a few weeks before the Election, Churchill himself had come to Islington to campaign. Frankie had been very excited at the prospect of actually seeing, in person, the nation's hero, so on the morning of the Rally, which was to be held outside Beales restaurant on the corner of Holloway Road and Tollington Road, he made quite sure he got a front position right by the dais where the Prime Minister was due to speak. Unfortunately, the poor man was denied the chance to say anything, for among the huge crowd who had turned up to hear him was a sizeable gang of thugs who created such chaos with booing and jostling, that Mr Churchill couldn't even reach the dais. However, Frankie wasn't nearly as interested in politics as Eric. Indeed, he was only too relieved that he wasn't allowed to vote until he was twenty-one.

Frankie hadn't seen any of the Merton Street gang since Prof's funeral. Although he had been grateful that they at least made the effort to pay their last respects, he could never really forgive Jeff or Patty for what they had done to him on the bike trip. Alan Downs was a different matter. Frankie felt sorry that he had to knock around with the others. But Frankie knew why he did it. He was just crazy for Patty Jackson.

On the Saturday afternoon after the General Election, Frankie was due to go with Eric to the Arsenal Football Stadium where 'the Gunners' were playing a summer special home game. In the morning he went to Woolworth's in Holloway Road to buy his sister Helen, who was now only two weeks off from having her baby, some of her favourite macaroon biscuits. Whilst he was waiting in a queue at the counter, he was surprised to see Jeff Murray just coming in through the Enkel Street back entrance of the store.

Frankie had recently heard that Jeff, who was now almost eighteen years old, had received his call-up papers, and was due at any minute to go into the Royal Navy to do his two years' National Service. A few minutes later, Patty Jackson came through the same door, and although it was quite clear that she was with Jeff, she made off in a different direction towards the nearby electrical counter.

For the next few minutes, Jeff wandered in and out of the shoppers, casually glancing at the different counter displays. He spent most of his time at the gramophone record counter where he sorted through the latest releases and listened to the song the assistant was playing sung by a new comedian called Danny Kaye from his film, *Wonder Man*. After a while, Patty also joined the crowd at the record counter, but curiously, she did not acknowledge Jeff's presence there.

Frankie reached the front of the queue he was standing in, and paid for his biscuits. But as he mingled with the other shoppers, his attention was constantly drawn towards Jeff and Patty, who were behaving in a very odd way, ignoring each other at opposite ends of the record counter. Frankie had a nasty feeling that they were up to something.

A few moments later, Jeff casually wandered across to the jewellery counter close by. There he paused to browse through the tatty selection of cheap rings, necklaces, bracelets, and brooches.

At the gramophone record counter nearby, Patty Jackson peered carefully over her shoulder to check what Jeff was doing.

Frankie hung around the stationery counter, watching Jeff and Patty's every move. Their behaviour was making him nervous, for it seemed as though they were plotting something quite daring. Frankie hated the way they were always doing stupid things that could get them into trouble.

Jeff finally found something that appealed to him, a pair of men's cufflinks attached to a small piece of cardboard and marked at sixpence. But, Frankie noticed, he didn't pick them up until he was sure that the assistant had her back turned towards him and was serving a customer on the opposite side of the counter. Frankie who had by now himself reached the jewellery counter, made quite sure that he kept carefully concealed behind some other browsing shoppers.

As soon as he was confident that no one was watching him, Jeff briskly snatched the cufflinks, covered them with his hand, and quickly tucked them into his trousers pocket.

Frankie watched with growing horror. Over the heads of the other shoppers he could see Jeff make a quick dash towards the Holloway Road entrance, unchallenged by anybody. Patty, who had hardly been able to conceal her excitement, then followed at a safe distance behind.

'Excuse me, sir. May I see what you just put in your pocket?'

Jeff stopped dead as a burly brown-coated store assistant appeared from nowhere and blocked his exit. 'Wot yer talkin' about?' he spluttered, indignantly.

'I just saw you take something from the jewellery counter.' The assistant was polite, but firm. 'If you don't mind, I'd like to see what it is.'

Patty looked on in horror from a safe distance nearby.

Jeff, now white-faced with fright, tried to pass it off with his usual bravado. 'Yer've got a bloody cheek! You tryin' ter accuse me of nickin' or somefin'?'

'Turn out yer pockets, son!' This time it was a different voice that approached him. 'Come on now. We 'aven't got all day!'

The sight of a Police Constable stopping someone at the entrance immediately drew a crowd of onlookers. But not Patty. Despite a look of desperation from Jeff for help, she was out of the store in a flash.

Although Frankie couldn't hear what was going on near the store entrance, he could just see Jeff with the Police Constable. The stupid, mindless git! What a thing to do! He'd really dropped himself in it and he deserved all he got! But despite his bitter resentment of everything Jeff had ever done, Frankie felt his stomach churning over inside. There was only one thing to do, he thought. Quickly pushing his way back through the shoppers, he went straight to the jewellery counter.

Realising that there was now nothing he could do but obey the Police Constable's command, Jeff took the cufflinks out of his pocket, and gave them to the store assistant.

'Thank you, sir. Do you have a receipt for this item?'

'Of course I don't 'ave a bloody receipt!' Jeff was trying to bluff his way out by becoming aggressive. 'The gel never give me one.'

The assistant exchanged a knowing glance with the Constable. 'I find that hard to believe, sir,' he said, rather grandly.

'Well, she didn't. An' if yer keep me 'angin' 'round 'ere my old man'll be onter your manager. Everyone knows my dad up the Town 'All!'

The crowd of onlookers gasped as they watched the Police Constable take hold of Jeff's arm. 'You'd better come along wiv me, son. You can tell us all about yer old man back at the Station.'

'I tell yer I didn't nick it! I paid wiv it – wiv me own money!'

'That's absolutely untrue, Constable,' said the store assistant, very proud to have caught a shop-lifter red-handed. 'There's no receipt. It's perfectly obvious that the cufflinks haven't been paid for.'

'That's not quite true, Constable. *I* paid for them.'

Everyone turned to look at Frankie, who, breathless, had pushed his way to the front of the crowd.

'That was right, wasn't it?' Frankie said to an absolutely astonished Jeff. 'That *is* wot yer give me the money for wan't it? Ter buy the cufflinks?'

Jeff was so flustered, he didn't know what to say. But he eventually caught on and answered quickly, 'Yeh! Yeh, that's wot it was for.'

Frankie sighed with mock relief. 'Oh, fank goodness! I give the girl a tanner. That was the price, wan't it?'

'Yeh! Yeh! That's it! A tanner!' The colour was gradually returning to Jeff's face.

'I presume you have a receipt for the item?' repeated the store assistant, not believing a word Frankie had said.

'Course I got a receipt! Wot d'yer take me for then? I ain't no shop-lifter, yer know!'

To the assistant's intense irritation, he took the receipt that Frankie was wagging in front of his face. The burly man scrutinized it carefully.

'Of course, if yer don't believe me, yer could always go an' ask the gel at the counter.'

The Police Constable awaited a nod from the assistant that the receipt was indeed genuine. When he got it, he let go of Jeff's arm. 'On your way, son.'

'Can I 'ave my cufflinks back, please?' Jeff held

out his hand triumphantly to the store assistant.

The assistant dropped the cufflinks into the palm of Jeff's hand. 'If I was you, I'd be careful next time.'

'Same goes for you,' Jeff came back with a smug grin on his face. 'If I may say so?'

As the assistant was about to go, Frankie then held out his hand. ''Scuse me. My receipt, I believe?'

The assistant slammed the receipt into Frankie's hand. Then he and the Police Constable turned their backs, and strolled off together, probably blaming each other for the blunder.

'So?' Jeff snarled at the crowd of onlookers. 'Wot you all gapin' at then?'

'Let's go!' snapped Frankie anxiously, trying desperately not to draw any more attention to themselves.

The crowd quickly dispersed, allowing Jeff and Frankie to make their way together out of the store and into Holloway Road. They only spoke when they reached the Nag's Head pub on the corner of Holloway Road and Seven Sisters Road.

'Fanks a lot, Frank,' Jeff said, incongruously patting Frankie on the back. 'I'll pay yer the tanner back next time I see yer.'

'Keep it!' Frankie's reply was like stone. 'Spend it on gettin' yerself a brain-surgeon!'

'I only did it fer a dare. It was that bleedin' Patty. She put me up to it.'

Frankie turned to go.

'Looks like I owe yer one, Frank?' Jeff held out his hand for Frankie to shake.

Frankie looked at Jeff's hand only briefly then slapped something straight into it. 'Yer owe me nuffin', Jeff! Absolutely nuffin'!'

Jeff watched Frankie as he turned and walked off down Seven Sisters Road. Then he looked to see what it was that Frankie had slapped into his hand. It was the receipt, together with the second pair of cufflinks, Frankie had quickly bought in order to get a receipt. Then, with a shrug of the shoulders, Jeff also turned, and hurried off.

Elsa told Frankie that she wanted him to look after the shop in the afternoon, on the following Monday week, because she had made an appointment to see her solicitor. Ever since she'd told him that she had been advised to sell the shop to Jack Barclay, Frankie had not stopped trying to persuade her that it would be a mad thing to do. He made no secret of the fact that he didn't trust Barclay and Elsa always listened intently to Frankie's advice and concerns, without ever letting on that she had absolutely no intention of selling the shop to anyone. Despite her solicitor's anxieties about the strain on her health, the shop meant far more to her than just money. But there was no doubt that these days, for certain reasons, Frankie's help was becoming more important than she had ever imagined.

When Frankie and Winston arrived at the shop first thing on the Monday morning, they were both angry to see Jack Barclay's car parked near the traffic lights.

'Ah, there you are! Good morning, young man!'

The moment he entered the shop, the sound of Barclay's voice made Frankie feel sick and he had to keep a tight hold of Winston's collar, for the dog was growling and bearing his teeth at Elsa's unwelcome visitor.

'I've been hearing what a great help you've been around the place.' Barclay, sipping from a cup of Camp coffee, looked up and smiled brightly at Frankie. Since the last time he met the boy, he had decided that it would not be in his interest to antagonise someone who had become so friendly with his sister-in-law. 'It's such a good idea your working here full time. Poor Elsa could do with the rest.'

'Elsa isn't *poor* Elsa!' she snapped quickly. 'And she doesn't need anything of the sort! We're too busy to think about rest.' Then she turned to Frankie, and asked haughtily, 'Isn't that so, Frankie?'

Frankie knew exactly what she meant him to say. 'Yes, Elsa.'

'Busy?' Barclay put his cup back on to the saucer and looked around the shop. 'Is it always as *busy* as this?'

'Don't be stupid, Jack!' Elsa snapped. 'You don't expect customers at this time of the morning.'

Barclay raised his eyes with a curious smile. 'Then why open so early?'

'Monday mornin's are always quiet,' said Frankie, speaking for the first time. 'It picks up later.'

'Oh really?' Barclay gave Frankie a sneering look, forgetting briefly that he was supposed to be nice to the boy. But he quickly put things right again with another big smile. 'I can see how lucky Elsa is to have someone like you working for her. I'll bet you're a wonderful salesman.'

Frankie did not respond. He wasn't taken in for one minute by Barclay's new-found admiration of him.

Barclay put his cup and saucer down on to the counter and got up from the high stool he was sitting on. Winston immediately started to growl at him again, so Frankie had to take him to the back room.

'I wonder,' said Barclay, resting both hands in the pockets of his tweed jacket. 'I wonder if there will still be a need for places like this in years to come?'

'If you need to wear clothes, you need a shop to buy them in,' Elsa replied, wryly.

Barclay started wandering around the shop, inspecting not only the goods on sale, but also the walls, ceilings, and plumbing pipes. 'What I mean is, as soon as the war with the Japs is over, things are bound to be different – business will want to invest in new ways of selling and buying.'

He stopped briefly to peer back at them from between a row of shelves containing a large selection of home-made pickles and sauces. 'I've heard that in America people are now doing their shopping in places called *supermarkets*. It's apparently one big shop where you can buy absolutely everything.'

'Can't see it catchin' on 'ere,' said Frankie, firmly. 'Not wiv this new Labour Government in power.'

Barclay's smile faded immediately. 'Even a Labour Government can't ignore the march of progress!' he snapped.

To Elsa's delight, the first customer of the day walked in, an elderly lady who was looking for a table-fan to keep her husband cool during the current terrible heatwave. To his dismay, Frankie couldn't help her. 'Sorry, madam,' he said, in his best shop-manner voice. 'I'm afraid we're out of stock just at the moment.'

After the woman had gone, Barclay had his best opportunity to force home a point. 'You see what I mean? In a small shop like this, you can't sell everything. It's not worth it, Elsa. It's just not worth it.' Then he cast his glance upwards. 'I mean, just look at the place . . . that huge crack in the ceiling. And the plumbing, the woodwork, the wiring. . . . The building's in a terrible condition, Elsa. If you're not careful, you'll have the Council condemning the place as unsafe.'

So *that* was it, thought Frankie! That's what

the git's up to, trying to scare Elsa into thinking the place'll be condemned if she doesn't sell it to him. The crafty, conniving sod!

Barclay was watching eagerly for Elsa's reaction. 'And you know what will happen once the Council start poking their noses in!' He shook his head in false concern. 'You'll have an office block or a *supermarket* here quicker than you can say Jack Robinson!'

'I don't care if they want to build an Ice Skating Stadium here!' Elsa snapped back. 'They'll have to carry me off in my coffin if they want to get me out of this shop!'

Frankie's spirit surged with excitement. If what Elsa had just said was true, it sounded as though she wouldn't be taking her solicitor's advice after all.

Realising that he had made yet another futile visit, Jack Barclay put his cup and saucer down on to the counter and made an excuse to leave. By the time he reached the shop door his initial attitude towards Frankie vanished. 'Oh, by the way, young man,' he said. 'Would you mind telling your parents that from next week I shall be putting up the rent. It's quite unavoidable, I'm afraid.' He opened the door and turned back with an apologetic smile. 'These are hard times we're living in.'

Frankie glared angrily at Barclay, and Elsa had to grab hold of his arm to restrain him.

Barclay left and within a few minutes Elsa

and Frankie heard his car roaring off down Hornsey Road.

That afternoon, Elsa went off to see her solicitor, leaving Frankie to manage the shop on his own. He had four customers within an hour, and it gave him great satisfaction to think how much Jack Barclay would have disapproved. He made the princely sum of seven shillings and sixpence, which included the sale of two kitchen chairs, a velvet-covered cushion, two empty pickling jars, an enamel bucket, and a pair of children's shoes. Feeling very pleased with himself, Frankie made a cup of tea and sat back to share a few broken Lincoln biscuits with Winston.

Just before four o'clock, Frankie had yet another customer. This time it was Bert Gorman. As usual, he was wearing a plain blue short-sleeved shirt with a blue and white polka dot bow tie, and, as the sun was still burning out of a clear blue sky outside, he wore a white flat cap.

''Ow are yer, young Frankie, young feller-me-lad? And 'ow many millions 'ave yer made for Mrs Barclay terday?'

Frankie had a broad grin on his face. Even though they always told the same old jokes, he found the Gorman brothers a breath of fresh air. 'It's bin a good day, Mr Gorman. If business carries on like this, we'll 'ave ter open anuvver shop!'

Bert laughed. 'Oy – watch it! I tell the jokes 'round 'ere!' He took off his cap, and used his handkerchief to wipe the sweat from the top of his thinning head of hair. 'I'm 'ere as a payin' customer. I wanna buy somefin'.'

'Anyfin' special, Mr Gorman?' Frankie followed him around.

'Yeh! I'm lookin' fer a weddin' present.'

'Oh – right. 'Ow much d'yer wanna spend?'

'It's gotta be somefin' nice,' said Bert, picking up some second-hand kitchen saucepans. 'After all, 'e is me bruvver.'

Frankie swung him a startled look. *'Pardon?'*

These days Bert had to look up to Frankie, who was now taller than him. 'I want a weddin' present fer Mike. 'E's gettin' married in a coupla weeks.'

Frankie couldn't believe what he was hearing. He imagined that the Gorman brothers must be in their late seventies at least, and was sure he hadn't heard right. 'Mr Gorman – Mr *Mike* Gorman – your bruvver – gettin' married?'

Bert responded as though he was surprised by Frankie's reaction. 'Yeh. Why not? 'E *is* old enough, yer know.' Again, he laughed at his own joke. But it was a hollow laugh.

For a brief moment, Frankie left him to continue looking through the pots and pans, and then asked, 'Who's 'e gettin' married to?'

Bert stopped and turned. 'Edie, of course. Edie Robson – number 49 next door. Luvely woman. They'll make an 'ansome couple.'

Frankie was absolutely amazed. He couldn't imagine two people of that age getting married.

'But Mrs Robson's been livin' at number 49 for years. Isn't it – well, a bit sudden?'

'Sudden?' This time Bert didn't look up, but continued with looking over a china tea-set. 'Yeh. I suppose it is a bit sudden. Anyway, I'm sure they'll be very 'appy. Let's face it, Mike won't be very far away. 'E's moving in wiv Edie next door.'

For the first time, Frankie noticed a slight reticence in the old boy's voice. He had known the Gorman brothers all his life; they were practically the first people he remembered when he was still in his pram. And Frankie couldn't remember a time when he had not seen the brothers together. Not only were they identical to look at, they also dressed alike, and thought and acted as one person. How would Bert cope without his other self?

'Still, if two people like each uvver enuff, why shouldn't they get tergevver. It don't matter 'ow old yer are. Yer've gotta make the best outa whatever time yer've got left.' Bert paused briefly while he pretended to look at some table-linen, then added with a sigh, 'Yeh. I suppose I will miss 'im though.' He quickly snapped out of his temporary lapse into feeling sorry for himself, and reverted to the old comedy patter again. 'Never mind, me old feller, me old son! As the farmer said to the turkey on Christmas Eve – 'ere terday, gone termorrer, eh?'

Frankie didn't think it was a funny joke, but he laughed because it was quite clear that poor old Bert needed someone to laugh with.

'Still, after wot's 'appened terday, it looks as though we'll soon be rid of them nasty littel yeller people.' Bert picked up a chunky-looking bronze statue of *Adonis*, and inspected it. 'Mind you, if anyone starts doin' the same fing to us, I'd say we'll all be in the same boat – 'ere terday, gone termorrer!'

Frankie looked puzzled. 'Wot d'yer mean, Mr Gorman? Wot *'as* 'appened terday?'

Bert slowly turned round to look at Frankie. 'Din't yer 'ear it on the news?'

''Ear wot on the news?'

'About the Yanks. They've dropped a bomb – a real biggun. On Japan.'

Chapter Twenty-five

And so the second great world war of the twentieth century finally came to an end with the surrender of all Japanese armed forces on Wednesday, 15 August 1945. The two horrific atomic bombs that were dropped on Japan – one on Hiroshima and then Nagasaki – were not only the end of a brutal reign of terror that stretched right across the Pacific Ocean, but also the start of a new era of fear and confrontation around the entire world.

It was also the beginning of a new era in Merton Street.

In the middle of August, Helen and Eric Sibley had their eagerly awaited first child, a little girl they called Josie Sandra. Everyone thought she was a pretty little thing but apart from Eric, the one who was most excited by the new arrival was Frankie. The idea that he was now an uncle made him feel immensely proud, and as he was now earning a regular wage at the shop, he immediately opened a Post Office Savings

Account for his little niece, and started it off with a contribution of two shillings and sixpence.

When September came, Frankie's fortunes weren't quite so happy. He had failed to pass his Matriculation exams though he had got his School Certificate. He was disappointed with the result, even though he'd never really expected to do any better, but, as always, it was Elsa who offered him what he considered the wisest advice: 'If you read books, you learn as much as any school can teach you,' she said. And how Frankie read books! He must have read over a hundred of them, since he first met Elsa, by authors as diverse as Charles Dickens and Captain W. E. Johns. As he had decided to stay on at the shop full-time, he had ample opportunity to choose and read as many books as he wanted.

For the rest, the best part of Frankie's life was being with Maggs. However, their relationship was put to the test when, early the following year, they accidentally bumped into Patty Jackson again, at a dance in Islington Town Hall.

With Jeff now away doing National Service, Patty was currently going strong with Alan Downs. But it was easy to see that Patty was merely stringing him along, and that she would drop him for the first bloke who came along that she really fancied. When she caught sight of Frankie being taught to dance a waltz by Maggs, she clearly thought the time had come to try her luck again.

'Din't ever think I'd see you on a dance floor, Frank.'

Frankie and Maggs turned with a start to find Patty and Alan dancing alongside them.

'Maggs,' said Frankie, reluctantly, raising his voice to be heard above the sound of the three-piece band. 'This is Patty Jackson and Alan Downs.'

Maggs had never met Patty before, and her smile froze on her face. 'Hallo.'

Alan looked uneasy. ''Ow are yer, Frank?'

'This is Maggs Fletcher,' Frankie said, and added pointedly. 'My gel.'

Patty grinned at Maggs. 'You used ter go ter Highbury Fields Girls' School, din't yer?'

'I still do.'

Frankie was only too aware that Patty was wearing a shoulderless black dress that left nothing to the imagination. 'Maggs is stayin' on an extra year,' he said. 'She might go on ter University.'

'Oh yes?' Patty was having to shout above the fractured sound of the music. 'One o' the brainy types, eh?'

'That's right,' Maggs yelled back. 'There are one or two of us around.'

Patty liked that. She sensed a duel, and wanted to get into it as soon as possible. 'Why don't we all 'ave a drink tergevver? It's too crowded here ternight.'

'No fanks, Pat,' Frankie said immediately. 'We're not stayin' late.'

'Don't be a spoilsport, Frankie. I'm feeling a bit thirsty.'

Frankie was flabbergasted to hear Maggs respond to Patty's invitation. He couldn't believe what was happening when she suddenly took hold of his hand and led him off the dance floor. As they were all under age to buy alcohol, the four of them finished up at the tea-counter in the hall outside.

'So,' said Patty, stirring her tea, ''ow long you bin comin' up 'ere then, Frank? The last time you an' me 'ad a dance tergevver at your school do, you preferred ter sit it out.'

Frankie knew what Patty was trying to suggest in front of Maggs, but he refused to rise to her bait. 'We in't bin 'ere before. You know I'm no dancer.'

'Don't listen to him,' Maggs said, sipping her tea with one hand and holding Frankie's hand with the other. 'He was doing very well.'

'Yeh,' leered Patty, her eyes watching Maggs slyly over the top of her teacup. 'Wot 'e needs is a good teacher.'

Maggs smiled back gracefully. 'Oh, I can assure you, Frankie has very little left to learn.' She turned to look at him, and he returned her smile.

Patty didn't like that. She licked the tea on her heavily lipsticked lips, and used her spare hand to beat time to the music they could hear coming from the Dance Hall. Frankie tried hard not to catch her eye, knowing it would be disastrous, and he hated the way she had tarted herself up with so much make-up, for she was a good-looking girl with a lovely complexion, and had no need to present such a false image.

'Pat had a postcard from Jeff the other day,' said Alan, suddenly changing the subject. 'Sounds like 'e's enjoyin' navy life.'

'Oh yes, 'e's doin' very well,' said Patty, putting her cup and saucer down on to the counter. 'Last time he was 'ome he bought me these.' To Frankie's horror, she pulled up her dress as far as she dared, and showed off the expensive pair of stockings she was wearing. 'Sheer nylon,' she purred, gliding her hand up her leg seductively, to demonstrate what she meant.

Frankie knew exactly what she meant, and turned his eyes away. But once again, 'his gel' surprised him.

'It's amazing what servicemen can pick up in the NAAFI,' Maggs said, looking down to admire Patty's nylons. 'Apparently, they get most things cheap.'

Patty looked hurt and lowered her dress, and Maggs immediately wished she hadn't made the remark. Patty was clearly vulnerable.

'Jeff says he's on active service out at sea somewhere', Alan said. 'He can't say where, of course, but it sounds like he's on quite a big ship –

probably a cruiser or something. Trust Jeff!'

Frankie responded with a dismissive, 'Yeh.' He knew that everything Alan had just said about Jeff was rubbish. It was common knowledge in Merton Street that when Jeff had been called up for National Service, he had been posted to a Naval Training Depot in the north of England, where he had remained ever since.

Maggs was still feeling guilty about her snide remark to Patty, so she made an effort to be nice. 'Patty. I need to go to the Girls' Room. Feel like joining me for a chat?'

Frankie darted a look of horror at Maggs.

Patty was taken aback, too. 'A chat? Wot about?'

Maggs grinned. 'About how awful blokes are!'

Patty actually laughed. 'Yeh! Why not!' she said, flicking a mischievous look at the two boys.

Frankie and Alan watched in disbelief as the two girls marched off together and disappeared into the Ladies' toilet.

'So what's goin' on there, then?' Alan asked tentatively.

'I dunno,' replied Frankie, biting his lip anxiously. 'But I don't like it.'

'I wouldn't worry too much if I was you.' Alan was doing his best to regain the friendship he used to enjoy with Frankie. 'Maggs seems like a really nice girl. I'm sure she can take care of herself.'

'She can.' There was a sour edge to Frankie's

reply. 'Unfortunately, so can Patty.'

'Not any more, Frank.' Alan lowered his eyes as he spoke. 'She's pregnant.'

Frankie looked as if he'd been struck by a thunderbolt. 'Yer mean – ?'

'No! It's not me. It's not Jeff, either.' Clearly embarrassed, Alan took out a packet of cigarettes, and offered one to Frankie, who shook his head. 'It's some bloke she met here at a dance, just before Christmas. She doesn't know who he is or where he comes from.'

'Christ Almighty!' Frankie couldn't get over what he had just heard. 'Pat can't 'ave a baby. She's only sixteen!'

'She's seventeen next month.'

'Even so. It's far too young ter . . . Stupid cow! I know the same fing 'appened ter my sister, but at least she loved the bloke.' He sighed and scratched his head. 'Wot's she gonna do now?'

'Get married – I hope.' Alan lit his cigarette.

'Yer mean – this bloke's agreed to marry 'er?'

Alan shook his head.

'Then if she's 'avin a kid, 'ow's she gonna get anyone ter marry 'er?'

Alan inhaled a small puff of smoke and waited for it to settle on his lungs. 'Because *I've* asked her.'

'Let me get this straight, Alan. Yer know Patty's 'avin someone else's kid, and yet you're prepared ter marry 'er?'

'If she'll have me – yes.'

Frankie waved away the smoke from Alan's cigarette, which was beginning to sting his eyes. 'Yer mean – she *'asn't* agreed?'

'Not yet. But I'm still hoping. I've asked my old man, and he says I can do what I want. Actually, he couldn't care less what I do.' He flicked his ash on the floor, and looked up at Frankie again. There was an air of desperation in his voice. 'Patty's always wanted to get married, you know she has, Frank. It's just a question of finding the right man.'

'Well, she's certainly 'ad plenty of good tries!'

'Don't be unkind, Frank,' pleaded Alan, stubbing his cigarette out on the floor. 'There are a lot of good things about Patty. She just needs a chance, that's all.'

'But – do yer love 'er, Alan?'

'Yes, Frank.' Alan stared Frankie straight in the eyes. 'You know I've *always* loved her.'

'But does *she* love you?' Frankie could barely grasp this conversation. It all seemed so – wrong!

'No. But she will.'

A few minutes later, Maggs and Patty returned from the Ladies' to announce that they actually got on well together, and had arranged to meet up again soon.

Frankie watched them in disbelief, and, glancing from Patty to Alan, decided that he didn't know anything about people any more.

At the beginning of March, Patty and Alan

married at Islington Registry Office. Patty's parents wanted nothing more to do with her, but Alan's widowed father helped them to get a one-bedroomed flat on the top floor of a house in Windsor Road. Then, a few weeks later, Patty told Alan that because she was desperate to get away from home and start a new life of her own, she had lied about being pregnant. What she didn't tell him, however, was that gaining Alan's sympathy had been part of her plan, and his offer of marriage was just what she'd been looking for to break loose from her 'stinkin' lousy' mother and father as she called them. Alan said that it made no difference to him. Indeed, he only hoped that it wouldn't be too long before they had kids of their own. Patty, however, wasn't so sure about that . . .

Towards the end of April, Alan received call-up papers for his National Service, and by the end of June, he was posted to an Army command in West Germany.

Frankie decided that he did not particularly want to make contact with either of them again. He had moved on and away from them in too many ways . . .

Through most of 1946, Elsa's shop continued to struggle against hard times. The post-war period was proving to be very depressing, for there was no sign of an end to rationing, and some food was even more difficult to get than during the war years. Frankie was only too aware that very little money was being made in the shop, and he often felt guilty about taking a weekly wage from Elsa. Although Jack Barclay had now cut down on his regular visits to put pressure on Elsa, the strain on her health was beginning to show. Not only had she lost a lot of weight, she was also becoming very absent-minded. On one occasion she had almost caused a disaster by leaving the sink tap on in the shop's back room. Frankie became even more worried when Elsa told him that she now found the tube journey to Swiss Cottage too wearisome and she was giving up her Thursday afternoon tea and cakes with Gertrude.

After a particularly unprofitable week at the end of September, Frankie came up with a plan of his own that he hoped might help relieve the situation.

'Give up your wages and work for nothing? Never! I wouldn't hear of such a thing!' It was Thursday morning, and Elsa was pacing up and down.

'But it's a good idea, Elsa – it really is.' Frankie grabbed hold of her hand and led her back to her stool in front of the counter, and made her sit down. 'Now listen. All I 'ave ter do is ter go out and find a daytime job. They're advertisin' for an office clerk at the coal yard up at the Archway. It'd bring me in all the cash I need, then I could work 'ere in the evenin's an' you wouldn't 'ave ter pay me any money at all. Now, don't that make sense?'

'No, it doesn't!' snapped Elsa.

'Of course it does! 'Ow many times do I 'ave ter tell yer – yer can't run a business wivout money.'

Elsa thumped her fist on the counter. 'And how many times do I have to tell *you* that it's not the money I worry about. It's customers!'

After Maggs, Frankie adored Elsa more than anyone else in the whole world. But it drove him mad that she had absolutely no business sense at all. 'Look, Elsa,' he said in desperation. 'Do yer want that bruvver-in-law of yours to get 'is slippery wet 'ands on this place?'

Clasping her hands together and looking up towards the ceiling as though praying, Elsa let out a loud wail of anguish.

'Well, then, be sensible!'

Now it was Frankie's turn to start pacing the shop floor. But as he did so, he was thinking out loud, trying to work out a rescue plan that would satisfy Elsa.

'Let's face it, we don't get more than a couple of customers in 'ere on any day of the week. And even when they come they only browse around wivout buyin' anyfin'. If yer can cut yer losses, and make even a tenner a week, yer could break even wivin a munff.' Then he quickly swung around to confront Elsa. 'And one way ter do that is ter cut out my wages!'

Elsa, arms crossed defiantly, was staring at the ceiling.

Frankie was extremely irritated by her obstinacy. 'Elsa, be reasonable! We've got ter do *somefin*! Last year Jack Barclay was warnin' yer that if somefin' in't done to make this place habitable, yer'd 'ave the Council down on yer like a ton of 'ot bricks. We've gotta make *some* profits, if only to pay for the repair work.'

'May I now say something, please?' Elsa finally spoke, but Frankie could tell she was putting on one of her acts of being a totally reasonable woman.

Frankie sighed in frustration, crossed his arms like Elsa, and stood with his back to the shop window.

'I have said – oh, so many times—' Elsa continued, 'I have said that if the only problem with this shop is finding the money to run it, then the money *shall* be found . . .' She quickly put her hand up to stop Frankie from interrupting.

'But if . . . *if* you are trying to tell me that you do not *want* to work in this shop with me any more, I shall not stand in your way.'

'Elsa!'

'Do I make myself clear, Frankie? That's all I ask.'

''Ow can yer say such a fing? Of *course* I wanna work for yer. I *love* this shop. It was the best day of my life when you asked me ter come and work 'ere. Yer know that, Elsa! Yer *must* know it!'

Winston's head was getting dizzy looking at one and then the other as they spoke.

'Things are different now, Frankie. You're not a boy any longer. You're a man. And I quite understand that you want to go out in the world to earn a proper wage and mix with people of your own age . . .'

Frankie suddenly got very angry. 'Stop it, Elsa! Stop it!'

'Well, it's true!' Elsa sprang up from her seat and went to him. 'Next year you'll be eighteen, Frankie. It's time you did things for yourself. You don't need an old woman like me hanging on to your tail.'

Frankie looked straight at her. 'You're not an old woman, Elsa! But are you giving me the sack?' he asked, accusingly.

Elsa turned away. 'Don't be so foolish!'

'Come on now – out wiv it! Is that why yer want ter get rid of me? 'Cos yer've 'ad enuff of me 'round the place?'

Elsa clasped her hands together. 'Dear Maker! What did I do to deserve this?'

Frankie turned her around to face him. 'Come on now – own up! D'yer want ter get rid of me – or don't yer?'

There followed a very long pause whilst they glared at each other. But gradually, a faint smile appeared in Elsa's eyes which slowly spread across her entire face. Then the same thing happened to Frankie, and soon they found themselves roaring with laughter.

'Yer artful old devil!' yelled Frankie as he threw his arms around Elsa and hugged her. 'Yer've been 'avin' me on, in't yer? You was just testin' me?'

'Old friends should always be truthful with each other,' Elsa said with a sly grin, pressing her face up against Frankie's chest.

After that, Frankie never brought up the subject again. But three weeks later, Elsa received a letter from the Islington Borough Council Health and Safety Department, advising her that she would shortly be receiving an official visit from a Council surveyor . . .

Chapter Twenty-six

Over the past year, Gracie and Reg Lewis had made huge efforts to come to terms with their life together. The painful row between them following Helen and Eric's wedding had finally stirred them into talking to each other, more than they had done in all the years since they married. It turned out to be an extraordinary experience. They learned about each other's likes and dislikes, their fears and anxieties, their hopes for the future. They talked about the people they had met, the ones they knew and the ones they wished they still knew. They talked about the kids – or, at least, what Helen and Frankie were like when they were kids. They still had rows, but in time they found a way to keep their disagreements in perspective. When Gracie wanted to listen to her favourite Sunday night radio programme, Reg listened with her. But perhaps the most important development took place one night as they lay in bed, both wide awake, waiting, hoping. And without a word, it happened, for the first time in more than ten years. And after it had happened, Gracie wept, for it seemed that her life was at last beginning to take on a new meaning . . .

Frankie spent most Saturday afternoons at Highbury Stadium watching football matches with Eric. Sometimes Maggs went with them; although she still didn't share Frankie's enthusiasm for cycling, she did enjoy a good game of football. After the game, they all went back to Eric's place where Helen was waiting with tea, bread and jam, and home-made cakes.

During the past few months, however, Frankie was disturbed to notice that there were one or two little tensions developing between his sister and brother-in-law. They appeared to be as much in love as ever, but when Helen announced that she was expecting again, Eric had grown restless. And Helen wasn't happy that Eric had become more and more involved with politics. He had recently joined the local Labour Party and although Helen too was a fervent Labour supporter, political meetings and rallies scared her; everyone seemed to get so aggressive. It didn't help that the country was in such a state of depression, what with food shortages, overcrowded schools, poor wages and a lack of jobs for ex-servicemen. But she knew it was inevitable, that Eric and his father-in-law would not always hit it off together, for Reg was an ardent Tory.

The crunch came in October, during one of Gracie's recently established Sunday afternoon tea parties for the family. Eric was in a truculent mood, and, to Helen's concern, was chain-smoking. Maggs was at the table, helping Helen to feed little Josie, while Frankie, Reg and Eric were getting a little hot under the collar about the news during the week that Hermann Goering had managed to commit suicide and escape the hangman after having been found guilty at the Nuremburg Trials in Germany.

'I still say he couldn't'a done it wivout 'elp from the inside,' said Eric, both elbows leaning on the table and constantly flicking ash off his fag into a saucer. 'I tell yer – someone was determined 'e wouldn't go ter the gallows.'

'They said on the wireless that 'e 'ad a cyanide pill hidden under his tongue,' said Frankie, finishing off the last of a bowl of winkles.

Eric pounced on that. 'Yeh! But who gave it to 'im?'

'Wot does it matter?' said Reg, rolling one of his own fags even though he had a dog-end behind his ear. 'As long as we get rid er the bastard!'

'Please, Reg!' Gracie was cutting bread. 'No swearin' in front of Josie.'

'What yer don't understand, Dad,' Eric continued relentlessly, 'is that there's an important point 'ere. ''Ow do we know that Goering isn't still alive? I mean, we've only got the Yanks' word for it. Suppose they didn't want 'im dead? Suppose there was some conspiracy ter keep 'im alive 'cos 'e 'ad somefin' that us and the Yanks wanted? Maybe it 'ad somefin' ter do wiv the Commies? We all know 'ow much Churchill and Truman' ate the Commies.'

'Bloody load of old rubbish!' Reg blew out the match he was using, and flicked it into the empty fire-grate. 'Yer don't know wot you're talkin' about, son!'

'You can say that, but I 'eard 'em talkin' down the Club the uvver night. Apparently in the first year of the war, Churchill tried ter do some kind of deal wiv 'Itler. That's why Rudolf 'Ess flew over 'ere ter meet up wiv 'im.'

Reg leaned back in his chair and roared with laughter.

'Laugh all yer want, Dad! But you mark my words,' Eric wagged his finger provocatively at his father-in-law. 'Churchill got up ter fings that we'll never know about!'

Reg laughed even louder. 'Churchill an' 'Itler! Now that's wot I call *really* funny!'

Eric hated to be laughed at and was now getting really hot under the collar. 'Yeh! You would say that – wouldn't yer! Votin' Tory all yer bloody life!'

Reg stopped laughing and leaned forward in his chair. 'That's right, mate, and fank Gord I 'ave – when yer see the mess your lot 'ave got us into since they pushed Churchill out!'

Helen, worried with the way Eric and her father were getting at each other, suddenly got up from the table. 'Josie needs a walk. I'll take 'er round the corner.'

Frankie could see his sister's agitation so he also got up. 'Come on, 'Elen. I'll come wiv yer.' He looked anxiously at Maggs.

'Don't worry about me,' Maggs said with her usual understanding. 'I'm going to help your mum wash up.'

A few minutes later, Helen and Frankie were walking little Josie down Merton Street. Josie was a big girl for fourteen months, but she was still a toddler, so they had to move quite slowly while the child stopped to inspect everything in sight.

Although it was still only six o'clock in the evening, the light was showing signs of fading, for it was October.

Helen, Frankie, and little Josie gradually made their way past the familiar front gates, glancing only casually to see if anyone they knew was looking out from behind their curtains. But Merton Street these days was becoming very different to what it was only a year or so before and, even if anyone were to suddenly appear at their front door, all you would get would be a brief, courteous smile before the door was quickly closed again.

'I wonder what our street'll look like in ten years' time?' reflected Helen, as they paused briefly at the corner of Herslet Road and looked back.

'Probably full of offices, or council flats,' grinned Frankie, but deep down such a prospect was a terrible one. He loved the street, with its two long rows of terraced houses, the endless different-sized chimney-pots, some of which were already shedding thin palls of black coal-fire smoke, small front gates still waiting to be repaired a year after the end of the war, and gas-lamp-posts newly painted in dark green paint.

And he loved being with Helen: he had grown even closer to her since she married Eric and it was Helen he had turned to for advice when he first started going out regularly with Maggs – and Helen considered Maggs to be the best thing that had ever happened to her young brother. Since Frankie had stopped her from having an abortion, Helen had never stopped being grateful to him. They had absolutely no secrets from each other.

'Frank, if I tell yer somefin', will yer promise not ter let on ter anyone else? It's about Eric.'

Frankie, immediately concerned, looked at her. 'Is anyfin' wrong?'

'No. Not really. Look, Eric's bin ter see the doctor, Frank. Did yer know that?'

Frankie was disturbed. 'No, I didn't. Wot's up wiv 'im?'

'Nuffin' serious – well, not *really* serious. It's because of wot 'e went through in that POW camp. It's not so much 'is body that's suffered – it's 'is mind. The doctor says that if we're not careful, 'e could 'ave a nervous breakdown. 'E wouldn't be able ter go ter work or do anyfin' except rest – maybe fer weeks or munffs. Oh, Frankie, it's terrible ter 'ear 'im sometimes at night – tossin' and turnin' and groanin' in 'is sleep. It's as though 'e's livin' it all again.'

Frankie sighed. 'Wot yer gonna do about it?'

'We bin talkin', Frank – me *an*' Eric.' She paused for a second, then spoke decisively. 'We both fink 'e needs a complete break. The fing is, Frank, I love this country. It's where I was born and brought up. Eric loves it too – Gord knows, 'e nearly gave 'is life for it. But since the war, it's bin such a depressin' place ter live in.' Helen was clearly having difficulty in what she was trying to say. 'It'd be a terrible fing ter 'ave ter leave.'

Frankie abruptly stopped strolling and turned to her. 'Leave? Wot yer talkin' about?'

Holding on to little Josie as if for comfort, Helen's face crunched up with anguish as she told him. 'Yer mustn't tell Mum and Dad, Frank – not just yet. But me and Eric – well – we've decided to emigrate – to Australia.'

In the first floor bathroom of number 19 Hadleigh Villas, Elsa weighed herself on a pair of ancient scales that she had bought for one shilling and sixpence. Since the last time she had weighed herself just a few days ago, she had lost another two pounds. With a shrug, she stepped off and took a casual look in the mirror. She couldn't see any real difference – just a few more lines on her face, which, she muttered to herself, she could easily cover with make-up and rouge. She had also lost a few more hairs from the small wisp that she had left, but that also made very little difference, for nobody – except shrewd old Gertrude – knew that the carefully coiffeured hair they always admired on her was, in fact, a hairpiece. She leaned forward to take a closer look at her face, screwing it up in disapproval. 'Alte Frau!' she snapped, scolding herself for being an old woman. So she pinched her cheeks with her fingers to bring some life back into them, then set about smothering them with as much make-up as she dared.

Back in her bedroom, Elsa dressed quickly, and left the house to go to the shop.

She completely ignored the three boxes of different coloured pills, one of each of which she had been ordered by the Specialist at the Royal Northern Hospital to take, four times a day . . .

Elsa took her time to walk down Berriman Road towards the shop. These days she moved more slowly than she used to, and even though it infuriated her to do so, she had to rely on a walking-stick – '*but only as a weapon*', as she would assure Frankie when he'd become concerned.

When she eventually reached the shop, Elsa was furious to discover that the builders still hadn't turned up to continue the repairs to the ceiling and walls that they had started the previous Monday morning. However, Elsa consoled herself with the fact that, much to Jack Barclay's disappointment (for it was obviously he who had notified the Health and Safety Department at the Town Hall), the 'man from the Council' turned out to be very sympathetic and did not condemn the shop as unsafe. But the place did need some urgent repairs, and, much to Frankie's astonishment, she had somehow found the money to have them done.

'So doesn't anybody know how to get out of bed in the mornings any more?' she snapped, tetchily, as Frankie and Winston came through the door, nearly five minutes late. 'If you ask me, the war has made the English worker very lazy!'

'Sorry, Elsa.' Frankie looked miserable and he seemed to have no life in him.

Elsa instantly felt guilty. Ever since last Monday when Frankie had told her about his sister deciding to emigrate to Australia, she knew how down in the dumps the boy had been. She quickly covered up her tactlessness, and went to the biscuit tin to give Winston his usual morning treat. 'So – what news about your sister?' she called, as she tried to manoeuvre around one of the many pieces of scaffolding that had been erected above the counter.

'They're goin' in April.'

Elsa could hardly hear his reply it was so soft and solemn. But then, when Frankie was suffering about something, he never really made any effort to conceal it.

'You mean – they've definitely decided to go to Australia?'

'Oh yeh. Wot she didn't tell me last Sunday was that she an' Eric 'ad already bin to Australia 'ouse and got the papers. Apparently they 'ad an interview a few weeks ago, and it's all arranged.' Suddenly, he felt a momentary surge of anger and he showed it by kicking a large second-hand mattress that he was covering. 'It'll take 'em six weeks on the boat.'

Elsa knew only too well what a loss it would be for him to part with the sister he loved and admired so much. As she lit the new gas ring to boil up a kettle of water for her cup of tea, she sighed, not really sure what comfort she could give the boy. 'Such a stupid idea! Who wants to go to Australia! All that sunshine and silly kangaroos!'

'When yer fink about it, it's not such a stupid idea, Elsa.' For a moment or so, Frankie stopped what he was doing. 'When yer fink about the state this country's in well, if I was old enough I'd take Maggs and we'd go, too.'

Elsa swung round with a start. She couldn't believe what he had just said. 'Are you mad, Frankie? How can you say such a thing about this country – *your* country. You only just won a war.'

'Yeh – fer what!' Frankie replied, sourly.

'Oh, stop feeling so sorry for yourself!' she said brusquely.

'Australia's a smashin' place, Elsa. *Everyone* says so!'

'And zo is *zis* country!' She was so angry that she momentarily lapsed back into an accent. 'It takes time, Frankie. Six years of war is a long time, and it doesn't matter whether it is Mr Attlee or Mr Churchill – you cannot re-build a country *or* it's people overnight! And so – when are *you* going to Australia, may I ask?'

Frankie sighed. 'I'm not going anywhere, Elsa. I only said that *if* – only *if* I was old enuff, I wouldn't 'esitate.'

'Really? And what would you do with poor Winston? Would you just cast him out in the street like so many so-called English animal-lovers seem to do when they don't have any more use for them?'

At the sound of his name, Winston's ears pricked up, hoping that this would mean another biscuit for him.

As Frankie watched Elsa, hands on hips, glaring at him disapprovingly, he suddenly felt guilty. For some time now he had noticed how frail Elsa was looking. Her body seemed to be all skin and bones, and her dresses were virtually hanging off her and she no longer made or ate her much-loved apple cake.

'Take no notice of me, Elsa,' he said, sheepishly, going to where she stood. 'It's just that – well, yer know 'ow much I fink of my sister. I can't bear ter fink I won't see 'er no more.'

'What do you mean, you won't see her any more! Australia isn't on the moon, is it? You can save up money and visit her?'

For the first time that morning, Frankie smiled. Elsa was right – yes, of course she was right – as always. 'I'm sorry,' he said, and went to cuddle her.

Elsa immediately reciprocated by throwing her arms around him. For a moment she felt totally warm and secure, as though it was her own son embracing her . . . 'Try always to remember, Frankie,' she said, her voice now soft and sympathetic, 'when you part from someone, it's so different from losing them . . .'

Their moment together was abruptly broken by the arrival of two of the builders, who strolled into the shop brightly. 'Mornin', missus!' they called in unison. 'Don't you missus, me!' yelled Elsa, once again losing her perfect English accent, 'if you expect me to pay you good money for starting verk half-way through the day, you can zink again!'

The two men exchanged a look of horror.

Elsa went back behind the counter and turned

off the tap of the gas ring under the boiling kettle, opened the back room door, and yelled again: 'And if you vant to have a cup of tea – you can make it yourself!'

With that she disappeared into the back room, and slammed the door behind her.

Frankie roared with laughter. He was delighted that Elsa was back to her old self again.

Now alone, Elsa turned on the light switch in the back room. Sorting through the letters she was holding, she found the particular one she was looking for, and put the others down on top of a pile of cardboard boxes. Sliding her finger through the top of the envelope, she gradually tore it open, took out the letter inside, and started to read it:

ROYAL NORTHERN HOSPITAL
HOLLOWAY
LONDON, N.7.

Mrs E. Barclay
19, Hadleigh Villas
Holloway, N.7.

14 October 1946.

Dear Mrs Barclay

We have now received the results of the blood

and pancreas tests you undertook on 4th October.

Your specialist, Dr. P. A. Carter has asked me to request that you make an immediate appointment to see him.

I look forward to hearing from you.

Yours sincerely, (signed)

J. Hartley (Mrs) Registrar.

Elsa read the letter impassively, folded it up again, then replaced it in the envelope.

Then she calmly tore it up and put the pieces into her dress pocket.

Chapter Twenty-seven

Gracie and Reg Lewis blamed themselves for Helen and Eric's decision to emigrate to Australia. When they heard the news it was as though their entire married lives had been thrown up to confront them. But despite their pain and anguish, and their knowledge that they would never again see their daughter, or be able to watch the growing-up of their granddaughter, Gracie and Reg vowed to use these last few months to do everything in their power to compensate Helen for all the mistakes they had made in the past.

Christmas 1946 turned out to be the happiest the Lewis family had ever known. Helen, Eric, and little Josie spent both Christmas Day and Boxing Day with Gracie, Reg, Frankie, and Winston at number 1 Merton Street, and even Maggs persuaded her parents to let her spend a good deal of the two days with Frankie and his family. The big surprise, hovever, turned out to be a visit from Eric's parents, who accepted the Lewises invitation to come and have a drink with them on Boxing Day after Gracie wrote a letter saying that she hoped they would accept her apologies for her behaviour after the wedding, and let bygones be bygones.

And so the Lewis family drifted into the new year of 1947, and as the days ticked by and the weeks rushed past, the dreaded month of April floated closer and closer, like a vast, black cloud heading for its final destination above number 1 Merton Street.

Before that, however, in the middle of March, Gracie and Reg Lewis had a very different problem to face up to; their new landlord, Jack Barclay.

'It's bad, Mr Lewis, very bad indeed.' Barclay stood in the hall passage of number 1, clipboard in hand, taking down notes as fast as he could scribble them. 'I'm sure you realise it's my duty as the freeholder to point out the poor state of decoration of your two upstairs bedrooms, the landing toilet . . .' As he spoke, he ticked off his notes. '. . . ceilings and walls above and alongside the staircase, this hall passage, ground floor scullery, and the two back and front living rooms.' He looked up, sighed, and shook his head to and fro in firm disapproval. 'You really have been very negligent, you know.'

Reg and Gracie Lewis both looked as though the blood had been drained from their bodies.

'It's not easy, Mr Barclay. We can't afford ter

bring in decorators, and by the time I get 'ome from the Barfs I in't 'ardly got time ter 'ave me supper and get ter bed.'

'With great respect, Mr Lewis, that is your problem – not mine. And it has to be said that your previous landlord felt exactly the same way as I do.'

'What, Mr Jackson?' said Gracie, indignantly. ''E never asked us ter do any buildin' work in the 'ouse. ''E always got uvver people ter do those sort of fings.'

Barclay was only too aware of the anxiety he was causing the Lewises. 'Mrs Lewis,' he said. 'Have you ever read the terms of occupancy inside the back cover of your rent book?'

Gracie exchanged a puzzled look with Reg. 'Why should we?' she replied, naïvely. 'We've always paid the rent on time.'

'They state quite clearly that the cost of all building repairs to the fabric of both exterior and interior of the property shall be borne by the freeholder – that's me. *But*—' He wagged a scolding gloved finger at Gracie. ' – the rent-holder shall be held responsible for the reasonable maintenance of good decorative order.'

'Wot's that supposed ter mean?' asked Gracie, again naïvely.

'It means we've gotta paint the place up,' replied Reg, gloomily.

'Precisely, Mr Lewis.' There was nothing menacing in Barclay's manner, and all the time he spoke he smiled politely. 'It is, after all, only fair that you keep to your side of the arrangement – don't you agree?'

Reg tried not to look at Gracie, who was clearly alarmed and distressed. 'Mr Barclay,' he said, after a brief moment's thought. 'Can I ask yer a question, please?' His tongue licked his lips, which were parched dry with anxiety. 'Mr Barclay. 'Wot 'appens if we can't find the cash ter do all this work?'

Barclay shrugged his shoulders and tried to look concerned. 'What can I say, Mr Lewis? I'd have no alternative but to ask you to vacate the premises.'

'Wot!' Gracie's eyes widened in horror. 'Yer mean – yer'd throw us out?'

'Mrs Lewis. I'm sure you know that the war has left a lot of people without decent homes. Many of them would give their right hand to find accomodation like this. The Council has a long, long list of people waiting to be rehoused.'

'But yer see, Mr Barclay – well – we don't 'ave nowhere else ter go,' Reg spluttered, hoping that Barclay would understand the desperate situation he and his family were in. 'It's not only me and Gracie. I've got my son, Frankie, ter fink about.'

If Reg Lewis had hoped that his plea for understanding would elicit Barclay's sympathy, he was sadly mistaken. The mention of Frankie's name was enough to seize up all the muscles in

Barclay's face, and his polite smile had a fixed glare. He had convinced himself that it was Frankie's interference that was preventing him from getting his hands on Elsa's shop, and that, if the only way to stop that interference was to put pressure on the boy's parents, then that's how it would have to be!'

'I'd like to help you, Mr Lewis, I really would. But agreements have to be honoured. It *is* the law, you know.'

Frankie fumed with anger. Unknown to Barclay he had been listening to the entire conversation out of sight on the first-floor landing, and everything he heard confirmed his worst suspicions. He was now positive that Barclay had only bought number 1 Merton Street so that he could have some kind of a hold over the Lewis family. But, as he listened quietly at the staircase bannisters, he still didn't know why.

'Please, Mr Barclay.' Gracie Lewis sounded as though she was begging. 'There must be *somefin'* yer can do ter 'elp?'

Barclay shook his head. 'I'm sorry, Mrs Lewis, there is nothing I can do. Unless, of course – '

Gracie eagerly seized on his hesitation. 'Yes?'

Barclay paused a moment, as though deep in thought. 'If you really *can't* do the work the house needs, there might be a place I could find for you in the country.'

Reg exchanged a puzzled look with Gracie. 'The country? Yer mean – outside London?'

'I have a friend who owns some small workmen's cottages up in Shropshire. If you want, I could have a word with him?'

'Shropshire?' asked Gracie, utterly bewildered. 'Where's that?'

Reg knew exactly where it was. 'We couldn't do that, Mr Barclay. Shropshire's *miles* away. What do I do about my job at the Barffs?'

Barclay shrugged his shoulders. 'I'm sure there are Public Bath Houses in Shropshire, too, Mr Lewis.'

'But wot about our Frankie? It'd break 'is 'eart ter 'ave ter leave the Jumble Shop.'

'I realise that,' Barclay replied, with a sympathetic smile. 'But I can assure you it would be for the best. For some time now my sister-in-law has been wanting to close down her shop – with her health the way it is, the place has become rather a burden for her. The only reason she stays there is – well – because of your son.'

On the landing upstairs, Frankie nearly had a fit. Blackmail! he very nearly shouted it out at the top of his voice. So that's what the old sod was up to! He wanted him, Frankie, out of the way so that Elsa had no one to take her side. The crafty, conniving old -!

'So you see, a move to the country could be a blessing in disguise – for all three of you.' Barclay paused just long enough to flick a quick glance at the Lewises. 'Don't you agree?'

Reg and Gracie exchange a muddled look. They

clearly didn't know *what* to think.

'Yer see – we're Londoners born and bred, Mr Barclay,' said Reg, finally.

And Gracie added, We don't know nuffin' about livin' in the country.'

'Very well,' replied Barclay, briskly. 'That's settled that then. Let's say I give you – shall we say . . . six weeks to complete the work.'

'Six weeks!' Reg was horrified.

So was Gracie. 'We'd never get all these rooms painted up and plastered in six weeks! We don't know anyfin' about decoratin'.'

'I'm sorry, Mrs Lewis. I'm afraid it's the best I can do for you.' He made one last entry on his clipboard. 'Let's say – the last day of April, shall we?'

After he left, Reg and Gracie went into the back parlour and flopped down on to facing chairs.

'Wot are we goin' ter do?' Gracie sat with her arms crossed in her lap, swaying slightly to and fro.

Reg was utterly drained. 'I don't know, Gracie. I 'aven't a clue.'

'Well I 'ave!'

They looked up with a start as Frankie came into the room.

'If that old sod finks 'e's goin' ter get away wiv this – well, 'e ain't!' He leaned on the table with both hands, shaking with anger. 'I 'eard everythin' 'e said, and I know *exactly* wot 'e's up to.

But I'm telling you 'ere an' now – we're not movin' from this 'ouse. We're stayin' right where we are!'

Reg waved a dismissive hand. 'Don't talk bloody nonsense, son! We don't 'ave the loot ter do no paintin' and decoratin'.'

'An' even if we did,' chimed in Gracie, 'we wouldn't 'ave a clue 'ow ter do it.'

'*You* may not 'ave,' snapped Frankie, thumping his fist firmly on the table. 'But *I* 'ave!'

During the next few days, Frankie was like a whirlwind. The first thing he did was to go through every secondhand book in the shop to find an instruction book about painting and decorating, and the one he eventually chose was clearly intended for builders for it contained wonderful step-by-step illustrations on how to plaster walls and ceilings. The next thing he did was to go to Elsa and borrow five pounds, which he promised to pay back in instalments. The money was needed to buy several tins of paint, and also some lime and sand to make up plaster for the ceilings and walls. Then he set about practising on a small hole in the wall in the back parlour. Working meticulously from the instruction book, the experiment was judged to be an astonishing success by both Reg and Gracie Lewis. The real test, however, was yet to come.

Using the only stepladder the family had ever possessed, a rickety old wooden contraption that hadn't been used for years, Frankie started to repair the cracks and holes in the walls and ceilings in different parts of the house. His first attempt took several hours, for the plaster kept drying up on the trowel he had borrowed from Mr Mitchinson, the caretaker of Pakeman Street School, and he had to keep running down into the back yard to add more water. When he had eventually finished, he left it overnight to set. The next morning his father went into his bedroom to tell him what he had never believed possible: Frankie's plastering was an unqualified success.

And so, with Frankie in charge of the painting and decorating, his mum and dad helped him start the great facelift of number 1 Merton Street.

It was a welcome distraction from that great black cloud of April, which had now arrived overhead.

Gracie and Reg Lewis always said that it would be much too painful for them to go to Liverpool Street Station to say goodbye to Helen, Eric, and little Josie, but Frankie gradually talked them into it, saying that if they didn't go they would regret it for the rest of their lives.

And so, at nine o'clock on one overcast morning in April, 1947, the Lewis and Sibley families gathered on the stark and featureless Platform 1 at Liverpool Street Station to watch their children take their leave of their birthplace and everyone and everything connected with it. There were many other families crowding on to the platform too, for the Boat Train to Tilbury was already packed with other hopefuls, all on their way to a new life in a strange country. Frankie and Maggs watched them, some weeping, some putting a brave face on a terrible ordeal.

'I'll write as soon as I get there, Mum – promise.' Helen had one arm around her mother's waist and another holding little Josie's hand. 'In any case, once we've got settled and made a bit o' money, we'll come back for a visit. Or maybe we'll save up enuff fer you and dad ter come over and see us.'

Gracie smiled bravely. She knew that what Helen had suggested would not, and could not, ever happen. 'As long as yer drop me a line from time ter time,' she said, fixing her face into a smile. 'I'd like a snapshot of Josie – just ter see 'ow she's gettin' on.'

Helen thought her heart would break. Only a couple of years ago she would have welcomed the idea of getting away from her mother and number 1 Merton Street. But as she watched Gracie lovingly cuddling her little grand-daughter for the last time, Helen wished that life could stop being so cruel . . .

Eric was finding it painful to say goodbye to his own parents. Phyll and Mick Sibley had been dreading this day and Eric's married sister,

Louie, was so upset by the thought of losing her young brother that her make-up was streaking down her cheeks. For several minutes, Eric hugged all three of them, none of them able to speak.

With only six or seven minutes to go before departure, Helen left her mother talking with Josie and went across to say her final farewells to Frankie and Maggs.

'You two take care of yerselves, now,' Helen said, her voice hoarse with emotion. 'Yer've gotta lot of good fings comin' up for yer.' Then she turned to Maggs with as big a tearful smile as she could muster. 'I fink yer' a smashin' gel, Maggs. If 'e lets *you* go – I'll smash 'is face in!'

Although she also smiled, Maggs was having difficulty in holding back her own tears. 'Have a safe journey, Helen.' She leaned forward and the two girls hugged each other. 'Don't forget to make lots of money!' Then Maggs moved away to allow Frankie a last minute alone with his sister.

For one brief moment, Frankie and Helen stared straight into each other's eyes. Tears were running down Helen's cheeks and Frankie's face was a deathly white.

'I'm going' ter miss yer, 'Elen. Don't forget all about us, will yer?'

'Ferget *you*?' Helen raised her hand, and gently touched her young brother's face. ''Ow could I ever do a fing like that?'

Frankie was standing absolutely still, as if his

legs were made of stone. 'Goodbyes are a bugger, in't they?'

Helen responded to this by throwing her arms around him, clasping him as tight to her as she possibly could.

'Frank . . . Before I go, I want yer ter know somefin'.' Helen now had her head resting on his shoulder. 'If it 'adn't bin fer you, I wouldn't 'ave wanted ter go on living. You're special, Frank.' The tears were now tumbling down her cheeks. 'Yer know that, don't yer?'

Frankie gradually eased her back and looked straight into her eyes. ''Elen. Are you sure yer know wot yer doin'?'

Helen swallowed hard, then slowly shook her head. 'No, Frank. I'm *not* sure. But we 'ave ter try.'

And then it came. The one sound they had dreaded, the shrill blast of the train guard's whistle.

Helen and Frankie quickly rushed across to join up for one last farewell with Gracie, Reg, and little Josie. For one breathless moment all five of them stood there in a small, poignant group, hugging each other. Then Eric helped Helen and little Josie to get into the train compartment where they had already left their luggage.

Last to get on was Eric, and before he did so, he hugged Frankie with a 'Keep an eye on the *Gunners* for me, mate!' After turning to give one last wave to his own parents, he pulled Gracie and Reg together, whispering 'Fanks fer givin' me 'Elen, you two. I promise I'll take good care of 'er.' Then he quickly leapt on to the train before he made an absolute fool of himself. Once on the train, Eric slammed the carrige door and immediately pulled down the window.

Helen's face appeared at the open window and Eric lifted little Josie up to join her. Now three strangely lost faces peered down onto a platform brimming with other lost families, all of them struggling to understand why their lives were being thrown into such turmoil and anguish.

The train guard brought down the green flag, sounded his hated whistle for the final time, and gradually the train started to move off.

Watching it go, all huddled tightly together, the Lewis family couldn't really hear what Helen or Eric or little Josie were calling to them because of the yelling and shouting and waving and whistling from the other relatives and friends, some of whom were running alongside the train as it gathered speed.

Frankie took a quick glance up at the huge, white-faced station clock which was suspended over the concourse. Its black hands showed that it was exactly ten o'clock.

And, as the boat train disappeared on its journey to Tilbury and its even longer journey of hope and ambition to the other side of the world, all the Lewises could now see were three tiny, distant figures, waving and waving, until finally they became no more than a fleeting memory . . .

Chapter Twenty-eight

Frankie hadn't been to Harringay Arena since the last years of the war. There used to be a time when he went ice-skating there regularly with the Merton Street gang, but after nearly a month of painting, decorating, and plastering every evening, a full day's work at the jumble shop during the day, and the trauma of seeing Helen and Eric off to Australia, a couple of hours' diversion with Maggs seemed like a good idea.

The Arena itself was enormous with a wide concrete concourse leading up to the main entrance turnstiles, a Greyhound Racing Stadium plonked right alongside, and a British Railways main line running between the two.

During the war, the Arena had been damaged several times by bombs and doodle-bugs, but it had escaped with nothing more serious than broken windows and a few holes in the vast roof caused by incendiary bombs and stray pieces of white-hot shrapnel from anti-aircraft fire.

As soon as they got there, Maggs could see

that Frankie loved the place, for, after paying a shilling each for their skate hire, he couldn't wait to lace up his boots and get on to the ice. As Maggs had never been ice-skating before, she suggested that Frankie go off on his own for a while and while she waited for him to come back she was left to struggle around the edge of the rink, clutching on desperately to the wooden barriers with the rest of the beginners. Frankie, though, was like a professional ice-skater as he rushed off at an enormous speed, hands clasped behind his back, weaving in and out of the dazzling array of skaters wearing multi-coloured sweaters, gloves, and bobble-hats. With the sound of pop songs echoing out on a faulty Tannoy system from the Hammond Organ, Frankie was in seventh heaven.

But even in Harringay Arena, exhilaration was to be short-lived.

''Ow are yer, Frank?' said a familiar voice. 'Long time no see!'

''Allo, Jeff.' Despite the lingering resentment he still felt for his former mate from the Merton Street gang, Frankie shook his hand. ''How long 'ave yer bin 'ome then?'

'Got five days' compassionate leave. My old man died.'

To Frankie, this seemed an odd kind of place to hear this kind of news. 'Oh – I'm sorry ter 'ear that.'

'One of those fings, Frank.' These days Jeff's

blond hair was short and regulation navy-cut, but it was still long enough to get ruffled during high-speed skating. He took out a comb from the inside pocket of his sailor's monkey jacket, and started to comb it. 'So when are you comin' up fer *your* two years? Yer turned eighteen now, in't yer?'

'I go for my medical in a couple of weeks. I'm tryin' ter get in the RAF.'

'The RAF! Wot d'yer wanna be a Brylcreem boy for? Yer should join up wiv my mob. It's a great life out at sea, yer know. An' the pay's good. Did yer know I was a signaller now?'

'No, Jeff. I didn't.' Frankie felt a sense of despair. Although Jeff seemed noticeably more mature he still had a slightly bombastic manner. Why oh why, thought Frankie, did Jeff have to show off about being a signaller out at sea when everyone in Merton Street knew that he hadn't set foot off dry land?

'Did yer 'ear about Patty then?' Jeff was already getting bored, and was looking everywhere else except at Frankie. 'She's left Alan.'

'Wot!'

'It was bound ter 'appen. Let's face it – she only did it ter get someone. She didn't really love 'im and Alan's still posted out in Germany.' Without warning, Jeff suddenly dashed off again, and, just to show his expertise, he went backwards this time, crossing one foot over the other, showing off his flashy style. But, to Frankie's horror, he could just hear what Jeff called back as he disappeared into the seething mass of multi-coloured sweaters: 'Patty's around somewhere. I'll tell 'er yer 'ere!'

Only a voice on the Tannoy system snapped Frankie out of his shock.

'Clear the ice, please! Dance period begins.'

Frankie immediately joined the other skaters in getting off the ice and when he reached the wooden barrier on the dressing-room side of the rink, he looked around for Maggs. And then he remembered that he had arranged to meet her for a cup of tea in the Café bar, so he stepped carefully back on to the well-worn lino outside the barrier.

As he did so, his heart sank. Patty Jackson was coming towards him.

'Good ter see yer again, Frank.' She had put on a little weight, but it suited her. And she had grown her hair to about the same length that Maggs had hers – but Frankie found her skating frock much too short and he was embarrassed.

''Allo, Patty.' He responded awkwardly. 'I didn't expect ter see you 'ere.'

'Likewise.' Patty smiled slightly. But the last year had softened her usual more mischievous expression.

'I'm sorry to hear your news,' he said, fumbling for something to say. 'About you and Alan.'

Patty shrugged her shoulders. 'Times change, Frank. So der people. That's life.'

Both of them watched the last few skaters clear the ice in time for the dancing session.

'So – 'ow's that nice gel yer used ter 'ave?'

'Maggs is fine, thanks. She's waitin' for me in the Caff.' He made a movement to leave, but Patty had other ideas.

'We 'ad a lovely talk that evenin', yer know,' she said, – 'when we met at that dance at the Town 'All – remember? She told me all about yer,' she said, with a twinkle in her voice. 'Well – nuffin' I didn't know already . . .'

'Sorry, Pat – I've gotta go.'

As he spoke, the Tannoy system suddenly burst forth with the sound of *I'll be Your Sweetheart*. Before Frankie even had time to protest, Patty grabbed hold of his hand. 'Come on, Frank! We 'aven't 'ad a dance on the ice tergevver fer ages!'

Frankie tried to pull away. 'No, Patty! I've gotta get back ter Maggs!'

But Patty held on, and tugged him harder until he had one skate back on the ice. 'Oh, come on, Frank! She won't mind!'

Before he could say another word, Frankie found himself back on the ice, partnered by Patty, joining the select group of dancers who were straggling on and showing off in time to the skating version of the foxtrot.

For the next few minutes, Frankie was on tenterhooks as his eyes scanned the whole Arena for a glimpse of Maggs. This clearly irritated

Patty, for every now and then she tried to divert his attention by swirling him around to make him skate backwards.

While the dance was going on, Maggs had got fed up with waiting in the Café and decided to go and watch the dancers.

When she reached the barrier, it took her several minutes to notice that Frankie was involved on the ice with Patty, and that the two of them were dancing cheek to cheek.

Maggs watched with incredulity. She herself had seen what a terrible dancer Frankie was, but he had never at any time told her about his skill as a dancer – on ice. And so, for the next ten minutes, Maggs had to watch Frankie and Patty complete the entire dance period. Time and time again she thought she would just take her skates off and go home. But she decided the least she could do was to wait and talk to Frankie about not only his dancing, but also about the partner he was dancing with.

When the Hammond organ music finally came to an end with a false roll of drums and a clash of symbols, Patty suddenly slipped over on the ice pulling Frankie down on top of her. From where Maggs was standing she couldn't tell whether it was deliberate or not, but she could see Frankie helping Patty up again. And then, to the accompaniment of cat-calls and wolf-whistles from some of the spectators, Maggs watched Patty fling her arms around Frankie's neck, and kiss him passionately on the lips.

This was more that Maggs could bear. She quickly turned away and returned to the Ladies' changing-room. When she came out a few minutes later, Frankie was waiting for her.

'Maggs!'

Maggs looked more hurt than angry. 'Go away, Frankie. It's quite pointless.'

She started to make for the exit, but Frankie, still on skates struggled to follow her. 'No, Maggs! Yer don't understand. I din't wanna dance wiv 'er! She dragged me on! She was up to 'er old tricks again!'

'Oh, I see,' said Maggs, at the exit. 'And there was nothing *you* could do to stop her – is that it?'

Frankie was beside himself. 'I din't know she was, 'ere, Maggs, 'onest ter God I din't. She come 'ere wiv Jeff – Jeff Murray. She's just split up wiv Alan.'

'How very convenient for you!' Maggs still didn't raise her voice. She just turned and passed through the exit turnstile. But she stopped for a moment on the other side and called back, 'Now you can have as many dances together as you like! And I hope you enjoy yourselves!'

Elsa usually spent the best part of Sundays in bed at her house in number 19 Hadleigh Villas. She called it her 'bliss day' because it was the one day of the week that she didn't have to go to the shop, and she could pamper herself by having tea and some lightly buttered toast at regular intervals whilst spending as much time as she liked reading the *Sunday Chronicle* and *Picture Post* from cover to cover. It was a little different today, however, for during the night she had not felt very well and had to get up several times. Apart from the bouts of nausea, which these days she was getting quite frequently, she had also been plagued with a fierce cough, which resulted in her spitting up some blood. As usual, she took little notice of it, only too aware that practically no part of her body was functioning properly. She therefore felt a little too tired and weak to go all the way down the stairs to make her toast and collect her newspaper. She decided to try and catch up on a little sleep.

'Elsa! Where are yer, Elsa? Are yer still in bed?'

'I'll be down in just a minute, Frankie!' she said, shouting out as loud as her weak little voice would allow. But Frankie's arrival brought an eager smile to her face, and she got out of bed as quickly as she could. She was already wearing her long woollen dressing-gown, but before going she made quite sure that she did not forget to put on either her ginger-coloured hair-piece, or an instant application of powder and rouge.

As Elsa came down the stairs to the hall, Frankie was pleased to see that she appeared calm and relaxed, and didn't look quite as pale as when he had seen her in the shop the previous afternoon – even though she did seem to be wearing rather more rouge on her cheeks than usual.

'I know this is your rest day, Elsa,' Frankie said, breathlessly. 'I'm really sorry ter get yer up.'

'What's the matter, Frankie?' Elsa added as she reached the bottom stair. 'I thought you were supposed to be spending the day with Maggs?'

'It's terrible, Elsa! It's all over wiv 'er 'an me'.

'What! What are you talking about?'

'We went ice-skatin' tergevver – up at 'Arringay.' As he told Elsa what had happened, he was like a cat on hot bricks.

Elsa put her hand up. 'I blame you, Frankie. Whatever Patty did – you could have stopped her.'

'No, Elsa! Yer don't understand!'

'Oh but I *do* understand. When a young man thinks that he is desirable to a young woman, he is vain enough to enjoy the experience. You enjoyed the experience, Frankie. That is why you did nothing to prevent it.'

'But I *'ate* Patty Jackson,' complained Frankie. 'I dunno why she keeps playin' these tricks on me.'

'Because she needs to have love in her life, Frankie. You should not be angry with her, – no. You should understand her. We all need love in some way or another. Without it, how can we feel wanted?'

Frankie was confused. 'I don't understand, Elsa. 'Ow can I stop Patty Jackson doin' fings like – well, like wot she did this mornin'?'

Elsa stretched her hand across and covered his hand. 'By being strong, Frankie. You're not a boy any longer, you're a *man*. If you don't think before you act, you can hurt an awful lot of people.'

'But it's Maggs I love! I wouldn't 'urt 'er fer all the tea in China.'

'Then go and tell her!' said Elsa firmly.

'I can't! I've been up to 'er 'ouse and 'er mum and dad keep tellin' me she don't wanna see me!'

Elsa made a dismissive sound with her mouth. 'Nonsense! Do you love this girl – or don't you?'

'Of course I love 'er!'

'Then tell her so!'

It was four o'clock by the time Frankie reached Canonbury Square. It was a Sunday afternoon and there was no one around. Frankie had a sudden vision of all the residents either having a snooze or listening to a play on the wireless.

Propping his bike up against a lamp-post, Frankie quickly made his way to the front door of the Fletchers' house. When he had called earlier, Jennifer and Sidney had both come to the door to tell him that their daughter wanted nothing more to do with him. They had conveyed their message reluctantly, for once Maggs started bringing Frankie to tea, they had warmed to him, although they were appalled by his fractured London accent.

'I'm sorry, Frankie,' Jennifer Fletcher said now, looking sad and anxious. 'Maggs is up in her bedroom and she's told me that she won't come down to see you for any reason at all.'

'Fank yer very much, Mrs Fletcher,' replied Frankie, politely. 'Would yer mind tellin' Maggs from me that if she don't come down, I'm goin' ter yell my 'ead off 'til she does?' And, with a cheeky smile, he added, 'I'd 'ate ter wake up the 'ole of Canonbury . . .'

In her bedroom a few minutes later, Maggs was resisting the endless shouts and chanting from Frankie on the pavement below.

'I love Maggs! I love Maggs! Where are yer, Maggs? Where are yer?'

Maggs couldn't have been more embarrassed. There was no doubt that every resident in Canonbury Square would be peering out of their windows to see what all the noise was about. So, finally, she opened her own window, and called down.

'Go away, Frank! I've told you – I never want to see you again!'

From her window on the top floor of the tall house, Frankie seemed no more than a slight figure on the pavement below. But his yelling more than made up for it, for it boomed out above the passing traffic on its way to nearby Chapel

Street and Highbury Corner.

'Come down, Maggs! I want ter see yer!'

'And I don't want to see *you*, Frank! If you don't go away, my father will call the police!'

'Just let me explain, Maggs. That's all I ask! Please?'

'There's nothing to explain!' Maggs suddenly realised that she was yelling out just as loud as Frankie, so she quickly lowered her voice. 'There's nothing to explain! Go back to Patty Jackson. You can tell *her*!'

'Please, Maggs! Please!' Frankie fell to his knees as if praying. Then he picked up a roll of white cardboard, straightened it out, and held it out for her to read the large words he had printed out in black ink. And, as he held it up for her to see, chanting 'Maggs! Maggs! Maggs!' windows were being thrown open all around the Square.

Maggs leaned out of her window as far as she dared, and strained to see what Frankie had written:

I LUV YOU

Maggs started to laugh. And so did all the other residents of the Square who were peering out of their windows, and applauding.

A few minutes later, much to the relief of Jennifer and Sidney Fletcher, their daughter went off for a stroll with Frankie Lewis . . .

Twenty-nine

The third week of April 1947 was still very cold and many people, especially the elderly, found it difficult to pay the huge electricity bills. Practically every industry seemed to be going on strike, and, as always, it was the public at home that suffered. In the House of Commons, Attlee and Churchill clashed daily on how the country should or should not be run, and these days Elsa hardly ever read her *News Chronicle* because it was full of gloom and doom and full of endless articles about how and when India was going to be given independence.

The only person who seemed to be happy was Frankie, for now that Maggs had forgiven him for the silly Patty Jackson encounter at Harringay Arena, he felt that life was really worth living again. Things were also looking more promising at number 1 Merton Street, for Frankie had not only plastered all the cracks and holes but had painted the walls and ceilings in practically every room in the house. With less than a week to go to the expiry of Jack Barclay's ultimatum, Frankie felt that he could confidently leave the decorating of the stairs and landing to Reg and Gracie.

The shop, too, had undergone a transformation. Once the builders had finished their repair work, Elsa paid them extra to paint the place for her, because she had firmly refused to allow Frankie to do decorating work both at home and in the shop. It took a long time and a lot of hard work to put all the secondhand goods back on show again, but Frankie got Maggs to help him, and, by the time they had finished, the place looked just like Aladdin's Cave. The only one who didn't care for the new look was Winston, who sniffed disdainfully at the new paint and seemed to prefer the old, worn lino and his own scratch-marks on the back-room door.

In the last few weeks or so Frankie had also been building up a nice collection of regular customers, and for the first time there were signs that business was picking up. But despite his determination to make the shop a good business proposition, Frankie was becoming increasingly concerned about Elsa's health. These days she took twice as long to walk the short distance from Hadleigh Villas as she used to, and when she got there she spent most of the day sitting in a wicker chair staring out of the window. But she absolutely denied there was anything wrong. For Frankie, it was a tragedy, but when he came to work on the last Wednesday of the month, he at least found a way of cheering her up.

''Ere, Elsa! Wot d'yer fink of this?'

Elsa turned from her mug of tea to find Frankie had tried on an overcoat and a bowler hat that were at least four sizes too big for him. It did bring a huge smile to her face. 'Frankie,' she said, '*What* do you think you're doing?'

'Wot's up? Don't it suit me or somefin'?' He quickly discarded both coat and hat. 'OK, then. 'Ow about this?' He disappeared behind a rail of secondhand coats and jackets and after a short pause reappeared, this time wearing a lady's feather boa and huge cartwheel hat.

This time, Elsa roared with laughter. 'Frankie! You are *such* an idiot!'

Once he had started to raise her spirits, Frankie was determined to go on, so for the next few minutes he made a succession of quick-changes of coats, jackets, workmen's overalls, vast-sized wellington boots, and a variety of different styled hats – both men and women's. Then he went across to an old upright piano, which had been waiting to be sold ever since he first started to work in the shop. Opening the lid, he pounded out the most awful sounds on the keyboard with his fists, and pretended that he was accompanying himself as he sang 'Honeysuckle Rose' in the most dreadful soprano voice. Winston raised his nose towards the ceiling and began howling his head off too.

'Bravo! Bravo!' called Elsa, who for a few brief

moments had forgotten her frail condition. 'An actor! I always knew that you were an actor!'

As Elsa applauded his performance, Frankie bowed deeply. 'Fank yer! Fank yer!' Then, still acting the fool, he leaned forward and announced triumphantly: 'Yer in't seen nuffin' yet!'

Jack Barclay arrived at Number 1 Merton Street just as Reg Lewis was listening to the six o'clock evening news on the wireless. Gracie had been painting all day and was now perched on top of the step-ladder finishing off part of the ceiling above the narrow first-floor landing.

'So wot' d'yer fink, Mr Barclay? Not bad for amateurs, eh?'

Reg hadn't felt so good for a long time, for every room that he took Barclay into smelt of fresh paint, and the place positively gleamed with loving care and attention.

'You've done very well, Mr Lewis – I have to admit.' As he looked up at ceilings and inspected walls, Barclay appeared to be impressed by the transformation. In reality, of course, the last thing he wanted was for the Lewises to keep to the terms and conditions in their rent book, because that would mean he would have no power to evict them. And evict them he must, for getting this wretched family out of the neighbourhood was the only way, as he saw it, to block Frankie Lewis's ever-growing influence over his sister-in-law.

In the kitchen, Reg eagerly pointed up to the ceiling where only a few weeks ago there had been an ugly hole revealing the wooden slats. 'Just look at that! You'd never know there'd been an 'ole up there. Be 'honest now – would yer!'

'Very good,' agreed Barclay, nodding his head. 'Really very good.'

'An yer know who done it, don't yer? Not any of these jerry builders – oh no! It was our young Frank!'

'Really?' Barclay tried hard to disguise the coolness in his voice. Once again he had miscalculated Frankie's shrewdness. The boy had clearly accepted Barclay's challenge – and won. No court in the land would allow him to evict a family who had refurbished his property to such a high standard. 'Very impressive,' he said, the words practically sticking in his throat.

They finished up in the hall passage, where Gracie, now balancing precariously at the top of the ladder, could hear them talking.

'So where do we stand now, Mr Barclay?'

Reg felt so good that he took out some already rolled fags from his tobacco tin, and offered Jack one. Barclay smiled courteously and shook his head.

'We've met yer deadline – three days early, eh?' Reg lit his fag and excitedly blew out smoke. 'I trust that means yer won't frow us out onter the streets now?'

'No, not at all, Mr Lewis. I'm delighted what

you've done here. It does you great credit—' He called up the stairs to Gracie. '*All* of you!'

Gracie ignored him and carried on working while Reg beamed with pride and immediately exhaled a circle of blue smoke from his fag.

'However,' continued Barclay, as he made his way towards the front door, 'now that you've made such a good job of the place, it is worth considerably more so I'm afraid this means a much higher weekly rent.'

'Wot!' Reg swallowed some smoke, and had a violent coughing fit.

'Wot yer talkin' about?' Gracie called down the stairs. 'You only put it up a little while ago!'

'You have to realise, Mrs Lewis,' Barclay called back, 'that this house is now a valuable asset. There are plenty of potential tenants around who would pay a good deal of money to live in a beautifully decorated place like this.'

Reg, at a loss for words, was spluttering helplessly. 'But . . . you was the one that insisted we do this 'ouse up. We'd never 'ave done it unless . . .'

'You sod!' yelled Gracie, brandishing her paintbrush from the top of the stepladder. 'You got us ter do up this place so's *you* could make money out of it! Crafty old bleeder!'

'All I have ever asked you to do, Mrs Lewis,' Barclay called up the stairs, 'is to return this property to the good state of repair that is called for in the terms of your rent agreement and you have complied with those terms. And, as the freeholder of this property, I intend to implement my right to charge whatever rent I consider appropriate. Good morning!'

With that, Barclay tipped his hat to Reg and left.

'Yer soddin' old rat-bag!' Gracie yelled down the stairs. 'Money-grabbin' old sod!'

'Don't Grace! It won't do any good!' Reg yelled back at her.

'After all we've done!' Gracie shrieked hysterically. 'After all the hard work Frankie's put into this place . . .!'

'Stop it, Grace! It's not worth gettin' upset.'

'I'll tear 'is bleedin' guts out!'

Reg suddenly noticed that the ladder was creaking badly. 'Be careful, Grace! Don't move about on that ladder!'

But Gracie was too worked up. ''Ow could someone do a fing like that! The old sod! The schemin' old git . . .!'

As Gracie spoke, the step-ladder suddenly collapsed beneath her and her terrified scream carried right to the top of the house.

'Grace . . .!'

Reg's horrified shout could be heard outside in the street. But it was too late. Before he could reach her, Gracie came tumbling down the entire flight of stairs.

At about the same time, Frankie locked up the

shop, and, with Winston leading the way on his leash walked Elsa back home to Hadleigh Villas. Arm in arm, they strolled very slowly along Tollington Road, stopping every now and then to look at some quite ordinary things that neither had noticed before. First it was a street door that had recently been painted in a totally unsuitable bright red. Then they saw a white cat with each eye a different colour and a chopped off-tail. As they passed the creature, it arched its back and hissed at Winston, who totally ignored it, and across the road at the Globe pub, they could hear old Florrie thumping away at the upright piano, urging the early evening customers to yell their heads off in a rowdy chorus of *'Allo! 'Allo! Who's yer lady friend?*

As they turned into Berriman Road, they caught two small boys and a young girl crouched on the kerbside together, passing a fag around between them. They couldn't have been aged more than nine or ten years.

'Stupid! All of you stupid!' Elsa yelled brandishing her walking-stick at them to let them know that she meant business. She and Frankie watched all three rush off, shrieking and yelling abuse at her until they disappeared over the debris of the blitzed houses alongside the railway line in Tollington Road.

'What is their future, Frankie?' Elsa asked. 'What is the future for all you children of the war? Sometimes, I wonder.' For a brief moment she raised her head to look up at the sky. For the third time that week it was very overcast, and the dark grey clouds were low and intimidating. But when she felt the cold breeze caressing her cheeks, Elsa closed her eyes and smiled. It was a strange smile, one that Frankie had never seen before, as though in her mind she was having a loving conversation with somebody. Then, quite unexpectedly, with her head still raised up towards the sky and her eyes closed, she squeezed Frankie's arm with her own arm, and said, 'Oh, I'm so pleased to know you, Missster Frankie Lewis!'

Elsa's odd behaviour was really beginning to worry Frankie. In the last few days he had watched her write an extraordinary amount of letters and he had no idea who they were all to. It puzzled him that she never gave them to him to post.

By the time they reached number 19 Hadleigh Villas, Elsa was quite breathless, so Frankie had to open the street door for her. But before she went inside, she stopped to ask him yet another curious little question.

'Tell me, Frankie. Do you remember that cold, foggy November night? The night when you played that silly game and knocked on my door?'

Frankie shrugged his shoulders. 'Of course I remember,' he replied. ''Ow could I ferget it? It was my lucky night.'

Elsa smiled. 'Yes, but did you ever think at the

time how much that knock on my door would change your life – and mine?'

Frankie didn't have to think about that. Yes, knowing Elsa *had* changed his life. It had entirely changed the way he had used his mind; it had changed his relationship with his own mum and dad, so that for the first time in his life they could sit down and actually *talk* to each other, and share one another's problems. It had given him the strength and courage to help his sister Helen at a time when she needed advice and support. And it had shown him how to love and be loved, and how to think for himself. But most of all, Elsa had changed his life that night by just being there when he knocked on her door, for his call was not only a silly game of 'Knock Down Ginger'. It was a cry for help . . .

In those few brief seconds, Elsa too, considered how her life had changed since she first pulled Frankie into her hall. How had it been possible for this young boy, who had hardly known how to put two words together, to help her live with her past? How was it possible for him to give her the energy to fight Jack Barclay and his attempts to take the shop away from her? And why was it that the only person in the world she could trust was a teenage boy from a back street in North London? It was because somewhere inside Misster Frankie Lewis there was a quite beautiful flower that was just waiting to come into bloom. Oh, thought Elsa, sadly, if only I could have lived long enough to see the flower grow . . .

'I'd better be goin',' Frankie said. 'I've gotta 'elp Mum and Dad finish the paintin'.'

Elsa turned to smile at him. Then she did yet another curious thing, something that she had never done before. She stretched out her hand and traced the outline of his face with the tips of her fingers. Then, with a warm smile on her face she leaned forward and gently kissed him on the forehead. 'Goodnight, Misster Frankie Lewis,' she said simply. 'Goodnight, Winston.' And she gave him one last stroke behind his ears.

''Night, Elsa.'

Frankie paused a moment to watch her go into the house. Only when she had closed the door did he and Winston start to make their way back home again, this time along Seven Sisters Road.

Frankie hadn't even got the key in the door of number 1 when he heard Bert Gorman's voice calling to him from the front garden gate behind.

'Don't go in, Frankie!'

Frankie and Winston both turned with a start.

Bert Gorman was standing there with his brother Mike's wife Edie, who was crying. 'I'm sorry, boy. I've got some bad news for yer . . .'

Ten minutes later, Frankie was sitting with his father in the waiting room of an Emergency Unit at the Royal Northern Hospital.

Thirty

It was after four-thirty the following morning when Frankie and his father got back home. The walk back along Manor Gardens from the Royal Northern Hospital only increased their feeling of desolation, for the back streets were dark and deserted. There was also still quite a stiff breeze blowing, and when they turned into Windsor Road an empty tin of garden peas was dancing up and down the pavement as though it was desperately trying to find its lost contents.

Waiting in the hospital all night had been a grim experience for both Frankie and his father. When Gracie arrived at the Emergency Unit she was still unconscious, and it wasn't until after the operation in the early hours of the morning that she showed signs of coming to. The doctors were non-commital in everything they reported about Gracie's condition. All they could say was that she had clearly had a very nasty accident, for apart from the bruises which covered her body, the X-Rays had shown that her spine had been fractured in two places. Although she had at least survived the ordeal, she was still on the critical list and it would be a long time before they would know what Gracie's future prospects of full recovery were likely to be.

'It was my fault, son.' Reg was sitting at the back parlour table, resting his head on one hand and smoking a fag with the other. 'I should never 'ave let 'er go up that ladder. I always knew the bloody fing was a deff-trap!'

Frankie came in from the scullery bringing two cups of tea. 'It's got nuffin' ter do wiv the ladder, Dad.' His voice was weary, but bitter. 'If yer wanna blame anybody, blame that bastard, Jack Barclay.'

Reg tried to sip the hot tea, but he was still too distressed, and preferred to pull at his fag. 'We was only just beginnin' ter start livin' our life tergevver – fer the first time since we got married, yer muvver 'an I 'ad got so much goin' fer us.' He paused briefly to wipe his already swollen red eyes with the back of his hand. 'If anyfin' 'appens to 'er, I wouldn't wanna live.' His voice suddenly cracked and, for the third or fourth time that night, he broke down.

Frankie rushed across to comfort him. 'Don't keep goin' on like this, Dad. Nuffin's gonna 'appen ter mum. She's gonna come fru' this wiv flyin' colours, you'll see.' He put his arm around his father, and held him tight. 'Come on now, drink yer tea. Mum wouldn't like ter see yer like this.'

After he made sure that his father had got to bed, Frankie switched off all the lights and went to his own room where Winston was half-asleep on his rug, probably wondering why everybody wanted to stay awake all night.

For the next half-hour or so, Frankie just lay in bed, eyes wide open. In the next room, he could hear his father sobbing his heart out, clearly blaming himself over and over again for all the wasted years he had spent not caring for Gracie. The sound tore Frankie's heart apart. But gradually, as his eye-lids grew heavier and heavier, he was consumed with fury about the real cause of his mum's accident. If he saw Jack Barclay in Merton Street just once more, he would probably punch him right in the face . . .

Eventually his eyes closed, and he fell into a deep, deep sleep.

Frankie woke up to find Winston on the bed beside him, licking his face to remind him that dogs require an early morning walk followed by a substantial breakfast if they are to be of any use to their masters during the course of the day. It was seven o'clock, and Frankie had had exactly two hours' sleep.

He took his father a cup of tea at eight-thirty. He had already decided that he wouldn't go in to the shop until after he and his father had been back to the hospital at nine o'clock.

When they got there, they found the Emergency Unit jammed with people. Overnight it seemed as though the entire population of Islington had either cut themselves, had a road accident, or swallowed a fish bone. The Receptionist told them that Gracie had been transferred to the main orthopaedic ward, but when they got there she was still too ill to have visitors. Reg decided that he wanted to wait around until he was certain that Gracie was no longer in danger, so Frankie went home to collect Winston, then, after calling on his dad's boss, made his way to the shop. When he got there he was surprised to find the door locked, and the *CLOSED* sign still in the window.

After he had opened up and turned on the shop lights, Frankie lit the paraffin heater and made himself a cup of tea. As he waited for the kettle to boil, he became more and more uneasy. This was the first time that he could remember that Elsa had not been in the shop on the stroke of nine. Something was terribly wrong, and it worried him. However, it was important that the shop be kept open, and so, yawning from his lack of a night's sleep, he set about his daily tasks – dusting the displays, going through the paperwork for the previous few day's earnings, unpacking newly arrived secondhand clothes from cardboard boxes, and chatting up any customer who wandered in.

His chance to go and see Elsa came at lunchtime, when he decided he could safely shut up shop for one hour. First of all, though, he gave Winston his usual bowl of biscuit-meal covered in hot Bisto, then they both left for Hadleigh Villas.

Frankie could hardly believe that it was only the evening before that he and Elsa had strolled along this same route. Somehow it seemed like an eternity since they had stopped in Berriman Road where Elsa had scolded the kids for smoking a fag. Life, thought Frankie, had such a peculiar way of carrying on – and, at the present moment, he didn't much care for it.

Frankie entered number 19 Hadleigh Villas with his own key, but the moment he did so, he knew something was not right. For one thing, although it was the middle of the day, all the house lights were on.

'Elsa!' he called, and his voice echoed around the large hallway. 'Where are yer, Elsa? Are yer all right?'

The first thing he did was to go into the sitting room. But she certainly wasn't there, for the fire was out and the room freezing cold. That, for a start, was unlike Elsa. She *hated* to be cold.

He came out into the hallway and called again. 'Elsa! It's Frankie!' He waited a moment. There was no response. So he went into the kitchen at the back of the house.

Frankie was surprised to find the light on in

there, too. And even more alarming was that one of the gas burners had been lit, with no kettle or pan on top of it. But at least it had warmed the room.

Frankie was now becoming anxious, so he hurried out into the hallway again, and quickly made his way up the stairs, calling as he went.

'Elsa! Are yer up there? I'm comin' up!'

It was only when he reached the first-floor landing that his stomach started to churn over.

'Elsa!' As he approached the door to one of three rooms, his voice was sounding more and more tentative.

He knocked on the door of the first room, and called out gently. 'Elsa! It's me – Frankie. Are yer all right?' He knocked again. 'Can I come in, please?'

There was no response, so he went in.

It was a small bedroom that had clearly hardly ever been used.

Frankie came out and approached another door. Once again, he knocked gently. 'Elsa? Are yer there? May I come in, please?'

Again there was no response, so in he went.

This, however, was quite clearly Elsa's bedroom. It had several of her personal possessions scattered around the place, and a dressing-table crammed with boxes and tubes and tubs of make-up. But Frankie's attention was soon distracted from everything in the room.

'Elsa?'

At first he thought that she was fast asleep, for she was sitting in a comfortable armchair beside her bed, with her head resting to one side. As he approached, however, he saw that her eyes were open, but were quite lifeless. 'Oh God, Elsa – no!' His initial alarm now turned into grief.

He slowly knelt down in front of her. There was nothing he could say, nothing he could do. She was *gone*. And the only words he could hear were from the evening before, on the steps outside the house: 'Goodnight, Misster Frankie Lewis.' He remembered the wonderful warm feeling he had had when Elsa touched his face with her fingertips. Now, he wanted to do the same to her. Just one last time. But as his own fingertips lightly touched Elsa's forehead, it felt as cold as ice, and the thick rouge on her cheeks made her face look like wax. In death, Frankie thought Elsa looked utterly beautiful. There were no lines on her face now, and her complexion looked as it might have looked when she was a young girl at the Synagogue in Germany all those years ago. But the biggest revelation of all was her hair. Frankie had never had any idea that Elsa's ginger hair wasn't her own. And yet here he was seeing her for the first time with her own natural growth, a few wisps of silvery white hair protruding out of a perfectly shaped head. For Frankie, it was an extraordinary experience, and one that he would not forget for the rest of his life. But then, Elsa was the most extraordinary person he had ever met, and he would never forget her.

As he knelt at her feet, he laid his head on her lap. Then he found himself talking to her as if they were still having a cup of tea together over the paraffin heater in the shop.

'Oh Elsa. This is a fine fing ter do ter me. 'Ow d'yer fink I'm gonna manage now, eh? 'Ow'm I gonna get customers if yer're not there to nag me? It's *your* shop, Elsa. It'll always be yours. An' yer know why? 'Cos yer've always loved the place so much, that's why. Wot was it yer said ter me? *We all need love in some way or anuvver. Wivout it, 'ow can we feel wanted?*' He paused for a moment, then stood up again. 'G'bye, Elsa . . .'

Then he turned, and left the room. There was moisture on Elsa's delicate hands, tears which had come from Frankie.

It was the first and only time he had ever wept in front of her.

On the following Thursday, Elsa was buried in Finchley cemetery, in the same grave as her husband. It turned out to be a lovely day, and the few mourners who were there, including the two Gorman brothers and Mike's wife, Edie, Mrs Mitchell from the newsagents shop in Hornsey Road, brought daffodils and other spring flowers to put on the grave. Frankie and Maggs, however, had a special wreath made with Elsa's favourite red and white tulips. Gertrude Rosenberg brought along a Rabbi, who said a few words in Hebrew over the grave, despite the fact that Elsa hadn't been to a synagogue in years.

The great surprise came after the funeral service itself, when Frankie discovered that Gertrude was Maggs' godmother from Swiss Cottage. It was also a revelation to Maggs that this godmother, whom she hadn't seen since she was a small child, was Elsa's best friend. When Frankie had talked about the New Years' Eve dinner he had spent with Elsa and 'this crazy friend of hers', he had never actually mentioned Gertrude by name, and so Maggs had never for one moment imagined that Elsa's 'friend' and Auntie Gertrude were the same person.

Neither Elsa's brother-in-law, Jack Barclay, nor his wife, Celia, attended. Jack sent a message to say that, as he was deeply attached to his late sister-in-law, he would find it far too painful to attend her funeral. The truth of the matter, however, was that Frankie Lewis's presence would pose a real threat to the Barclay's veneer of concern. Jack Barclay was also only too aware of the hostility the boy was feeling towards him, especially after what had happened to Gracie Lewis following his last visit to number 1 Merton Street. No, an ugly scene at Elsa's graveside would not be helpful. It was essential he maintained the utmost dignity throughout this period of mourning – or at least, until he had had the chance to claim his natural inheritance as Elsa's only next-of-kin.

After everyone had left the graveside and returned to the two funeral cars, Frankie asked Maggs if he could stay behind on his own for a few minutes. Maggs understood perfectly, and went off to walk with her godmother . . .

Frankie stood on the edge of Elsa's grave and looked down at her tiny coffin. The last time he had stood in the same position, he had been with Elsa herself, and he looked back to that wonderful day when he had watched Elsa from the distance as she talked to her husband's grave as though he was having a cosy chat with her. How different it was now, thought Frankie. There she is, reunited with the man she loved. Until that moment, the impact of Elsa's passing had not really sunk into Frankie's mind. Now the tears came freely, trickling down his cheeks and on to the soil that would soon be covering his old friend's remains. But although she had gone, she had left her mark of guidance and wisdom on him forever . . .

Thirty-one

A week later Frankie received a letter from the RAF to say that, following his recent medical examination, he had been classified as A4. This meant that, because of his asthmatic condition, he would not be called upon to do his two years' National Service. Frankie was grateful that he would not be parted from either Maggs or Elsa's shop.

The past week had been one of the most traumatic of Frankie's life and perhaps the worst part was knowing that it was more than probable that his mother would never walk again. But it was astonishing to see how the tragedy had given Reg Lewis the will and determination to support his wife.

At ten minutes to nine on the same morning, Frankie, with Winston on his lead, left home to walk the short distance to the shop. Before he got there, he stopped at the newsagent's shop to buy the current week's edition of the *Picturegoer* magazine.

'So what's goin' to 'appen to the poor old jumble shop now?' asked the amiable Mrs Mitchell. 'Now it's bin closed down, I suppose that means that sooner or later we'll all end up on the rubbish dump?'

Frankie was surprised by what she said. No one had told him anything about what was going to happen to the shop, and, until they did, he was going to keep on running it. 'It's not closed down, Mrs Mitchell. Not as far as I'm concerned anyway.'

'Really?' Mrs Mitchell went to her window and looked out to the kerb outside. 'Then what's goin' on out there?'

Frankie joined her at the window. To his horror he saw Jack Barclay's car parked at the kerbside right outside the jumble shop. Winston immediately started snarling.

Frankie rushed out of Mrs Mitchell's to find Barclay pacing up and down the pavement immediately in front of Elsa's shop. 'Ah! There you are!' Barclay's face lit up the moment he saw Frankie. 'Good morning, young man.'

Winston, eyes blazing red, bared his teeth at Barclay, and Frankie had to hold the dog firmly by his collar.

All Frankie could think about was how Barclay was responsible for his mother's accident, and how he would like nothing better in this world than to smash his face in. Fortunately, he was distracted by the sound of someone hammering in nails. Practically pushing Barclay to one side, he rushed straight past him to find that a workman had already boarded up the jumble shop's windows, and was now doing the same to the front door. 'Wot's goin' on 'ere!' Frankie yelled at the top of his voice.

Barclay came up behind him and placed a driving-gloved hand on his shoulder. Lips quivering with mounting anger, Winston watched Barclay's every move. 'Nothing for you to worry your young self about, my boy. This property is now *my* possession.'

Frankie angrily wrenched his shoulder away from Barclay's hand. 'Who bloody says so? You in't got no right!'

'Oh, but I have.'

Hearing the disagreement going on behind him, the workman briefly stopped what he was doing. But he quickly continued when Barclay's bossy signal ordered him to do so.

'You clearly aren't aware that in the absence of a will, I am the sole beneficiary of my brother's Estates.'

Frankie could feel the blood rising in his veins. 'This shop belonged ter Elsa. She told me so lots er times!'

Barclay smiled apologetically and shook his head. 'Wrong again, I'm afraid. Both properties – this shop and number 19 Hadleigh Gardens were in both my *brother's* name and hers. Elsa *Lieberman* had no heirs.'

Frankie could feel the tension in his breathing, and he hoped he would not humiliate himself by having an asthma attack in front of Barclay. He'd always known in his heart of hearts that this day was bound to come. After all, he was only an employee who was paid a weekly wage to work in the shop. But as the workman carried on knocking nails into the wood across the front door, he felt as though every one of them was tearing into his own flesh.

'I understand you have a key to the shop, and to number 19 Hadleigh Villas?'

Frankie refused to answer. He just kept looking past Barclay to watch what the workman was doing.

Barclay held out his gloved hand. 'If you'd be so good?'

Barclay was lucky that Winston didn't bite his hand off, for the sudden movement angered the dog even more, and he was now straining at his leash.

Frankie slowly turned to glare straight at Barclay. But Frankie knew that this was as far as he could go, so he reached into his trouser pocket and pulled out both sets of keys and slammed them angrily into Barclay's suede-gloved hand.

'Thank you so much.' Barclay quickly put the keys into his jacket pocket, but by the time he had done so Frankie and Winston had already rushed across the road at the traffic lights. Barclay called after him. 'Oh – by the way! There'll be a week's wages coming to you – in lieu of notice!'

Now on the opposite pavement, Frankie stopped only briefly to turn back and give Barclay the aggressive 'V' sign he deserved.

It did not, however, have the same connotation that Winston Churchill had intended . . .

Hurrying off down the road, Frankie didn't know which road he was in or which direction he was heading towards. What he had just gone through had devastated him. The shop – Elsa's shop – that wonderful Aladdin's Cave that he had loved ever since he first set foot inside the place – gone forever! Jack Barclay had won the day.

It didn't bear thinking about, not even the idea of Barclay walking around the shop and touching all the 'junk' that he and Elsa loved so much. Where was the justice in this world, Frankie kept asking himself? This is not what Elsa would have wanted. The more he thought about it, the more shattered he felt. He now had no idea in which direction life would be taking him.

A few weeks later, Frankie applied for a job as a shop assistant in Jones Brothers Department Store in the Holloway Road. The wages were pathetic, and, to his way of thinking, some of the assistants there were a bit on the snooty side. However, he had to earn his keep somehow, for his meagre savings were rapidly dwindling. But working in Jones Brothers – or anywhere else for that matter – depressed Frankie, for his heart was still amongst all that secondhand 'junk' in what had once been called the 'Aladdin's Cave of Hornsey Road.'

It was after three o'clock in the afternoon when Frankie got back to number 1 Merton Street. At the other end of the street, they were carrying old Clancy's coffin out of number 78 to the hearse waiting at the kerbside. The usual group of neighbours were gathered outside, like a flock of crows, Frankie thought, gaping and gawping with mock sympathy, and paying Clancy more attention than they ever did when he was alive. Nobody appeared to know what the poor old thing had died of, only that he'd been taken to hospital two weeks before and that he 'passed away' there. But then, all that tight little group of women with their kids in prams were really interested in was an opportunity to pass a few minutes of idle gossip on a hot afternoon in June. Frankie didn't wait for the hearse and its solitary mourners' car to leave the street. He saw no point.

To his surprise, as soon as he turned the key in the lock Maggs threw herself into his arms and hugged him. For Frankie, it was like a breath of fresh air. It was over a week since he had seen her, and the way he was feeling right now, he needed her more than ever before.

'Is that you, Frank?' Reg called from the front room.

'Come inside, Frank,' whispered Maggs. 'There's someone waiting for you.'

Thoroughly mystified, Frankie went into the front room where he found his father and two other people, one of them Gertrude Rosenberg and the other a dumpy middle-aged man, smartly dressed in a dark pin-stripe suit with a small red carnation in his buttonhole.

'Ah! There yer are, son,' Although he was looking less strained than he had been over the past few weeks, Reg seemed a little nervous about his visitors' presence. 'This lady and gentlemen have come ter see yer. I fink yer know Miss—'

Frankie went straight to Gertrude, who was sitting on the sofa smoking one of her exotic cigarettes. ''Allo, miss. It's good ter see yer again.'

Gertrude sniffed, but held out her limp hand without getting up. 'Personally, I never knew vot Elsa could see in you,' she said, acidly.

Frankie exchanged a sly smirk with Maggs, and shook Gertrude's hand. He was relieved to know that Elsa's friend hadn't changed a bit since he'd joined them both for that memorable New Years' Eve dinner party at number 19 Hadleigh Villas!

'How d'you do, Frankie,' said the man who was sitting at the side of Gertrude on the sofa, as he got up to shake hands. 'My name is Michael Carrington.' Frankie thought he had rather a posh voice. 'I'm very pleased to meet you.'

'Mr Carrington is Elsa's solicitor, Frankie,' said Maggs, rather mysteriously.

Frankie looked as bewildered as ever, and could only respond by shrugging his shoulders. 'Wot's it all about?'

The solicitor picked up his briefcase, and brought out a wad of papers. 'Frankie, I've been acting on behalf of Mrs Barclay for several years now. I want to talk to you about her will.'

''Er will?' Frankie looked genuinely surprised. 'I din't know there was one.'

The solicitor smiled. 'As a matter of fact, neither did I. If it hadn't been for Miss Rosenberg here we could have assumed that one didn't exist.'

Maggie could see how confused Frankie was looking, so she decided to try and explain. 'It seems that over a year ago, Elsa gave a copy of the will she'd made to Auntie Gertrude.'

'So what happened to the original?' asked Frankie, trying hard to fathom it all out.

'A good question,' replied the solicitor, referring back to his notes. 'Her brother-in-law, Mr Jack Barclay, assured me he had searched for it in both the shop and number 19 Hadleigh Villas. Apparently it had mysteriously disappeared.'

'Ha!' grunted Gertrude, clenching her teeth tightly on her cigarette holder. 'Jack Barclay!' She sniffed, and snapped her fingers indignantly.

Maggs slipped her arm through Frankie's.

'We'd never have known anything about the will if it hadn't been something my mother said quite casually to her cousin who still keeps in touch with Auntie Gertrude. It was about you being – well, my friend, and how after all the hard work you'd done for Elsa, you'd been thrown out of the shop.'

'I'm sorry,' said Frankie, utterly bewildered. 'I don't understand all this.'

'What seems to have happened,' explained the solicitor, 'was that when she heard about you being thrown out of the shop, Miss Rosenburg became suspicious that Mrs Barclay's will had not been executed. And since it appeared that Mrs Barclay had died intestate, everything had gone to her brother-in-law, Mr Jack Barclay.'

Maggs again joined in. 'Luckily, Auntie Gertrude tracked down Mr Carrington here.'

'Yes!' snapped Gertrude, wagging a reprimanding finger at Frankie. 'And you should know the trouble it took to do so!'

Frankie suddenly felt guilty, as though he was somehow responsible for all the fuss. 'But I still don't understand,' he said, weakly. 'Wot's Elsa's will got ter do wiv me?'

'Ha!' Gertrude slapped her knees disapprovingly, and practically bit off the end of her cigarette holder. 'Vell you may ask!'

'Frankie,' continued the solicitor, calmly. 'Mrs Barclay has made you her chief beneficiary.'

''Er wot?'

Gertrude clasped her hands together and directed them up towards the ceiling as though calling for divine intervention. 'I knew it! I knew it! Elsa, you *are* a *dumm Frau*! Didn't I always tell you zo!'

Poor Mr Carrington had clearly had quite an afternoon with Gertrude, and he sighed in frustration. 'It means, Frankie, that as soon as you reach the age of twenty-one, you will be inheriting everything that Mrs Barclay had bequeathed.' Before continuing, he referred to the copy of the will which was spread out on his lap. 'There are, of course, one or two personal bequests, such as some clothes, jewellery, and a small amount of money to Miss Rosenberg . . .'

'Ha!'

Carrington was determined not to let Gertrude interrupt again. 'But Mrs Barclay was emphatic that the bulk of her Estate should come to you.' He looked up to take in Frankie's reaction.

The news was too much for Reg Lewis to take in, so he quickly sat down in the armchair nearest to him.

All Frankie could do was to stand in the middle of the room with his mouth and eyes wide open. '*Me*!' he spluttered, in total disbelief. 'Elsa's left everyfin' she 'ad – ter *me*?'

'Yes, Frankie.' The solicitor looked up from the will, a warm smile on his face. 'From the things she's written down, she had a deep affection for you. I'd say she saw in you the son she never had. Clearly you made the last years of her life the happiest she had known since her husband died.'

Frankie was stunned. 'But – wot about Jack Barclay? When 'e 'ears about this, 'e's goin' ter cut up rough, ain't 'e?'

'Yes,' replied the solicitor, immediately becoming strict and business-like again. 'I'm well aware of what Mr Barclay will do – or at least *try* to do. I think you can take it that I am more than prepared for the dialogue I intend to have with *him*.'

Frankie stood in the middle of the room, still bewildered by the enormity of all that had taken place during the past few minutes.

He exchanged a brief smile with Maggs, and then turned to Gertrude. 'But miss, surely yer must 'ave known? When Elsa give yer the will – din't yer know she was goin' do – all this?'

Gertrude sat bolt upright on the sofa. 'Know?' she snapped indignantly. 'Do you think I would open a sealed envelope, marked *PRIVATE AND CONFIDENTIAL*? Do you think I am a common criminal – like Jack Barclay!'

'But, Mr Carrington,' said Maggs, stepping in to stem Gertrude's outrage, 'if Elsa was so determined not to let Jack Barclay have her property, why didn't she get you to draw up a proper will for her?'

'I think I know why.' This time Frankie felt confident enough to answer. Remembering what

Elsa had told him about her experience with the authorities when she was interned on the Isle of Man during the war, he replied with a smile, 'She 'ated officials. No matter where they come from. She just din't trust 'em.' Then he quickly turned to the solicitor, adding, 'No offence meant, sir.'

Mr Carrington smiled. He wasn't at all offended.

'Zo! Vot are you going to say to me, Misster Frankie Lewis?'

For the first time in ages, Frankie's face broke out into a broad grin. 'Fank yer, miss! I'm very grateful to yer for all yer've done.' Then he turned to the solicitor again. 'I'm grateful ter you, too, sir.' Then suddenly, his thoughts seemed to wander. 'An' I'm grateful ter Elsa.' He lowered his eyes, and for a brief moment he was silent. 'The fing is though – it's goin' ter be funny 'avin' all this wivout 'er bein' – 'ere. I'm tellin' yer, if yer could get 'er back fer me, I'd give it all back.'

There was a hushed silence, only broken by the sound of Gertrude sniffing and wiping the tears from her eyes. 'It's time we were going!' she said, hurriedly. Both she and the solicitor got up, and made for the door. Maggs kissed her godmother goodbye, and both she and Reg thanked the solicitor for all he had done.

Before leaving, Gertrude allowed Frankie to kiss her on the cheek. Life without her dearest friend would never be the same again . . .

Once Gertrude and the solicitor had gone, Frankie had a lot to talk over with his father and Maggs. After all, he would soon have a business of his own to run, and that needed an awful lot of planning. As soon as he could reopen the jumble shop, Frankie was determined to make it the sort of place that Elsa had always wanted it to be – a place that everyone in the whole neighbourhood could be proud of.

Elsa would have approved of that.

The rest of the year continued to be a time of great depression throughout the country. In June, London recorded the hottest day for forty years, but during the winter there were strikes in all parts of industry, and it was so cold that the Minister of Power, Emmanuel Shinwell, had to ration the supply of electricity and gas.

But for Frankie, it was a very different story, with the second half of 1947 turning out to be a milestone in his young life. Although Elsa's property and assets were placed in a trust until he reached the age of 21, Frankie was allowed to take over the shop and run it as a viable proposition. Before that took place, however, the executors of Elsa's estate took Jack Barclay to court with a writ that charged him with confiscation of property that did not legally belong to him. The outcome was that he was made to return every item of goods that he took out of the shop, and anything that had been destroyed had to be replaced. By the autumn of that year, Barclay's jumble shop on the corner of Hornsey Road had not only been given a bright new coat of green paint, but it also became a favourite meeting place for the people who lived near by.

After an agonising four months in hospital, Gracie Lewis was finally allowed home in August. But once again she had to learn how to start a new life, confined as she was to a wheelchair for the rest of her days. However, what she lost in personal freedom, she gained in the love of her family. Reg gave up his job at the Hornsey Road Baths and dedicated his life to looking after his wife. Frankie promised his parents that, as soon as he came into his inheritance, he would buy them a really nice little cottage in the country. But Gracie said she hated the country, and would sooner stay in good old London where she belonged, and they were comforted by fortnightly letters from Helen, who kept her promise to send Gracie snapshots of little Josie, and also of the new addition to the family, a seven pounds four ounce baby boy called Martin.

During this time, Frankie and Maggs fell even more deeply in love. They often wondered whether they would ever see Patty Jackson again – Alan, fed up with his wife sleeping around had divorced her and remarried, and somebody in Merton Street said that Patty had gone off to America with a GI she had met at a dance on a US Air Force base in England. Somebody else swore that she had been seen working as a waitress in a Lyons Corner House Café in Streatham. As for Jeff, well – navy life apparently suited him, so he'd signed on for another seven years.

And so, as Merton Street prepared to move into another year, Frankie and Maggs joined them all in a New Years' Eve party in the main hall of Pakeman Street School. Despite the fact that for the rest of the year hardly any of the neighbours ever seemed to talk to each other any more, come New Years' Eve it was just like wartime, when people stood at their front garden gates and nattered about anything or anyone that came into their heads; when they all joined together as ARP Wardens, and kept a look-out for stray incendiary bombs from enemy aircraft (while still managing to down the odd glass of brown ale as they did so!). Yes, but for this one night of the year, Merton Street was now a very different place, and it would never be the same again.

The snow on New Year's Eve was just like it was in the pictures, but it was the kids and teenagers who had the most fun. Nobody who put their face outside their doors was safe from snowballs – and when snooty Mrs Robinson was pelted by kids as she made her way to a midnight service at the Emmanuel Church, they never heard the last of it.

Frankie and Maggs had a great time at the New Year's Eve party. Of course, Frankie still hadn't learnt to dance a step (not on a hall floor, that is), and despite Maggs' valiant efforts to make him do the 'jitterbug', the two of them invariably finished up falling flat on their backs on the school hall floor.

At about two minutes to midnight, Maggs began to get a little concerned when she realised that Frankie had been away at the toilet for rather a long time and she decided to go and look for him. However, when she met up with her friend, Iris, she was told that Frankie was outside in the school playground.

Maggs came out to find the playground absolutely deserted. There was about two feet of snow around, glistening in the bright moonglow of a bitterly cold winter's night. For a moment, she just stood there, rubbing her arms to try and keep warm, for she had no top coat on and was only wearing her red and white velvet party dress. Frankie was obviously not out there, so she turned to go back inside again.

'Miss . . .'

Maggs turned with a start. Someone was calling her.

'Over here, miss. Wot's up wiv yer? You blind or somefin?'

Maggs knew it was Frankie's voice, but all she

could see was a huge snowman that someone had built beneath the large oak tree in the school playground.

'Come on then! Don't tell me yer scared of someone like poor little me?'

With a broad grin on her face, Maggs went to the great white figure and looked closely at it. It had a friendly face, with two buttons for eyes, a tattered old scarf tied around its neck, and an old trilby hat that had been put on at a rakish angle. After a moment, she spoke to it directly.

'Frankie?'

'Sorry, miss,' came the immediate reply. 'Don't know no Frankie. Will I do?'

Maggs smiled back, without giggling. 'Depends. What do you want?'

'I want ter marry yer, miss.'

Maggs was completely taken aback.

'I'm sorry I can't go down on me knees. But I do love yer, miss. And if yer could bear ter put up wiv a snowman fer the rest of yer life, I'd be ever so grateful.'

At that moment, Frankie himself stepped out from behind the snowman.

'So wot about it, miss? Yes – or no?'

Little rivulets of tears were streaming down Maggs' cheeks. But it was not because she was cold. Suddenly she threw herself into his arms and yelled. 'Oh yes please, Mr Snowman! Yes! Yes! Yes!'

As the two of them stood there with snow

half-way up their legs, the chimes of Big Ben could be heard booming out from at least three wireless sets in Pakeman and Roden Streets. And, as they chimed, the people from Merton Street joined together in song with all their neighbours from the other streets: 'Should Auld Acquaintance Be Forgot . . .' At the same time, the bells of the Emmanuel Church echoed out across the rooftops of Merton Street – Frankie's Street. Most people agreed that the bells had never pealed so loud and clear, for everyone could hear them for miles around. Everyone, that is, except the two young lovers who were locked in a tight embrace in the playground of Pakeman Street School.

It looked as though it was going to be quite a year for them . . .

The Silent War

Victor Pemberton

Sunday Collins is less than happy with her lot in life in bomb-blasted North London, working in the sweaty, steamy ëbagwashí, the laundry round the corner from the stark Holloway council flats where she lives. Although her adopted mother, Madge Collins, who found her abandoned on the steps of the Salvation Army as a baby, is as loving as any mother could be, to Sunday her affection is stifling, and sharing their cramped home with Madgeís lazy, bad-tempered sister Louie is far from easy.

Sunday longs for Saturday nights when, with her friend Pearl, she takes full advantage of her Betty Grable looks down at the Athenaeum Dance Hall where her motto is a defiant ëlife is for livin!í But Sundayís recklessly lived life is changed dramatically when, on a warm summer morning in 1944, the bagwash receives a direct hit from one of Hitlerís V-1s, and she finds she is suddenly and, she has to accept, permanently, deaf . . .

ëA wonderful storyí Nerys Hughes

ëNever a dull moment in this charming storyí *Romford Recorder*

ëA vivid story of a community surviving some of the darkest days in our history . . . warm-heartedí *Bolton Evening News*

0 7472 5322 6

HEADLINE

Our Rose

Victor Pemberton

A Young girl learns to take her place in a London at war

The second of six children born in the tiny flat above Mr Popov's Islington piano factory, Rose Humble is used to holding her own in the world. But as war begins to cast its shadow over her family, Rose realises there are some problems a quick wit and a ready tongue cannot solve. And as she grows older she also comes to see there are people who are not all they seem. Like her own sister, Queenie, and the charming young man Rose believes to be the love of her life.

Though Rose cannot forget how those she trusted hurt her, her disappointments are put into context when the bombing starts in earnest and, as an ambulancewoman, she witnesses suffering she never dreamed she'd see on the streets of London. Then she meets a young firefighter who forces her to re-think her world once more . . .

0 7472 4765 X

HEADLINE